# WOMEN IN GERMAN YEARBOOK

**10**

# EDITORIAL BOARD

Leslie A. Adelson, Ohio State University, 1992-94
Angelika Bammer, Emory University, 1992-94
Barbara Becker-Cantarino, Ohio State University, 1992-94
Jeannine Blackwell, University of Kentucky, 1992-97
Gisela Brinker-Gabler, State University of New York, Binghamton, 1992-97
Helen L. Cafferty, Bowdoin College, 1992-97
Susan L. Cocalis, University of Massachusetts, Amherst, 1992-97
Gisela Ecker, Universität-Gesamthochschule-Paderborn, 1992-97
Elke Frederiksen, University of Maryland, College Park, 1992-94
Katherine R. Goodman, Brown University, 1992-94
Patricia Herminghouse, University of Rochester, 1992-97
Ruth-Ellen B. Joeres, University of Minnesota, Minneapolis, 1992-97
Anna K. Kuhn, University of California, Davis, 1992-97
Sara Lennox, University of Massachusetts, Amherst, 1992-94
Ricarda Schmidt, University of Sheffield, England, 1992-94
Edith Waldstein, Wartburg College, 1992-94

# WOMEN IN

*Feminist Studies in German Literature & Culture*

# GERMAN

*Edited by Jeanette Clausen & Sara Friedrichsmeyer*

# YEARBOOK

**10**

*University of Nebraska Press, Lincoln and London*

© 1995 by the University of
Nebraska Press. All rights
reserved. Manufactured in
the United States of America.
Published by arrangement
with the Coalition of
Women in German.
⊚ The paper in this book
meets the minimum require-
ments of American National
Standard for Information
Sciences – Permanence of
Paper for Printed Library
Materials, ANSI Z39.48-1984.
ISBN 0-8032-4776-1 (cloth)
ISBN 0-8032-9771-8 (paper)
ISSN 1058-7446

# CONTENTS

Acknowledgments vii
Preface ix

**Richard W. McCormick** 1
Private Anxieties/Public Projections: "New Objectivity," Male Subjectivity, and Weimar Cinema

**Elizabeth Mittman** 19
Locating a Public Sphere: Some Reflections on Writers and *Öffentlichkeit* in the GDR

**Ruth-Ellen B. Joeres** 39
"We are adjacent to human society": German Women Writers, the Homosocial Experience, and a Challenge to the Public/Domestic Dichotomy

**Marjorie Gelus** 59
Patriarchy's Fragile Boundaries under Siege: Three Stories of Heinrich von Kleist

**Gail K. Hart** 83
*Anmut*'s Gender: The "Marionettentheater" and Kleist's Revision of "Anmut und Würde"

**Brigid Haines** 97
Masochism and Femininity in Lou Andreas-Salomé's *Eine Ausschweifung*

**Silke von der Emde** 117
Irmtraud Morgner's Postmodern Feminism: A Question of Politics

**Susan C. Anderson** 143
Creativity and Nonconformity in Monika Maron's *Die Überläuferin*

**Ruth Klüger** 161
Dankrede zum Grimmelshausen-Preis

**Karen Remmler** 167
Gender Identities and the Remembrance of the Holocaust

**Suzanne Shipley** 189
From the Prater to Central Park: Finding a Self in Exile

**Sigrid Lange** 203
Dokument und Fiktion: Marie-Thérèse Kerschbaumers
*Der weibliche Name des Widerstands*

**Miriam Frank** 219
Lesbian Life and Literature: A Survey of Recent
German-Language Publications

**Luise F. Pusch** 239
Ein Streit um Worte? Eine Lesbe macht Skandal im Deutschen Bundestag

**Jeanette Clausen and Sara Friedrichsmeyer** 267
WIG 2000: Feminism and the Future of *Germanistik*

About the Authors 273
Notice to Contributors 277
Contents of Previous Volumes 279

# ACKNOWLEDGMENTS

In addition to members of the Editorial Board, the following individuals reviewed manuscripts received during the preparation of volume 10.

We gratefully acknowledge their assistance.

Sigrid Bauschinger, University of Massachusetts, Amherst
Ruth B. Bottigheimer, State University of New York, Stony Brook
Ute Brandes, Amherst College
Barton Byg, University of Massachusetts, Amherst
Heidi Byrnes, Georgetown University
Linda Feldman, University of Windsor
Sandra Frieden, University of Houston
Marilyn Sibley Fries, University of Michigan
Marie-Luise Gättens, Southern Methodist University
Marjorie Gelus, California State University, Sacramento
Susan E. Gustafson, Rochester University
Sabine Hake, University of Pittsburgh
Beatrice G. Hanssen, Harvard University
Ingeborg Hoesterey, Indiana University
Ritta Jo Horsley, University of Massachusetts, Boston
Lynda J. King, Oregon State University
Julie G. Klassen, Carleton College
Susanne Kord, Georgetown University
Alice A. Kuzniar, University of North Carolina, Chapel Hill
Tobe J. Levin, University of Maryland, European Division
Myra Love, Boston, MA
Nancy Lukens, University of New Hampshire
Barbara Mabee, Oakland University
Ursula Mahlendorf, University of California, Santa Barbara
Biddy Martin, Cornell University
Claudia Mayer-Iswandy, University of Montreal
Richard W. McCormick, University of Minnesota, Minneapolis
Magda Mueller, California State University, Chico
Kamakshi P. Murti, University of Arizona, Tucson
Linda S. Pickle, Westminster College
Luise F. Pusch, Hannover, Germany

Roslyn Abt Schindler, Wayne State University
Monika Shafi, University of Delaware
Patricia A. Simpson, University of Michigan
Arlene A. Teraoka, University of Minnesota, Minneapolis
Margaret E. Ward, Wellesley College
Sabine Wilke, University of Washington
W. Daniel Wilson, University of California, Berkeley
Linda Kraus Worley, University of Kentucky
Susanne Zantop, Dartmouth College

Special thanks to Victoria M. Kingsbury for manuscript preparation and to Maggie Hofmann and MaryEllen Shea for technical assistance.

# PREFACE

With this volume, we have reached what feels like a milestone of sorts: ten years of the Women in German Yearbook, our first decade. A decade sounds more substantial somehow than a period of years such as eight or nine that has no special name; there is a sense of having "arrived." Of course, longevity alone would be a dubious achievement without quality—and the articles in this volume are, we believe, among the best our journal has offered: original, thought-provoking, and useful. Contributors from Germany, Great Britain, and the USA offer provocative new readings of literary works from the nineteenth century to the present and bring a range of theoretical perspectives to bear on issues of gender and sexual identity in literature, film, publishing house practices, and even parliamentary debates in German-speaking countries. As always, the articles resonate in unexpected and exciting ways with each other. Redefinitions of the public and private spheres are the focus of several articles and inform the analysis in several others. The instability of constructions of gender and sexual identity is a theme or subtheme of nearly every contribution. Feminist perspectives on the Holocaust yield new and sometimes painful insights into the complexity of gendered experience.

The volume opens with three articles that offer innovative approaches to theorizing the public and private spheres, building on recent work in cultural studies, history, political theory, feminist philosophy, and even the theory of letters. The first article, by Richard McCormick, focuses on the instability of the boundaries between those spheres in Weimar Germany as reflected in (and in part produced by) the new forms of mass culture that emerged during that period. Taking G.W. Pabst's 1926 film *Geheimnisse einer Seele* as emblematic of a "New Objectivist" sensibility, he shows how the cinema provided a "public" place to project "private" anxieties about gender identity, and argues that the politics of gender in Weimar culture can illuminate the relationship of national, class, and gender identities to public dialogue in Germany today. Turning to the issue of *Öffentlichkeit* under state socialism, Elizabeth Mittman proposes that we regard writers as actually embodying whatever public sphere existed in the former GDR up to 1989. She analyzes Christa Wolf's and Helga Königsdorf's 1989–90 extra-literary publications in light of the authors' need to negotiate new positions for themselves in the drastically altered post-*Wende* public sphere. Familiar definitions of the two spheres are also challenged by Ruth-Ellen B. Joeres in her examination of early nineteenth-century women writers' letters. Focusing especially on the Rahel Varnhagen/Pauline Wiesel and Bettine von Arnim/Karoline von Günderrode correspondences, she reads the homosocial content in their letters as suggesting the willful creation of a social sphere distinct from those usually identified as public or private, one responsive to the expression of their desires and the construction of their identities.

Two feminist revisions of Heinrich von Kleist's prose follow. Marjorie Gelus continues the challenge to traditional Kleist scholarship she began in WIG Yearbook 8 by analyzing the obsessive focus on sex and gender in three of Kleist's stories as the author's response to his own rejection of Enlightenment values. Rather than constructing ideological correctives to the loss of these values as did so many of his contemporaries, Kleist, she argues, focused on the threats to order, for him embodied in women and their sexuality. Kleist's famous "Marionettentheater" essay is the focus of Gail Hart's contribution. Contrasting Kleist's use of the word *Anmut* with that of Schiller, she shows how Kleist's de-humanization and de-feminization of that virtue reinforce the exclusivity of a male homosocial universe. A nineteenth-century woman writer's view of female sexuality is the subject of Brigid Haines's contribution. Working with turn-of-the-century as well as contemporary theories of domination and submission, she argues that Lou Andreas-Salomé's *Eine Ausschweifung* (1898) stands out both in its time and among Salomé's works for its treatment of the relationship between female erotic desire and masochism.

Two contributors offer fresh perspectives on literature from the former GDR. Silke von der Emde argues that the contradictory early reception of Irmtraud Morgner's *Leben und Abenteuer der Trobadora Beatriz* can be explained as critics' failure to recognize the author's use of postmodern strategies to promote feminist goals. She shows that, in raising questions of representation and the status of the subject as well as in deconstructing familiar concepts such as "nature," "history," and "difference," Morgner anticipated many aspects of today's debates about the intersections of postmodernism and feminism. Another work on which critics have disagreed, Monika Maron's *Die Überläuferin*, is the subject of Susan Anderson's essay. Analyzing the representation and role of fantasy and memory, she argues that Maron's narrative affirms the destabilizing and self-emancipatory effects of creative action.

Another cluster of articles, this time offering feminist perspectives on the Holocaust, is introduced by Ruth Klüger, our guest at the 1993 WIG conference. Klüger's "Dankrede zum Grimmelshausen-Preis," her speech accepting the Grimmelshausen Prize for her 1992 autobiographical work *weiter leben. Eine Jugend*, establishes the link between gender and remembering the past that is the focus of the next three articles. Karen Remmler concentrates on the relationship between structures of memory and the portrayal of female bodies in two recent works, the one an autobiographical account by Austrian writer Mali Fritz of her experiences in Auschwitz-Birkenau, and the other a novel by Polish writer Marie Nurowska. Based on her reading of these works, Remmler argues that texts on the Holocaust should be read not just as universal examples of suffering, but as examples of how survivors can reclaim agency through a gendered recollection of painful memories. Suzanne Shipley, working with the autobiographies of Franzi Ascher-Nash and Stella Hershan, two little-known women who fled 1930s Austria for the USA, identifies five stages in their experiences that, she hypothesizes, may also apply to others writing in exile. She tentatively suggests that for women emigrating under similar circumstances, the exile experience can be crucial in finding a self. Sigrid Lange introduces readers to Marie-Thérèse Kerschbaumer, another Austrian writer, whose *Der weibliche Name des Widerstands* documents the experiences of seven women, all of whom died in the death camps. She sees the work as Kerschbaumer's challenge to Austria's attempts to forget or minimize its own role in the Nazi persecutions.

The final two articles offer complementary perspectives on lesbian issues. Miriam Frank introduces her survey of German-language Lesbian literature with an analysis of Lesbian/Gay politics and culture in Germany as compared to the USA. The publications she discusses reflect widespread international influence and document the existence of Lesbian subcultures in the former GDR, in Switzerland in the 1930s and 1940s, and in Germany under National Socialism. Luise Pusch reports a recent attempt at language censorship in which leaders of the German parliament tried to enforce the use in official documents of the words *Lesbierinnen* and *Homosexuelle* rather than *Lesben* and *Schwule*, the terms preferred by the Lesbian and Gay communities. The case provides the basis for her reflections concerning homophobia and language, including the act of coming out as a complex and widely misunderstood speech act. The volume closes with the editors' thoughts on Women in German after twenty years.

With this volume, Jeanette Clausen brings to a close her many years of work as WIG coeditor and begins a term as chair of her department. She and Sara Friedrichsmeyer welcome Patricia Herminghouse of the University of Rochester as the new coeditor to lead the Yearbook into its next decade.

Jeanette Clausen<br>
Sara Friedrichsmeyer<br>
August 1994

# Private Anxieties/Public Projections: "New Objectivity," Male Subjectivity, and Weimar Cinema

Richard W. McCormick

The so-called "New Objectivity" in the arts and culture of the Weimar Republic was characterized by an erosion of the boundary between the "high culture" associated with the bourgeois public sphere and new forms of mass culture directed at other classes in the emerging modern consumer society. Related to this erosion of boundaries were anxieties about the destabilization of traditional models of (national, ethnic, class, gender, sexual) identity. Change seemed especially threatening in its effect on traditional ("natural") gender roles, as can readily be demonstrated in G.W. Pabst's film *Geheimnisse einer Seele* (1926). Similar anxieties about gender are also crucial to subsequent developments in German culture and society. (RWM)

I. The Relevance of Weimar

An examination of the sexual and social politics underlying the culture of Germany's Weimar Republic is especially relevant to the study of modernity and modernization—in general, and in a specifically German context. If it is true that the value of Habermas's concept of the "public sphere" lies in the postulation of a fourth entity mediating between state power, the power of the "private" economy, and the realm of family and sexual relations (Hansen, Foreword xxvi), then the relation of that "public sphere" to modern forms of mass culture is especially significant. The Weimar period was characterized both by the development and the celebration of new forms of mass culture. With regard to the cinema in particular, it was during Weimar that the German Left first became aware of "a democratic potential inherent in the structure of cinematic representation" (Hansen, "Early Silent Cinema" 172).

Equally important, if not more so, is another point about Weimar culture and politics. In Weimar culture, explicitly thematized anxiety about gender roles characterized much public discourse, including popular culture. Sexual anxieties are especially evident in films produced in

Germany during the 1920s, and this article explores their relation to competing social and political discourses in the Weimar Republic. For the politics of gender within Weimar culture is not merely of historical interest, but is relevant to contemporary Germany and to the relationship of national, ethnic, class, and gender identities with any public dialogue in that nation.

In 1970 Helmut Lethen made the point that the construction of a democratic identity for West Germany in the 1950s was achieved by means of a selective identification with the Weimar Republic, especially with an idealized version of the so-called "stabilized period" beginning in 1924 with the Dawes Plan and Stresemann's elimination of inflation (1).[1] Certain typical attitudes of the 1950s (in West Germany and elsewhere)—the proclaimed "end of ideology" and the valorization of a "neutral," "value-free" technocracy—had definite parallels in the prevailing "Neue Sachlichkeit" or "New Objectivity" of the stabilized period of the Weimar Republic, when the "isms"—Expressionism, romantic anticapitalism, revolutionary socialism, indeed any utopianism—seemed exhausted, and accomodation with capitalist modernization seemed the only pragmatic option.

The West Germany of the 1980s that quite unexpectedly (and ambivalently) inherited East Germany with the collapse of the Soviet Bloc had in many ways turned its back on the turbulence of the 1960s and 1970s. In those decades a different legacy of the Weimar Republic, its specifically leftist tradition, had enjoyed currency. Marked correspondences between the 1950s and the 1980s were noticeable in the nostalgia for the 1950s within popular culture and in electoral debates as well (for instance, NATO was a topic of heated debate in the early 1950s and in the early 1980s, won by the Cold War party both times). Helmut Kohl's West Germany saw itself as a conservative technocracy with a strong consumer culture, and the origins of this self-image in the 1950s were clear. It was precisely this image of a *Wirtschaftswunder*-Land characterized by "no experiments" (no *socialist* experiments) that the majority of East German voters found so appealing in 1990.

These events of the latter half of the twentieth century are not unrelated to earlier ones, including crucial developments of the Weimar Republic's stabilized period (1924–29). During that period the so-called "New Objectivity" emerged, the cultural disposition most unique to Weimar—as opposed to Expressionism or Dada, which had older origins. Not only did Berlin gain recognition as *the* modern European metropolis during this period, but modern consumer culture first became prominent in Germany, and the new class of white-collar office workers became influential. At the same time mass culture was being evaluated in a new way; indeed, even members of the leftist avant-garde were embracing it as a weapon against bourgeois culture. The cinema became important in a new way during this era, as the German and American film industries became ever more entwined in Dawes-Plan-type financing. In a sense this brief era anticipated the consumer culture that would become dominant in Western Europe and North America after World War II, which in turn led ultimately to a "postindustrial" or "third stage" of capitalism.

Thus any attempts to define the potential or the reality of a "public sphere" in Germany or anywhere else in the so-called "developed" world can benefit from some examination of the developments in the Weimar Republic. For lurking beneath its new and happily distracted consumerist culture, of course, were all sorts of anxieties about its destabilization of traditional identities—above all class, gender, and national identities—and these anxieties would have drastic consequences after the economic bubble burst at the end of 1929. I would assert that such anxieties, especially those relating to gender, remain a problem within industrial and postindustrial modernity up to the present.

The emphasis on the destabilization of gender roles can in turn be connected to discussions of the role of gender in the formation of the bourgeois public sphere, a crucial one according to such "revisionists" as Joan Landes, Nancy Fraser, Mary Ryan, Geoff Eley, and others. They assert that access to that public sphere has always been limited, in spite (or because) of its universalist rhetoric, by the effective exclusion of the interests of those marginalized because of gender, class, ethnic, and sexual identities. From the beginning, gender exclusion especially played a formative (if invisible) role in the constitution of that sphere, since it was defined in relation to a "private" realm of subjectivity, intimacy, and domesticity identified with women. This identification, aside from any positive symbolic value it might have had, nonetheless meant in real terms the confinement of women within this private realm (upon which the public sphere depended) and the denial of any public agency to women, fully in accordance with the new conceptions of "natural" gender roles that also were being consolidated with the rise of the bourgeoisie and the hegemony of its particular "public." And whereas the subject of the bourgeois public sphere was supposedly universal but implicitly male, in Weimar culture and especially in "New Objectivity" one finds an overt thematization of anxiety about gender directed (in its dominant version) at an explicitly male subject.

## II. Weimar Culture and "New Objectivity"

I am using the term "New Objectivity" in its broadest sense to characterize a cultural sensibility that connects a wide variety of social, political, and artistic attitudes and endeavors in Weimar culture. There is considerable agreement that the term cannot be used to define a particular artistic school or movement; neither, for that matter, can it be applied to a particular political movement (Petersen). Indeed, it is difficult to restrict it to either end of the traditional political spectrum, and this confounding of ordinary Left-Right distinctions makes it almost "postmodern." This quality enabled ready appropriation after World War II for the proclaimed "end of ideology."

The term "New Objectivity" was initially coined by Gustav Hartlaub at the Mannheim Museum in 1923 to define the return to objective realism in German painting in the aftermath of Expressionism and Dada (Schmied, "Neue Sachlichkeit and German Realism" 9). Already at this point, while still limited to painting, the term encompassed at least two trends, a socially critical, naturalistic "verism," and a more conservative "magic realism."[2] By the late 1920s the term could be applied to trends in architecture, literature, and film, as well as to political attitudes and even "emancipated" (sober/cynical/desentimentalized) sexual behavior. And although the stabilized period ends with the stock market crash in 1929, the "New Objective" sensibility can be said to continue until 1933, albeit in decline, most typically perhaps in the attitude of supposedly "freischwebende" intellectuals who document the chaos of the end of the republic as well as their own paralysis and impotence in the face of it.

Siegfried Kracauer ascribes "New Objectivity" to social resignation and cynicism, and cynicism is of course the term Peter Sloterdijk uses to define this era of Weimar, which provides the central historical model for his critique of Western intellectual history. But the era was much more ambiguous than such negative terms can imply, as valid as they are. John Willett, for instance, defines the period much more positively, in part by translating "Neue Sachlichkeit" as the "New Sobriety"; he stresses the willingness of avant-garde artists to give up their disdain for modern civilization, and instead to apply their skills to a modern, democratic design for the life of the masses (*Art and Politics*). Their commitment to a functional, political art can be seen as reflecting hopes that a truly democratic public sphere was emerging and that its formation could be assisted and influenced by artists.

This move is typified by the Bauhaus's shift from a mystical, "organic" Expressionism to a rectilinear functionalism, certainly in the ideals behind this shift if not necessarily always in its results. Many writers were influenced by journalists and the genre of reportage (as practiced by the Communist Egon Erwin Kisch), especially its social engagement with contemporary events and its accessible journalistic style. Other writers (like Döblin) moved toward a style that attempted to approximate filmic montage; the appropriation of mass culture against high bourgeois art was still a favored avant-garde practice in the 1920s.

It should be noted that the avant-garde dreams of the 1920s about using mass cultural forms as weapons against high culture—the kind of culture crucial to the classical bourgeois public sphere—bear some resemblance to the concept of a "counter-public sphere" as developed by

Oskar Negt and Alexander Kluge in their 1972 book *The Public Sphere and Experience*. Negt and Kluge saw the potential for an oppositional public sphere, as Hansen has written, "in the contradictory make-up of the late-capitalist public spheres of production," that is, within the very processes of capitalist modernization that Habermas blamed for the decline of the classic bourgeois sphere. Within those processes there was the possibility of "a medium for the organization of human experience in relation to—rather than, as in the classical model, separation from—the material sphere of everyday life, the social conditions of production" ("Early Silent Cinema" 156). Of course, it has to be stressed that Negt and Kluge had no illusions about capitalist mass culture per se; they were arguing for a counter-public sphere that "was a fundamentally new structure opposed to both the classical-representative and the market-oriented types of public sphere" ("Early Silent Cinema" 156). They were not guilty of any naive optimism about mass culture.[3] Such optimism had still been possible in the 1920s, but it became much more difficult to maintain after the uses to which fascists and Stalinists (and capitalists in Hollywood) would put mass culture in the 1930s.

Related to this optimistic attitude toward mass culture in Weimar was an uncritical fascination with (an idea of) America, but the influence of the Soviet avant-garde, from Constructivism to Eisenstein and Vertov, was equally important. This is particularly noticeable in the German cinema, especially after the overwhelming popular success of Eisenstein's *Potemkin* in Germany. The attraction to the cinema and to technical innovation in the cinema may have been naive, or doomed, like the general technological optimism of the Left avant-garde, but Willett is right to stress a positive moment, even if he underplays the disillusionment and cynicism that was also undeniably related to the overall mood of the period.

Related to Americanism and the infatuation with modern mass culture in "New Objectivity" was the widespread popularity of jazz and the type of entertainment personified by the Tiller Girls (an English troupe of dancers whose chorus line routines could be said to fuse the display of female legs with the mechanized ethos of the assembly line) as well as the fascination with sports—especially boxing. Brecht liked boxing so much he cited it as a model for a more democratic theater (Bathrick 130-36). The general enthusiasm for sports included the glorification of outdoor activity; mountain-climbing became the subject of a very popular genre of films.[4] Indeed, the preoccupation with sports, the outdoors, and the cult of youth can be noted in films across the political spectrum, from Brecht and Slatan Dudow's *Kuhle Wampe* (1932) to Hans Steinhoff's pro-Nazi *Hitlerjunge Quex* (1933). All of these elements can be considered positively as part of the rejection of "high" bourgeois art, with its inwardness, elitism, and traditionalism—and more negatively as symptoms of the new consumer culture with its commodification of leisure time and reinforcement of youthful narcissism. This cult of youth was a part of the fascination for the new and the modern so central to "New Objectivity." The most famous aspect of that fascination was of course the glorification of technology, science, and rationalistic "objectivity."

Uniting most of these amorphous elements is the gendering of "New Objectivity": the subject that seemingly produced it, that it glorified, and to whom it was addressed was obviously, explicitly, indeed defensively *masculine*. "New Objectivity" is typified by boxers, athletes, technicians, engineers, scientists, journalists, and the spectators for whom the Tiller Girls displayed their legs.[5] In 1929 Kurt Pinthus actually defined "New Objectivity" in post-Expressionist literature specifically as "masculine" in an essay titled "Männliche Literatur." He defines literature from 1910 to 1925 not as "effeminate" but as immature, as literature of the "Jüngling." In this definition, "masculine" literature means "mature" literature; Oedipal crises have been resolved, and the process of maturation seems to involve coming to terms with wartime experiences (328–33). Willett also defines the experience of World War I as central to this generation of artists (*Art and Politics* 20). Although he does not state it explicitly, he means the experience of male artists, and thus he reproduces the male bias that is so striking in the art of the Weimar Republic. In his view it is the male rite of passage in World War I—the horrors of the trenches and gas warfare—that cures this generation of both nationalism and romantic utopianism.[6]

The move in unprecedented numbers by women into the work force during the war tended to exaggerate male distrust and resentment of women. This resentment did not dissipate after the war, when women were granted unprecedented rights by the Weimar Republic's constitution[7]; it can be connected to a more widespread "crisis of male subjectivity" in the aftermath of Germany's defeat in World War I.[8] Even after the postwar chaos—revolution, counter-revolution, hyper-inflation—had been "stabilized," the authoritarian Right still felt humiliated and had by no means given up hope of re-establishing the traditional order; and socialists and communists still felt the disillusionment of having had their revolutionary hopes of 1918 dashed. This led to feelings of "emasculation" on the left as well. Lingering post-inflationary fears about insecure economic and social status were combined with specific fears about the instability of gender roles: in the popular press the new consumerism was being symbolized by an emancipated—and androgynous—"New Woman." There were also campaigns for legalized abortion and homosexual rights, as well as much more open lesbian and gay subcultures in the large cities, especially Berlin.

I would therefore interpret the "New Objectivity" at least in part as a response to such underlying anxieties during the stabilized period, above all for middle-class males. Indeed, the position of intellectuals especially was so fragile after the chaos of inflation that accomodation with mass culture, or rather the budding "culture industry," can be seen in terms of economic necessity; resignation and cynicism ought only to be expected, although genuine commitment on the part of some to playing a "public" role within the new society cannot be discounted (nor can the possibility of mixed feelings on the part of many). But the idea of the public still seemed to exclude women, who in turn were seen primarily as an obstacle to public rationality. In "New Objectivity" there is an obvious gesture of disavowal of the underlying anxieties about gender and modernity, an attempt to re-achieve "masculine" mastery through objectivity, science, technology.

Willett summarizes the advice of a 1928 primer on photography by the Berlin "Constructivist" Werner Graeff with the assertion that "there is no reason on earth for the camera to obey the same laws of perspective and balance as the human eye. It can twist, foreshorten, superimpose, blur and cut; *all that matters is that the photographer should remain in control*" (*Art and Politics* 140-41; my emphasis). The stress is on control and mastery, which the increasingly marginalized modern artist seems here able to reclaim. Graeff's advice is by no means aimed at a merely "realistic" or "documentary" use of the camera, but its relation to the cult or fetishization of technology is clear. The "excess" in this joy of technological control is typical of German cinema in these years, even among its most "realistic" directors, such as G.W. Pabst, whose best work is traditionally lauded for its "social realism" and who indeed is the only film director Kracauer discusses in his chapter on what he calls "The New Realism" (165-80).

III. "New Objectivity" and Weimar Cinema: Pabst's *Geheimnisse einer Seele*

Pabst's *Geheimnisse einer Seele* (1926) demonstrates the joyful "excess" of cinematic technology while containing it within a realist narrative in the service of a "scientific project"—the cure of male neurosis and impotence, no less, through the wonders of psychoanalysis. But what meaning does "New Objectivity" have for the German cinema? The German cinema that became internationally famous after World War I was the "Expressionist" or "fantastic" cinema epitomized in films like Robert Wiene's *The Cabinet of Dr. Caligari* (1919) and F.W. Murnau's *Nosferatu* (1922). Expressionism, it should be noted, came to the cinema when it was just about exhausted already in the theater and had long been moribund in painting.

As the German cinema became more technologically advanced, there was a move toward more realistic stories in more contemporary settings, a development accelerated in the stabilized period by the attempt to approximate American filmmaking. Thomas Elsaesser sees fears about social mobility displaced into fantastic nightmares in Expressionist cinema (16–20); indeed, he labels that cinema "fantastic," not Expressionist. Similar fears appear in increasingly "realistic" forms in "New Objectivity." The same can be said of anxieties about destabilized gender and sexual identity, also obvious if displaced in the earlier films and still present but in much more conventionally realistic form in later films. A certain technical "excess" also remains, and this is probably what most clearly distinguishes Weimar realism from Hollywood realism—or for that matter from the entertainment cinema of the Third Reich.[9]

The technical excess in cinematic "New Objectivity" is not merely a formal or stylistic matter; it is intricately related to the gender anxieties foregrounded in this article. Women—especially "emancipated" women—were of all the "Others" in Weimar society the one group whose activities many male intellectuals across the political spectrum found most threatening. Technology and science—as thematized in cinema and as manifested in cinematic technique—seemed now to function primarily as tools for examining and controlling precisely the destabilization women were seen to represent: decadent excesses that threatened the stable, rational, scientific modernity with which the male subject was now identified. Stabilizing modernity came to mean stabilizing threats to male subjectivity, and male anxieties were foregrounded in very explicit ways as part of this project of "curing" them.

The cinema's primary function by the mid-1920s was to provide the perfect "public place" to project private fantasies and anxieties; but, in spite of the potential such a public mediation might have meant, it seems that the main (commercial) intention was to exploit, exorcise, and/or contain these private sentiments. Many German films considered "artistic" (as opposed to the melodramas disparaged for their direct address to women) openly thematize male anxieties about women. They project onto images of women supposedly "private" fears that represent social anxieties as much as (if not more than) purely psychological or sexual ones. Thus a film like *Geheimnisse einer Seele* becomes especially emblematic as a publicly projected attempt to contain sexual and social anxieties through "science"—not just through the technological apparatus of the cinema, but via the new science of psychoanalysis as well.

The hero of the film is a chemist—played by none other than Werner Krauss, who had portrayed Dr. Caligari in 1919.[10] This scientist has his ordered bourgeois existence disturbed by various anxieties, most memorably depicted in a dream sequence that is the technical highlight of the film, due primarily to masterful use of camera and optical printer by the pioneering German cinematographer Guido Seeber. Two disciples of Freud, Karl Abraham and Hanns Sachs, served as advisors to the film, which was produced by Ufa's "Kulturfilm" department. The film received the rating "volksbildend" and was a critical success, praised for its use of "everyday" reality and its basis in a supposedly real case, for its technical virtuosity in depicting private anxieties and the dream state, for its accessible introduction to the science of psychoanalysis, and for its explication of disturbing but common human fantasies.

The protagonist's subjectivity is penetrated here for the purpose of objective analysis and control. Thus while the dream sequence with its exotic mise-en-scene, superimpositions, and trick photography owes much to the Expressionist or "fantastic" cinema of the early 1920s, as Lotte Eisner stressed (31), the "fantastic" is mobilized with the ostensible intention of demystifying it, so that it can be integrated into the realist narrative just as the disturbed protagonist will be re-integrated into his marriage as a potent, virile husband and—finally—a father.

The film begins with the main character's reaction to certain unrelated incidents one day, notably a woman's murder in the neighborhood and a letter announcing the return of a favorite male cousin of the hero's wife from his travels in Southeast Asia. These events combine to affect the hero's unconscious such that he has a terrifying dream that night, and the next day he develops such a severe phobia about knives that he cannot cut his food, and he ends up moving in with his mother. Luckily, however, at his (all-male) club he has met a psychoanalyst who explains to him some of his "Fehlleistungen" ("Freudian slips").

This silent film then goes on to depict the "talking cure," a nice paradox that Anne Friedberg has pointed out (46). During this section of the film we shift continually from the psychoanalyst's office to depictions of earlier episodes, including scenes from the dream. All these disparate and disturbing flashbacks are ultimately tied to a childhood memory; the protagonist is cured and can return to his wife. In the epilogue we see the hero fishing in the great outdoors and then running up a hill to embrace his wife; they now have a baby, which he holds up to the sky.

Except for this "happy end," the film is set mostly in interiors: the psychoanalyst's office; the husband's lab, where two women (his lab assistant and a client) are shown smirking at him; and above all his comfortable bourgeois home, associated with his wife and the onset of his anxieties about her. The ultimate interior in the film is the mind of the protagonist, of course, the "site" of his terrifying dream, where the camera must penetrate to document his anxieties, just as the psychoanalyst must rationally explain them before we can leave that troubled interior for the virile world of sport and the outdoors. In the dream, the wife's cousin, carrying a rifle and wearing a (phallic) pith helmet, appears threateningly, and the wife appears in a number of exotic settings in which she seems to be betraying her husband with the cousin. At one point an Italian village springs up—apparently the scene of the hero's honeymoon with his wife—and a (very phallic) bell-tower grows up from the ground. At the top of the tower three bells are ringing, and they transform into the faces of three women laughing at him: the two smirking women we saw earlier in his lab and his wife. The protagonist is then shown in his lab, striking at a hallucination of his wife with the cousin's ceremonial sword, as the assistant looks on. Finally there is a trial scene in which the protagonist is apparently found guilty of murder.

The anxieties depicted so elaborately in the dream sequence are explicit references to the so-called crisis of male subjectivity so evident in Weimar cinema, and Weimar culture in general. I have referred in another article to that crisis as a "discourse of castration," a somewhat hyperbolic term that seems especially appropriate for this film, with its knife phobia, phallic images, fear about betrayal, impotence, childlessness, and rage directed at a projection of woman. In Weimar cinema this male crisis tends to be depicted in order to displace fears about the loss of social autonomy into the sexual realm.

Especially interesting is how much more technical skill goes into depicting the crisis than into crafting a satisfactory resolution. Kracauer later rebuked Pabst for not fulfilling a "public" responsibility, asserting that Pabst had been more interested in technical virtuosity than in the resolution of what he felt to be the genuine problems to which it alluded—male "retrogression" (Kracauer 171-72). By this term he seems to mean emasculation/infantilization/feminization—becoming "weak," less than fully masculine. Thus Kracauer, attacking the film both for its exploitation of popular anxieties and for Pabst's "private" aestheticism, actually argues for a *more* affirmative cinema—a cinema whose public function would be to shore up the subjectivity of middle-class males.

But Kracauer is right that the "cure" in the film is in some ways unsatisfactory: certainly there are a number of obvious visual motifs—especially the phallic ones—to which the "talking cure" does not refer; they are not mentioned in the intertitles. This omission is obviously not a failing typical of psychoanalysis; it is probably due to the censors (Zglinicki 581). As Eric Rentschler suggests, the happy ending in the great outdoors can also be read to be a bit more subversive than it initially might seem (7-8). Even if any irony here is the unintentional effect of a sentimental, obligatory, and formulaic happy ending (relieved by some intentional humor), the fact that the ending is unequal to the anxieties that the film mobilizes is certainly significant: again, there is an excess, an admission of instability, a lack of resolution, for which there would be little if any room in Nazi cinema.

Indeed, perhaps in the end all this excess occasioned by attempts to represent anxieties about gender in modernity did have a positive function—one that might correspond to something like a genuine public debate on gender. It was certainly no debate among "equals," given the obvious masculine bias of the film industry, but the very thematization of social anxieties about gender was bound to interest those less invested in such bias—above all women.

IV. Women and "New Objectivity"

In any case, it is the explicit depiction of male anxieties in Weimar cinema that enacts a destabilization not adequately contained, excessive to the closure. It is for this reason Patrice Petro finds Weimar cinema to be interesting from the perspective of female spectators—the *female* subject absent in so much discussion of Weimar culture. The marking of males in crisis as "impotent" or "feminized" in Weimar cinema, which from the dominant heterosexual male perspective represented anxieties about loss of power, would necessarily be received somewhat differently by women, whose relation both to power and to social constructions of what "femininity" entails was obviously different (Petro, e.g., 25). The excess associated with gender destabilization in Weimar cinema also "exceeds" male paranoia and any misogynistic intentions. To some extent, then, the cinema served a public function in addressing spectators of both genders and of various classes concerned about their roles and status within Weimar society.

Indeed, women "were both stars of the cinema and its major audience" (Bridenthal et al. 13). Given the numbers of female filmgoers (one of the reasons the cinema had from the beginning seemed so dangerous to Germany's upper classes), it is impossible to define Weimar cinema solely in terms of male spectatorship and subjectivity. However, beyond the obvious significance of female subjects in Weimar culture with regard to questions of address and reception, there were also some women involved in its production. There were women authors in the Weimar Republic, and two women directed famous films before 1933: Leontine Sagan (*Mädchen in Uniform,* 1931) and Leni Riefenstahl (*Das blaue Licht,* 1932).[11]

Even in its most narrowly defined sense, "New Objectivity" was not produced solely by men; indeed, Pinthus, who called its literary manifestation "masculine," claimed for it works by two women authors, Marieluise Fleißer and Anna Seghers. What did he find so "masculine" in their works? In Seghers it was an absence of sentimentality, but in Fleißer it was the demystification of romantic love (331–32). Much more recently, Livia Wittmann has noted that all the typical formal characteristics of literary "New Objectivity" can be found in the works of Fleißer and Irmgard Keun. She then questions why their novels were not canonized with other classics of "New Objectivity" like those by Erich Kästner or Hans Fallada. Seghers was canonized within the Marxist tradition, but Fleißer and Keun were suppressed in the Third Reich and then for the most part had difficulties after the war. Only in the late 1960s and the 1970s would these writers be rediscovered. Why were they so long neglected? Because they were women, and because their "New Objectivist" demystification of romantic love from the perspective of *female* characters was somehow more threatening than what one finds in the novels of the men, a reaction noted already in the responses of contemporary critics (Wittmann 56–63).

The apparent threat posed by such writing must be seen in connection to the concerted effort after about 1930 to restore traditional conceptions of family and motherhood. There was a clear renunciation of the emancipated, androgynous "New Woman" all the way from the fashion magazines to Kästner's *Fabian,* a novel that in terms of gender politics is definitely a nostalgic lament. In January of 1933, just days before Hitler would take power, Alice Rühle-Gerstel wrote bitterly that the restorative trend was evident among women as well (359–60). In the Third Reich, any anxieties or doubts about "natural" roles determined by gender—and "race"—would be much more forcefully disavowed. This had its effect on the cinema where, in contrast to Weimar cinema, female characters would soon be trivialized to the point where they would no longer be allowed even to represent any serious threat (Gleber).

V. Historical Lessons?

The tracing of historical continuities since the end of the Weimar Republic has relevance for Germany today, and gender is related to such continuities in interesting and crucial ways. In a cursory overview of subsequent German history, I shall suggest a few of them:

In "New Objectivity" and in late Weimar we note a public fascination with the instability of traditional, fixed gender identities in modernization as well as an attempt to "control" them—and that attempt seems to be related to tendencies toward homogenization and control in popular culture in general, and in the entertainment film in particular. In contrast to "New Objectivity," National Socialism provided a much more definitive "answer" to such consequences of modernization as destabilized identities, subversive or divisive elements in mass culture, and other problems of national resolve. As a "reactionary modernism" (Herf), fascism was an emphatic disavowal not so much of modernity as of its heterogeneity, and the new managerial class whose fate was tied to modernization opted—cynically, according to Sloterdijk—to acquiesce in this disavowal for the sake of a strong, "masculine," and homogenous national identity. This included, especially in the cinema, a program for a unitary, "middle-brow," and predominantly escapist mass culture.

After the war, there was yet another attempt to maintain a homogenous and stable national identity and culture. In West Germany the Nazis themselves became marked as a "decadent" modern perversion of an otherwise classical, enlightened German culture.[12] There was thus a certain rehabilitation of the classic bourgeois sphere, and a certain autonomy was granted (via repressive tolerance?) to dissident literati such as those in *Gruppe 47*. But mass culture and consumerism played a greater role than ever in the "economic miracle." The postwar German film industry in the West, although decentralized, nonetheless changed very little from its pre-1945 identity in terms of personnel and the type of escapist genre films produced.

The same cultural and political continuity can be noticed for West German society in general with regard to gender relations: in discourse from politicians and church officials as well as in films, Germany's postwar problems were blamed on women who had become too independent (Fehrenbach). This was another attempt to restore a stable national identity through the re-establishment of traditional gender roles.[13] This time the campaign was free of the ideological trappings of fascism, but instead based on "Christian values" and "value-free" market imperatives. The blend of a rapidly developing consumer economy with "stable," "traditional" gender roles was typical of the 1950s, and not just in Germany. While this "idyllic" stabilization was neither idyllic nor even very stable for long, it became the postwar ideal of the "good old days" as well as of a Cold War identity meant to be clearly distinct from what a different managerial elite was putting into place in the GDR.

Given the technocratic, masculinist self-image of the GDR, it is somewhat ironic that after its collapse it was so often gendered "female" in discourse, but of course in patriarchal cultures that is how the loser tends to be gendered. One of the more common tropes in the public discourse around the trauma of reunification is a concern about the "emasculation" of the men of the ex-GDR. Such discourse ignores the plight of women in the ex-GDR, which is arguably much worse.[14] Meanwhile acts of violence against minorities provide an even more disturbing parallel with the late Weimar Republic.

But the relevance of the Weimar Republic today is to be found not in any too specific construction of historical parallels, but rather, I would suggest, in its formative role as a site where the "stabilization" of identity in a modern state with an emergent consumer economy was in flux and openly thematized. As long as this "stabilization" remained incomplete, the illusion of homogenous identity and of a "universal" public sphere was also impossible; a field of competing "publics" and multiple identities was possible. "New Objectivity," and specifically the cinema I have associated with it, was, in spite of its predominantly masculinist, misogynist intentions, still a cultural space in which anxieties about gender and sexual difference were more or less openly conceded, and thus its spectators were addressed in a sort of public debate.

In the history of the German cinema there seems rarely to have been a time when the medium had such mass appeal and at the same time at least the potential for such debates—a potential that would be closed off as the Weimar Republic ended, just as any public tolerance of sexual emancipation or sexual ambiguity would be closed off in the Third Reich. The "New German Cinema" that did emerge in West Germany during the 1960s was often genuinely oppositional—and within it (or at its margins) an impressive number of women were able to begin making films and contribute to the creation of a feminist cinema (see, e.g., Knight; Frieden et al.). Nonetheless the New German Cinema was ultimately not able to reach or create a broad public, a failing that Alexander Kluge himself criticized early on (Hansen, Foreword xxiv).

It may be that the potential for genuine and democratic public contestation among competing interests (or publics) still exists in popular culture within advanced consumer societies; whether the cinema any longer represents a space in which such potential might be realized is another question. Yet one must hope that there are still spheres of cultural activity in which diversity can be articulated to counter effectively any mythic constructions of homogenous public, ethnic, or national identities. For such constructions are all too prevalent—whether in the "new" Germany plagued by xenophobia, in the USA with its homophobic right wing and with many of its "liberals" only too willing to blame economic decay on "welfare mothers" and undocumented immigrants, or anywhere in our "new world order." The investigation of such cultural phenomena in modernity is essential, and for such a project Weimar culture remains a crucial site—and one that cannot be understood without reference to its gender politics.

## Notes

[1] The identification of the Federal Republic of the 1950s with the Stresemann era was made quite explicit by a 1957 West German film entitled *Stresemann* (directed by Alfred Braun), seen at the time as an all too obvious glorification of Adenauer.

[2] Hartlaub saw precedents for the trend in painting he labeled "Neue Sachlichkeit" going back a decade, but the term he coined only caught on in the mid-1920s, and that is the era most closely associated with it. Many famous artists (some of whom were associated earlier with other movements like Expressionism and Dada) worked in a "New Objectivist" vein during the mid- and later 1920s, including Otto Dix, Christian Schad, Max Beckmann, George Grosz, and Hanna Höch. See Lethen (10-11); Schmied, "Neue Sachlichkeit and German Realism" (8-10); see also Schmied, *Neue Sachlichkeit und Magischer Realismus*.

[3] This is not to say that their concept of a "proletarian" counter-public sphere is itself unproblematic; see Hansen ("Early Silent Cinema" 157, note 22;

159). For a more in-depth (and more recent) evaluation, see Hansen's Foreword to the English translation of Negt/Kluge.

[4] For a differentiated discussion of the ideological implications of this genre, see Rentschler ("Mountains and Modernity"). It was not so unambiguously "anti-modern" or even right wing as many critics (most notably Kracauer) have often asserted.

[5] One can get a feeling for the hard, scientific "masculinity" of the era defined as "New Objectivist" just by noting the shift in the designs of the Bauhaus from the rounded, "organic" Expressionism of Erich Mendelsohn's architectural work in the early 1920s to the rectilinear functionalism of Walter Gropius's designs in the mid- and later 1920s. Compare also Walter Gropius's 1926 design for the Törten housing project to Erich Mendelsohn's 1920 "Einstein Tower" in Potsdam (Willett, *The Weimar Years* 30, 53).

[6] Thus, although he does not ignore important women artists like Hanna Höch and Käthe Kollwitz—or indeed the influential activity of women artists in the Soviet Union—Willett produces his own version of a common narrative about Weimar: what Patrice Petro in her book on Weimar cinema and photojournalism has called "male subjectivity in crisis" (13).

[7] Beth Irwin Lewis has called attention to the striking gender dynamics in paintings by men like George Grosz and Otto Dix even before their work would be classified as "New Objective." The fascination with the prostitute is already obvious in modern art and literature by the turn of the century, but in Dix and Grosz what one notices is a fascination with the mutilated corpses of the female victims of "sexual murders."

[8] See Silverman's second chapter for a discussion of that male crisis in a different historical context—the USA in the mid-1940s.

[9] In that excess one can perhaps note some resistance to the homogenizing tendencies toward the "classical" model of realist cinema that would become consolidated in the 1930s in Hollywood, a model the German cinema of the Third Reich would for the most part emulate.

[10] In his very long career, he would go on to act in Veit Harlan's notoriously anti-semitic film *Jud Süß* (1940), in which he played a number of Jewish roles.

[11] Neither of these two directors would seem especially "New Objectivist," but nonetheless they can be related to its sensibilities. The Social Democrat Sagan directs a film that bears an important relation to sexual emancipation. Riefenstahl's film is a mountain film, a genre closely related to the cult of youth, sports, and nature.

[12] This distinction between the Nazis and the German tradition must be problematized somewhat, if only for the cultural mobilization of the eighteenth century in the Third Reich. For a thorough and incisive discussion of this mobilization, see Schulte-Sasse.

[13] As the Nazis had once labeled the Weimar Republic decadent and inimical to traditional values, now they themselves were marked as decadent (indeed, they often became inscribed in popular culture as "perverse," even—ironically

enough for such a homophobic movement—homosexual). In films as varied as Willi Forst's *Die Sünderin* (1950) and Bernard Wicki's *Die Brücke* (1959) the Third Reich and/or Nazis are associated with dissolute morals.

[14] I cannot attempt to trace the GDR's specific development here, but it is fairly obvious that its "scientific socialism" and technocracy had roots in "New Objectivist" scientism.

## Works Cited

Bathrick, David. "Max Schmeling on the Canvas: Boxing as an Icon of Weimar Culture." *New German Critique* 51 (1990): 113-36.

Bridenthal, Renate, Atina Grossman, and Marion Kaplan, eds. *When Biology Became Destiny: Women in Weimar and Nazi Germany*. New York: Monthly Review, 1984.

Calhoun, Craig, ed. *Habermas and the Public Sphere*. Cambridge, MA: MIT, 1992.

Eisner, Lotte. *The Haunted Screen: Expressionism in the German Cinema and the Influence of Max Reinhardt*. Trans. Roger Greaves. Berkeley: U of California P, 1969.

Eley, Geoff. "Nations, Publics, and Political Cultures: Placing Habermas in the Nineteenth Century." Calhoun. 289-339.

Elsaesser, Thomas. "Social Mobility and the Fantastic in Weimar Films." *Wide Angle* 5.2 (1982): 14-25.

Fehrenbach, Heide. "The Fight for the 'Christian West': German Film Control, the Churches, and the Reconstruction of Civil Society in the Early Bonn Republic." *German Studies Review* 14.1 (1991): 39-63.

———. "*Die Sünderin* or Who Killed the German Male? Early Postwar German Cinema and the Betrayal of the Fatherland." Frieden et al. Vol. 2: 135-60.

Fraser, Nancy. "Rethinking the Public Sphere: A Contribution to the Critique of Actually Existing Democracy." Calhoun. 109-42.

Friedberg, Anne. "An *Unheimlich* Maneuver between Psychoanalysis and the Cinema: Pabst's *Secrets of the Soul* (1926)." Rentschler. *The Films of G.W. Pabst*. 41-51.

Frieden, Sandra, Richard W. McCormick, Vibeke R. Petersen, and Laurie Melissa Vogelsang, eds. *Gender and German Cinema: Feminist Interventions*. 2 vols. Providence, RI: Berg, 1993.

Gleber, Anke. "Das Fräulein von Tellheim: Die ideologische Funktion der Frau in der nationalsozialistischen Lessing-Adaption." *German Quarterly* 56.4 (1986): 547-68.

———. "Only Man Must Be and Remain a Judge, Soldier and Ruler of State." Trans. Antje Masten. Frieden et al. Vol. 2: 105-16.

Habermas, Jürgen. *Strukturwandel der Öffentlichkeit: Untersuchung zu einer Kategorie der bürgerlichen Gesellschaft*. Darmstadt: Luchterhand, 1962.

Hansen, Miriam. "Early Silent Cinema: Whose Public Sphere?" *New German Critique* 29 (1983): 147-84.

———. Foreword. Oskar Negt and Alexander Kluge.

Herf, Jeffrey. *Reactionary Modernism: Technology, Culture, and Politics in Weimar and the Third Reich*. Cambridge (UK): Cambridge UP, 1984.

Huyssen, Andreas. "The Vamp and the Machine." *After the Great Divide: Modernism, Mass Culture, Postmodernism*. Bloomington: Indiana UP, 1986. 65-81.

Kaes, Anton, ed. *Weimarer Republik: Manifeste und Dokumente zur deutschen Literatur 1918-1933*. Stuttgart: Metzler, 1983.

Knight, Julia. *Women and the New German Cinema*. London: Verso, 1992.

Kracauer, Siegfried. *From Caligari to Hitler: A Psychological History of the German Film*. Princeton: Princeton UP, 1947.

Landes, Joan. *Women and the Public Sphere in the Age of the French Revolution*. Ithaca: Cornell UP, 1988.

Lethen, Helmut. *Neue Sachlichkeit 1924-1932: Studien zur Literatur des "Weißen Sozialismus."* Stuttgart: Metzler, 1970.

Lewis, Beth Irwin. "*Lustmord*: Inside the Windows of the Metropolis." *Berlin: Culture and Metropolis*. Ed. Charles W. Haxthausen and Heidrun Suhr. Minneapolis: U of Minnesota P, 1990. 111-40.

McCormick, Richard W. "From *Caligari* to Dietrich: Sexual, Social, and Cinematic Discourses in Weimar Film." *SIGNS: Journal of Women in Culture and Society* 18.3 (1993): 640-68.

Negt, Oskar, and Alexander Kluge. *The Public Sphere and Experience: Toward an Analysis of the Bourgeois and Proletarian Public Sphere*. 1972. Trans. Peter Labanyi, Jamie Owen Daniel, and Assenka Oksiloff. Minneapolis: U of Minnesota P, 1993.

Petersen, Klaus. "'Neue Sachlichkeit': Stilbegriff, Epochenbezeichnung oder Gruppenphänomen?" *Deutsche Vierteljahresschrift für Literaturwissenschaft und Geistesgeschichte* 56.3 (1982): 463-77.

Petro, Patrice. *Joyless Streets: Women and Melodramatic Representation in Weimar Germany*. Princeton: Princeton UP, 1989.

Pinthus, Kurt. "Männliche Literatur." 1929. Kaes. 328-33.

Rentschler, Eric. Introd. and ed. *The Films of G.W. Pabst: An Extraterritorial Cinema*. New Brunswick: Rutgers UP, 1990.

———. "Mountains and Modernity: Relocating the *Bergfilm*." *New German Critique* 51 (1990): 137-61.

Rühle-Gerstel, Alice. "Zurück zur guten alten Zeit?" 1933. Kaes. 359-60.

Ryan, Mary. "Gender and Public Access: Women's Politics in Nineteenth-Century America." Calhoun. 259-88.

Schmied, Wieland. "Neue Sachlichkeit and the German Realism of the 1920s." Trans. David Britt and Frank Whitford. *Neue Sachlichkeit and German Realism of the Twenties*. London: Arts Council of Great Britain, 1978. 7–32.

_____. *Neue Sachlichkeit und Magischer Realismus in Deutschland 1918–1933*. Hannover: Fackelträger Verlag Schmidt-Küster, 1969.

Schulte-Sasse, Linda. "The Never Was As History: Portrayals of the 18th Century in the National Socialist Film." Diss. U of Minnesota, 1985.

Silverman, Kaja. *Male Subjectivity at the Margins*. New York: Routledge, 1992.

Sloterdijk, Peter. *Critique of Cynical Reason*. 1983. Trans. Michael Eldred. Minneapolis: U of Minnesota P, 1987.

Willett, John. *Art and Politics in the Weimar Period: The New Sobriety, 1917–1933*. New York: Pantheon, 1978.

_____. *The Weimar Years: A Culture Cut Short*. New York: Abbeville, 1984.

Wittmann, Livia. "Der Stein des Anstoßes: Zu einem Problemkomplex in berühmten und gerühmten Romanen der Neuen Sachlichkeit." *Jahrbuch für Internationale Germanistik* 14.2 (1982): 56–78.

Zglinicki, Friedrich von. *Der Weg des Films: Die Geschichte der Kinematographie und ihrer Vorläufer*. Berlin: Rembrandt, 1956.

# Locating a Public Sphere: Some Reflections on Writers and *Öffentlichkeit* in the GDR

Elizabeth Mittman

The article examines some recent extra-literary writings by Christa Wolf and Helga Königsdorf in order to approach historical and theoretical questions about the constitution of *Öffentlichkeit* in the GDR. As the conditions for communication and publicity changed in 1989-90, these writers found themselves compelled to reflect, within the emerging new forums, upon their own status as carriers of a public sphere, and hence as institutions. A reading of their reflections reveals some of the structural contradictions that shaped GDR writers' self-understanding and literary production. (EM)

*In einem Staat, der den Mangel an bürgerlichen Freiheiten zur Doktrin erhebt, sammelt sich die verbotene Öffentlichkeit in den verbleibenden Rinnsalen der Kommunikation: in privaten Zirkeln, in den Kirchen, in der Kunst. Der konspirative Diskurs wird zu einer Form des Widerstands. Diese leidvollen Bedingungen bescherten den Schriftstellern und Künstlern der DDR ihre exklusive Bedeutung. Wie selbstverständlich wuchs ihnen das Recht, sogar die Pflicht zu, im Namen der zum Schweigen gezwungenen Mehrheit zu sprechen.* —Maron, "Das neue Elend der Intellektuellen" 85

A scant four months after the fall of the Berlin Wall, Monika Maron published the essay from which these words are taken—in a West Berlin newspaper. There is a certain irony at work in her post-wall musings on *Öffentlichkeit,* for Maron's own biography tells of a highly conflicted relationship to the notion of a GDR public sphere: while she began her writing career as an East German journalist, none of her later literary texts (novels, short prose, and dramatic pieces) were ever published in the GDR. Her first novel, *Flugasche,* which was published in West Germany in 1981, took as its theme precisely the struggle in and for a public space. The protagonist in this text is Josefa, a journalist, who writes some critical reportage on industrial pollution in the GDR. When this work is suppressed, she breaks all of her ties with society, entering a kind of internal exile—and with the novel's suppression in the GDR, Maron herself joined the ranks of those writers living in the internal exile of nonpublication.[1] After several years of total censorship of her work in the GDR, she left the country permanently in 1988. Thus, unlike many of her fellow GDR writers, Maron was not confronted with the need to justify or recast her role as a writer in 1989. The essays she wrote after her move to West Germany articulate the privileged position of the outsider, unimplicated in the turmoil of uprising, revolt, and unification, who can perform her critiques of both states and their institutions with the freedom of that distance. While her own literary work recognizes the value of literature as resistance and intervention (most notably in *Die Überläuferin*), Maron is skeptical of the conferring of moral authority upon writers who would speak for the "zum Schweigen gezwungene[ ] Mehrheit" invoked in the passage above.

The situation is dramatically different for writers who remained in the GDR and, more importantly, were consistently published in the GDR and hence inhabited that often contradictory space of literature between communication and censorship. In the fall of 1989, two significant changes occurred for these personally invested figures. First, their sphere of influence came into flux; the loosening of strictures on the media in the GDR radically altered the possibilities for public verbal communication. As a result, many writers and artists found themselves propelled (or propelled themselves) into new spaces, from radio interviews to soapbox oratory at mass demonstrations (culminating in the November 4 rally on the Alexanderplatz), in countless newspaper articles, and, at least until the March 1990 elections, in the work of numerous roundtables. Second, within this changing nexus of institutions, their status was not simply reinforced; it was also challenged precisely by these new forums, and by the entrance of new participants into them. I will argue that this unique confluence of events provides a critical point of departure for a new look at the status and function of intellectuals, and of writers in particular, in the GDR before 1989. I focus my reflections around Christa Wolf and Helga Königsdorf, two writers who have been particularly important for American feminist Germanists, and who played highly visible roles in the popular uprising of 1989. Their activism during this period left its visible trace in the form of an extraordinary number of new texts, largely nonfiction, journalistic writing. Each of these women published three books in 1990–91: Wolf produced autobiographical fiction (*Was bleibt*), a volume of essays, speeches, and articles (*Im Dialog: Aktuelle Texte*), and one of readers' letters (*Angepaßt oder mündig? Briefe an Christa Wolf im Herbst 1989*); Königsdorf, a collage of letters, poems, and speeches (*1989 oder ein Moment Schönheit*), a more straightforward collection of journalistic work (*Aus dem Dilemma eine Chance machen*), and a volume of *Protokolle* (*Adieu DDR*).

This simple listing already demonstrates the common point of departure for these publications in a rapidly shifting landscape of communication. In a time of enormous change, both Wolf and Königsdorf exploited the opportunities open to them. These opportunities—both to speak and to expect that they would exercise some influence in an increasingly non-literary public sphere—reflect not only that which was new and different (e.g., the lifting of censorship), but also that which the writers brought with them from the past, namely the considerable role that they had played in the GDR for the previous forty years. In the following, I will discuss some of the ways in which the texts in these volumes articulate the struggle around *Öffentlichkeit* and its manifold effects on authorial voice. The temporal gap that opened up in 1989-90 between one set of conditions and another evoked a reflective moment for Christa Wolf and Helga Königsdorf. In the process of coming to terms with new structures of publicity, each of them struggled to sort out the different strands of their status as carriers of a public sphere in the GDR. At the same time, the strategies that each of them employed reveal some informative points of divergence in their respective status and self-understanding as GDR writers.

Theorizing the Public Sphere

Before turning to the texts at hand, it is important to clarify the notion of the public sphere as I will be using it. In the GDR, literature often functioned as an informational *Ersatzöffentlichkeit*, while the newspapers were largely controlled by the official discourse of a ruling party that conducted its affairs in cameralistic privacy. This is not a new insight; far from it, it has served as a widely accepted commonplace among Western GDR scholars for years. But if the relationship of literature to journalism in the GDR had been purely one of functional substitution, then one could plausibly assert that, in 1989, literature lost its previous informational function to a newly open journalistic realm and became irrelevant. While most would reject such a peremptory statement, discussion of literature in or as public sphere in the GDR has largely taken the form of the examination (often specific case studies) of the dynamics of censorship, publication, and reception. In other words, this focus on the text as product effectively forecloses a critical-reflective debate about the implications of this condition of culture for literature and its creators.

Theoretically, the bourgeois split between state and society had been overcome in the GDR; social structures (such as labor unions) that had previously possessed some degree of either regional or institutional autonomy were subsumed by the larger apparatus of the state. Literature and its material means of production were no exception, and in the GDR, cultural politics were given particularly high priority: the "Revolution von oben" that founded the GDR as an independent state after World War II was in desperate need of legitimation from below, and literature was seen as one important means of achieving this goal. Not only were writers integrated into state-run institutions (e.g., the *Schriftstellerverband* and most of the publishing houses); as David Bathrick has shown, the importance placed upon their profession made it possible for the more renowned among them to achieve a certain degree of political autonomy "...that is without parallel in the other societal realms of this public sphere.... In this way they all became institutions to some extent which, directly or indirectly, provided for the articulation of societal interests, but also for forms of dissidence or opposition" (64).[2]

Two aspects of Bathrick's articulation of this relation are of interest to me here. The first is his conceptualization of the author as institution. Looking at writers not merely as participants within a public sphere, but as embodying such a space themselves, opens up a potentially different and productive way of talking about GDR literature beyond the polar binarism we have inherited from the Cold War, according to which a writer was either a fully integrated part of the state apparatus ("Staatsdichter") or a dissident. This brings me to the second aspect of Bathrick's formulation: namely the implicit possibility for the simultaneity of both moments—the "articulation of societal interests" and "forms of dissidence or opposition"—within one author or one text. Recent theoretical work by historians and social theorists has revised the notion of the public sphere away from Habermas's unitary, homogeneous structure and toward a multivocal, often conflicted one.[3] I find Geoff Eley's formulation of the public sphere particularly helpful, namely as "the structured setting where cultural and ideological contest or negotiation among a variety of publics takes place" (306). Following this line of thought, the public sphere, or *Öffentlichkeit,* then, would not be an ontologically secure space, but rather a complex network of discursive relations that permeate a given society and culture.

But how does this model apply in a state whose structure challenges the legitimacy of such a public sphere altogether? Nancy Fraser describes this condition of state socialism as a "conflation of the state apparatus with the public sphere of discourse and association" (109–10). Such a collapsing of state and society—spheres that in other political systems are functionally separate—carries important implications for the theorizing of a literary public sphere in the GDR. Returning to Bathrick's implication of simultaneity, it becomes productive to ask what marks imaginative literature in the GDR in terms of structural function. Through their very activity, writers would seem to give the lie to the hypothetical conflation of state and society; they squeeze their writing between that line. Or, put differently, we may regard the writer as actually embodying whatever public sphere existed in the GDR—both in the texts that the writer writes and in the texts that are written upon the writer's body. This may make it possible to look at the writer's relationship to the rest of society—that which is not the state, and which some may term civil society—in a more differentiated manner as well. As a site for the production and communication of subjectivity, for the expression of the non-collective, in and through the voice of the writer, literature produced under the structural conditions of state socialism bears witness to a persistence of dissonances between two antagonistic discursive realms—the official discourse of the state and a plethora of other, "private" voices that would, through their public articulation, contest the dominant discourse. In Wolfgang Emmerich's words: "Damit ist der DDR-Schriftsteller, ob er will oder nicht, in Widersprüche hineindefiniert, die an die Wurzeln seiner Existenz reichen und ihm die alltägliche Herstellung seiner Identität zur manchmal kaum noch lösbaren Aufgabe machen..." (30).

Through the writing of her/his own "I," the writer was effectively handed the task of putting into public (i.e., open, accessible) circulation matters of public (i.e., general, social) concern. For many writers, then, the literary public sphere in the GDR was a conflict-ridden space, within which they often tried to work from two different directions at once: on the one hand institutionally embedded within a totalizing, statist public sphere, and on the other hand counter-institutionally responsible for the articulation of those particularities that resisted incorporation into the collective. In a certain concrete sense, the writer bore the inscription of the difficult task that all GDR citizens faced in negotiating their individual and corporate selves. By exposing the seam between these different selves, the writer was reproducing a fundamental trope of daily life.

Christa Wolf: The Author as Institution

In the summer of 1990, on the eve of German unification, a debate raged in the pages of the West German intellectual press about Christa Wolf.[4] The issues covered by this "Literaturstreit" ranged from the political and moral culpability of writers in the GDR to the possible political and aesthetic positions remaining for those on the Left in this particular German landscape. What is particularly striking about this discussion is its exclusive concentration on the figure of Wolf. The 1990 publication of *Was bleibt,* which had first been drafted in 1979, drew the spark for this inter(intra?)cultural fire. On the surface, what is at issue in the public discussion of this text is the question of Wolf's relative complicity in the former system of the GDR, as she chose not to attempt to publish the story in 1979 (when it could only have appeared in the West, an option that she consistently rejected to avoid being cast as a dissident), and as her sufferings (which are described in the narrative) paled in comparison with the incomparably more severe political persecution of many nameless people. Indeed, Wolf enjoyed the status of a world-renowned writer whose country knew in turn to benefit from her reputation and granted her such privileges as the relative freedom of travel.

Several scholars have convincingly argued that the journalistic debate says more about the state of West German intellectual life in the new post-wall era than it does about Wolf herself. For indeed, many of those West German feuilletonists had previously championed the writer they now so quickly stigmatized as the GDR's poet laureate.[5] It is, however, relevant to ask why Christa Wolf served so well as a scapegoat. While recognizing the Western domination of the terms of this debate, it seems important to me to try to place it within the complex configuration of the literary public sphere in the GDR. Therese Hörnigk draws a clear connection between the debate and Wolf's status as author and institution: "Hauptangriffspunkt, das wurde schnell deutlich, war die Problematisierung einer in der Person Christa Wolfs repräsentierten traditionsreichen Institutionalisierung öffentlicher Rede und mit ihr die identifikationsstiftende Funktion von Literatur, konkret: DDR-Literatur" (4). In other words, it was at least in part a problem of crosscultural misunderstanding: *Was bleibt* is deeply embedded in, and can only be understood through, specifically East German patterns of communication. The simple fact of the text is remarkable, as it represents Wolf's first literary attempt at an utterly unveiled critique of, and confrontation with, the state within which she had lived and negotiated her identity as writer and citizen for forty years. As such, it breaks the rules to which all of her previously published work at some point had ultimately adhered. In the "old" context the mere fact of its having been written would have constituted a radical act. In the "new" context of 1989-90, however, the (literary) public sphere according to whose presuppositions the text had been written was undergoing drastic changes. Upon its publication the text was read *not* as GDR literature by or for a GDR public; rather, it was inserted into a dynamic, often verbally violent journalistic public discourse, in which East and West Germans were only beginning to face what would become a period of extreme anxiety on all sides. As documentary fiction, *Was bleibt* offered immediate fodder for the contesting of the legitimacy of East German identities, and for the questioning of the role of literature in the GDR.

In *Im Dialog,* Wolf casts her existence as a writer in the GDR in terms of her struggle, over three decades, to create an oppositional space within. Beginning with her own university days during the height of Stalinism, she traces a crisscrossing path back and forth between identification with the ideals and rejection of the realities of the system within which she lived. With the experience of fascism as the historical backdrop, her life story becomes a narrative constructed around the problem of identification. The horror she registered at the power of the identification of Germans with National Socialism—"eine solche unheilvolle Identifikation" (72)—led her to search for new, better objects of identification. In several different speeches, interviews, and articles, she explains how desperately they—what she calls her "generation," those who came of age in the early post-war era—needed the alternative that socialism offered, and how much they identified with the antifascists and communists who had resisted Hitler. As these heroic figures occupied the seats of power in the new, socialist GDR, Wolf offers this piece of biography as a kind of apologetics for her generation's conflicted relation to the state:

> Wir fühlten eine starke Hemmung, gegen Menschen Widerstand zu leisten, die in der Nazizeit im KZ gesessen hatten. Wir haben zwar intellektuellen Widerstand geleistet—das war bei mir seit Anfang der sechziger Jahre ganz klar—, aber eine massenhafte oder nur nennenswerte politische Oppositionsbewegung hat sich nicht formiert... (136).

Wolf presents the relationship between individual and state in very personalized terms. The state is not initially perceived as a monolith, but rather as a collective of individuals who in their own time had performed awe-inspiring resistance against another institution. In addition, by positioning herself in terms of another "we," she sublates the level of a potentially individuated "I." By identifying with the founders of the GDR and their socialist principles and simultaneously opposing certain of their policies, her generation, as Wolf constructs it, finds itself in a difficult relationship to the notion of resistance per se.

The conflicted nature of the discursive space thus created is echoed in Wolf's self-construction as author in the confessional texts of 1989-90.[6] In short, Wolf projects her authorial self as existing on a seam between the collective and the individual. By insisting on both strands, and defining them as affirmation and opposition, she locks herself into a polarized duality and in effect sublates those differences into the identificatory-yet-resistant voice that characterizes her writing. Wolf's stance bears much in common with that of any modern writer who perceives her/himself as social critic—but given the extremely small, collapsed space of public discourse in the GDR, the effects are unique. For the writer in this situation is not simply speaking as a private individual; s/he is always already enmeshed in an institution of cultural production that is understood to be part and parcel of the state apparatus. In a sense, the texts in *Im Dialog* can perhaps be regarded as Wolf's "coming out" as public sphere, in which she reveals just how difficult she found this existence. This revelation of the author's personal (as opposed to authorial) self to the world at large is significant: she can finally—for the first time really—tell her story. This is the light in which *Was bleibt* must also be read.

Elsewhere Wolf describes how, in the wake of the Biermann affair in 1976,[7] she (along with several other artists) was cut off from "öffentliche[r] Wirksamkeit" (*Im Dialog* 106), by which she means the possibility of publishing political articles in the print media and appearing on radio and television (*Im Dialog* 106, 126). Part of the ensuing shift in her relationship to the state included a distancing from state institutions, most notably the *Schriftstellerverband*. The internal exile in which she felt herself to be was not perhaps readily apparent from the outside, for she kept writing, and indeed continued to be published in the GDR, unlike others (such as Maron). But in response to some hostile letters she received in October 1989, she writes: "Ich sehe, die Politik der Trennung von 'Intelligenz' und 'Volk', die über Jahrzehnte mehr oder weniger zielgerichtet betrieben wurde, wirkt weiter—nicht bei vielen, vielleicht, aber sie wirkt" (*Im Dialog* 125).[8] For Wolf, the effect of that ban from appearing in the GDR mass media for a decade was the creation of a growing chasm between the writers and their audience, an ever-increasing disengagement from "the people." Wolf would likely assert that what the people saw were the privileges she and others enjoyed, and not the writers' pain of being caught in the middle.

What I find particularly interesting here is that at least implicitly, she perceived herself as having been previously integrated into a kind of ideally functioning public sphere—that is, a discursive space in which individual voices participated in open debate and were heard. For Wolf, the limitations on her possibilities for expression intensified the *Ersatzfunktion* of literature, not just for the readers, but also for the writer. As an author functioning within ever more strictly defined parameters of public speech—i.e., the institution of literature—her role became ever greater. The adjustments she made in order to keep writing in a situation of increasing conflict with the official collective voice (with which she had sought and indeed continued to seek points of identification) made some form of distance necessary. From the mid-1970s onward, she shifted her allegiance further away from the specific ideology of the GDR government in a number of different directions, turning to a German intellectual tradition (as evidenced in her increasing use of historical material, particularly German Romanticism [*Im Dialog* 142]), mythology (*Kassandra*), and feminism.

Despite her disillusionment with real existing socialism, in 1989 Wolf is optimistic about the potential that the new grassroots groups might promote "sozialistische Umgangsformen und Strukturen in der DDR..., die die Gesellschaft in eine Richtung verändern sollen, in der viel mehr Bürger als jetzt sich mit ihr identifizieren könnten" (*Im Dialog* 80). It was not the moment of resistance or criticism to which she responded, but rather the possibility that greater *identification* with the state might become possible. The notion of a public sphere of continuous debate and conflict seemed almost unbearable to Wolf; I would argue that this is the legacy of a life spent embodying a space that theoretically ought not to have existed in the GDR. In other words, at some point she internalized the Marxist telos described by Nancy Fraser, that would collapse state and society into one homogeneous whole. This is underlined in her response to the mass exodus of 1989:

> Ich kann selbst noch nicht sehr viel dazu sagen, was psychologisch, sozialpsychologisch dahintersteht, wenn eine Generation—oder Teile dieser Generation—so wenig Bindung hat aufbauen können; wenn sie sich so wenig hat identifizieren können mit—ich will nicht sagen: dem Staat—, aber mit bestimmten Institutionen, oder besser: bestimmten Zielen. Oder auch mit ihren Eltern. Was ist denn da gewesen? Hat es je ene Bindung, ein Gespräch gegeben? Wenn nein, warum nicht? (*Im Dialog* 84–85)

In a tense historical moment, language betrays its speaker through a string of retractions and modifications—from "Staat" to "Institutionen" to, finally and most neutrally, "Ziele." This aporia leads Wolf, in a later, similarly entangled passage, to apologize for the breakdown of her language: "Ich drücke mich vorsichtig und verschwommen aus..." (*Im Dialog* 85). In this particular vagueness, however, the desire for identification reveals itself.

Simultaneously, and somewhat paradoxically, Wolf made these comments in a context of direct oppositional resistance. They are part of a radio interview given in West Berlin on Sunday, 8 October 1989, the day before what many feared might become a violent showdown between police and Monday demonstrators in Leipzig. Wolf deliberately gave this interview, which was re-broadcast throughout that Monday, in order to lend her voice—a voice of authority and mediation—to the situation. The appeal for peaceful, non-violent, reasonable behavior that she makes elsewhere in the interview is a direct extension of her sense of social responsibility—and of the real power inhering in her role as writer and institution.[9] In effect, Wolf transfers her authority from the previously existing literary public sphere to newly emerging spaces, intervening repeatedly and in many different forums, in this interview as well as in two letters (published in the same volume) to institutions of the state: the Party's youth newspaper, *Junge Welt,* and the attorney general of the GDR.[10] References to her role as mediator between the state and the newly vocal people in the fall of 1989 ("Mir geht es darum, zu vermitteln" [79]) surface at many different points in these writings, and reinforce the complicated position she occupied between them. In a 1987–88 interview (one of two pre-1989 texts included in this volume), Wolf expresses a simultaneous discomfort with and acceptance of her role:

> Diese Problematik gehört zum schwierigsten in meinem Leben, oft sehe ich sie schlicht als Unglück an.... [D]er lebendige Mensch wird institutionalisiert.... Vor allem: Ich weiß, daß nicht ich gemeint bin, sondern das Bild, das man sich von mir macht. Es fällt mir schwer, dem standzuhalten. (*Im Dialog* 65).

While recognizing the phenomenon of institutionalization, she appears to take herself out of the equation by locating its point of origin in those (presumably her readers) who respond to her in this way. Identifying the "problem" as one produced by others, Wolf ultimately forecloses the possibility of reflection upon her own emmeshedness within this relationship to the voices of State and "Volk" that flank her on either side.

These complications do not disappear with the dramatic shift in the structures of public discourse in 1989; on the contrary, Wolf finds herself challenged to rethink her own evolving position; the people will no longer need artists as their representatives, "weil viele von ihnen gelernt haben, für sich selber zu sprechen" (*Im Dialog* 167). She is left to ask questions:

> Aber was ist inzwischen mit der Kunst? Der Posten ist vakant, den sie so lange besetzt hielt. Diese Entlassung aus einer Dauer-Überforderung erleichtert, aber ich beobachte auch Irritationen.... Klage und Selbstmitleid halte ich für verfehlt, angebracht finde ich die Frage, ob wir nun etwa aus der Verantwortung entlassen sind oder wofür wir in Zukunft gebraucht werden—wenn auch sicherlich stärker marginalisiert als bisher (*Im Dialog* 161).[11]

The intensely moral tone of Wolf's language—which circles around notions of responsibility and duty—is one more indicator of just how much she has internalized her own institutionalization. The prospect of being suddenly freed from her "post" leaves her adrift, uncertain what do with the parts of her self that are in fact *not* subsumed by that role as mediator, moral authority, cultural and social institution:

> Ich enthalte mich aller Ratschläge.... Ich glaube daran, daß Menschen sich verändern können, weiß es auch von mir. Und: Gibt es nicht auch produktiven Schmerz? Wie einer der Briefschreiber es ausdrückt: "Es tut weh zu wissen: Ich darf mit Selbstverständlichkeit *ich* sagen" (*Im Dialog* 127).

It is an interesting reprise of that most famous Wolfian phrase that already echoed throughout *Nachdenken über Christa T.*, placed into the mouth of a correspondent. By allowing this anonymous citizen to speak what are widely known to be her words, as it were, Wolf gives up a little of her authority, and takes perhaps a first step toward confronting her own very particular difficulties in saying "I."

## Helga Königsdorf: Imagining a New Forum

While Helga Königsdorf was active in many of the same forums as Wolf in the fall of 1989, the strategies she employs in her extra-literary writings offer a significant contrast to Wolf. Most notably, she appears to find ways of negotiating a new position that avoids the structural quagmire in which Wolf finds herself, yet without rejecting her past position. Her texts document the emergence of a different understanding of public sphere in the GDR, and consequently of her status as author/institution. In this discursive space, Königsdorf establishes connections between her different and often conflicting identities as "private" individual, well-known writer, mathematician, full member of the Academy of Sciences, and SED Party member. The public sphere as she ultimately stages it here is a space where her own multiple identities go public and, in that going-public, speak to each other. I would suggest that this process of re-formation—one that includes reflection upon her past role—gave her a resilience, a flexibility that escaped Wolf. To be sure, some of these differences may be the result of her less prominent status; unlike Wolf, she had not been transfigured into a cultural icon. At the same time, it is possible that Königsdorf's rather different response to changing circumstances is connected to a different history of embeddedness. Within the GDR she was personally and professionally at home in several different institutions, not only that of the literary *Ersatzöffentlichkeit*. Indeed, her best-known literary texts are satirical stories about academic and scientific institutional life.

On 28 October 1989, Königsdorf attended a meeting of artists in the *Erlöserkirche*.[12] In a lengthy article that appeared in the *Wochenpost* three weeks later, she uses this experience as a springboard for some reflections upon her own complicated and contradictory use of voice in literary and extra-literary writings. She describes her walk home from that meeting:

> Nie habe ich mich so verlassen gefühlt. Nie habe ich das Alleinsein so gebraucht. Plötzlich war mein Leben in Frage gestellt. Und ich habe nicht mehr viel davon.
>
> Ich dachte an meinen Text, der fertig zu Hause lag. Das Manuskript zu einem Vortrag "Menschenwürde". Fertig also. Wohldurchdacht. Eine Menge sich klug gebärdender Sätze. Und doch kein guter Vortrag. Warum wollten mir solche Vorträge nicht gelingen, während sich bei den meisten meiner literarischen Texte doch das sichere Gefühl in der Magengegend einstellte. Als ich nachts nach dieser Veranstaltung nach Hause wanderte, wußte ich plötzlich den Grund. In diesem Vortrag sage ich nicht ein einziges Mal "Ich". Über mich selbst konnte ich überhaupt nur sprechen, indem ich vorgab, in Wirklichkeit nicht über mich zu reden, indem ich mir Geschichten ausdachte, die scheinbar nichts mit mir zu tun hatten und in denen ich

doch die Schmerzgrenze überschritt. Trotzdem blieb es eine Kunstwelt, in der zwar jede Figur etwas von mir hatte, aber doch niemals ich war, sondern bereits ein repariertes Ich. Wußte ich das nicht immer? Was hatte ich noch alles gewußt? Gewußt und verdrängt (*1989* 58).

Königsdorf's encounter with the radically new and different public space of that meeting serves as the catalyst for an explicit transformation of herself as public sphere, that is, an extra-literary voice. The voice that she had consciously constructed in order to speak in another public forum (the lecture on "Menschenwürde") denied the first person, making reflection upon her own relationship to either her collective or her personal identities impossible. And the authorial voice of her literary texts was always already "a repaired I," as she calls it, rendered safe by the veil of fiction. By confronting her own absences in those other instances of publicity, Königsdorf opens herself to a new challenge, namely the attempt to develop a different kind of personal voice, a new public subjectivity.

Given her attention to voice, it is particularly interesting to note that the collection containing this article (*1989 oder Ein Moment Schönheit*) begins with a text from 1987 entitled "Von der Schwierigkeit, 'Ich' zu sagen." The title indicates Königsdorf's indebtedness to Wolf; yet her reflections lead her toward some different conclusions for her own constitution as public sphere within the GDR. Not coincidentally, I think, this early articulation of the problems addressed above occurred in the context of literary production. In this contribution for discussion at the Tenth Writers' Congress of the GDR, Königsdorf places the importance of saying "I" in a global rather than a local context, but even here it models a public sphere conceived as the conscious intersection of "I" and "we":

> ...nicht zuletzt heißt Schreiben für mich auch, gemeinsam mit dem Leser, "Ich" sagen. Und "Ich" sogleich wieder in Frage stellen. Es erneut, auf neue Weise also, mit kollektiver Identität konfrontieren und diese gegebenenfalls auch verändern. Das ist ein unbequemer Vorgang, und in diesem Sinn soll und muß meiner Meinung nach Literatur unbequem sein, muß unbequeme Literatur unter die Leute, auch in unbequemen Zeiten. Dann erst recht (*1989* 9).

Literature may have been displaced by the opening of new public spaces in 1989, but Königsdorf had already been at work developing a model that would allow her to move with the changes around her, both in terms of her relationship to the reader and to the collective. What was couched in global terms there allows re-imagining in local terms later.[13]

For Königsdorf, the first step in this direction is the brutal recognition of her own complicity with the state: "Spätestens in dieser Veranstaltung [in der Erlöserkirche—e.m.] hatte ich begriffen, daß auch ich Täter war" (*1989* 59). In Königsdorf's confessional texts, this new voice both exposes and breaks open the uneasy relationships between the collective "we" and the writer, and between the writer and the "I" that is so many things, so many places. The "I" intrudes upon the "we" in a way that forces a dialogue between two who are not opposites, but partners—and Königsdorf is contained within both of them. The complexity of the position that she must negotiate for herself can be read as a metaphor for the systematic disjunction of particular and collective identities in the GDR—*both* of which inhabit, and are inhabited by, the personal. The self-reflective moment that emerges with this move takes Königsdorf in a radically different direction from Wolf. Also in November 1989, she addressed fellow Party members in front of the offices of the Central Committee by saying:

> Ich spreche hier zu euch nicht im Namen, im Auftrag.... Nein, ich spreche hier in meinem eigenen Namen. Auch wir Genossen müssen lernen, ich zu sagen. Wir lassen uns nicht mehr auf *eine* Meinung verpflichten und erst recht nicht auf keine Meinung. Wer ist denn die Partei? Die Partei bin ich. Und du. Und du. Das Volk hat es uns vorgemacht. Sagen wir, unsere Partei, das sind wir (*1989* 83).

Once again we see Königsdorf drawing upon the example of the new forum created by the people ("Das Volk hat es uns vorgemacht") and extracting as its most essential element the assertion of a (multi-voiced?) subjectivity. The hopefulness with which she formulates this particular appeal does not last; but more than a year later, when the German Democratic Republic has literally ceased to exist, she maintains this connection between individual identity and corporate Party identity with a self-reflective "we": "...daß wir jetzt so wehrlos sind, ist die Folge ununterbrochener Demütigung, die wir erduldet und weitergegeben haben.... Die meisten von uns haben diese Politik bis fünf nach zwölf mitgetragen" (*Dilemma* 60-61).[14] The leverage that she gains with this strategy allows her to produce ongoing criticisms of the Party and its politics without falling into the aporia of defending/blaming. She is able to keep talking.[15]

As a process of saying "I," this talking must allow for collisions of "I's"—and "we's"—that are markers of different interests. The notion of a capacity for conflict is central to many of these writings, and Königsdorf's different voices emerge—sometimes conciliatory, sometimes contentious, always grounded in a position from which an "I" is speaking: "Heimat, das habe ich im Herbst begriffen, ist der Ort, wo man sich einmischen darf. Nun darf ich mich plötzlich in ganz Deutschland einmischen" (*Dilemma* 51). The critical content of many of her articles moves Königsdorf toward a notion of the public sphere as a site of meddling, of interference—an interventionary strategy that is visible, for example, in her attempts to recognize and name the vulnerabilities of conflicting groups.[16] But there are examples of other ways in which she "meddles": a self-help group advertises in the *Berliner Zeitung*; a woman who cannot attend their meeting writes to the group out of a sense of utter disorientation at the collapse of her state; Königsdorf, apparently a member of the group, responds; the exchange is published in the *Berliner Zeitung,* and once again in a volume of speeches and articles.[17]

As I have noted above, Christa Wolf engaged in a similarly active way with events around her in 1989–90. The difference in self-perception, and hence strategy, emerges in the conclusions Königsdorf draws for her future role as a writer and intellectual: "Es wird nun für die Dichter etwas Neues beginnen. Die Leser lesen Zeitungen. Ich habe immer gewarnt und prophezeit, daß wir uns mit unseren Forderungen nach Glasnost selbst das Wasser abgraben. Nur wollte niemand auf mich hören, nicht einmal ich selbst" (*1989* 93). When GDR intellectuals began speaking from platforms in the fall of 1989, they were, in a certain sense, doing what they had done before, only more freely, more openly. They were still acting as a mouthpiece of the people, themselves constituting a space within which competing interests could meet and speak. Like Wolf, Königsdorf understands that the revolution was precisely about the people learning to speak for themselves, taking their own "I's" public. What is different is her assessment of the conflicts and contradictions that had marked their lives and given the writers their function: "Erst einmal sind wir vom Sockel gestürzt, auf dem wir zwar dem Wind ausgesetzt waren, auf dem es sich doch hochgemut stehen ließ. Und dieser Sturz ist gut. Für uns und für die, die uns stürzen" (*Dilemma* 9).

*1989 oder Ein Moment Schönheit* echoes the transgression of boundaries that was occurring in the political arena on another level as well. While this collage, as Königsdorf has subtitled it, can certainly be read as documentary literature, it is at least as interesting to read it as an aesthetic composition. Königsdorf traces many crossings between "private" and "public," or "personal" and "political" genres here, from love letters to soapbox oratory. In the juxtaposition of delivered speeches and published articles with poems, she aestheticizes the whole in not completely unfamiliar ways. But when these texts—speeches, articles, poems—are in turn interrupted by what are clearly her own private letters, letters that bear witness to the beginning and the ending of a love affair, that reveal her doubts and frustrations with the SED and with her own sick body (Königsdorf suffers from Parkinson's disease), the effect of this indiscretion is remarkable. The mere act of making the previously invisible visible in the context of the GDR is explosive; Königsdorf seems intent on underlining this fact by upsetting the public/private split from top to bottom, or rather, from inside out. "I" writes: "Ich lege Morgenluft, Harzduft und Vogelgezwitscher in diesen Brief" (30); "I" also writes: "Ein kulturelles Gegengewicht zu den bedrohlichen Entwicklungen muß heute auch die Wirksamkeit oder die eventuelle Nichtwirksamkeit von ökonomischen und politischen Strukturen berücksichtigen" (24); and finally, "I" writes:

Ihr Worte
Meine schönen Kinder
Wenn ich jetzt gehe
Steht für mich
Sehr allein war ich
Und allzu oft
In schlechter Gesellschaft (130).

Königsdorf's radical juxtaposition of domestic and political texts clearly transgresses traditional boundaries. Returning once again to the notion of embodiment, one could speculate on the ways in which the writer's body not only displays itself as the slate upon which texts have been inscribed, but also makes its very bodiliness known. In one of Königsdorf's earlier literary works, *Respektloser Umgang* (1986), the narrator's body plays a critical role as the stage upon which different identities perform and upon which they leave their marks. No single unified position of identification exists in this text. Similarly, the "I" in Königsdorf's extra-literary, post-1989 writings is not a single essential GDR identity, nor does it strive in that direction. Rather, it reflects upon its shifting institutional status—exploring and rendering visible that network of discursive relations between and among the various "publics" out of which it is constituted.

There is much historical and theoretical work that remains to be done with regard to the relations between author, state, and society in the GDR. Indeed, the West's eager Stasi-fication of the GDR intelligentsia in the wake of unification is hardly an improvement upon the previously available categories of "Staatsdichter"/dissident. While the historically and thematically parallel texts by Wolf and Königsdorf offer rich material for a generic discussion of GDR *Ersatzöffentlichkeit* in themselves, my selection of these two women is marked by another, less explicit motivation. For American feminist Germanists, the work of GDR women writers—Wolf and Königsdorf central among them—has often provided an access to alternative visions for a society beyond both capitalism and patriarchy. Yet the search for those commonalities that would bind us with them has just as often pushed us past a critical assessment of differences between our political and cultural locations. Seemingly straightforward terms—such as author, gender, individual, and institution—need to be made more complicated, as do the relationships between and among them. By theorizing the relationship of author and institution in this article, I have attempted to demonstrate that it is just as problematic to assume a conceptually clear divide between the individual and the state as it is to assume their total congruence. For feminist work on the GDR, this raises important questions about agency and resistance, about body and voice. Reading these texts as the expression of a complicated set of relations can perhaps help us to develop new images with which to think and talk about the GDR and its citizens—not simply as victims of Stalinism or Western cultural imperialism, nor as Stasi agents, but as heterogeneous, discursively inscribed bodies. This would seem to be what Königsdorf is experimenting with herself, as she develops and articulates new ways of saying "I" within the context of a changing public sphere: "...von den Intellektuellen, von den Andersdenkern also, denkt per Definition ein jeder anders als der andere. Wenn ich also von uns spreche, so meine ich durchweg mich" (*Dilemma* 7).

## Notes

I am very grateful to Assenka Oksiloff, as well as to the anonymous reviewers and the editors of the Yearbook, for their extensive and thoughtful criticisms of earlier drafts of this article.

[1] Having failed to gain entrance to a public sphere at home, Maron explored other possible publics, most importantly that of the Federal Republic of Germany, where her books were read. The most notable example of this is the correspondence between Maron and a West German writer-journalist, commissioned and published weekly by *Die Zeit* between July 1987 and March 1988 (subsequently published in book form as *Trotzdem herzliche Grüße*). At that time, *Flugasche* was in fact being considered for much-delayed publication in the GDR, but the *Zeit* correspondence caused East German authorities to reconsider and her contract with the publisher was cancelled.

[2] Bathrick's article offers an excellent introduction to the notion of a literary public sphere in the GDR, as well as a fascinating discussion of the reception there of Ulrich Plenzdorf's *Die neuen Leiden des jungen W.*

[3] See the volume edited by Craig Calhoun, *Habermas and the Public Sphere,* for several examples of this work.

[4] This debate is by now well-documented by articles and anthologies too numerous to mention. The original texts of the debate, as well as some analysis, can be found in Deiritz/Kraus and Golombek/Ratzke. See also the forum articles in *GDR Bulletin* 17.1 (Kuhn, Hörnigk, Fries, Rossman). Andreas Huyssen provides a particularly helpful discussion of the larger terms of the debate in the Federal Republic.

[5] As Anna Kuhn so succinctly puts it: "The Christa Wolf of these reviews bears little resemblance to her earlier persona as constructed by the West German literary establishment. The image of a cowardly, servile, opportunistic, authoritarian personality has replaced the once familiar image of Wolf as a scrupulously honest, self-searching, critical writer, someone worthy of the Federal Republic's most prestigious literary and political awards…. Overall,

they seem intent on destroying the literary icon West Germany had been so instrumental in helping to establish" (9).

[6] See my "Christa Wolf's Signature in and on the Essay: Woman, Science, and Authority" for a discussion of the problem of authorial voice in Wolf's earlier essays.

[7] Christa Wolf was one of several prominent writers in the GDR who publicly protested the expatriation of Wolf Biermann, a popular singer and social critic. Biermann's forced expatriation led to a period of significant upheaval in cultural circles, as many other artists also left the country permanently.

[8] Of the particular action taken after the Biermann affair, she says "...natürlich ging eine ganze Dimension von öffentlicher Wirksamkeit verloren, gingen auch ganz bestimmte Schichten der Bevölkerung, die eben weniger lesen und mehr fernsehen, uns Autoren absolut verloren. Genau das war die Absicht. Das haben wir auch als Absicht erkannt" (*Im Dialog* 106).

[9] Of another speech, given 4 November in Berlin, where rumors of violence circulated as well, she says: "Alarmiert durch Warnungen, feilte ich in der Nacht noch einmal an meinem Redetext, um jede provozierende Wirkung auszuschließen" (*Im Dialog* 12).

[10] See *Im Dialog* 90–92. In the letter to *Junge Welt,* Wolf lambasts the paper for using her name to denounce a book that is critical of the GDR; in the other letter, she criticizes the attorney general for blaming police brutality on supposed provocations by demonstrators in Berlin (7–8 October 1989).

[11] She clearly regards this social function as a moral responsibility, even when transferred onto others: "Wie schön, wenn jetzt Journalisten, Soziologen, Historiker, Psychologen, Gesellschaftswissenschaftler, Philosophen ebenfalls öffentlich *ihre Pflicht* tun werden" (*Im Dialog* 97, my emphasis).

[12] Wolf also participated in this gathering, during which protocols documenting the mistreatment of demonstrators earlier that month in Berlin were read aloud.

[13] The other pre-1989 piece included in this volume that was originally a "public" text, namely a speech given in Marburg on the concept of home [*Heimat*], also addresses problems of personal and collective identity.

[14] "Dem Alten keine Chance geben" was first published in *Neues Deutschland,* January 1991, on the occasion of the PDS Party Conference. While Königsdorf remained in the Party and drew this part of her GDR existence into her ongoing reflections, Wolf left the SED in the summer of 1989. This fact, and her lack of discussion of it in the published texts, presents another interesting point of contrast.

[15] Another explanation for her ability to keep talking can be found in the way in which she is able to translate her role as a writer into a conscious articulation of a democratic public sphere in terms of political theory. The *Wochenpost* article is, among other things, a sweeping analysis of precisely that. Königsdorf employs the tripartite (Habermasian) model of public sphere-state-economy, delineating what she sees as the potential responsibilities of each of these areas

of public life. Interestingly, she refuses to limit herself to the realm of (literary or journalistic) public sphere: she proposes economic policies and considers at one point the possibility of a candidacy for the PDS in the Federal Parliament.

[16] One example of this is her account of the attempt of the *Linke Liste* and the PDS to form a coalition: "Die Westlinken, vom Kollaps des Kommandosystems in Mitleidenschaft gezogen, höchst verletzlich; die unabhängigen Ostlinken, von der SED irgendwann in Mitleidenschaft gezogen, ebenfalls höchst verletzlich..." (*Dilemma* 56-57).

[17] "Ein Glück für uns alle? Ein Briefwechsel" (*Dilemma* 19-25). Other examples of her engagement with different parts of the new public sphere can be found in her correspondence with another woman (*1989* 103-07) and in her volume of protocols entitled *Adieu DDR,* which documents the responses of some of her fellow citizens to the end of the order in which they lived until 1989.

## Works Cited

Bathrick, David. "Kultur und Öffentlichkeit in der DDR." *Literatur der DDR in den siebziger Jahren.* Ed. Peter-Uwe Hohendahl and Patricia Herminghouse. Frankfurt a.M.: Suhrkamp, 1983. 53-81.

Deiritz, Karl, and Hannes Kraus, eds. *Der deutsch-deutsche Literaturstreit oder "Freunde, es spricht sich schlecht mit gebundener Zunge": Analysen und Materialien.* Hamburg: Luchterhand, 1991.

Eley, Geoff. "Nations, Publics, and Political Cultures: Placing Habermas in the Nineteenth Century." *Habermas and the Public Sphere.* 289-339.

Emmerich, Wolfgang. *Kleine Literaturgeschichte der DDR: 1945-1988.* Darmstadt: Luchterhand, 1989.

Fraser, Nancy. "Rethinking the Public Sphere: A Contribution to the Critique of Actually Existing Democracy." *Habermas and the Public Sphere.* 109-42.

Fries, Marilyn Sibley. "When the Mirror is Broken, What Remains? Christa Wolf's *Was bleibt.*" *GDR Bulletin* 17.1 (1991): 11-15.

Golombek, Dieter, and Dietrich Ratzke, eds. *Facetten der Wende: Reportagen über eine deutsche Revolution.* Frankfurt a.M.: Institut für Medienentwicklung und Kommunikation, 1991. Vol. 2.

*Habermas and the Public Sphere.* Ed. Craig Calhoun. Cambridge, MA: MIT Press, 1992.

Hörnigk, Therese. "Von 'Mutter Wolfen' zur 'bösen' Wolf. Oder: Die fremdgesteuerte Metamorphose einer Schriftstellerin im Jahr der deutschen Einheit." *GDR Bulletin* 17.1 (1991): 3-5.

Huyssen, Andreas. "After the Wall: The Failure of German Intellectuals." *New German Critique* 52 (1991): 109-43.

Königsdorf, Helga. *Adieu DDR: Protokolle eines Abschieds.* Reinbek: Rowohlt, 1990.

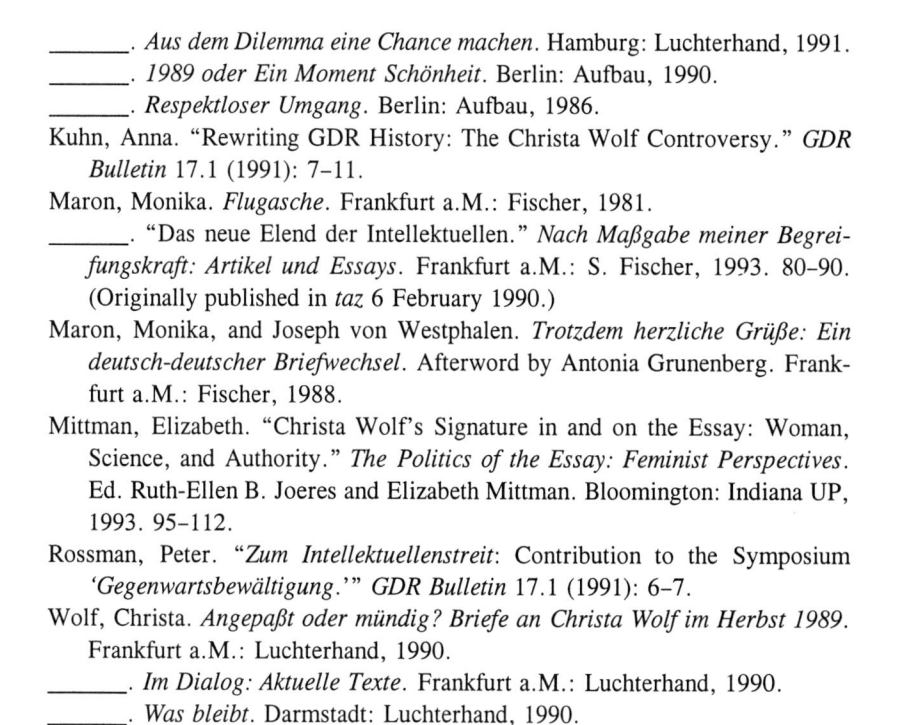

———. *Aus dem Dilemma eine Chance machen*. Hamburg: Luchterhand, 1991.
———. *1989 oder Ein Moment Schönheit*. Berlin: Aufbau, 1990.
———. *Respektloser Umgang*. Berlin: Aufbau, 1986.
Kuhn, Anna. "Rewriting GDR History: The Christa Wolf Controversy." *GDR Bulletin* 17.1 (1991): 7–11.
Maron, Monika. *Flugasche*. Frankfurt a.M.: Fischer, 1981.
———. "Das neue Elend der Intellektuellen." *Nach Maßgabe meiner Begreifungskraft: Artikel und Essays*. Frankfurt a.M.: S. Fischer, 1993. 80–90. (Originally published in *taz* 6 February 1990.)
Maron, Monika, and Joseph von Westphalen. *Trotzdem herzliche Grüße: Ein deutsch-deutscher Briefwechsel*. Afterword by Antonia Grunenberg. Frankfurt a.M.: Fischer, 1988.
Mittman, Elizabeth. "Christa Wolf's Signature in and on the Essay: Woman, Science, and Authority." *The Politics of the Essay: Feminist Perspectives*. Ed. Ruth-Ellen B. Joeres and Elizabeth Mittman. Bloomington: Indiana UP, 1993. 95–112.
Rossman, Peter. "*Zum Intellektuellenstreit*: Contribution to the Symposium 'Gegenwartsbewältigung.'" *GDR Bulletin* 17.1 (1991): 6–7.
Wolf, Christa. *Angepaßt oder mündig? Briefe an Christa Wolf im Herbst 1989*. Frankfurt a.M.: Luchterhand, 1990.
———. *Im Dialog: Aktuelle Texte*. Frankfurt a.M.: Luchterhand, 1990.
———. *Was bleibt*. Darmstadt: Luchterhand, 1990.

# "We are adjacent to human society": German Women Writers, the Homosocial Experience, and a Challenge to the Public/Domestic Dichotomy

Ruth-Ellen B. Joeres

---

With the help of several Anglo-American theoretical texts from philosophy and political theory, the thesis is put forth that the expression of friendship/love that is conveyed by homosocial correspondences between middle-class German women in the late eighteenth and early nineteenth centuries allowed for the creation of another sort of social sphere. This sphere in turn made room for the expression of desire and the construction of identities that the rigid ideology of public and private spheres did not acknowledge. Examples from a letter by Rahel Varnhagen and the epistolary novel *Die Günderode* by Bettine von Arnim are used to illustrate the thesis. (R-EBJ)

---

*...and I thought how unpleasant it is to be locked out; and I thought how it is worse perhaps to be locked in...* —Woolf 24

In a pathbreaking 1983 article, the feminist political theorist Carole Pateman declared that the dichotomy between the public and private spheres "is central to almost two centuries of feminist writing and political struggle; it is, ultimately, what the feminist movement is about" (281). It is, in other words, hardly a new issue that is the subject of this piece: whether it is Jürgen Habermas putting forth his concept of the bourgeois public sphere, or whether it is feminists challenging the idea that there have ever been two discrete entities called the public and private spheres, this is a topic with which many of us coming from very different perspectives are familiar. But for those of us who are involved in the study of literature and history and who have also chosen to work in the area of feminist theory, certain specific questions arise. Where does writing, specifically women's writing, fit into the concept of spheres, for example, especially when the writers were German and were active in the eighteenth and nineteenth centuries, when little in the way of public participation was available to them, and when they chose ostensibly "private" genres like the letter in which to present themselves? How does gender fit into the discussion, especially given the particularly slow path toward a public life that was taken by German women? Does their slow pace imply that they were, at least well into the nineteenth century, inhabitants of a virtually sealed-off enclosure labeled the private sphere? How did the women view themselves? Were they entirely dependent for the definition of their location on the patriarchy that ruled and determined them? Was the marginality that they represented imposed on them, or was it in any way chosen by them?

These and other questions have had me reading in political theory, in the theory of letters, and in letters themselves. What I have been left with is the sense that my set of questions is immensely fluid, and that, in fact, dealing with any group located at a particular time and place may well not provide a useful model for anything more than that momentary spatial and temporal site. Nevertheless, I have found an interesting response that some middle-class (and therefore literate, in the literal sense of the word) German women began to make in the late eighteenth and early nineteenth centuries to a world that was barely of their making and that often viewed them in an oddly prescriptive fashion. If we can assume that "public" implies at least the possibility of a very small circumference—a group, for example, of two, such as two correspondents—then I will claim that these women set up an alternative public sphere that represented a challenge to the status quo. I will try not only to establish that counter-sphere as something different from either the public or private spheres as they have generally been defined, but also to think about the consequences of such an alternative sphere, including the issue of power. The philosophical and theoretical basis for the assertion of a counter-sphere is grounded in ideas presented by various non-German political theorists, philosophers, and literary scholars, most notably Marilyn Friedman's work on friendship, Iris Young's ideas about the problematic nature of communities, Thomas Laqueur's musings on body and gender, and Rita Felski's preliminary thoughts on alternative feminist public spheres.

Numerous feminist scholars have challenged the rigid dichotomization of the public and private sphere ideology: the anthropologist Michelle Rosaldo, for example, indicated already in the 1970s that women might well select the option of forming another sphere while they were in the process of entering what is traditionally viewed as the male public sphere.[1] Certainly the idea that the eighteenth-century bourgeois German world was divided into the neat categories of public and private was questioned as well by Habermas, whose blurring of boundaries is frequently evident in *The Structural Transformation of the Public Sphere*. But by choosing to concentrate on the middle- and upper-class German women who wrote in the late eighteenth and early nineteenth centuries, I have selected a group that was, to all intents and purposes, indeed confined to the home. Aside from the salons that several of them established and that served to bring the outside world into their private world, there was little on any concrete level that touched on what Habermas has defined as the public sphere. It was, in fact, through their writing that connections were initiated that moved them beyond the immediacy of their homes. And it was not only through their letters that they figuratively moved out of the home, connecting with others but also often engaging in debates of issues beyond the domestic sphere; it was, for a few of them, the real step into publishing, often in the letter-related form of the epistolary novel.

The question that I am asking, however, has to do with both the given (the isolation of a domestic sphere) and the way in which that given was interpreted and dealt with by the women whose roles were prescribed by it. Is there a possibility that what Elisabeth Lenk has called "pariah consciousness" might indeed be viewed positively, particularly if one allows the variable of choice to be contemplated: a possibly deliberate choice on the part of Rahel Varnhagen, Bettine von Arnim, Caroline Schlegel-Schelling, and others not to join what Lenk terms the homogenous world of normative male culture but to remain in their marginal heterogeneity and to find value in their difference?[2] Clearly, that choice might amount to replacing one myth—the passive, pliable, dutiful woman who embodies the home—with another, the subtle, sexual being who breaks rules, but who will do little harm and is still relegated to the margin. It might result in the sort of mystification that in the end locates the woman in a place as isolated and as powerless as the traditionally understood private sphere. Or it might lead to the sort of sentimentalization of women that will be viewed as poor and unscientific analysis, ultimately nothing more than an anecdotal blip.

At the same time, it seems to me that the matter of agency and choice can indeed change the picture. A look at various theoretical texts, especially those concerned with community, difference, and friendship, may allow for a different interpretation of the apparently isolated situation of these women that neither mystifies nor sentimentalizes what appears to have occurred. My assertion is that, given a situation in which there was very little that they could do to enter what was traditionally understood as the public sphere—and given that they may have been skeptical about the benefits of such a move in any case—a number of bourgeois German women chose an alternative route by creating a sphere that was neither public nor private (at least as those terms were understood), by breaking the boundaries and deliberately selecting another way that focused on homosocial relationships, i.e., social relationships with members of the same sex.[3] The literary form that best embodies this idea of public and private and that has specific relevance to Germany in the era in which I am interested is the letter, a form that ostensibly was private but that—at least in the eighteenth century—rarely remained so. The public that was involved also often extended beyond the letter's recipient and may well not have involved a single gender. At the same time, I am particularly interested in the homosocial aspects of letter-writing as well as in the extension of the letter into the public form of the epistolary novel.

By concerning myself with what I see as a counter-sphere, I am also inclined to think about the dichotomies not only of the public and the domestic, but also the individual and the community, an issue of particular concern to feminists. Focusing on the individual—by emphasizing the "female voice," "the female self," etc.—has been called into question in recent years by the growing preponderance of a postmodernist preference for critiquing, indeed doing away altogether with, the idea of the unified self. For women who are now learning to stand on their own, to claim individuality, this is obviously a problem. But even if the individual is allowed to remain in the picture, it still is located in opposition to community, which also conflicts with the aims of a feminist movement, with its emphasis on the need for community, for mutual support, for coalition-building. As Bernice Johnson Reagon says, "you don't do no coalition-building in a womb" (359).

The concept of a community itself is also hardly unproblematic. As Iris Young has remarked, individuals as well as communities are very rarely diverse: we speak of the individual, and we generally mean a man; feminists speak of the "female voice" or the individual woman, for example, and in the past, at least, have often meant white, western, middle-class women. The very idea of a community—the inclusivity that it implies—is, according to Young, improbable, since communities are often only set up in contrast to other, different communities, with an aim to disregarding or getting rid of differences within a specific group. In other words, identity politics can only go so far, and ultimately one ends up right back at individualization and isolation. There is no guarantee that a community is in any case more than a sometime thing, a group of people who join together for a specific and temporary purpose and who tend to separate again.[4]

To raise the flag of community to describe these women, then, is not as useful as it might initially seem. To see Rahel Varnhagen, Bettine von Arnim, Karoline von Günderrode, and others among their contemporaries in Germany during the late eighteenth and early nineteenth centuries in some sort of communal set-up is too imprecise. And that is why I have moved away from community to the more specific, more limited, but perhaps more useful concept of friendship. It is here that the philosopher Marilyn Friedman has offered several ideas that echo Iris Young's skepticism about community and suggest another model. Although she sees power in the idea of the "self as deriving its identity and nature from its social relationships, from the way it is intersubjectively apprehended, from the norms of the community in which it is embedded" (144), Friedman recognizes great limitations to the communitarian philosophy that, at least in the past, has been particularly detrimental for women and other marginal groups who are often excluded or exploited in the formation of communities. She mentions, for example, the communitarian emphasis on the traditional idea of "the family," which shows little regard for the feminist stress on "the need for change in all the traditions and practices which show gender differentiation" (149).

Where the idea of community becomes interesting for Friedman (and for me) is in the examination of communities in terms of their being discovered or chosen. Discovery implies already-existing communities—churches, labor unions, schools, etc.—that one enters. These are givens, particularly helpful for individuals who are beginning to reflect on their own identities. But choice implies creativity, "communities of choice, supplementing, if not displacing, the communities and attachments which are merely found" (152)—i.e., discovered. The discovered communities, as important and useful as they always are, may not represent us in entirely satisfactory ways; they may indeed "harbor ambiguities, ambivalences, contradictions, and oppressions which complicate as well as constitute identity and which have to be sorted out, critically scrutinized." But "our theories of community should recognize that resources and skills derived from communities which are not merely found or discovered may equally well contribute to the constitution of identity" (153). And the particularity that is implied here—that which makes us specifically who we are—may well require something very different from that which already exists, the pool on which we normally draw.

Friedman then moves into the specific realm of friendship, one that has implications and applications for what I have found in the writings of Varnhagen, Arnim, and others. Friendship itself fits into the realm of choice, rather than discovery: it is based on voluntary choice, which Friedman defines in this instance as emerging from "motivations arising out of one's own needs, desires, interests, values, and attractions, in contrast to motivations arising from what is socially assigned, ascribed, expected, or demanded" (154). Friendship was widely encouraged in the eighteenth century, but unlike family, it remained an option, a choice. It may well have been the site for resolving some of the contradictions between prescription and desire that women like Varnhagen and Arnim experienced in their narrow world of acceptable activity. And because friendship, unlike family, may involve tolerance for certain deviant behaviors and ideas that a family will not accept, it has "socially disruptive possibilities, for out of the unconventional living which it helps to sustain there often arise influential forces for social change" (154-55).

In other words, friendship could result in something involving the presence and production of power. One need only think of the feminist movement, of consciousness-raising groups, and other activities of the 1970s, to recognize a connection between friendship and social, revolutionary change. The homosocial activities that arose in that movement—the chosen move from (given or found) communities into communities of choice that were based on gender as well as political convictions—indeed became a basis for social, philosophical, and political transformation.

Communities of choice, like friendship, says Friedman, "may be sought out as contexts in which people relocate the various constituents of their identities.... While people in a community of choice may not share a common history, their shared values or interests are likely to manifest backgrounds of similar experiences, as, for example, among the members of a lesbian community. The modern [in this case, the new, or reconstituted] self may seek new communities whose norms and relationships stimulate and develop her identity and self-understanding more adequately than her unchosen community of origin, her original community of place" (157). And the fact that such selves may well be viewed in their communities of origins as "deviants and resisters" (certainly a common accusation among those arbiters of public taste in eighteenth- and nineteenth-century Germany who scorned the entrance of women into the public world of publishing) makes their move into a chosen community—however that community may be defined—a sign of elected difference.

Thus far, it seems to me, much of what Friedman has said and I have paraphrased and discussed is probably, but not necessarily, gender-specific. The common oppression shared by the community of women who wrote in the eighteenth century was an oppression certainly experienced by numbers of men as well, albeit within a different set of social dimensions—one need only read Karl Philip Moritz, for example, or think about class or race or ethnic rather than gender differences. Where the discussion becomes gender-specific may be when we begin to consider "politics and the biology of two sexes," as Laqueur calls it in his examination of the role of sexual difference in the establishment of private and public spheres (194). Here it becomes a matter of the rationalization for a separate public sphere in the first place, and it is important to note that, (the mostly gender-neutral) Habermas notwithstanding, sexual difference played a considerable role in the defining of both private and public spheres. As Laqueur comments, "[t]he creation of a bourgeois public sphere...raised with a vengeance the question of which sex(es) ought legitimately to occupy it. And everywhere biology entered the discourse" (194). What is overridingly significant in this biological differentiation, however, has to do with desire or the presumed lack of it: in this case, the pacification of women, reducing them to an essentially pure, pedestalized, but passive, desireless state, and the always-present dichotomous position of men who own all the desire. When women were described by numerous eighteenth-century theorists of the letter as "natural," and as in that way reflecting what was considered appropriate for the letter, there was the assumption that "natural" also implied "the male domination of women, of sexual passion and jealousy, of the sexual division of labor and of cultural practices..." (196). What amounts to "a biology of sexual incommensurability," as Laqueur calls it, allowed those who dominated to call upon nature to point out the passivity and subordination of the female in nature, to justify a separation of spheres, to establish what Laqueur calls "the discursive creation of difference" (198). And the result—thanks to Diderot, Rousseau, and others—is the creation of an ideal woman who can be consigned to a private space because she essentially belongs there. "To be a woman in civil society," remarks Laqueur, "is to be modest, to create but not to have desire. To be otherwise is to be 'unnatural'" (200). With the permission granted to be creative (albeit without desire), certain "'polite accomplishments'" (John Millar [1793] quoted in Lacquer 201) are granted to women, who are viewed in this scheme as different but not unequal—thus the aligning of the letter genre with women, since in its preferred form it so obviously resembled the natural and unsophisticated (and in that way law-less) realm of women. The letter was hardly a revolutionary challenging of any gender role; it was instead viewed as the successful carrying-out of what it is that women, given their make-up, are capable of. The lack of desire, the passionlessness that are assumed to be part and parcel of the domestic sphere may also be reflected in the letter, which was prescribed by the eighteenth-century theoreticians writing on the letter as a form that was governed at least by a certain sense of propriety.[5] The letter, after all, was frequently seen as a mirror of friendship: letters were exchanged not only between lovers, but also between friends.[6]

But the "biology of cosmic hierarchy" that involved a move away from discussions of equality versus inequality into the realm of difference also "required interpretation and became the weapon of cultural and political struggle" (Laqueur 207). Certainly, the concept of separate-but-equal espoused by Rousseau and others emerged from this hierarchy and was as contradictory as any simultaneous grouping of the concepts of equality and hierarchy is bound to be. In the writings of Varnhagen and Arnim it is this very interpretation of difference that I find so intriguing. I see them offering an alternative way, not only in what they write but also in their choice of the letter form, with both the confining and the extending elements that the letter entails—the distances but also the closenesses that are implied in a letter. To illustrate my point, I want to cite, then discuss, a passage from a letter from Rahel Varnhagen to her friend, the actress Pauline Wiesel, that includes the quotation I used in my title:

> And we have been created in order to live truth in this world. And coming from different directions we have arrived at the same point. We are adjacent to human society. For us there is no location, no office, no vain title! Lies all have [such a location]: Eternal Truth, the proper life and feeling that lead back in unbroken form to the innermost human dispositions, to the nature that we can grasp! And in this way we are shut out of society—you, because you insulted it. (I congratulate you on that! at least you got something out of it, many days of pleasure!) I, because I cannot sin or lie to it [society] (Varnhagen to Wiesel, Berlin, 12 March 1810).[7]

One cannot read a passage such as this and see only the mystification or sentimentalization of the woman. Varnhagen does not allow us to think in that way. Her language is so rich in contradictions, in ambiguous interpretations of the role she and Pauline Wiesel are meant to fulfill, that, when it comes to defining their outsider status as women, their lack of a concrete presence at least in the public sphere, the question of insiderdom inevitably arises as well: to hear this quotation and to see beyond the words[8] is to discover considerably more about that which is most essential, namely the perception of place and role that Rahel Varnhagen—viewed because of her gender as well as her religion as part of a marginal group—represented.

In the years in which Rahel Varnhagen lived and wrote and held her salon, women were by virtue of their biological sex, their sexual role definition, their lack of self-created tradition and history, and their position within the scheme of thinking that produced such a concept as a public sphere, outsiders, marginal to the seats of power and influence.[9] They were, as Varnhagen comments, "adjacent to human [i.e., male] society," devoid of public standing, place, professional status, title.[10] Yet the quotation from her letter to Pauline Wiesel begins with a "we," that is, with the establishment of a group in and of itself that perhaps shares no common history, but that has come together and now makes up a unit whose purpose is, according to Varnhagen, to represent the truth. And a group that is still uncertain and disjointed: the middle section of the quotation is awash in ambivalences and mystifications, particularly with the illusion of woman as the carrier of Eternal Truth (as opposed to the simple, unadorned truth mentioned in the first sentence) and as the representative of feeling and nature, a role that Rousseau, Campe, and others had assigned to her to give her a sense of importance that she might otherwise have lacked, but that really made of her an unreal, a "metaphorical woman," to use Jonathan Culler's term for such an uneasy position.[11] The complex syntax of Varnhagen's letter makes the ambivalence even more apparent; the colon after the assertive statement about the lies that govern her life is confusing, the sudden expression of prescriptive thoughts on the woman's purpose and role is somehow tacked on, yet insistent. But this digression is followed by a return to the sense of the unifying force of the "we," the group. The reassertion of their status as women is by no means gloomy and indeed is marked by congratulatory, praising words and a joyful acceptance of another grouping: we, the rebels, we, the honest ones, have formed a group of our own, we, the pariahs, view ourselves as a supportive unit—indeed as a supportive universe—unto ourselves. We are our own chosen public sphere. The acknowledgement of difference thus formulates the basis not for a grouping in passivity, but rather a new alignment, a new assertion of subjecthood, one from the perspective of which the rest of the world now takes on alien, Other status. There is no sense of isolation or passivity or of lack of desire in Varnhagen's letter; instead, the move from muted to dominant position, from ineffective inhabitant of the passive and isolated private sphere to a new and dynamic definition of another public space, is paramount. And this new and chosen community is significantly one of women.

It is not only Rahel Varnhagen's friendship with Pauline Wiesel that reveals this new status, this band of those who live truth. Bettine von Arnim's memorial to her friend, *Die Günderode,* is a paean to outsiders as new center, the creation of a sphere of friendship, another "we," who are by virtue of their gender—as well as their beliefs—not a part of the ruling patriarchy. Arnim and Günderrode go beyond the externals of friendship, in fact: they actually establish a new religion for their group, a religion based on no male god, no male savior, on no central figure at all, a religion, one might say, of the margin, rich in borrowed elements, to be sure, but elements that have also been reappropriated and transformed to be flexible, open-ended, non-dogmatic. Their group thereby begins to take on defining characteristics, establishes its separate identity, becomes a valid alternative viewed very much from its own perspective at the center of its own sphere. In the world of difference that they created, the words remained essentially the same, the language often indeed highly imitative of their male counterparts. Where contrasts emerged was in the imagery, which appeared, as it does in Varnhagen's letter to Wiesel, ambivalent and fragmentary, a mixing of patriarchal normalization, social commentary, as well as a further element, an effort to define and locate themselves as women. The creation of a countersphere as a reaction to a world in which their outsider status meant essentially that they were defined by others and belonged only in the place/sphere assigned to them was a positive response to whatever might be lacking in their acculturated roles.

For Varnhagen, Wiesel, Arnim, and Günderrode, friendship is the chosen model of sociability, a friendship that has at its focus the homo-social connections among women. It would perhaps be possible to define such a relationship in terms of what is commonly understood as the private sphere, the sphere that encompassed the family. But these women were not members of a related family, and the manner in which they communicated with one another involved, most certainly in the case of Arnim's biographical/autobiographical novel, the public sphere: it was published, it was printed, it was read by many more readers than simply the correspondents themselves. Letters too were often read "publicly," that is, they were to be shared by many more than the single recipient. And as to Friedman's talk of revolution when she discusses friendship, the very homosociality represented in these epistolary exchanges is a change from the usual and the expected. The passionate language of these correspondents of the same sex subverted at least on a symbolic level what was the expected and only acceptable form for sexual love, the heterosexual relationship between women and men.[12]

One can challenge Laqueur's perception of desireless women by using the example of *Günderode,* a volume that fairly bursts with an active, questing desire. Arnim and Günderrode show a robust passion for one another, in language that, even if it seems at times to resemble the ardent but formulaic friendship characteristic of eighteenth-century letters, nevertheless contradicts the normative perceptions of appropriate and acceptable sexual relationships. These women are agents who choose and create something else: the loving and at times erotic epistolary relationship with one another, the establishing of a group of likeness, a collective consciousness on however limited a plane.[13] Rahel Varnhagen's letters to Pauline Wiesel created a discourse that not only intended communication, dialogue, and the awareness of connection—these were certainly aims that she had in her correspondences with women and men alike—she also drew gender-specific webs of connection to Pauline Wiesel, Regina Frohberg, and various other women. That she wrote to men as well as to women does not eliminate the power of her letters to Wiesel, with whom she established a particular homosocial alliance, an obvious "we." Bettine von Arnim wrote admiringly, worshipfully, not only of Karoline von Günderrode, but also of Goethe, Philipp Nathusius, her brother Clemens, and other males, yet it is in her tribute to her female friend that the sense of group formation and of alliances and commonalities comes most powerfully to the fore. She admires and worships Goethe hierarchically, as a child would worship a mentor—but she spends nights dreaming with Günderrode, she establishes a religion with her, she shares her self with her, she feels equal to her. Günderrode herself writes passionate epistles to Gunda and Bettine Brentano and receives her most intimate and self-identifying letters from Lisette Nees; here too, relationships were formed that are in a sphere far removed from the male sphere that generally dominated her thinking and her writing.[14]

Personal letters—those exchanged between friends or lovers—have been described by Janet Altman as "mediators of desire in the communication process" (19). As she comments, on one level they represent the metaphorical lover in the epistolary situation, conjuring up interiorized images and comparisons; on another, by virtue of its physical contact with the recipient, with the beloved, the letter stands for the metonymic lover. Altman sees letters as straddling the gulf between presence and absence, for two persons who "meet" through the letter are neither totally separated nor totally united, thus increasing the possibilities for the expression of desire (43). By so doing she also manages to counter Laqueur, for if the letter expresses desire—and is also a form that is considered appropriate to women—then women can hardly be seen as desire-less. What often occurs in epistolary novels like *Günderode* is, in fact, a tension between what Altman labels *amitié* and *amour,* which "seems to derive from the nature of the epistolary exchange itself, which sets up two essential categories of letter writers, lovers and friend-confidants, who speak two fundamental kinds of language: on the one hand that of candor and *confiance* [which she defines elsewhere as "self-confidence, faith in others, willingness to confide" (63)], on the other that of coquetry, mystification, and dissimulation" (81). With friends, in other words, one tends to be honest, direct, open; with lovers, indirect, masked, possibly even dishonest. Restraint will be shown with a lover; real sentiments will be confided to a friend. The divisions are drawn.

But are they? In Altman's study of epistolarity there is also a frequent emphasis on friendship, much as there is in the critical literature on the letter written in Germany in the eighteenth century: friendship was a focus in discussions of the letter, along with the philosophical extensions that centered on communication among individuals and the more encompassing ideas of "Humanität." At the same time, the letters exchanged between the friends Bettine von Arnim and Karoline von Günderrode are not only honest, direct, and open, they also show considerable evidence of the lover's coquetry and flirtation, of fantasizing if not lying, of little restraint. The boundaries between love and friendship are thus blurred. There is a clear difference made evident here between the letter exchanges of a woman and a man, or as here, of two women: in the latter case, that of lover/confidante who expresses the desire and passion, the masking and coquetry characteristic of heterosexual love letters, but who writes as well with the self-confidence and directness characteristic of letters between friends. And as in all letters, there is the implied or stated longing for response: "To write a letter is not only to define oneself in relationship to a particular *you*; it is also an attempt to draw that *you* into becoming the *I* of a new statement" (Altman 122). Reciprocity, connection, desire, often passion: these are the elements that are found in the letter exchanges between the women whom I have included here. And in that back-and-forth there is the continuous sense of a space, a homosocial sphere, that is being chosen and created by the women who are engaging in the exchanges. At least in the realm of the written texts, women are creating relationships among themselves that expand and re-shape the rest of their prescribed lives.

Descriptive words are inexact and inadequate in a discussion like this. "Friendship" is no more appropriate than "love" in my effort to describe what was transpiring between these women. "Loving friendship" sounds bland, bordering on sentimentalization. "Friendly love" is too banal. What occurred is something that crosses any number of boundaries, attempts to break down barriers created by role expectations, normalizing gender role processes, gender definitions, not to mention understandings of the realms we have in retrospect labeled public and private spheres. There is considerably more here in the way of active, dynamic choice, of rebellion, of a powerful creative effort to revise and re-vision the parameters of existence. Whether the word "power" is in any way appropriate in this discussion is a difficult question. Certainly the women who exchanged these letters and wrote the epistolary novels gained no political power in the commonly understood sense of the word; they did not expand their influence, wield power in a larger sphere, affect the state (although Arnim certainly affected the marketplace once her letter novels were published and available for sale).

At the same time, the very choice of these connections between friends seems to me to expand and strengthen the idea of marginality well beyond the usual realm of the powerlessness it has until recently been presumed to represent. In this instance, the margin assumes the importance of location: as Trinh Minh-ha says in her wonderful essay on marginalization, "[t]he margins, our sites of survival, become our fighting grounds and their site for pilgrimage" (17). Bourgeois women's letters in the eighteenth century were indeed a "site for pilgrimage" for the patriarchy which, while it clearly retained the role of prescription and assignation, nevertheless allotted a certain amount of influence and power to the women whose letter-writing style it wished men to emulate. And as to the women who were consigned to the margin: it is a matter of perspective as to whether they saw that positioning as entirely negative and powerless or as a site from which to engage in choice and creativity. To be marginal may grow out of imposition or necessity; that does not rule out choice. In this context, I am reminded of Marilyn Frye's comment on the role of agency in the positive choice of marginalization:

> For the benefits of marginality to be reaped, marginality must in some sense be chosen. Even if, in one's own individual history, one experiences one's patterns of desire as given [in Friedman's terms, found, discovered] and not chosen, one may deny, resist, tolerate or embrace them. One can choose a way of life which is devoted to changing them, disguising oneself or

escaping the consequences of difference, or a way of life which takes on one's difference as integral to one's stance and location in the world. If one takes the route of denial and avoidance, one cannot take difference as a resource. One cannot see what is to be seen from one's particular vantage point or know what can be known to a body so located if one is preoccupied with wishing one were not there, denying the peculiarity of one's position, disowning oneself (149-50).

Certainly, the wish not to be present is not evident in Varnhagen's letter to Wiesel, or in Arnim's exuberant letters to Günderrode. There are congratulation and triumph in the Varnhagen letter; there is joy in the Arnim/Günderrode exchange, a sense that there is benefit for both of them in their communication with one another. What this might say about power is that it is perhaps a power of appropriation, the appropriation of gendered role definitions and the re-writing, re-thinking, re-conceptualizing of those roles in ways that will grant power to those who are doing the appropriating.

The counter-sphere that I see created through this medium—this choice—of the letter among German women also has an element of disinterest in the other spheres, certainly as they have been defined for us. There is little in these letters that indicates an interest in the prescribed culture of the eighteenth-century private sphere, the assigned location of women, or in the public sphere, at least as far as that sphere was concerned with matters of politics and the state.[15] These letters represent another social grouping, one centering on homosocial friendship and love and the dynamic power inherent in the matter of choice: the choice of friends, of companions, of seeking out likeness. Here, in other words, is more evidence of power: the power of creativity, of creating a sphere for one's self and for others who resemble that self.[16] There is, to be sure, a sense of an exclusive community that will shut out those who do not resemble the community, but at the same time, there is the strength that those who were marginalized because of their gender (if not because of their class) might gain from finding each other. Within the context of eighteenth- and early nineteenth-century Germany, there was in these exchanges between middle-class, articulate women evidence of a primitive, limited, but nevertheless impressive identity politics. And the epistolary form—with its capacity for expressing the sentiment of friendship—provided the tools for such a significant step.

In her book *Beyond Feminist Aesthetics,* Rita Felski introduces what she chooses to call the "feminist counter-sphere," a concept that is a product of this century and not the era to which I have been referring. The sphere that she sees in current feminist literature is based on a knowledge of oppression as the factor uniting all of those who are a part of the sphere. It has a dual function: internally, it entails a generating of a gender-specific identity "grounded in a consciousness of community and solidarity among women." And externally, it seeks to convince the society as a whole of the "validity of feminist claims...political activity...theoretical critique" (168). It does not really resemble the realm that has been the focus of my attention in my reading of Rahel Varnhagen and Bettine von Arnim. It involves, at least in part, very much an outer-directed movement: an effort to convince the rest of the world of the importance of women and of feminism. In that way, it takes on the more familiar contours of a public sphere in Habermasian terms: a reasoning body of human beings, in this case feminist women, who unite and use their *Räsonnement* to exert influence on the state. Unified under the banner of oppression, it forms an exclusive community of those who perhaps share nothing more than their common oppressed status as women. The fact that they are feminists narrows the group somewhat, for these are women who are not only aware of their oppression, they want to do something about it.

What a difference a century and a half (or more) make. The alternative sphere that I see developing among German bourgeois, literate women at the turn into the nineteenth century could not have been more private, at least in terms of its intended effect on the larger community of the state. Yet in its communicative function, its aims to find likeness and points of connection, its establishment of the "we," its appropriation and transformation of rigidifying gender constructs into what might be viewed as startlingly different possibilities, it indeed had the potential of being revolutionary. The fact that it did not connect with the wider world of the public sphere does not mean that it did not have public consequences, on however subtle a level.

The choice of friendship in a gendered margin made it possible to create a sphere that was as full of desire as it was of connection. Rahel Varnhagen's and Bettine von Arnim's articulation of their status is often joyful and innovative, an answer to the oppression of that other sphere in which they played such a prescribed role. The creative strength of their alternative way of thinking and living provides feminist critics today with an enlightening and broadening view of how the re-definition of reality and knowledge was (and is still) possible and productive. In practical terms, these women continued to reside on the fringes, but in their perception of themselves and of their female friends they had begun to think in terms of a group, a sphere. It is, after all, all a matter of perception: Virginia Woolf's realization of that fact upon being barred from the "Oxbridge" library thus echoes the re-visionary thinking begun so long before her and our time.

## Notes

[1] See in particular her "Woman, Culture, and Society: A Theoretical Overview."

[2] A point of differentiation: Bettine von Arnim certainly entered a public sphere in ways that Varnhagen and other contemporary women did not. She published, after all; she also involved herself in matters of the court. But I still want to include her here primarily because of her epistolary novel/biography *Günderode,* which presents what I view as a clear move toward another sort of heterogeneity—not to mention its wonderful display of the homosocial pattern I am pinpointing in this article.

[3] "Homosocial" is a descriptive word that appears frequently in the writings of queer theory: see, for example, Eve Kosofsky Sedgwick's *Epistemology of the Closet* (88), in which she speaks of a "continuum of male or female homosocial desire," in a reflection of Adrienne Rich's well-known "lesbian continuum." Despite Sedgwick's stated belief that "...people of the same gender, people grouped together under the single most determinative diacritical mark of social organization, people whose economic, institutional, emotional, physical needs and knowledges may have so much in common, should bond together also on the axis of sexual desire" (87), homosociality is distinguished from homosexuality by an absence of a sexual component.

[4] June Jordan provides an illustrative comment in this regard: "'It occurs to me that much organizational grief could be avoided if people understood that partnership in misery does not necessarily provide for partnership for change; when we get the monsters off our backs all of us may want to run in very different directions'" (quoted in Adams 28).

[5] There is a growing body of feminist literary-critical work specifically centering on German women and their use of the letter, a list too long to detail here. That research is not entirely pertinent to the particular focus of this paper. Notable US Germanist contributions in this area include Kay Goodman's two articles in 1980 and 1982 and Liliane Weissberg's "Turns of Emancipation." Both offer useful insights particularly into the letters of Rahel Varnhagen. "Leben als Text: Briefe als Ausdrucks-und Verständigungsmittel in der Briefkultur und Literatur des 18. Jahrhunderts," Barbara Becker-Cantarino's contribution to the anthology *Frauen Literatur Geschichte* gives a helpful overview of the topic of German women and letters in the eighteenth century. Several German/Germanist contributions to the topic have emerged in recent years. A very good new anthology that shows particular sensitivity to the issue of gender in the letter theory of eighteenth-century Germany is *Brieftheorie des 18. Jahrhunderts: Texte, Kommentare, Essays.* A companion volume to this anthology is *Die Frau im Dialog: Studie zu Theorie und Geschichte des Briefes.* Another recent volume that discusses the particular connections between friendship, letters, and (on occasion) women is *Frauenfreundschaft—Männerfreundschaft: Literarische Diskurse im 18. Jahrhundert.* A further investigation of the topic of my article and

of the related issues of self-representation makes up part of a volume I am completing on labelling and self-representation in the writings of nineteenth-century German women.

[6] And letters were read aloud, thus expanding their immediate audience. Letters that are read aloud also gain a power of sorts through that expansion: a current example is provided in Jutta Brückner's film *Kolossale Liebe,* whose text consists primarily of the letters—spoken aloud—of Rahel Varnhagen. Here letters become dialogue and take on an even more powerful life of their own; letters are visible, heard, almost tangible.

[7] The original German for this literally translated quotation from Varnhagen's letter to her friend Pauline Wiesel is as follows: "Und wir sind geschaffen, die Wahrheit in dieser Welt zu leben. Und auf verschiedenem Wege sind wir zu Einem Punkt gelangt. Wir sind neben der menschlichen Gesellschaft. Für uns ist kein Platz, kein Amt, kein eitler Titel da! Alle Lügen haben einen: die ewige Wahrheit, das richtige Leben und Fühlen, das sich unabgebrochen auf einfach tiefe Menschenanlagen, auf die für uns zu fassende Natur zurückzuführen läßt, hat keinen! Und somit sind wir ausgeschloßen aus der Gesellschaft, Sie, weil Sie sie beleidigten. (Ich gratuliere Ihnen dazu! so hatten Sie doch etwas; viele Tage der Lust!) Ich, weil ich nicht mit ihr sündigen und lügen kann" (*Rahel Varnhagen* 56).

[8] See Mary Daly: "In the beginning was not the word. In the beginning is the hearing" (424).

[9] I am aware of the danger of universalizing in using the unqualified label "women" in a discussion in which I am concerning myself exclusively with those German women of the middle and upper classes who were articulate and literate, who wrote and were published and thus left a record for us of their various positions. They were, of course, an exclusive group, their "confinement" to the private sphere a result of wealth, privilege, and/or the good luck at finding a husband to support them. No working-class woman had the luxury of such a location, and for her, the matter of public and private spheres certainly had little, if any meaning. That fact does not detract, however, from the importance of studying the written records that we do possess, and trying to determine, despite the complexities of distance and time-based perception, what those women thought of their own specific location. It is within that context that my piece should be read and understood.

[10] Habermas himself essentially equates the German terms "menschlich" and "männlich": at the point where he is working on establishing a definition of the public sphere and its inhabitants, he comments: "The status of private man combined the role of owner of commodities with that of head of the family, that of property owner with that of 'human being' *per se*" (28-29).

[11] "Celebrations of woman or the identification of woman with some powerful force or idea—truth as a woman, liberty as a woman, the muses as women—identify actual women as marginal. Woman can be a symbol of truth only if she is denied an effective relation to truth, only if one presumes that

those seeking truth are men. The identification of woman with poetry through the figure of the muse also assumes that the poet will be a man. While appearing to celebrate the feminine, this model denies women an active role in the system of literary production and bars them from the literary tradition" (Jonathan Culler 166–67.) I am struck by the statements of such critics as Laqueur and Culler: in their agreement that women have been mistreated, oppressed, and treated mostly as marginal objects, they run the risk of marginalizing women even more in the process—certainly of ignoring the possibilities for power and desire that I am beginning to recognize.

[12] My cautious language is intentional. Despite the fact that Marilyn Friedman uses a lesbian community as an example for the chosen community of friends she is trying to characterize, my awareness of the common use of passionate language in eighteenth-century letters between women and my sense that it borders on the formulaic hold me back from assuming anything more than a passion of words, not of actions, even if, according to Adrienne Rich, their language would place these women somewhere along the lesbian continuum. Although Carroll Smith-Rosenberg's widely acclaimed *Signs* article makes a strong case for seeing the letters of nineteenth-century American women as indicative of something certainly bordering on sexuality, given my present knowledge I am able only to go so far with this—indeed, to conclude, as Smith-Rosenberg also ultimately does, that this language implies a "spectrum of emotions between love, sensuality, and sexuality" (27).

[13] Toni A. H. McNaron has, in fact, taken this idea of likeness to form the basis of a new theoretical way of formulating a lesbian aesthetic in the study of literature.

[14] For the Lisette Nees letters, see Max Preitz.

[15] At a March 1992 conference in Montreal on women artists and art theorists, a commonly heard refrain was the disinterest on the part of the artists in what they called the public sphere, which many of them view as damaging to their freedom of expression and their creativity. Certainly the backlash that questioned the existence of the NEA during the Reagan/Bush years also brought forth comments from artists who see the agency as far too prescriptive and who would indeed prefer withdrawing from any public support because of their sense of the constraints that are placed on them via that support.

I am also reminded of Dorothy Dinnerstein's *The Mermaid and the Minotaur: Sexual Arrangements and Human Malaise*: in a passage on the "immunity," as she calls it, that women obtain, essentially by living according to patriarchal prescription, she comments that "…the immunity life offers woman is immunity not only from the risks and exertions of history-making, but also from the history-maker's legitimate internal misgivings about the value of what he spends his life doing" (213).

[16] There is also a certain challenge to the privileging of the public sphere in this ignoring of its characteristic elements: the contempt of a Hannah Arendt, for example, when she writes of the private sphere in contrast to her ideas of how

the far more important sphere of politics is formed, does not play a role here at all, where it is more a matter of disinterest in the usual substance of either the public or private spheres as they are traditionally defined (see Brown on Arendt).

## Works Cited

Adams, Mary Louise. "There's No Place Like Home: On the Place of Identity in Feminist Politics." *Feminist Review* 31 (Spring 1989): 22–33.

Altman, Janet. *Epistolarity: Approaches to a Form.* Columbus: Ohio State UP, 1982.

Arnim, Bettina von. *Die Günderode.* Frankfurt: Insel, 1983.

Becker-Cantarino, Barbara. "Leben als Text: Briefe als Ausdrucks- und Verständigungsmittel in der Briefkultur und Literatur des 18. Jahrhunderts." *Frauen Literatur Geschichte: Schreibende Frauen vom Mittelalter bis zur Gegenwart.* Ed. Hiltrud Gnüg and Renate Möhrmann. Stuttgart: Metzler, 1985. 83–103.

*Brieftheorie des 18. Jahrhunderts: Texte, Kommentare, Essays.* Ed. Angelika Ebrecht, Regine Nörtemann, and Herta Schwarz. Stuttgart: Metzler, 1990.

Brown, Wendy. "Arendt: The Fragility of Politics." *Manhood and Politics: A Feminist Reading in Political Theory.* Totowa, NJ: Rowman, 1988. 23–31.

Culler, Jonathan. *On Deconstruction: Theory and Criticism After Structuralism.* Ithaca: Cornell UP, 1982.

Daly, Mary. *Gyn/Ecology: The Metaethics of Radical Feminism.* Boston: Beacon, 1978.

Dinnerstein, Dorothy. *The Mermaid and the Minotaur: Sexual Arrangements and Human Malaise.* New York: Harper, 1976.

Felski, Rita. *Beyond Feminist Aesthetics: Feminist Literature and Social Change.* Cambridge: Harvard UP, 1989.

*Die Frau im Dialog: Studie zur Theorie und Geschichte des Briefes.* Ed. Anita Runge und Lieselotte Steinbrügge. Stuttgart: Metzler, 1991.

*Frauenfreundschaft—Männerfreundschaft: Literarische Diskurse im 18. Jahrhundert.* Ed. Wolfram Mauser and Barbara Becker-Cantarino. Tübingen: Niemeyer, 1991.

Friedman, Marilyn. "Feminism and Modern Friendship: Dislocating the Community." *Feminism and Political Theory.* Ed. Cass R. Sunstein. Chicago: U of Chicago P, 1990. 143–58.

Frye, Marilyn. "Lesbian Feminism and the Gay Rights Movement: Another View of Male Supremacy, Another Separatism." *The Politics of Reality: Essays in Feminist Theory.* Trumansburg, NY: Crossing, 1983. 128–51.

Goodman, Katherine. "The Impact of Rahel Varnhagen on Women in the Nineteenth Century." *Gestaltet und Gestaltend: Frauen in der deutschen Literatur.* Ed. Marianne Burkhard. Amsterdam: Rodopi, 1980. 125–53.

———. "Poesis and Praxis in Rahel Varnhagen's Letters." *New German Critique* 27 (Fall 1982): 123-39.

Habermas, Jürgen. *The Structural Transformation of the Public Sphere: An Inquiry into a Category of Bourgeois Society.* Trans. Thomas Burger and Frederick Lawrence. Cambridge, MA: MIT Press, 1991.

Laqueur, Thomas. *Making Sex: Body and Gender from the Greeks to Freud.* Cambridge: Harvard UP, 1990.

Lenk, Elisabeth. "Indiskretion des Federviehs: Pariabewußtsein schreibender Frauen seit der Romantik." *Pauline Wiesel. Rahel Varnhagen: Briefwechsel 1808-1832.* Berlin: Edition Sirene/Verlag Ausprunk und Peters, 1982. 141-70.

McNaron, Toni. "Mirrors and Likeness: A Lesbian Aesthetic in the Making." *Sexual Practice, Textual Theory: Lesbian Cultural Criticism.* Ed. Susan J. Wolfe and Julia Penelope. Cambridge: Blackwell, 1993. 291-306.

Pateman, Carole. "Feminist Critiques of the Public/Private Dichotomy." *Public and Private in Social Life.* Ed. S.I. Benn and G.F. Gaus. London: Croom Helm, 1983. 281-303.

Preitz, Max. "Karoline von Günderrode in ihrer Umwelt." *Jahrbuch des Freien Deutschen Hochstifts* (1962). 208-306.

*Rahel Varnhagen: Jeder Wunsch wird Frivolität genannt: Briefe und Tagebücher.* Ed. Marlis Gerhardt. Darmstadt: Luchterhand, 1983. 56.

Reagon, Bernice Johnson. "Coalition Politics: Turning the Century." *Home Girls: A Black Feminist Anthology.* Ed. Barbara Smith. New York: Kitchen Table: Women of Color Press, 1983. 356-68.

Rosaldo, Michelle Zimbalist. "Woman, Culture, and Society: A Theoretical Overview." *Woman, Culture, and Society.* Ed. Michelle Zimbalist Rosaldo and Louise Lamphere. Stanford: Stanford UP, 1974. 17-42.

Sedgwick, Eve Kosofsky. *Epistemology of the Closet.* Berkeley: U of California P, 1990.

Smith-Rosenberg, Carroll. "The Female World of Love and Ritual: Relations between Women in Nineteenth-Century America." *Signs* 1.1 (Autumn 1975): 1-29.

Trinh T. Minh-ha. "Cotton and Iron." *When the Moon Waxes Red: Representation, Gender and Cultural Politics.* New York: Routledge, 1991. 11-26.

Weissberg, Liliane. "Turns of Emancipation: On Rahel Varnhagen's Letters." *In the Shadow of Olympus: German Women Writers Around 1800.* Ed. Katherine R. Goodman and Edith Waldstein. Albany: State U of New York P, 1992. 53-70.

Woolf, Virginia. *A Room of One's Own.* New York: Harcourt, 1957.

Young, Iris Marion. "The Ideal of Community and the Politics of Difference." *Social Theory and Practice* 12.1 (Spring 1986): 1-26.

# Patriarchy's Fragile Boundaries under Siege: Three Stories of Heinrich von Kleist

Marjorie Gelus

The works of Heinrich von Kleist (1777–1811) mirror the deep anxieties of his age in the face of challenges to Enlightenment values, but, unlike those of his contemporaries, they dwell at morbid length on the threats to order, rather than constructing ideological antidotes to them. In these works, it is particularly women and their sexuality who embody the threat to one of patriarchy's foundational gestures: the drawing of boundaries that allow all that is Self to cohere by constituting an Other that is purged, at whatever level—the individual, the gender, the family, the tribe, the nation, the religion, the race, etc. Even the apparently most objective political upheavals—e.g., the French and Haitian revolutions—are thus filtered through this Kleistian lens of the embattled subject. (MG)

To neglect male-authored texts in the name of feminist purity is not only to pass over arenas promising some of the richest results precisely for *feminist* engagement with cultural products, but also, indefensibly, to allow the literary canon to stand uncorrected by feminist analysis. The canon needs not just expanding to include other voices, it also needs reconstructing, so that it is not stamped with quite so much patriarchal orthodoxy and myopia.

The works of Heinrich von Kleist (1777–1811) are one of the most obvious examples of a canonical *oeuvre* packed with fertile material for feminist revision.[1] His works, like those of his contemporaries, mirror the deep anxieties of his age in the face of challenges to Enlightenment values.[2] The social, economic, and political upheavals in the era of Rousseau and the French Revolution are everywhere evident in contemporary cultural products,[3] and literature commonly thematizes fears about the instability of identity in both class and gender hierarchies (see, e.g., Cora Kaplan). Women's role, in particular, became the focus of an intense effort at regulation and relegation to the private sphere because of the various threats that women were seen to pose to the new social order.[4] But Kleist's works dwell at morbid length on the threats to order, rather than constructing ideological antidotes to those threats, as do works by Goethe and others of his contemporaries.[5] Kleist's is a nightmare vision staging one onslaught after another on the existing order by the most potent forces of disruption: marginalized race, class, and sex/woman. His works are also the battlefield for his own idiosyncratic collision of values, enacting the split within himself between the steadfast upholder of patriarchal values and the androgynously subversive dismantler of stable meaning.

In Kleist's works, we see characters seeking to uphold rounded fictions of personal agency, and to enforce narrow class, gender, and racial identities in the face of constant slippage. The self is to be firmly delineated against that which it purges as Other, yet is repeatedly compromised by the stain, the fever, the disease that have found their way back in. But although issues of class and race occupy prominent positions in the *oeuvre,* it is issues of sex and gender that become the obsessive focus. Rape, pregnancy, childbirth, nursing, illegitimacy, incest, adultery, sexual passion and repression, fetishism, voyeurism, cannibalism, necrophilia, and passion-related fevers and fugue states are the staples of this work. Although most characters are not actually having sex, most are caught up in its *danse macabre* that has something of the energy and cadence of the fugue state of the damned brothers in "Heilige Cäcilie." And although both men and women are its victims, the destructive force of it is strongly identified with women. Women and their sexuality embody at the personal level the threat to a foundational gesture of patriarchy: the drawing of boundaries that allow all that is Self to cohere by constituting an Other that is purged, at whatever level—the individual, the gender, the family, the tribe, the nation, the religion, the race, etc. Let us consider some of the intriguing constellations of these issues that feminist analysis may detect in specific works.

"Das Erdbeben in Chili"

Set in seventeenth-century Chile, the story tells how Donna Josephe is banished to a convent by her aristocratic father when he discovers her tryst with her tutor Jeronimo. There she falls down in labor on the steps of the cathedral during a solemn procession of nuns, and is soon thereafter condemned to death by beheading. She is saved at the last moment by a catastrophic earthquake, and rejoins Jeronimo and her infant son for an idyllic night on a hill outside of town where all survivors seem united into one human family. This so-called "Eden" interlude is brief: the lovers are lynched the following day by a mob outside the cathedral, despite the heroic efforts of Don Fernando, who had taken them and their child into his protection.

The "Eden" interlude can be seen as a world reduced to the visible, or the pre-symbolic. When the power structure is leveled by the quake, with it goes that most abstract and invisible reality, the reality of paternity, whose authority the entire patriarchal system—including its signifying system—is set up to assert. What is left is Josephe's breast milk, which asserts, uncontested, the authority of maternity, separate from all law that had made it an offense punishable by death before the quake.[6] As Maggie Berg says, citing Lacan's *Écrits*:

> The distinction between paternity and maternity in Lacan's system is that paternity depends on signification; maternity, apparently, does not: "There is no need of a signifier to be a father, any more than to be dead, but without a signifier no one would ever know anything about either state of being" (Berg 62).

Josephe's maternity is as visible now in her breast milk as it was first in her belly and then, appallingly, in her public labor on the steps of the cathedral.[7] In fact, one of the telling signs of the world about to emerge from the quake—and perhaps intended as the most terrifying of all of Kleist's images of a world out of control—was the vision of women all over the city giving birth before the eyes of men during the quake:

> Man erzählte, wie die Stadt gleich nach der ersten Haupterschütterung von Weibern ganz voll gewesen, die vor den Augen aller Männer niedergekommen seien; wie die Mönche darin, mit dem Kruzifix in der Hand, umhergelaufen wären, und geschrieen hätten: das Ende der Welt sei da! (151)

This juxtaposition of lurid exposure of the most taboo details of female biological functions with those most ascetic embodiments of the patriarchal drive toward abstraction, the monks (panicked in the face of nature), is a memorable (and quintessentially Kleistian) emblem of a world gone awry.[8]

There is nothing novel in noting the female or maternal stamp on the Eden interlude. Many critics have remarked on the ascendancy of the female or maternal here during the brief eclipse of the corrupt patriarchal order. But the motherhood commonly evoked by critics is generally far more conventional than the one that I see emerging. It is a relative of that sacred calling ("heilige Bestimmung") that was deemed women's highest mission at the time, familiar to us from Kleist's letters to his fiancée, Wilhelmine von Zenge, and from books like Betty Gleim's on the education of women, published in 1810. The latter, cited by Friedrich Kittler as the sort of "motherliness" that replaces "phallocentrism" in the Eden scenes, sees mothers as the key to the restoration of a golden age of more noble humanity:

> Ihr werdet nur oberflächlich helfen, wenn Ihr nicht da anfangt, wo der einzige Anfangspunct alles Besserwerdens ist, wenn Ihr nicht die Mütter reformiren, wenn Ihr sie nicht mit einem lebendigen Gefühl ihrer hohen

Würde, ihrer heiligen Bestimmung, und der Wichtigkeit des ihnen anvertrauten Amtes, erfüllen könnt (cited in Kittler 31).

Schneider, too, discusses the "maternal" interlude, and describes the purpose of the story's last scene as "die Wiederherstellung der patronymen Gewalt der Gesellschaft, die durch die uneheliche Geburt verletzt worden war und die im 'mütterlich' geprägten Zwischenteil der Novelle suspendiert war" (122). Lorenz notes the instability of all claims of paternity, compared with maternity, and the threat that that constitutes to the patriarchal order (279). René Girard, coming closer to my point about the collapse of the signifying system, sees the quake's aftermath as a collapse of the symbolic order—a "Krise der Nicht-Unterscheidung," "Zerfall des kulturell-symbolischen Systems" (135-36)—though he does not note the gendered nature of the fallen order. And Josephe, far from representing a threat to that order in Girard's view, here begins the process of its restoration, the "Wiedergeburt der Kultur" whose centerpoint is the family. This she does by offering the food of her body to the community, and by virtue of being "die vollkommene Frau, als Mutter und Geliebte zugleich," in comparison to the other women: "Die anderen Frauenfiguren weisen alle bestimmte Mängel auf; zwei sind unverheiratet und Donna Elvire wurde so schwer verwundet, daß sie ihre mütterliche Pflicht nicht länger erfüllen kann" (145). (Fortunate as Elvire may be in not suffering the female deficiency of being unmarried, she may well feel singled out for particularly bizarre punishment in finding herself unable to nurse due to wounds to the feet.) The ideological baggage that Girard attaches to Josephe thus settles her securely back in patriarchy's mold.

The mother that I see emerging here is far more dangerous, because she has briefly slipped outside of the system entirely. The signifying chain of patriarchy permits approximately three meanings for women: virgin, madonna, and whore, and Josephe had unequivocally progressed to whore in that system. Here, though, she is *mother,* the sole point of certainty in the new world, signifying in herself, without reference to the father and his signifying chain. That whole system of invisible truths has been rendered temporarily inoperative.

Josephe is the sole possessor of reproductive authority for as long as the lines of patriarchy are down, and it is this authority that is the most likely explanation for Fernando's exaggerated attraction to her. The extent to which Josephe and Fernando are presented as a pair is striking. As soon as he appears on the scene, Jeronimo is quickly displaced as Josephe's partner and would-be protector. Fernando firmly announces his claim on her (whom the narrator soon calls "seine Dame") by placing his own baby at her breast, by repeatedly touching and holding on to her, and by leading her on his arm back down to the city to worship, with Jeronimo mutely bringing up the rear:

> Hierauf bot Don Fernando, dem die ganze Würdigkeit und Anmut ihres Betragens sehr gefiel, ihr den Arm; Jeronimo, welcher den kleinen Philipp trug, führte Donna Constanzen; die übrigen Mitglieder, die sich bei der Gesellschaft eingefunden hatten, folgten; und in dieser Ordnung ging der Zug nach der Stadt (154).

So strong is this sense of a pairing between Fernando and Josephe that various critics have speculated whether there might not be an actual attraction between the two—or, more radically, whether Fernando might even be the father of Josephe's child—e.g., Lorenz (279), Bernd Fischer (424), Robin Clouser (135), and Terence Thayer (269). Although the text offers inadequate evidence to support this interpretation of Fernando's behavior in personal terms, its meaning in sociological terms is unequivocal: he is enacting one of the foundational gestures of patriarchy, claiming the woman. He is drawn to her first as a supplicant, asking for her milk for his baby. But Josephe is also deeply threatening in her capacity as sole bearer of reproductive authority. Thus Fernando, clearly one of the alpha males of the old system, quickly blends the role of supplicant with that of claimant, in a move to reinscribe patriarchy on her.

While there is ample cause to admire Fernando's gallantry, kindness, and bravery in first bringing the outcast family back within the human circle and then risking his life to defend it from the mob, there is more going on here than the humanitarian and the personal. His function, whether conscious or not, is also to nullify the threat that the unholy family constitutes to the patriarchal order, and to restore that order and his position in it. This becomes particularly evident in the climax of the story, the lynch scene. That there is a larger social agenda at work here is evident, first, in the large number of men attempting to shape Josephe's fate according to their will—in sharp contrast to the extent to which she either shapes her own fate or attempts to shape the fate of others. Secondly, there is extensive invocation of class markers in this struggle that expands its import beyond the personal. Fernando's role is to restore and defend the patriarchal order, and this he starts to do almost as soon as he sets eyes on Josephe.

This vision of Josephe as subversive "mother" is tenuous but real, one of several gestalts that shimmer over her figure. Representations and perceptions of her are unstable, shifting among fallen woman, madonna, mother outside the patriarchal signifying chain, and partner reclaimed by patriarchy. In this, her figure is like her ground, for representations of "Eden" shift, too, among various possibilities: a sanitized nature on Rousseau's model, a much more dangerous nature that nullifies the symbolic order on which patriarchy rests, and a barely veiled continuation of patriarchal relations.[9]

Very quickly, though, definition is fixed. Josephe is killed, and Fernando adopts her child. The system can tolerate neither ambiguity in paternity, nor, most especially, the possibility of the only certainty lying in maternity (where it always lay), and Josephe must be claimed. That she must finally die is a further indication that she represents simply too great a threat for rehabilitation, in both her sexual self-determination and her self-signifying. Only her son is allowed to survive, and with his adoption by Fernando, he takes his place in patrilineage and the rehabilitation is successful.

"Die Marquise von O..."

This story is about almost nothing *but* gender and sex—and about the fervor with which that realm is suppressed. The Marquise's pregnancy is the focus of the entire story—already a startling departure from contemporary norms—but it is in the questions asked about the pregnancy that the story takes its truly Kleistian turns. At issue is, first, how this young, widowed mother of immaculate reputation became pregnant, and the answer that soon emerges—for the reader at least—is that she was raped, while unconscious, by the count who had gallantly saved her from being raped by a band of his own soldiers during an attack on her father's fortress. But the main question is why it takes her so long to find out how she became pregnant—and, incidentally, why she feels that her most effective recourse would be to place an advertisement in the local newspaper seeking the father of her unborn child. Finally, there is the scene of reconciliation between father and daughter that is drenched in reciprocal sexual desire, and that manages only by the most studious misconstruction possible not to be acknowledged as such by the principals. This is the molten core of the danger that finds such various expression here without ever fully finding representation.

For all the foregrounding of sex, it is oddly invisible in its manifestations here as rape, pregnancy, and incest. The rape at the heart of the story deserves most of our attention, but first let us consider the pregnancy and the incest. The entire later pregnancy occurs, utterly without narration or audience, in six lines of text on the story's last page. The birth itself is relegated to a subordinate clause in one of these six lines explaining how it came about that the Count was invited to the baptism: "Nur seinem zarten, würdigen und völlig musterhaften Betragen überall, wo er mit der Familie in irgend eine Berührung kam, hatte er es zu verdanken, daß er, nach der nunmehr erfolgten Entbindung der Gräfin von einem jungen Sohne, zur Taufe desselben eingeladen ward" (143). When next we see the Marquise, she is sitting up combed and curried on her "Wochenbette," "mit Teppichen bedeckt," approximately as sexual as a piece of furniture under her rugs, and receiving gifts for her newborn son in a recuperation that is downright Madonna-like. The physical presence of the pregnancy is thus minimal when compared with the actuality of nine months of pregnancy and the birth. It may occupy center stage, but we stare at it with averted eyes.

One is hard pressed to remember depiction of even the most chaste kiss in Kleist's work, and yet in the scene of reconciliation between father and daughter we hear in lurid detail of a father engrossed in his daughter's mouth, claiming it with lips and fingers. When the mother tiptoes into the room, this is what she sees:

> [Sie] sah nun—und das Herz quoll ihr vor Freuden empor: die Tochter still, mit zurückgebeugtem Nacken, die Augen fest geschlossen, in des Vaters Armen liegen; indessen dieser, auf dem Lehnstuhl sitzend, lange, heiße und lechzende Küsse, das große Auge voll glänzender Tränen, auf ihren Mund drückte: gerade wie ein Verliebter!...Die Mutter fühlte sich, wie eine Selige;...Sie...sah ihn, da er eben wieder mit Fingern und Lippen in unsäglicher Lust über den Mund seiner Tochter beschäftigt war...von der Seite an (138-39).

In Kleist's world, characters seek at almost any cost to avoid awareness of the hungers that drive them. The Marquise speaks for all when she says, in italics, "Ich *will nichts* wissen," shoves the Count away from her, and vanishes (129). To the extent that consciousness *is* retained as characters approach the dreaded realm, it is generally a consciousness altered by passage through a tortuous system of channels and locks erected between the two realms, so that it does not have to be fully operative: when threatened with awareness, characters faint, they rage, they become speechless, they fire guns, they are afflicted with fevers and delirium, they lose their minds, they enter fugue states. And yet here we see father and daughter sunk in deep and deliberate passion while awake and conscious to a degree that even permits speech—the mother hears a "Gelispel" when she first approaches the closed door. To any reader familiar with Kleist's work, the shock of hearing speech from deep inside such a realm is considerable.

There are, however, just barely enough safeguards still in place to allow them finally to retreat back out to the world that they *are* willing to know. The danger of consciousness symbolized by their speech is slight, since it is speech in its most rudimentary form. It is a "Gelispel," of indeterminate content and origin, followed by silence. The Marquise's eyes, too, are "fest geschlossen," suggesting a state one step removed from the fainting that preceded her rape by the count. But the crucial factor permitting their unanimous retreat from consciousness is the mother's absolute refusal to allow the scene to signify what it signifies. Not for an instant does she allow herself to flinch at what she sees, or waver in her interpretation of it. Instead, she boldly rewrites the story, by manifesting a seamless fond pleasure toward this scene as one of "himmelfrohe Versöhnung" between estranged father and daughter, and she moves quickly to impart her construction of it to its principals. The father's crossness when she does so speaks volumes about how little his actions have to do with "himmelfroher Versöhnung," but he allows her version to stand, allows her defusion of the electric tension with a joke to work. Here, too, then, as with the pregnancy, we are not seeing what we are seeing.

What we see instead, as we stare fixedly at this invisible sexual center, are the contortions of the principals trying to make it signify without short-circuiting precariously balanced cognitive systems. Confronted with the pregnancy, the Count tries to cover it quickly by marriage, the Marquise with a Madonna scenario, and her father with a violent objectification and distancing, reviling and disowning her, and threatening to murder her. A good deal of desperation accompanies these efforts, because the signifying system and the subjectivities that it employs are fundamentally incompatible with the material they are trying to incorporate. In Kleist's world, this blood-deep hunger that constantly erodes the self's clean boundaries from Other is the danger zone not only for identity, but for all signification and the difference that it is predicated on. What the pregnancy is the incest is too: an exercise in staring with averted eyes, a near suicidal flirtation with annihilation. This is the danger inherent in a world so invested in boundaries and difference.

The rape itself is famous for its representation as only a dash in the text. Stained by the sexual chaos erupting among the "rabble" of soldiers (as usual, class plays a role, too) about to gang-rape the Marquise, the rescuer himself succumbs to desire, but only after the Marquise's fainting removes the last witness to the act: "Hier—traf er, da bald darauf ihre erschrockenen Frauen erschienen, Anstalten, einen Arzt zu rufen; versicherte, indem er sich den Hut aufsetzte, daß sie sich bald erholen würde; und kehrte in den Kampf zurück" (106). Some more recent critics understandably wish to give the rape a prominence commensurate with its effects in the story, but they do so with mixed results. Susan Winnett does so in order to reveal the "broader cultural processes that relegate to the 'heroine's plot' particular untold stories of male violence" (170), but her insights tend toward the broadly ahistorical, and are achieved at the expense of a convincingly accurate representation of important issues particular to this story and its heroine. Horn sees the issue as less a moral problem than a class problem, arising from the question of why the Count is not shot dead for his rape as his soldiers were for their own attempt. The dash, he feels, represents an ideological veiling of reigning morals that is no longer possible in the wake of the Revolution (99–100). Overly eager to make his point that contemporary society was unwilling to recognize its own transgressions in this mirror that Kleist was holding up, Horn somewhat carelessly locates society's mirror image in the Marquise's suppression of her own impossible truths—the rape and what he sees as her unconscious complicity in it—and dismisses the rape as "nur technisch eine Vergewaltigung, in Wirklichkeit aber bereits ein Akt der Liebe mit ihrer (unbewußten) Zustimmung" (105). This conclusion is by no means justified, and it is symptomatic of a perspective insensitive to the importance of social markers other than class, and to the rape's status as something more than suppressed truth. It is also surprisingly inconsistent with Horn's earlier insistence on the full equatability of the soldiers' and the Count's acts. Thomas Fries, intent on portraying the Count's predicament as "the dilemma of an author" (1319), argues that "the whole story is told from the point of view of the sign-receiver, not the sign-author (whose feelings and insights are hardly discussed)" (1320). He thus implies that the "real" story that is thereby veiled, as always, lies with the phallus, in its invisible microsecond of activity, and that the subsequent nine months of hullaballoo and tasteless visibility constitute the (secondary) "reception" of the "sign." Despite some provocative insights, there is a disconcerting failure of the text to resemble itself in Fries's rendering of it that suggests a lack of familiarity with both the primary and the secondary literature—hinted at when he twice (1320, 1324) implies that the novella is a drama. Robert Glenny, too, tends to distort and domesticate the rape, first by excusing the Count because of the strain he is under, second by asking us to question the validity of defining people through their acts, and third by equating the Count's and Marquise's plights (119, 120, 178). Also, in his rather sunny assessment of the Marquise's psychic development (184–87) Glenny seems to miss most of the sexual longing and terror that fire the story—especially the Marquise's.

Linda Dietrick's provocative essay constructs the elided rape as the unrepresentable Kantian *Ding-an-sich* that finds its fullest representation in another scene in the story: the Count's description of his hallucinatory dream of himself as a child throwing mud at the white swan, who in turn merely dives under the fiery waves on which she is swimming and emerges pure again, to continue on her way in utter indifference to the boy:

> Hierauf erzählte er...daß ihm besonders eine Erinnerung rührend gewesen wäre, da er diesen Schwan einst mit Kot beworfen, worauf dieser still untergetaucht, und rein aus der Flut wieder emporgekommen sei; daß sie immer auf feurigen Fluten umhergeschwommen wäre, und er Thinka gerufen hätte...daß er aber nicht im Stande gewesen wäre, sie an sich zu locken, indem sie ihre Freude gehabt hätte, bloß am Rudern und In-die-Brust-sich-werfen...(116).

It is an image deeply imbued with the constructing subject and shimmering with competing meanings. While most critics see the swan as representing the Marquise, Dietrick sees androgyny as one of its most important characteristics—an indeterminacy that allows it to represent not only the Marquise being sullied by the rape, but also the sullying of the

Count's honor, and, more generally, the wish of most of Kleist's characters to cleanse themselves from the sullying of embodiment, the matter of origination—a wish that only Jupiter can realize (as he does, for example with Alkmene in *Amphitryon,* or, as a swan, with Leda). It is the same wish, Dietrick argues, evident in Kleist's poetics ("Brief eines Dichters an einen Anderen"), that the language "embodying" the thought be as transparent as possible, come as close as it can to disappearing:

> Nur weil der Gedanke, um zu erscheinen, wie jene flüchtigen, undarstellbaren, chemischen Stoffe, mit etwas Gröberem, Körperlichen, verbunden sein muß: nur darum bediene ich mich...der Rede. Sprache, Rhythmus, Wohlklang usw....sind...ein...notwendiger Übelstand; und die Kunst kann, in bezug auf sie, auf nichts gehen, als sie möglichst *verschwinden* zu machen (Kleist 347–48).

The swan's androgyny, Dietrick claims, is part of the larger cultural tradition. It appears "as a divine image on countless prehistoric artifacts" in Europe, and witnesses "to an ancient matriarchal religion centred on a powerful nature goddess with androgynous and parthenogenic...characteristics" (325). In this scheme, cosmic generation was "an immanent process...without an origin extrinsic to itself" (325). With the advent of the Olympian gods, the scheme changes:

> ...the swan lived on in a later, patriarchal mythic tradition that sharply divided male and female roles in the Olympic pantheon, and that converted the earth goddess, under her many names, into the consorts of heavenly male gods. Thus the story of Jupiter's descent to Leda in the form of a swan appears to have been constructed from the remnants of an older narrative about an androgynous divinity already fruitful and rooted in the immanent, organic world. In order for the forms of the material world to originate, even the male spirit gods of the later tradition still had to go down and muck around with the mortals (325–26).

At this point, Dietrick concludes that a residue of the more archaic conception of the swan inheres in Kleist's image, giving it a "shimmering instability" that evokes Hélène Cixous's *écriture féminine,* or "writing that undermines the sharp, 'clean' dichotomies of male-centered discourse." She emphasizes here that androgyny "does not mean an overcoming of difference or the projection onto the image of some 'pure,' sexless and disembodied ideal" (326) but rather, presumably, a productive blurring of boundaries in an image well rooted in matter and sex. By the end of the essay, however, Dietrick's description of the image has shifted. Now the Count's dream "speaks of the unattainable desire for a guiltless androgyny, for an origin that transcends the boundaries of time and the body, for an 'immaculate' conception" (328)—a picture with enough vertical transcendence, purity, and escape from the body to place it squarely back in the patriarchal tradition. What has happened?

The problem lies with what the swan is doing: being sullied and cleansing itself. That the image of the swan may shimmeringly, androgynously evoke the Marquise or the Count or Jupiter seems a less significant factor than that in all cases it is being sullied and cleansing itself—a dual action that is the quintessential expression of patriarchy's boundary fetish, its ideal of purity: the need not just to set self off from other, but to purge all other and emerge untarnished from defilement, whether at the level of the individual, or gender, or tribe, or class, or nation, or political persuasion, or religion, or race, or ontological status (spirit versus matter). What is excluded from the boundaries thus drawn is, as Judith Butler says, the "constitutive outside" of the subject, "what has to be excluded for those economies to function as self-sustaining systems" (35). This swan that is cleansing itself is affirming purity more than it is shimmering androgynously. The only trace of sex is the oblique representation of conception, but conception here is nothing but mud that needs washing off, not immanent, parthenogenic, unbifurcated generation.

Moreover, the image is so charged with patriarchal messages that it becomes difficult to press it into the service of also giving expression to the quite different violation that the rape represents to the Marquise. That the Count sees the Marquise as sullied by his act—however generously he then allows her to restore her purity in his vision—stems from an age-old patriarchal credo that women penetrated in any but the most narrowly prescribed way are damaged goods. But this is a sullying so trivial compared to that experienced by the raped woman that one word cannot adequately cover both phenomena. Similarly the tarnishing of the Count's honor that Dietrick cites: it derives more from the violation of the social code proscribing rape than from the rape itself, and from the Count's silence while the other, would-be, rapists are tried and executed, and is, in the scheme of things, a rather abstract and luxurious injury compared to the Marquise's (and the would-be rapists'). And finally, the boundary violated by having to "muck about in matter"—a squeamishness shared by the Marquise and the Count—is laughably inessential compared to the one violated by rape; there is precious little violence in the former violation, whereas the rape forcibly transgresses the most intimate boundaries of the Marquise's body and her self. Boundaries there must be—if no self could be constituted, nothing would ever move or act—the question is only how rigid and narrow they are to be, or how capacious and permeable.

In sum: by making the sullying/cleansing the focus in the swan dream, the narrator has significantly stabilized the androgynously shimmering instability that inheres in the swan, but he has not eliminated it. This is a classic example of the split in Kleist cited at the beginning of this essay, between the steadfast upholder of patriarchal values and the androgynously subversive dismantler of stable meaning. Dietrick's apparent uncertainty about which one Kleist was doing is indicative of precisely this indeterminacy.

A last point about Dietrick's essay: it reminds us that the threat of permeable boundaries is two-way—a horror not only at the self being contaminated by Other, but also at seeing the stain of self on the world, which is the main issue of the *Kantkrise,* where "the knower is always subjectively involved in what is known," where the "things-in-themselves, and indeed other subjects, had receded beyond the direct reach of the knowing self, while at the same time being deeply involved with and related to the self" (318). The task of setting and maintaining boundaries is so difficult precisely because of this two-way permeability, of self to world and world to self. The leaks are incessant because of the fundamental fluidity of things that we are up against when we try erecting these dikes.[10]

"Die Verlobung in St. Domingo"

If the "Marquise" offers Kleist's readers the epitome of the sexual threat in a domestic setting, "Verlobung" offers a paroxysm of upheaval combining all the worst threats—marginalized race, class, and sex—on a global scale. The French Revolution—the consummate emblem of upheaval—is here expanded to include its colonial repercussions, the uprising of Blacks against their French rulers on the Caribbean island of Santo Domingo (to found today's Haiti). In Kleist's depiction of the latter revolution especially, the privileged are confronted with the most potent symbols of destabilization: murderous Black rage, disease transmitted sexually by vengeful Black women, and unlicensed sexuality reigning supreme in fornication, whoring, and bastardy. As an index of the extent to which Kleist's contemporaries felt under siege, this story could stand for the era. Its depiction of external assault on an orderly universe combines with the inner instability that marks all of Kleist's characters to escalate the threat to unprecedented levels.

"Verlobung" is the story of Gustav von der Ried, a Swiss officer in the French army who has come to Santo Domingo in 1803 to quell the Black uprising. When Fort Dauphin falls and all its whites are killed, he flees with his family toward Port au Prince, in hopes of reaching it in time to defend it against the onslaught of General Dessalines. One night he seeks refuge with the mulatto Babekan and her daughter Toni, who have been instructed by Congo Hoango, Babekan's common-law husband, to lure any whites they can into the house to await their death at his hands when he returns from battle. Gustav is terrified and wary, but eventually makes love with Toni, partly as a test, and partly because she has begun to resemble his fiancée Mariane, who died to save his life during the

French Terror. Toni is so profoundly affected by the encounter that she begins to transform herself into white Mariane, and tries by desperate ruse to save Gustav from his certain death when Congo Hoango returns. But Gustav thinks she has betrayed him, and he kills her and then, learning what he has done, himself. His family buries the bodies side by side at their home in Switzerland.

A good deal of critical commentary on this story, especially recently, focuses on what the story has to say about the social and historical issues of revolution, imperialism, slavery, and racism on which it draws for its material. Surveys of Kleist literature (e.g., Klaus Kanzog in general, Uerlings and Horn on "Verlobung") show that earlier criticism tended to cast Kleist as somewhat of a reactionary, either implicitly (an ostensibly objective and politically neutral assessment that in fact saw and affirmed reactionary positions—cf. Horn 136, 138) or explicitly (concluding that Kleist identified with the position of his narrator and Gustav). More recent criticism has tended to revise that assessment and see Kleist as liberally, even radically, questioning prevailing cultural assumptions and absolutes. Critics disagree, however, on the design of the critique and on the extent of the radicalism, some finding, for instance, that what appears to be a sympathetic portrayal of alterity may in fact be a rather sentimental construction of an Other domesticated by European values (does the figure of Toni offer a critique because she is a Black woman with virtues that her white lover lacks, or because the "white" values that she embraces destroy her?)—or merely a conventional expression of sympathy that does not constitute a serious challenge to existing norms.

Angress is among those who see subversive tendencies in the story. Comparing it to *Hermannsschlacht,* she argues that its basic premise is that of "slavery and imperialistic domination as an ultimate evil" ("Imperialism" 17), and that Kleist's treatment of the "politics of revolution" is unprecedented and shocking because it makes a case for total politics (embodied here in Congo Hoango and Babekan) that goes against humanist values (embodied in the narrator and Gustav), e.g., of "fair treatment of the individual" ("Imperialism" 19-20). Hiebel warns against identifying the "christlichen, humanistischen, eurozentrischen Versatzstücke" of the narrator and Gustav with Kleist's perspective (171), and Horn details ways in which the story undermines racist and antirevolutionary assumptions of its narrator and protagonist. Fleming locates the critique in the way the story pits Gustav, who represents what he calls the reformist element in Post-Enlightenment society (the one that imagines, e.g., that there is a "correct" way to treat slaves [312]), against Babekan, the radical revolutionary element. Gilman argues that Kleist is critiquing the "aesthetics of blackness" of the earlier eighteenth century (in which darkness is "the source of...fear and horror" [88]), and suggesting instead an "aesthetics of ambiguity," modeled on Wieland and Lessing, that emphasizes the relativity of aesthetic categories. Weigel also argues that Kleist is challenging prevailing norms, but she focuses more on Toni's lethal conversion to "white" values (as does Gilman, less convincingly) than on sympathetic portrayals of Blacks ("Körper"). Impatient with critics whose comments on racism derive too exclusively from analysis of the attitude of narrator and characters, she concentrates on historical analysis of concepts and discursive patterns in the story. The collision of historical events with seemingly stable worldviews was particularly shocking and unsettling in the case of Haiti, she says, given how greatly these Blacks diverged from their image in pre-Revolutionary discourse on "savages." One particularly provocative outcome of Weigel's discourse analysis is her construction of Toni's death as a "white death"—of being made to conform to common concepts from eighteenth-century discourse on the feminine, "treue Seele, schöne Seele"—in contrast to the "black death" evoked by the "plague-ridden" slave's deliberate infection of her master. Uerlings feels that contemporary critics have tended to go too far in aligning Kleist's sympathies with revolution and Blacks, and against slavery. He bases this claim on impressive reconstruction of relevant historical context that suggests, for example, that the sympathy Kleist shows here for Blacks "überschreitet an keiner Stelle das Maß des in der Anti-Sklaverei-Literatur des ausgehenden 18. Jahrhunderts Üblichen" (193), and does not necessarily entail a consistent position against slavery and colonialism, or for revolution (192). Nor does Kleist go far in this story, claims Uerlings, toward transcending racial stereotypes or embracing cultural relativism: Toni is cast in the currently popular role of the noble savage[11] who is noble precisely to the extent that she acquires "European" values. Uerlings's historical contextualizing provides a useful check against a too-eager revision of Kleist into a multicultural post-structuralist, but there still seems to be more subversive instability in Kleist's texts than Uerlings is willing to concede—evident, e.g., in how he considers Toni simply interchangeable with Mariane, or simply white, rather than charged with the ambiguity that will be discussed below.

While the increased attention to the political/historical aspects of the story is a welcome change from what Horn criticizes as the all-too-metaphysical or psychological, or what Gilman criticizes as the anachronistically existential, it would be misleading to draw too sharp a line between the political and all else. Two essays may serve as cautionary examples: those of Ruth Angress and Sander Gilman. Angress sees this as a story of private and public worlds clashing in which, finally, "the heart is crushed in the mills of ineluctable social change" ("Imperialism" 32). She posits erotic love as "the antithesis of political engagement" ("Imperialism" 27), and sees the private sphere in general as a potential refuge from political currents: "For Gustav, the private man, cannot escape the turmoil around him, and in attempting to steer clear of the main currents and to seek salvation in intimacy, he leaves a trail of blood behind him" ("Imperialism" 29). Yet Gustav is in important ways *not* "the private man," there is a good deal of the political mixed up in this love of theirs, and intimacy is anything but a haven: to see love as "crushed in the mills of social change" is to seriously underestimate its inherent pathology in Kleist's world. Even were he not an officer in the French army, actively seeking to quell the uprising, Gustav, as a privileged white European of the upper classes, steeped in that culture's values and blind to its biases and abuses, is not politically innocent. His and Toni's love is equally enmeshed in the political: an important motivation for his overtures to her is to test "whether she has a heart," find out what side she is on; much of what he is doing with her is remaking her in a European image; and Toni's original mission is to seduce and ensnare him for delivery up to Congo Hoango. Finally, it does not take "ineluctable social change" for love to derail into catastrophe: the two are constant companions in this *oeuvre*.

Gilman's essay suffers from a similar problem. He insists that the story is dealing primarily with aesthetic issues: that it illustrates "human reaction to general philosophical patterns" (83), or that it is Kleist's "major *essay* on the relativity of aesthetic categories" (89, emphasis mine). It is a breathtakingly overconfident subordination of the entire, clamorous historical situation to aesthetic issues that Gilman defends on the grounds that the story was composed during a year when Kleist was preoccupied with Kant and perception, and that Kleist was not "writing history" (85).[12] Why anyone would imagine that Kleist was not capable of entertaining more than one concern at a time is hard to understand, particularly given the intrusiveness of that particular historical era, and the well-documented, lively engagement of European culture in general and Kleist in particular with events in France and Haiti (Gilman himself has examined "twenty volumes in English, French, German, and Spanish written about the Haitian revolution between 1791 and 1800" [83]).

The separation between the political/historical and all else is simply artificial. As Weigel points out, discourse *is* history, and, although the "history" that Kleist presents tends to be told more in the cadences of myth and legend than of historiography, there is more history than there may appear to be, "und zwar in Gestalt der Denkmuster und Vorstellungen, der Diskursfiguren und Metaphern, die in historische Erfahrungen eingehen und diese strukturieren" ("Körper" 205). This essay, then, will focus more generally on the threat that alterity represents, on the struggles of characters both to sustain clean boundaries that separate them from it and to domesticate it by recuperation, on whatever level it is manifested in this story—on the level of individuals, or differing gender, or race, or nationality, or class, or political persuasion, or ethos. Thus the political upheaval depicted in the story is part of a spectrum of assaults—including the Kantian—on the embattled Kleistian subject, and the instability with which Kleist invests all received wisdom, from the most overtly political to the most intimate, is his hallmark.

The story tracks the horror of experiencing the instability and dissolution of these boundaries, from assaults both external and internal. We watch as its protagonist, Gustav von der Ried, keeps trying to cordon off the "bad" from his "good," to no avail. But the reason it is to no avail turns out to be not so much because of the ferocity of the onslaught from the outside, but because of the stain within, the dispossessed self that keeps seeking out its like on the outside. What is dispossessed is mostly hunger, the impulse that thwarts the safety of perfect self-containment, and gives the lie to the split between self and other.

In a flashback, we learn of the first great blow to Gustav's sense of who he is: the guillotine death in Strassburg of his fiancée Mariane during the French Terror. He had carelessly provoked the terrorists and then mistakenly thought he could protect himself by fleeing to a suburb. Too late he realizes that he has thus left himself vulnerable to appalling injury: he has not thought to protect Mariane, and, with her, the crucial part of self he has invested in her. He rushes to save her, but she denies knowing him, and the terrorists cut off her head before his eyes. His conscious self abdicates and temporarily disintegrates: he finds himself—he has no idea how—a quarter hour later in a friend's house, where he succumbs to serial swooning and partial dementia, and is loaded like so much baggage onto a wagon and taken to safety (174). With appalling suddenness he is reduced to impotence, revealing how tenuous his hold on agency had been. This is a recurring motif in the *oeuvre:* it is precisely the alpha men who may be subject to the mortification of serial swooning. What brought Gustav to this state is, in large measure, his misprision of where self ends, and how to secure it. The shock of his sudden injury is overwhelming.

When next we see Gustav, his vigilance has escalated: he is now an officer in the military. He has fashioned more rigid armor against formlessness, but unfortunately, the Other is vastly more alien and menacing here in Santo Domingo, and the fragility of his defenses is palpable. It is as if that first breach of self's boundaries through Mariane had made possible this wild escalation of threat.[13]

The Black "villains," however, turn out to be so differentiated that their spectrum embraces the mestiza Toni as well, who ends up being the story's hero. And white Gustav turns out to be so spectacularly wrong that he is given the most grisly comeuppance in the *oeuvre:* he blows his brains out such that pieces are left hanging on the surrounding walls. Thus the story by no means offers the homogeneous perspective of an external evil threatening embattled patriarchal values. On the contrary, this blurring of boundaries is precisely the point. It is not just that the bad refuses to be uniformly bad, but the appalling extent to which the spectrum of possibilities can seem to exist simultaneously in things, defeating the very notion of boundaries.

One of the most effective emblems of this state of affairs is the strangely shared identity of three women in the story: the white European Mariane, the mestiza Toni, and the Black slave woman who avenges herself on her abusive white master by luring him to her bed in order to infect him with her yellow fever—*vagina dentata* personified (or what Hiebel calls the "Venus-Falle" motif [172]). Mariane's most obvious trait is her apparent saintliness, evident in her self-sacrifice and in Gustav's words: "...ich lernte den Inbegriff aller Güte und Vortrefflichkeit erst mit ihrem Tode kennen" (174). Toni seems designed for a position well beneath Mariane: she belongs to the Black camp, and she is used as a lure to draw white victims to their doom. The Black slave woman seems to occupy the bottom rung. Her defining deed is presented as such an execrable betrayal that the angels themselves would have to take up the cause against this threat to "human and divine order" (171). But these neat divisions quickly blur. Gustav and Toni not only fall in love, but Toni is soon seen to exhibit a strange likeness—"eine wunderbare Ähnlichkeit" (173)—to Mariane, and then to strive to assume a new identity close to Mariane's. Thus we see both the figure of Mariane and the figure of the killer seductress in Toni. Even her color is indeterminate. She is a light mestiza,[14] yet Gustav barely distinguishes her from black, and finds her color repugnant. She herself, on the other hand, begins to think of herself as white by the end of the story. She tells her family: "...ich bin eine Weiße, und dem Jüngling, den ihr gefangen haltet, verlobt; ich gehöre zu dem Geschlecht derer, mit denen ihr im offenen Kriege liegt" (191). She is also described as yellow, echoing the yellow fever with which the slave woman had infected her former master. The various shadings of color shimmer on her face depending on who is looking, and when. Finally, what all three women share is the deadly lure of hunger. The sexually transmitted, lethal infection is an old literary trope—one has only to think of Tristan's deadly groin wounds—and it is no stretch to see the fear even when the contamination is absent, as in Gustav's love for both Toni and Mariane. One also sees traces of Toni and the slave woman in Mariane: she was a greater threat to Gustav's unitary self than were the terrorists. Race and gender work together in this unholy trinity of women who shimmer strangely between one and three. As embodiments of the most alien Other, they show that the most potent threat to the boundaries of self comes from the stain within that seeks precisely to dissolve boundaries, and merge.

While some critics, like Fleming, seem not to notice the shadings of color in the story's "Black" characters, others notice them but see them as fixed—as are the identities of these three women under consideration. According to Burwick, Toni's resemblance to Mariane is merely an error of perception on Gustav's part, generated out of his need to see her as such (326). Burwick's later claim that by the end of the story Toni has "merged the two female images and given them new meaning" (324) not only fails to appreciate the fundamental fluidity and interconnectedness of these three apparently separate identities, but also indefensibly domesticates the lethal threat of the slave women, whose "new meaning" is apparently as "the black woman whose embrace *saves* the white man" (324, emphasis mine).[15] Glenny, too, sees Gustav's transformation of Toni into Mariane as the result of his desperate need to "simplify the complexities of fluid reality and reduce characters and phenomena by fixing them linguistically" (42).[16] Weigel, though she seems to fix Toni's color as yellow and therefore "ambivalent," does suggest that it can be interpreted anywhere on the spectrum represented by the three women: "Das Gelb von Tonis Haut...spannt die Möglichkeiten, ihre Hautfarbe zu deuten, zwischen dem Konzept der reinen, weißen Frau und der Vorstellung vom ansteckenden, schwarzen Körper auf" ("Körper" 216). But Weigel, as mentioned above, sees Toni's identity finally stabilized in her "white" death, in accordance with Gustav's need to recuperate her. Her death bespeaks the deadening that is inscribed in the white concepts applied to her:

> Während die Unsicherheit über das weibliche Geschlecht im Entwurf der "schönen Seele" Beruhigung sucht, wird in dessen Verkörperung die Entlebendigung, die diesem Konzept eingeschrieben ist, materialisiert: Im Tod vollendet sich die Nachahmung und Erfüllung des Entwurfs ("Körper" 213).

Only in death does the woman—the play of her meaning—finally become reassuringly fixed. The "white death," then, is "Tod als Effekt einer Vorstellung, die im Diskurs der Weißen in 18. Jahrhundert eine zentrale Bedeutung hatte," and it reflects "die Tötungstendenz, die dem Akt der Verkörperung weißer Vorstellungen eingeschrieben ist" ("Körper" 217). As Weigel makes clear, what Toni needed to be recuperated *from* by embracing this white death is her racial and sexual Otherness. That the two are collapsed in the word "Geschlecht" mirrors nicely the way in which the feminine sometimes came to stand for all the species of Other that needed subjugating and overcoming in Enlightenment discourse, and the extensive similarity between talk of women and of savages in particular in that discourse, as Weigel discusses in another essay (*Topographien* 118–19).

That the story focuses heavily on the dangerously destabilizing effect of "love" is particularly evident in the transformation that Toni undergoes once Gustav has touched her. After they have made love, she dissolves into an extended, sobbing fugue state from which nothing that Gustav says or does can rouse her. Finally, he carries her back to her own room like the lifeless burden he himself had become when Mariane was killed: "...er trug sie, die wie eine Leblose von seiner Schulter niederhing, die Treppe hinauf in ihre Kammer..." (176). Like the serial fainting, this fugue state is a staple of the Kleistian *oeuvre*. Characters descend into a place that enthralls and transfixes them, unmoored from the selves that they know. When next we see Toni, she is well on her way to becoming someone else: calling herself white, disengaging herself from her Black family and their values, and casting her lot with Gustav and his family in Europe.

What kills Gustav in the end is not what he expected. Just as the greater danger to him before lay not with the French terrorists but in his love for Mariane, so here the danger is less the Black rebels than his love for Toni. Like Mariane, Toni tries to save his life by pretending not to know or love him. Her only hope of saving him from her family's plot, she thinks, is to dispel any doubt that she has gone over to his side by tying him up, then secretly run to fetch help from his family. Predictably, Gustav is unable to see beyond the ropes with which she has tied him, and believes she has betrayed him. He manages to shoot and kill her, and then, realizing his error, to kill himself. It is thus not the Black plot that kills him, but the inner wound of loving, the wound of hunger that forever thwarts the safety of self-contained identity—just as in *Marquise,* the greater danger lay not in the Count's rape but in her desire for him, not in the rabble trying to rape her but in the savior who defended her from them, not in the gun her father fires but in his sex. The instability of identity, especially before desire, is sometimes lethal in Kleist's world.

\* \* \*

We need to remember that this view of things is not universal, but particular to Kleist. It is shaped by his own psychic makeup, which was notoriously fragile, and disturbed particularly in its relations with others. Some call the disturbance narcissistic.[17] But we can also see larger cultural assumptions at work here. Kleist had invested heavily in some of the classic tenets of contemporary patriarchy, numbingly articulated in his *Lebensplan*. When that self-prescribed mission derailed with his Kant crisis, its values were not simply jettisoned. Instead, they were liberally infused with the fears and doubts and hungers that had before been kept in check, resulting in a tone and color that sets Kleist's work apart within contemporary literary discourse. It is a tone of ideology imbricated with subversion. Feminist analysis is particularly well suited to this work, first, because of the conspicuous role that questions of sex and gender play in undermining the ideology that Kleist had embraced—stemming, as some have discussed, from androgynous disruptions/discontinuities in his characters and in himself—and second, because of the corrective that feminism tries to provide to the assumption that boundaries and difference are uniformly necessary and good. A more fluid sense of self and world can reveal the contingency of the dangers that may seem inevitable and universal in Kleist's world.

## Notes

[1] Such a revision is the aim of two of my previous essays "Birth as Metaphor" and "Josephe und die Männer."

[2] This is a central theme of many critical assessments of Kleist. See, e.g., Ruth Angress ("Abkehr"), Sigrid Weigel ("Körper"), and Susan Wells Howard.

[3] For their impact on Kleist's work, see, e.g., Peter Horn, Dagmar Lorenz, Helmut Schneider, and Helmut Koopmann. Bernhard Böschenstein offers good coverage of critical treatment of Rousseau and Kleist. Harry Steinhauer also discusses Rousseau at length. The Haitian revolution as a subtopic of the French Revolution has received extensive coverage from Kleist critics because of his "Verlobung in St. Domingo." See, e.g., my discussion of Angress, Horn, Roswitha Burwick, Herbert Uerlings, Hans Hiebel, Ray Fleming, Sander Gilman, and Weigel later in this essay.

[4] See my "Josephe" for more detailed treatment of this issue.

[5] A telling example of Kleist's penchant for thematizing social instability is in the way he rewrites historical fact to suit his aims in "Das Erdbeben in Chili": one historical record of the actual quake in Santiago (Moses 172-73) describes not scenes of sadistic lynching, as in Kleist's story, but scenes of mass penitence and self-flagellation.

[6] Schneider notes that this reversal in assessing her attributes is characteristic of the sacrificial figure in myth, which he sees as her main function: "Genau diejenigen Eigenschaften, die Josephe zum Außenseiter der Gemeinde machten und dadurch zum idealen Opfer, garantieren ihr jetzt ihre Stellung im Mittelpunkt der Gesellschaft, für die sie zum Quell neuen Lebens wird. Diese Umkehrung stimmt genau mit der Transformation überein, die beinahe jedes Opfer erfährt" (145).

[7] It is worth noting that the procession of nuns of which she was a part at the time was celebrating the Feast of Corpus Christi—merging with the body of the beloved bridegroom in the safely figurative way decreed by the patriarchal Church, rather than in Josephe's egregiously carnal way.

[8] See my more extensive coverage of this point in "Birth as Metaphor" (3-5).

[9] For a fuller treatment of this issue, and of Fernando's role as alpha male, see my "Josephe und die Männer."

[10] One is reminded of the defective sphincter of the "masturbating girl" that Eve Sedgwick finds in the character of Marianne in Jane Austen's *Sense and Sensibility*. "The particular muscle on which 'will' is modeled in this novel is a

sphincter, which, when properly toned, defines an internal space of private identity by holding some kinds of material inside, even while guarding against the admission of others. Marianne's unpracticed muscle lets her privacy dribble away..." (123).

[11] The noble savage motif was popular at the time, as Uerlings documents, through the widely disseminated versions of another interracial love story to which "Verlobung" bears many resemblances: the Inkle and Yariko story. Uerlings describes at some length the story's various incarnations and reception.

[12] Uerlings claims, however, that there is no trace of evidence that Kleist worked on the story before its appearance in 1811 (187)—contrary to Gilman's claim, or those, like Angress, who feel that the story bears the mark of the patriotic fervor that Kleist displays after the Prussian defeat by Napoleon in 1806. Gilman's rendering of the problem of Kantian epistemology is equally unsatisfying. Citing Kleist's famous "green glasses" letter (to Wilhelmine von Zenge, 22 March 1801), Gilman reduces the "Kant crisis" to the limitations on perception of truth caused by "the imposition of perceptual systems on individuals by society," or, an even more drastic reduction, "the preconceptions inherent in our individual and collective understanding of the world" (92). By tracing the obfuscation of "truth" to preconceptions or social encoding, he dismisses the more fundamental problem, namely the impossibility of determining which features of truth are the product of our modes of cognition. Even farther from the Kantian premise is Gilman's conclusion that "[t]he reality of existence can only be perceived...by an external observer" (92). Even casual reflection should remind us that nobody in Kleist's (or Kant's, or our) world—external observers included—escapes the pitfalls of consciousness.

[13] Burwick sees an "intense desire for personal safety" (325) as one of the driving forces behind Gustav's actions—as opposed to devotion to principle—and as a factor, along with an "inner aimlessness," in his difficulty in correctly assessing self and others.

[14] Uerlings performs a useful service in clarifying what many have seen as an error in Kleist's designation of her as a mestiza, citing documented contemporary usage that defines the term as "Mischlinge, Abkömmlinge von Europäern und Malayen, oder auch von Amerikanern und Mulatten"; earlier usage designated it as "Oberbegriff für jeden Nachkommen einer Verbindung zwischen einem europäischen und einem nicht-weißen außereuropäischen Elternteil" (193).

[15] Burwick concludes with the following assessment: "However, [Toni] is not the cold and 'pure' white virgin who saves her fiancé's life by publicly denying her love for him; she is the passionate black lover who gives herself physically and spiritually without any compromise" (324). This is racial stereotyping of a disconcerting banality, whose relevance to the characters at hand is hard to imagine. At the very least, it needs to be pointed out that Toni, too, quite conspicuously publicly denies her love for Gustav in order to save him when she ties him up.

[16] His treatment of Toni's development is as sunny as with the Marquise—she chooses to abandon "the lie she has been living," which "represents a prostitution of herself rather than any ethical or authentic existence," and is "brought...into being as a person of moral beauty" (187, 190).

[17] E.g., Gail Newman.

## Works Cited

Angress, Ruth. "Kleists Abkehr von der Aufklärung." *Kleist-Jahrbuch 1987.* Ed. Hans Joachim Kreutzer. Berlin: Schmidt, 1987. 98–114.

———. "Kleist's Treatment of Imperialism: *Die Hermannsschlacht* and 'Die Verlobung in St. Domingo.'" *Monatshefte* 69.1 (Spring 1977): 17–33.

Berg, Maggie. "Luce Irigaray's 'Contradictions': Poststructuralism and Feminism." *Signs* (Autumn 1991): 50–70.

Böschenstein, Bernhard. "Kleist und Rousseau." *Kleist-Jahrbuch 1981/82.* Internationales Kleist-Kolloquium 1981. Ed. Hans Joachim Kreutzer. Berlin: Schmidt, 1983. 145–56.

Burwick, Roswitha. "Issues of Language and Communication: Kleist's 'Die Verlobung in St. Domingo.'" *The German Quarterly* 65.3–4 (Summer–Fall 1992): 318–27.

Butler, Judith. *Bodies that Matter: On the Discursive Limits of "Sex."* New York: Routledge, 1993.

Clouser, Robin. "Heroism in Kleist's 'Das Erdbeben in Chili.'" *Germanic Review* 58.4 (Fall 1983): 129–40.

Dietrick, Linda. "The Immaculate Conceptions: The Marquise von O... and the Swan." *Seminar* 27.4 (November 1991): 316–29.

Fischer, Bernd. "Fatum und Idee: Zu Kleists 'Erdbeben in Chili.'" *Deutsche Vierteljahresschrift* 58.3 (September 1984): 414–27.

Fleming, Ray. "Race and the Difference It Makes in Kleist's 'Die Verlobung in St. Domingo.'" *The German Quarterly* 65.3–4 (Summer–Fall 1992): 306–17.

Fries, Thomas. "The Impossible Object: The Feminine, the Narrative (Laclos' *Liaisons Dangereuses* and Kleist's *Marquise von O...*)." *Modern Language Notes* 91 (1976): 1296–1326.

Gelus, Marjorie. "Birth as Metaphor in Kleist's 'Das Erdbeben in Chili': A Comparison of Critical Methodologies." *Women in German Yearbook 8.* Ed. Jeanette Clausen and Sara Friedrichsmeyer. Lincoln: U of Nebraska P, 1993. 1–20.

———. "Josephe und die Männer: Klassen- und Geschlechteridentität in Kleists 'Erdbeben in Chili,'" scheduled to appear in the 1994 edition of the *Kleist-Jahrbuch.*

Gilman, Sander. "The Aesthetics of Blackness and Heinrich von Kleist's 'Die Verlobung in St. Domingo.'" *On Blackness without Blacks: Essays on the Image of the Black in Germany.* Boston: Hall, 1982. 83–92.

Girard, René. "Mythos und Gegenmythos: Zu Kleists *Erdbeben in Chili.*" Wellbery. 130–48.

Glenny, Robert E. *The Manipulation of Reality in Works by Heinrich von Kleist.* Studies in Modern German Literature 13. New York: Lang, 1987.

Hiebel, Hans H. "Reflexe der Französischen Revolution in Heinrich von Kleists Erzählungen." *Wirkendes Wort* 39.2 (1989): 163–80.

Horn, Peter. *Heinrich von Kleists Erzählungen.* Königstein: Scriptor, 1978.

Howard, Susan Wells. *Die Gewalt der Geschichte: The Role of Historical Consciousness as a Model of Intelligibility in Selected Stories of Heinrich von Kleist.* Diss. U of Texas, Austin, 1989.

Kanzog, Klaus. "Vom rechten zum linken Mythos: Ein Paradigmenwechsel der Kleist-Rezeption." *Heinrich von Kleist: Studien zu Werk und Wirkung.* Ed. Dirk Grathoff. Opladen: Westdeutscher Verlag, 1988. 312–28.

Kaplan, Cora. "Pandora's Box: Subjectivity, Class and Sexuality in Socialist Feminist Criticism." *Making a Difference: Feminist Literary Criticism.* Ed. Gayle Greene and Coppélia Kahn. London: Routledge, 1985. 146–76.

Kittler, Friedrich A. "Ein Erdbeben in Chili und Preußen." Wellbery. 24–38.

Kleist, Heinrich von. *Sämtliche Werke und Briefe.* 2 vols. Ed. Helmut Sembdner. 6th ed. Munich: Hanser, 1961. Vol. 2.

Koopmann, Helmut. *Freiheitssonne und Revolutionsgewitter: Reflexe der Französischen Revolution im literarischen Deutschland zwischen 1789 und 1840.* Tübingen: Niemeyer, 1989.

Lorenz, Dagmar. "Väter und Mütter in der Sozialstruktur von Kleists 'Erdbeben in Chili.'" *Études Germaniques* 33 (1978): 270–81.

Moses, Bernard. *The Spanish Dependencies in South America: An Introduction to the History of Their Civilization.* New York: Cooper Square, 1965. Vol. 2.

Newman, Gail. "'Ich will mit Dir reden, als spräche ich mit mir selbst': Approaching Narcissistic Fusion in Kleist." Presented at the 1991 MLA Convention.

Schneider, Helmut J. "Der Zusammensturz des Allgemeinen." Wellbery. 110–29.

Sedgwick, Eve Kosofsky. *Tendencies.* Durham: Duke UP, 1993.

Steinhauer, Harry. "Heinrich von Kleists 'Das Erdbeben in Chili.'" *Goethezeit: Studien zur Erkenntnis und Rezeption Goethes und seiner Zeitgenossen: Festschrift für Stuart Atkins.* Ed. Gerhart Hoffmeister, Bern: Francke, 1981. 281–300.

Thayer, Terence K. "Kleist's Don Fernando and 'Das Erdbeben in Chili.'" *Colloquia Germanica* 11.3/4 (1978): 263–88.

Uerlings, Herbert. "Preussen in Haiti? Zur interkulturellen Begegnung in Kleists 'Verlobung in St. Domingo.'" *Kleist-Jahrbuch 1991*. Ed. Hans Joachim Kreutzer. Stuttgart: Metzler, 1991. 185–201.

Weigel, Sigrid. "Der Körper am Kreuzpunkt von Liebesgeschichte und Rassendiskurs in Heinrich von Kleists Erzählung 'Die Verlobung in St. Domingo.'" *Kleist-Jahrbuch 1991*. Ed. Hans Joachim Kreutzer. Stuttgart: Metzler, 1991. 202–17.

———. *Topographien der Geschlechter: Kulturgeschichtliche Studien zur Literatur*. Hamburg: Rowohlt, 1990.

Wellbery, David E., ed. *Positionen der Literaturwissenschaft: Acht Modellanalysen am Beispiel von Kleists "Das Erdbeben in Chili."* Munich: Beck, 1985.

Winnett, Susan. "The Marquise's 'O' and the Mad Dash of Narrative." *Rape and Representation*. Ed. Lynn A. Higgins and Brenda R. Silver. New York: Columbia UP, 1991. 67–86.

# *Anmut*'s Gender: The "Marionettentheater" and Kleist's Revision of "Anmut und Würde"

## Gail K. Hart

Schiller's famous essay "Über Anmut und Würde" establishes *Anmut* or *Grazie* as a feminine quality. Kleist, who seems to be parodying Schillerian argumentation on several levels, reduces Schiller's idealism to material terms by rupturing the link between *Geist* and *Grazie*, but he also cancels its association with women—de-humanizing and de-feminizing grace. By taking the arch-feminine virtue of *Anmut* and appropriating it to mindless or mechanized beings who are specifically gendered male, Kleist reinforces the exclusivity of the male homosocial bonds being developed between the narrator and Herr C.... (GKH)

Kleist's essay "Über das Marionettentheater" (1810) is both parasitic on and antagonistic to the theory of grace proposed in Schiller's "Über Anmut und Würde" (1793). It is parasitic because it relies on concepts that Schiller's essay labors to establish and antagonistic because it demolishes the most central of these concepts, namely the link between *Geist* and *Anmut* or *Grazie*. The relatedness of the two essays has been duly noted in the secondary literature and it is also evident in the most recent critical edition of Schiller's works, where Kleist's piece haunts the precursor as the editor annotates the passage, "Grazie hingegen muß jederzeit Natur...sein...und das Subjekt selbst darf nie so aussehen, als wenn es *um seine Anmut wüßte*" (*Theoretische Schriften* 350), with "Hier ist die Nähe zu Kleists *Über das Marionettentheater* (1810) offensichtlich" (1334).

The present study is less concerned with "Nähe" in the sense of concord than with the "nearness" that breeds discord, disagreement, and revision—*and with the uses of this revision*. By divorcing *Geist* and *Grazie*, Kleist "reduces" Schiller's idealism to material terms. Where Schiller carefully constructs an intricate theory of grace as proceeding from human spirit and never from "bloße Natur" (345, 362),[1] Kleist gives us wooden-headed puppets and a fencing bear. This radical difference in their respective concepts of *Anmut* and its origins overwhelmed most similarities for Benno von Wiese, leading him to conclude: "Es ist kaum anzunehmen, daß Kleist bei seiner Schrift an Schillers Aufsatz, 'Über Anmut und Würde' gedacht hat. Vielleicht kannte er ihn noch nicht einmal" (211). In many cases, we do not know what Kleist actually read—scholars are not even certain that his "Kant-Krise" was precipitated by reading Kant—but "Anmut und Würde" and its arguments were available to him[2] and a comparative reading of the two essays strongly suggests that Kleist responded either to the essay itself or to some version of its contents.

I will read "Marionettentheater" as (among other things) a corrective to the earlier essay, a successful revision that overwhelms the precursor not by superior rationality, but rather by its brilliant abuse of rational conventions. Scholars who have followed Schiller's philosophical investigations of the beautiful know that the results are anything but pretty. While trying to capture deep mysteries in reasonable formulas—a process requiring endless adjustment and qualification—Schiller often succeeds in making Reason an unattractive alternative to mystery or even ignorance. Whereas his investigative zeal has enriched our aesthetic tradition and opened up fruitful avenues of thought, Schiller's very sincerity in bringing Reason to the beautiful[3] has led to much graceless cerebration. It has also left him open to parody, especially in "Anmut und Würde." Kleist's piece seems to exploit this very weakness by mimicking the mannerisms of reasonable argument in the dialogue between the narrator and Herr C..., without submitting the results of their peculiar conversation to rational analysis. Thus, both form and content express resistance to Schiller, and this resistance is crucial to Kleist's project.

Though "Marionettentheater" certainly transcends any dependence on Schiller or his manner of philosophical inquiry, the conflict between Schiller's brand of animate grace and Kleist's inanimate variety, as well as Kleist's other variations on Schiller, have inspired some very interesting discussions, including the recent piece by Helmut Schneider detailing Kleist's attack on classical unity and classical hierarchies and the late essay by Paul de Man that remarks on Kleist's relentless revisions of Schillerian staples from classical argumentation to aesthetic education. Thus there is a fair amount of scholarly commentary on the Kleist-Schiller link and beyond this there is an immense amount of scholarly commentary on the "Marionettentheater." I am adding here to that aggregate of analysis and opinion because I hope to bring out a facet of "Marionettentheater" that remains unexplored by viewing the essay within the context of an argument I have been developing about the excision of women from certain segments of German literature.[4] The point of adopting this particular perspective is to focus on the rigorous exclusivity of the homosocial bonds being developed between the narrator and Herr C... and on the nature of the "world" they envision.

My larger project concerns the character and conditions of male homosocial bonds in the German literary canon from roughly 1750–1850. The term "homosocial" is by now familiar as the (re)invention of Eve Kosofsky Sedgwick in her seminal (and gestational) study *Between Men: English Literature and Male Homosocial Desire*, where she uses it to refer to "the spectrum of male bonds that includes but is not limited to the 'homosexual'" (85). It is a somewhat awkward usage because it so closely resembles and so regularly evokes the term it is intended to enclose and differ from. When we hear the prefix 'homo' we usually anticipate neither 'sapiens' nor 'social,' but rather 'sexual,' itself a highly charged and politically pregnant term/suffix, and the potential for confusion is strong.[5] Nonetheless, we do not really have an adequate vocabulary for describing the gamut of male-male relationships and Sedgwick's important, careful, and ground-breaking work compels the broader use of her terminology.

In *Between Men*, Sedgwick finds that women usually serve as a conduit for male homosocial desire (as in the traffic in or exchange of women) and that rivalry and cuckoldry (or fear of cuckoldry) are among the strongest of these bonds in English literature. Thus far, I have found that German literature of the period 1750–1850 does not regularly feature the same explicit structure of rivalry Sedgwick describes and that in many instances the strengthening of male homosocial bonds—toward which certain literary forms strive—results from the explicit removal of women. It is not so much the *absence* of women that I find interesting here, but rather the effort to effect and maintain that absence.

Previously I have examined *bürgerliches Trauerspiel* as a genre whose *telos* is the elimination of women from the family (all those dead mothers and daughters) in order to allow for a usurpation of the feminine by the masculine (father) figures—who can thus become mother-father figures like the male couples who take over the families in Lessing's *Miß Sara Sampson* and Klinger's *Sturm und Drang*. This particular usurpation is facilitated by *Empfindsamkeit*, which created a higher realm of emotional expression similar to that considered feminine, but ultimately inaccessible to women. As Kant explained: "Sie ist *empfindlich*, er *empfindsam*."[6] Now, I am beginning to look at other genres and forms to identify moments of forceful and deliberate exclusion of the feminine (in the form of women) from "the scene" of significant thought and action. Kleist's essay appears to constitute an interesting example of this process in its dialogue with Schillerian ideals.

In Schiller's treatise, the categories of *Anmut* and *Würde* are rigidly gendered. Not only does he follow traditional divisions of masculine and feminine qualities in defining his terms, but he specifically designates *Anmut* as a quality that occurs mainly in women:

> Man wird, im ganzen genommen, die Anmut mehr bei dem *weiblichen* Geschlecht (die Schönheit vielleicht mehr bei dem männlichen) finden, wovon die Ursache nicht weit zu suchen ist. Zur Anmut muß sowohl *der körperliche Bau* als der Charakter beitragen; jener durch seine Biegsamkeit, Eindrücke anzunehmen und ins Spiel gesetzt zu werden, dieser durch die sittliche Harmonie der Gefühle. In beidem war die Natur dem Weibe günstiger als dem Manne.... Anmut wird also der Ausdruck der weiblichen Tugend sein, der sehr oft der männlichen fehlen dürfte (372).

Even as he designates *Anmut* a womanly or feminine quality, Schiller appropriates beauty (*Schönheit*) for men and inasmuch as *Würde* pertains to women only in a highly modified form, as indicated in the poem "Würde der Frauen,"[7] *Anmut* is the only quality left to women that is of interest to an aesthetician. In "Über das Pathetische" (1793), which followed "Anmut und Würde" in the next issue of *Thalia*, Schiller excludes the more passionate and sentimental (feminine) types of *Rührung* from the realm of art, claiming that they are "durch einen edlen und männlichen Geschmack von der Kunst ausgeschlossen" (427). Interestingly, in this first printing of "Über das Pathetische," Schiller was more specific about non-art than in the final, revised version of 1801, taking time to exclude the works of Angelika Kaufmann from art and the beautiful immediately prior to the passage just quoted:

> Ich kann hier nicht unbemerkt lassen (wie sehr ich es auch dadurch mit dem Modegeschmack verderben mag) daß die beliebten Zeichnungen unsrer Angelika Kaufmann zu der nehmlichen Klasse d.i. zum bloß angenehmen zu rechnen sind, und sich selten oder nie zum Schönen erheben. Weit mehr hat es die Künstlerin auf unsern *Sinn* als auf unsern *Geschmack angelegt*, und sie verfehlt lieber die Wahrheit, vernachlässigt lieber die Zeichnung, opfert lieber die Kraft auf, als daß sie dem weichlichen Sinn durch eine etwas harte oder auch nur kühne Andeutung wahrer Natur zu nahe treten sollte (1362–63).

The 'noble and masculine taste' that excludes mere *Rührung* also moves Schiller to exclude Kaufmann, possibly the only prominent woman painter known to him. Clearly women have a very restricted role in Schiller's aesthetics where 'masculine' and 'feminine' represent well-established and value-laden polarities.

Although *Anmut* is feminine and *Würde* masculine in Schiller's bifurcated scheme of things, there is also a brief discussion of cases of male grace and female dignity and the possibility of both existing in the same person at the same time: "Da Würde und Anmut ihre verschiedenen Gebiete haben, worin sie sich äußern, so schließen sie einander in derselben Person, ja in demselben Zustand einer Person nicht aus" (385). This adjustment may result from Schiller's inclination to write plays about women who, if they were *anmutig,* would be resistant to the agonies of conflict and probably highly undramatic. Women who are resistant to conflict work much better in prose, where they often serve as stabilizing agents for conflicted male protagonists. Nevertheless, the division of qualities along gender lines, the femininity of grace and the masculinity of dignity, is fundamental to Schiller's development of his topic.

Now let us turn to the ways in which the gendered oppositions of "Anmut und Würde" are transformed in Kleist's essay, where only one of the terms is adopted for discussion, namely *Anmut* or *Grazie*. Kleist chooses the feminine side of Schiller's dichotomy for further discussion and revision in "Marionettentheater," but part of this revision—the part that has not yet been discussed to my knowledge—consists in emptying it of its feminine content. While it has long been acknowledged that Kleist removes the spiritual content of Schiller's term, or, as Schneider puts it, "de-humanizes" grace (220), it should be noted that he also cancels its association with women or 'de-feminizes' it. By taking the arch-feminine virtue of *Anmut* and appropriating it to mindless or mechanized beings *who are specifically gendered male*, Kleist reinforces the exclusivity of the male homosocial universe and approximates the effects achieved a generation earlier by the exaltation of a de-feminized *Empfindsamkeit*. He actively removes the feminine from an established feminine quality, subtracting the feminine from grace, and just as deliberately subtracting grace from the feminine.

The examples of true grace presented in the "Marionettentheater" are the marionette or "Glieder*mann*," as he is called here, the youth at the baths, and a male bear, who can parry sword thrusts and does not react to feints. All of these achieve their graceful moments by virtue of the absence of thought—thought being perceived as the source of awkwardness. Puppets have no cerebral functions, bears operate on instinct, and though the young man can think, he achieves or approximates grace while in a state of non-self-conscious reverie. Yet beyond their common incapacity for—or momentary lapse from—thought, these graceful movers are all male. Man-made limbs also enter the discussion briefly, but these are an extension of the *Gliedermann* or man-of-limbs principle. Women rarely figure in this account of a conversation between two men and when they do occur, it is as examples of failed grace. None are present and the two to whom Herr C... alludes are dancers who somehow fall short of the ideal. First of all, there is P..., a prominent, but clumsy ballerina whose soul has been seen to reside in her rump (or "in the small of her back" as a 1937 translation delicately puts it [Murray, 103]): "Sehen Sie nur die P... an, fuhr er fort, wenn sie die Daphne spielt, und sich, verfolgt vom Apoll, nach ihm umsieht; die Seele sitzt ihr in den Wirbeln des Kreuzes; sie beugt sich, als ob sie brechen wollte...." Whereas P...'s soul is profoundly misplaced, the very body of another ballerina, G..., is an impediment to graceful movement: "Was würde unsre gute G... darum geben, wenn sie sechzig Pfund leichter wäre, oder ein Gewicht von dieser Größe ihr bei ihren Entrechats oder Pirouetten, zu Hülfe käme?" (342).[8] One ballerina is plagued by lack of proper balance or center of gravity and the other is weighed down by her own corporeality, the "Trägheit der Materie" (342). Indeed, the art of graceful movement, the ballet, is represented not in the traditional manner by a ballerina, but by Herr C..., a male dancer who has the privilege of defining or delimiting grace. There is no further mention of women at all, except for a remark by the narrator in his anecdote about the youth at the baths. The boy at sixteen evinces "eine wunderbare Anmut," clouded only by the slightest traces of vanity, a blemish that the narrator blames on women: "nur ganz von fern ließen sich, *von der Gunst der Frauen herbeigerufen*, die ersten Spuren von Eitelkeit erblicken" (343). Thus women figure only peripherally in this inquiry into *Anmut* and then as despoilers rather than exemplars of grace.

The text also directs its reader—loudly and clearly—to the founding text of women's dis-grace (at least for the Judeo-Christian tradition), namely Genesis 1:3, where Adam must explain to an angry Lord that "the woman whom thou gavest to be with me, she gave me the fruit of the tree and I ate." God then punishes her by making her biological function unpleasant ("in pain you shall bring forth children") and reinforcing the hierarchy already implied by Adam's primogeniture ("and he shall rule over you").

More than a mere reference to the well-known story of the Fall, this particular Biblical passage is flagged in Kleist's essay as absolutely necessary to the comprehension of further discussion: "wer diese erste Periode aller menschlichen Bildung nicht kennt, mit dem könne man nicht füglich über die folgenden, um wie viel weniger über die letzte sprechen" (343). The narrator then seeks to demonstrate his understanding of the reference by elaborating on "welche Unordnungen, in der natürlichen Grazie des Menschen, das *Bewußtsein* anrichtet" (343, my emphasis), citing *consciousness* and its consequences as the moral of the Genesis tale. Indeed, consciousness is the fruit they ingested, and this is the primary thrust of the allusion, but the gender dynamics of the Adam and Eve story also resonate (or resound) in "Marionettentheater." Once again, the feminine side of the "opposition" will be eliminated.

In direct response to Herr C...'s Biblical allusion, the narrator offers his account of the beautiful youth losing his innocence as he notices or becomes conscious of his "grace" or more properly his resemblance to the statue of the *Dornauszieher* that he saw in Paris: "Ein Blick, den er in dem Augenblick, da er den Fuß auf den Schemel setzte, um ihn abzutrocknen, in einen großen Spiegel warf, erinnerte ihn daran; er lächelte und sagte mir, welch eine Entdeckung er gemacht habe" (343).

As we know, when the narrator challenged the boy to repeat his gesture, he was unable to do so, and his movements became clumsy and comical. Worse still, he then deteriorated into a vain worshipper of his own image, losing all of the charm he had once possessed:

> Er fing an, tagelang vor dem Spiegel zu stehen; und immer ein Reiz nach dem anderen verließ ihn. Eine unsichtbare und unbegreifliche Gewalt schien sich, wie ein eisernes Netz, um das freie Spiel seiner Gebärden zu legen, und als ein Jahr verflossen war, war keine Spur mehr von der Lieblichkeit in ihm zu entdecken... (344).

The role of consciousness or self-consciousness in eroding grace is more than obvious as we leave the poor vain boy looking vainly into the mirror in search of his former appearance. But there is another, more significant, connection between this scene and Genesis 1:3. First of all, both allude to the agency of woman in man's or mankind's expulsion from paradise inasmuch as the "Gunst der Frauen" disposed the narrator's youth to vanity and Eve persuaded Adam to eat the fruit. We could conclude that the two episodes share a common misogyny, being critical of women in general and the dangers they pose to orderly procedure. But this is perhaps too common a conclusion, and I think that the point of the Biblical detour lies elsewhere.

For "Marionettentheater," the reference to Biblical origins actually creates an opportunity to amend the history of the world (as in "das letzte Kapitel von der Geschichte der Welt" [345]) right at the origin by removing the woman from the scene of the Fall. Kleist's narrator recreates the Fall in the bathing incident of three years past, but the gendered couple of Genesis is here represented by a young *man* looking at his reflection in a mirror. This specular homosocial bond converts the Bible's gendered opposition to a scenario of *one* sex losing innocence as it admires itself and keeps company with itself. The "unlikeness" posited by Schiller and Moses and embodied in the gendered polarities of *Anmut und Würde*, Adam and Eve, becomes Kleist's "likeness" at the "Punkt, wo die beiden Enden der ringförmigen Welt in einander [greifen]" (343). The circle closes and the women are expelled, rather than encircled.

Behind the revision of a Schillerian polarity lies the more radical revision of the scriptural account of the origins of mankind. Herr C...'s 'last chapter of the history of the world' proceeds from a new first chapter that expunges the woman and substitutes a man staring admiringly at his own image—the most intensive and exclusive of all possible male homosocial bonds.

Turning from content to "form," it seems that "Marionettentheater" must be read with great normative heterosexual determination in order to miss the fact that heterosexual presumptions do not necessarily apply. The subtext for this discussion, which may in fact be the main text, is probably a homosexual encounter. Herr C... is identified as a dancer, a profession with a historically more visible concentration of gay men and thus the basis for a recognizable stereotype. The narrator has been observing him for some time and ultimately approaches him in the public garden, wanting to know why he frequents the puppet theater. This narrator says little about himself, but he does recall bathing with a very attractive sixteen-year-old boy with whom he has traveled to Paris and whose physical attractions he has studied closely. Interstitial remarks are often mysterious in their departure from the theme of the conversation being reported or they address the matter of whether the two discussants are *really* understanding each other, including Herr C...'s observation, "so sind Sie im Besitz von allem, was nötig ist, um mich zu begreifen" (345).[9] Finally, each speaker shows embarrassment—looking awkwardly toward the floor—during points of the discussion that do not seem capable of generating embarrassment. This has been noted and cited as an example of their own awkwardness in an intellectual discussion of a quantity that cannot coexist with intellect and rational reflection, but it also signals a greater and unnamed investment in the exchange as a manifestation of possible sexual tension.

Though the assertion of a homosexual exchange, also implied by Schneider, who writes of Herr C...'s rhetorical *seduction* of his dialogue partner (217),[10] could prompt a re-reading of "Marionettentheater" that would render many of its lines examples of double-entendre or the coded communication of a forbidden desire,[11] I do not think this is necessary to establish homosexual interest as an amplification of the exclusivity of the male homosocial bonds already in evidence. We need not scrutinize the details to note that the desire at the base of this dialogue is very likely one that excludes feminine participation and that women, already divested of their representative function (as "Graces" for example), also forfeit their customary erotic value.

The examples of feminine exile that I have developed elsewhere and referred to here concern the usurping of feminine functions in the (dramatic) *family,* and if we stage a more direct comparison of this highly theatrical essay and its movement to that of bourgeois tragedy, we find that the traditional family of that genre has been supplanted by a male couple, neither member of which appears to have formed any bonds that fall outside the category of male homosocial arrangements. They are for all practical purposes motherless, fatherless, and utterly detached from anything that can be construed as blood relations for the brief space of their recorded dialogue. Looking beyond the missing family ties to their circle of social contacts, they admit only to male friends and acquaintances, such as the youth and Herr C...'s friend in Russia, Herr v. G..., but there is a minute reference to family in connection with the latter. Herr v. G..., proprietor of the fencing bear, has two sons, and the father-son-brother relations are made relatively conspicuous through unnecessary repetition:

> Ich befand mich, auf meiner Reise nach Rußland, auf einem Landgut des Herrn v. G..., eines livländischen Edelmanns, *dessen Söhne* sich eben damals stark im Fechten übten. Besonders *der ältere*, der eben von der Universität zurückgekommen war, machte den Virtuosen, und bot mir, da ich eines Morgens auf seinem Zimmer war, ein Rapier an. Wir fochten; doch es traf sich, daß ich ihm überlegen war; Leidenschaft kam dazu, ihn zu verwirren; fast jeder Stoß, den ich führte, traf, und sein Rapier flog zuletzt in den Winkel. Halb scherzend, halb empfindlich, sagte er, indem er das Rapier aufhob, daß er seinen Meister gefunden habe: doch alles auf der Welt finde den seinen, und fortan wolle er mich zu dem meinigen führen. *Die Brüder* lachten laut auf und riefen: Fort! fort! In den Holzstall herab! und damit nahmen sie mich bei der Hand und führten mich zu einem Bären, den *Herr v. G..., ihr Vater*, auf dem Hofe auferziehen ließ (344, my emphasis).

Sons, brothers, father. In the midst of the anecdote, where the terms are separated by so much narration, the breach of economy constituted by the redundancy of twice designating Herr v. G... the father of his sons is not intrusive. Nevertheless, it establishes the only model for family available as an emphatically closed and fortuitously circular system of male relations (father-sons/brother-brother/sons-father). Herr C... appears to join this constellation at least figuratively during his description of his losing battle with the bear: "Jetzt war ich fast in dem Fall des jungen Herrn v. G..." (345). He is in a similar "fallen" state (Schneider 30)—unable to fence gracefully or convincingly—but perhaps also in a filial relation to old Herr v. G..., who encourages him from the sidelines. This family of men, fencing on their estate in Russia, receives only brief mention, but as a family or *the* family here, it is admirably consistent with the rest of a piece that works to create an exclusively male world. Obviously Kleist is not embedding a domestic plot in his brief essay and one would have to look elsewhere for an understanding of his use of family configurations. Other pieces, fictional and dramatic, suggest an approach to family that has more to do with the ambiguities of fatherhood than the expulsion of women—though there is also a fair amount of the latter. Nonetheless, "Über das Marionettentheater," so often cited as the theoretical "key" to Kleist's work (Kurz 264) is fully integrated into the movement of bourgeois tragedy toward a woman-less stage or family or world.

But now to take Herr C...'s advice and go back to the point where we began, namely to the removal of women from German literature (and creation), we see that *Anmut*'s gender is a matter of some importance. While the term is traditionally applicable to young boys (though often in their capacity as girl-substitutes), it is historically a feminine quality and Schiller's essay represents the rule rather than the exception on this matter. The willful reassignment of this quality to the masculine—though it underlies a more conspicuous reassignment of grace to the non-thinking or non-reflecting—represents a relatively strenuous effort to usurp women's position (here a position of grace) by removing them and redistributing their attributes. The most graceful of women, the ballerina, fails to exhibit grace here and is reduced to *anima*te buttocks (P...) and an earthbound mass of sluggish matter (G...). Yet as the *Gliedermann* dances and the youth dries his foot and the bear swats at his sweaty fencing partner, the spectacle of grace unfolds *and* the two men come to understand one another.

The matter of their understanding is the *telos* of their particular drama, the point toward which everything strives, as the narrator tells the tale of his rhetorical or pedagogical seduction by Herr C.... Their bond develops from guarded and excessively polite verbal sparring and disagreement to joyous concourse at the end as our narrator responds to Herr C...'s question about the bear story, "Glauben Sie diese Geschichte?": "Vollkommen! rief ich, mit freudigem Beifall; jedwedem Fremden, so wahrscheinlich ist sie: um wie viel mehr Ihnen!" (345). Given that this same narrator had protested at the beginning that he would never be convinced a marionette could exhibit more grace than the human body *and* given that the process of persuasion has taken us through the Bible and the history of the world, the ends achieved are by no means trivial. Rather than forming the woman-dependent bonds of rivalry or fear of cuckoldry that Sedgwick finds in her English sources, two men are uniting intellectually—and perhaps even physically—as they develop and accept a (problematic) notion of grace that prohibits feminine participation and obviates traditional rivalry. Inasmuch as this grace extends to origins and eschatology, it provides a new first and last chapter to the history of a world without women.

## Notes

[1] "[W]o die bloße Natur herrscht, da muß die Menschheit verschwinden" (362).

[2] Kant, some of whose work Kleist certainly did read, even refers his reader to the *Thalia* version of Schiller's essay in the second edition of *Religion innerhalb der Grenzen der bloßen Vernunft* in 1794 (Schiller, *Theoretische Schriften* 1323).

[3] See letter to Körner of 21.12.1792: "Den objectiven Begriff des Schönen, der sich eo ipso auch zu einem objectiven Grundsatz des Geschmacks qualificiert, und an welchem Kant verzweifelt, glaube ich gefunden zu haben" (*Theoretische Schriften* 1304).

[4] The working title for the project is "A Family Without Women: Gender and German Bourgeois Tragedy 1750-1850"; two essays from the book manuscript have already appeared: "A Family Without Women: The Triumph of the Sentimental Father in Lessing's *Sara Sampson* and Klinger's *Sturm und Drang*" (*Lessing Yearbook* XXII [1990]: 113-32) and "Voyeuristic Star-Gazing: Authority, Instinct and the Women's World of Goethe's *Stella*" (*Monatshefte* 82.4 [1990]: 408-20).

[5] Indeed, Sedgwick's next publisher, the University of California Press, confused the terms on the back cover of the first paperback edition of her subsequent book, *Epistemology of the Closet* (1990), identifying her as the author of *Between Men: English Literature and Male **Homosexual Desire***. The error was corrected in subsequent editions.

[6] Kant (*Anthropologie in pragmatischer Hinsicht: Werke in 12 Bänden*. Ed. W. Weischedel [Wiesbaden and Frankfurt a.M., 1960-64] 654). Cited from Bovenschen 161.

[7] "Ehret die Frauen! Sie flechten und weben" etc. (I: 448).

[8] There is, of course a third dancer, to whom C... refers, a male dancer who plays the role of Paris, who is, as Irmgard Wagner has reminded me, the judge of feminine beauty. The dancer's fall from grace occurs at the moment in which he is awarding the apple to Venus, thus declaring her the most beautiful of all: "Sehen Sie den jungen F... an, wenn er, als Paris, unter den drei Göttinnen steht, und der Venus den Apfel überreicht: die Seele sitzt ihm gar (es ist ein Schrecken, es zu sehen) im Ellenbogen" (342).

[9] The matter of *really* understanding a person and his/her soul is an important part of the romantic discourse of Kleist's letters to his fiancée Wilhelmine von Zenge. He praises her in the famous letter of 22 March 1801 for her interest in his "Innerstes" and warns her that she must hold *Bildung* and *Wahrheit* in great reverence "wenn Du den Verfolg dieser Geschichte meiner Seele verstehen willst" (*Werke und Briefe* 4: 199). The "Marionettentheater" was written in 1810, but takes place in "Winter 1801" (338) and the letter to Wilhelmine, which announces his spiritual crisis ("Vor kurzem ward ich mit der neueren sogenannten Kantischen Philosophie bekannt..." [200]), is dated one day after the end of Winter 1801.

[10] Ruth Klüger remarks on the general attention now being paid to homoerotic passages in Kleist's works: "Über homoerotische Passagen in Kleists Werken und Briefen wurde früher meist als Androgynität gesprochen oder sie wurden in die Rubrik Freundschaftskult der Epoche eingestuft. In letzter Zeit wird offener darüber diskutiert..." (Klüger 109-10).

[11] The most obvious example of potential double-entendre is Herr C...'s conspicuous remark, "Wir müssen die Reise um die Welt machen, und sehen, ob es [Paradies] von hinten irgendwo wieder offen ist" (342). Gerhard Kurz calls attention to the off-color character of this statement: "Auffallend ist auch der Kontrast zwischen der doch zentralen Hoffnung auf eine Rückkehr ins Paradies und ihrer nachlässig-burschikosen, *ins Derbe gehenden* Formulierung, '...und

sehen, ob es vielleicht von hinten irgendwie wieder offen' sei" (269, my emphasis). The "von hinten" remark has always had the effect of a very neat conclusion to a progression from paradise lost to paradise regained that is familiar to us from the Bible, the romantics, and western civilization. Yet despite this general appeal to familiarity, it has the ring of strangeness or mystery because it suggests that we must look for a back door somewhere behind paradise in our attempt to return to innocence or grace. What von Wiese has called "die geheimnisvolle Wendung [that] deutet einen neuen utopischen Zugang an" (206) does hint at another way, but in so doing, it may do double duty as a convincing part of the higher philosophical discussion and also as a coarse remark that is solidly within the spirit of the essay, as it merges the explicitly physical with the metaphysical just as grace can be produced by a wooden *Gliedermann* or a god. This new, utopian access to paradise would thus combine the crass physical scatology of the back-door entry with the eschatology of the realm to be entered.

## Works Cited

Bovenschen, Silvia. *Die imaginierte Weiblichkeit*. Frankfurt a.M.: Suhrkamp, 1979.

de Man, Paul. "Aesthetic Formalization: Kleist's *Über das Marionettentheater*." *The Rhetoric of Romanticism*. New York: Columbia UP, 1984. 263-90.

Kleist, Heinrich. "Über das Marionettentheater." *Sämtliche Werke und Briefe*. 2 vols. Ed. Helmut Sembdner. Munich: Hanser, 1970. Vol. 2.

——. *Werke und Briefe*. 4 vols. Ed. Wolfgang Barthel et al. Berlin: Aufbau, 1978. Vol. 4.

Klüger, Ruth. "Die andere Hündin: Käthchen." *Kleist Jahrbuch*. Ed. Hans Joachim Kreuzer. Stuttgart: Metzler, 1993. 103-15.

Kurz, Gerhard. "'Gott befohlen': Kleists Dialog 'Über das Marionettentheater' und der Mythos vom Sündenfall des Bewußtseins." *Kleist Jahrbuch*. Ed. Hans Joachim Kreuzer. Stuttgart: Metzler, 1981/82. 264-77.

Murray, Cherna, trans. "About the Marionette Theatre." *Life and Letters Today* 16.8 (1937): 101-05.

Schiller, Friedrich. *Gedichte: Schiller: Werke und Briefe*. 12 vols. Ed. Georg Kurscheidt. Frankfurt a.M.: Deutsche Klassiker, 1992. Vol. 1.

——. *Theoretische Schriften: Schiller: Werke und Briefe*. 12 vols. Ed. Rolf-Peter Janz et al. Frankfurt a.M.: Deutsche Klassiker, 1992. Vol. 8.

Schneider, Helmut. "Deconstruction of the Hermeneutical Body: Kleist and the Discourse of Classical Aesthetics." *Body and Text in the Eighteenth Century*. Ed. Veronica Kelley and Dorothea E. von Mücke. Stanford: Stanford UP, 1994. 209-26.

Sedgwick, Eve Kosofsky. *Between Men: English Literature and Male Homosocial Desire*. New York: Columbia UP, 1985.

Wiese, Benno von. "Das verlorene und wieder zu findende Paradies." *Kleists Aufsatz über das Marionettentheater: Studien und Interpretationen.* Ed. Helmut Sembdner. Berlin: Schmidt, 1967. 196–220.

# Masochism and Femininity in Lou Andreas-Salomé's *Eine Ausschweifung*

Brigid Haines

Beginning with a close reading of Lou Andreas-Salomé's *Eine Ausschweifung* (1898) within the contexts of her other work and of turn-of-the-century understandings of masochism, this article then explores the text's contradictory depiction of feminine masochism in the light of Deleuze's theory of the pre-oedipal origins of the phenomenon. Its originality lying in its locating of patriarchal power structures within women's subjectivities, the text's puzzling affirmation of masochism in women (despite the simultaneous cataloguing and condemnation of its pathological symptoms) is interpreted as offering resistance to oedipal repression. (BH)

*"Let's hope he starts to treat you better."*
*"I don't think I'd like that at all."*
*"God, you're such a pervert!"*
*"I am! I am!"*—Diski 132

*"[D]as Weib selber ist bereits der Effekt der Peitsche."*—Adorno 121

## I

Lou Andreas-Salomé's story *Eine Ausschweifung* (1898) presents a case of feminine masochism,[1] depicting it as a pathological state, but refusing to condemn masochism as an illegitimate response to the world. It is my intention to show, through a detailed reading of the text against its various contexts, that *Eine Ausschweifung* is unusual both for its time and within Andreas-Salomé's work because it posits a feminine subjectivity molded by patriarchal power structures in which masochism is rooted and because it maintains an ambivalence towards that masochism: recognized as a debilitating perversion, masochism is also, paradoxically, affirmed as a familiar channel for feminine desire. In all of this the text strikingly anticipates current debates in feminist and psychoanalytic circles on the causes, manifestations, and effects of feminine masochism.

## II

*Eine Ausschweifung* is unusual among Andreas-Salomé's literary works[2] for its exploration of the links between masochism in women, their erotic desire, and the confinements imposed on the expression of that desire by patriarchy, links that are visible in her other works but are not highlighted. An early collection of stories, *Menschenkinder* (1899), for example, shows the sexual awakening of her young female protagonists as an overwhelming experience that, however, they cannot channel into anything socially acceptable, or even articulate. While some rebel against constraints, some turn inwards and show masochistic tendencies, but their inability, and that of their narrators, to articulate what it is that is troubling them leads to frequent unresolved endings, unread letters, and expressive silences.[3] Sometimes submissive and masochistic behaviour is noted with approval, a typical example being the 1897 text "Amor," which begins with two men in a train discussing an incident in a newspaper of a girl "das ihrem Geliebten die Füße wusch" and referring to it as "dieses fast biblische Bild" (9). While one man dismisses the submissive behavior of the girl, who is later murdered by her lover, as exaggerated and hysterical, the other comments approvingly on the "Herrlichkeit" (10) of the archetypal scene.

Two novels of a slightly later period go so far as to glorify the masochistic sacrifices involved in motherhood, again without problematizing what this means for the women involved. *Ma* (1901) depicts a middle-aged widow, mother of two daughters, who rejects the chance of personal fulfillment through a second marriage and remains true to her vocation as mother. The novel *Das Haus* (1921) is an extended treatment of marriage and family life that supports stereotypical gender roles. For example, the novel unproblematically backs patriarchal authority when the daughter of the house Gitta, who functions as a younger version of her mother Anneliese, marries, leaves her husband when she feels constrained, but goes back to him when she comes to accept his authority. Masochism as such enters the text in the figure of Renate, a friend of Anneliese, who is passionately in love with a violent man of a lower social class, and who experiences "diese[n] wahnsinnige[n] Reiz der Unterordnung" (57). Though Renate functions as a negative example in this text, Anneliese, who affirms the positive effects of married life, also has to come face to face with her own masochistic tendencies. When Frank, her husband, suddenly gives way to her superior judgment in an argument they have been conducting, she has a momentary desire to be dominated, and she fantasizes in what are for her surprisingly violent terms, similar to those we shall meet in *Eine Ausschweifung*: "Sie sah die

Hand vor sich, wie sie das Briefblatt gegen die Tischkante schlug,—und wußte plötzlich, daß sie lieber noch sich hätte niederschlagen lassen von einer Faust, als ihn auf immer so kalt gewährend vor sich zu sehen,—so tot,—so, als sei er ihr längst gestorben" (198). However, when Anneliese realizes that she is experiencing what Renate has succumbed to and risks thereby losing the balanced home life she has gained, she bravely ("tapfer") suppresses her weakness, and the conflict within her is resolved. This moment is described approvingly in terms of a maturation: "in dieser Stunde ging sie hinaus aus ihrer Jugend, und sie weinte dabei" (199).

The eroticization of submission is here dismissed as a childish temptation to be overcome and is not dwelt upon as a natural, if extreme, consequence of women's submission and sacrifice, which are often noted approvingly in Andreas-Salomé's texts.

### III

*Eine Ausschweifung*, by contrast, provides an extended exploration of the theme. The story concerns a young woman Adine who, despite having succeeded in leaving her small home town and avoiding a constricting marriage to live independently as an artist in Paris, has failed to find peace of mind. At an early age she fell in love with her cousin Benno and became engaged to him, but from the beginning her passion for him was out of control. Although she viewed marriage with foreboding, she nevertheless desired it intensely and looked forward to bending her will to Benno's: "[d]as Ideal einer kleinen Brieger Hausfrau...trug für mich geheimnisvolle Märtyrer- und Asketenzüge; ich ging einen Weg der gewaltsamen Selbstkasteiung aus lauter hilfloser Liebessehnsucht" (79). Because of the damage this was doing to her health, Benno dissolved the relationship and Adine left to become an artist.

Returning home some time later, she realizes that the erotic desire for self-abasement before Benno is as strong as ever. But, paradoxically, when she discovers that he has become the kind of man the rational part of her can respect (he is now less self-obsessed, he has stopped being a workaholic, and he is developing his mind through reading), she no longer desires him: "Nie, noch nie bin ich ihm menschlich, in menschlicher Anteilnahme, mitempfindend so nahe gewesen,—nie aber auch war ich gleichzeitig so fern von ihm, so weit, weit fort,—als Weib" (105). Rather than hurting his feelings by telling him she no longer loves him, Adine lets him believe erroneously that she has had a lover during her time away, and he rejects her as unworthy of being his wife. And in this final moment of being once again "Staub zu seinen Füßen" (118) she feels intense pleasure. This "Ausschweifung," this wild excess, leaves her drained, unfulfilled, and incapable of love, and she seeks a kind of exorcism through writing about her experiences.

Adine is thus permanently scarred by her "Ausschweifung," which is repeatedly described in vocabulary denoting abnormality, trauma, and illness, as the reference to "Selbstkasteiung" shows. For example, the thought of her future together with Benno, living in close proximity to the prison and the mental asylum where he works, fills her with "wilde[ ] Verzweiflung" and "Gruseln" (76) which, however, make her cling to Benno all the more, especially as he turns her fears into a test of his hold over her: "Aber sie hätte mich ja nicht lieb, bliebe sie nicht hier" (77). A conversation with her feminist friend Gabriele makes her see that she is different from her friend, "denn ich war ja so leidenschaftlich bereit zu unterliegen, und sollte ich selbst darüber in tausend Stücke gehn," and leads her to analyze her feelings in terms that sound like a dictionary definition of masochism: "Durch diese gewaltsame Unterordnung unter ihn vermischte sich in meiner Leidenschaft das Süßeste mit dem Schmerzlichsten, fast mit dem Grauen" (79). When Benno dissolves the relationship she feels destroyed, thinking "daß er mich zu lauter jämmerlichen Scherben zertreten habe" (80), and she later diagnoses her feelings for him as "[k]eine Liebe,—etwas Dunkleres, Triebhafteres,—Unheimlicheres——" (92). When she realizes that Benno now no longer wants to dominate her she feels sadness and disappointment, and on finding out that the Baronesse Daniele, one of Benno's patients, is in love with and idolizes Benno as she herself used to, she uses the vocabulary of slavery ("Sklavenseligkeit"), intoxication ("zur bewußtlosen Selbstvernichtung berauscht"), and poison ("bis in die letzten Nervenfasern vergiftet") (107) to describe the malady from which they are both suffering. She longs for the danger of her passionate feelings: "Und Sehnsucht und Enttäuschung und ein Widerwille gegen alles, was nicht Abgrund und Gefahr sein wollte, wachten in mir auf" (110-11). And at the moment where Adine allows Benno to believe wrongly that she has had a lover and is therefore not as she was ("Wenn du nur bist, die du warst!" [117]), she experiences both a resurgence of her old masochistic feelings of enjoying being worthless in his eyes, described in the now familiar vocabulary of excess, and a new sense of triumph and of self-worth at having retained her freedom:

> "Staub zu seinen Füßen,—jetzt bin ich ihm das wirklich!" dachte ich nur noch dumpf, und irgendeine unklare Vorstellung dämmerte dunkel in mir auf, daß sich da soeben etwas Sonderbares begäbe: irgendeine wahnsinnige Selbsterniedrigung und Selbstunterwerfung,—irgendein sich zu Boden treten lassen wollen—.
> Und doch löste sich dabei etwas in meiner innersten Seele, was sich bis zum äußersten gestrafft und gespannt hatte wie ein Seelenkrampf,—und es überflutete mich mit einer zitternden Glut, und es schrie auf und frohlockte—— (118).

But this triumph is only partial, for while she realizes that she would now never be able to bear the love of a man "der mich wirklich auf die Knie festbannen oder mich in meiner Individualität ähnlich vergewaltigen wollte, wie Benno es ehedem unwissentlich versucht hatte," this realization will not help her to love "ohne diese furchtbaren Nervenreize" (118).

By means of this vocabulary of illness and excess, *Eine Ausschweifung* therefore depicts a woman who is permanently scarred by her masochism, but who nevertheless repeatedly seeks out the masochistic scenario, for her intellectual and erotic desires are out of step. Adine rejects her lover at the very moment when he stops wanting to dominate her (while allowing him to believe that he is rejecting her), indulges in fantasies of violence, and finds that her greatest pleasure lies in the enjoyment of subservience. Masochism is not something she can easily live with, and she realizes this: because of it her capacity to love has been permanently mutilated, her desire is forever masochistically organized, her sense of self is irrevocably split. Like the central character in Andreas-Salomé's story "Jutta: Ein Pfingsttagebuch," she is divided between the suffering and the observing self: "Da war nur Jemand, der litt zwischen Tod und Leben, litt wie ein gedrosseltes Tier, und Jemand, der auf dies Tier schweigend achtgab" (90).

## IV

The idea that feminine masochism could be seen as an illness is remarkable for the period. The medical and psychoanalytic theory of the time is dominated by two assumptions: firstly that masochism is primarily a female phenomenon and therefore constitutes normal behavior for a woman, and secondly that, as a result, pathological cases of feminine masochism are rare. While Krafft-Ebing, who named the phenomena known as sadism and masochism in his 1886 book *Psychopathia sexualis*, had noted a few cases where masochism in women had the proportions of a sexual perversion, he claimed that in general masochism was a primarily female condition resulting from women's physiology, and indeed that "eine Neigung zur Unterordnung unter den Mann...beim Weibe bis zu einem gewissen Grade als normale Erscheinung sich vorfindet" (152). A similar view is to be found in the thinking of sexologist August Forel:

> Ist der Masochismus beim Manne eine häufige Erscheinung, so tritt er beim Weibe mehr als Andeutung innerhalb der normalen Geschlechtsempfindung auf, weil er mit ihrer normalen passiven Rolle vielfach übereinstimmt.... Im übrigen sind ausgesprochene pathologische Formen des Masochismus beim Weibe sehr selten (244).

Freud shared this view, and although in his 1924 essay "Das ökonomische Problem des Masochismus," his last statement on the theme, he widened the concept of masochism and expounded the view that feminine masochism is not the primary form but, like moral masochism, derivative of the root form, erotogenic masochism, it was always central to his theory that women are inherently masochistic.

Despite the remarkable vehemence with which she catalogues the negative effects of her condition, Adine also, however, seeks to explain it in other ways that give it a more positive value, and, at times, vigorously to defend it, and it is here that the text becomes doubly interesting from a feminist point of view in that it shows the enduring attraction of masochistic behavior for women. Adine diagnoses her masochism as caused by pent-up sexual energy. But in her search for clarity this is not the only cause she gives. She also seeks to explain it in terms of a learned response to male violence instilled in her in childhood and to justify its appeal by locating it in a tradition of female submissiveness. One of her earliest memories is of her nurse being beaten by her husband, "während ihre Augen in verliebter Demut an ihm hingen," all the while laughing so that "mein Kinderherz meinen mußte, dieser brutale Schlag gehöre zweifellos zu den besondern Annehmlichkeiten ihres Lebens." The "fast wollustweiche[] Demut im Ausdruck der Blicke und Gebärden meiner Amme in jenem Augenblick" (72) remains one of her strongest memories, the result of which is "ein wunderlicher Schauer über den Rücken" (73).

In attempting to theorize women's masochistic tendencies Adine gives three possible causes:

> Sind es aber nicht tausendfach Zufälle, die unser verborgenstes Leben mit heimlicher Gewalttätigkeit durch das prägen, was sie früh, ganz früh, durch unsre Nerven und durch unsre Träume hindurchzittern lassen? Oder liegt es vielleicht noch weiter zurück, und zwitschert uns, schon während wir noch in der Wiege schlummern, ein Vögelchen in unsern Schlaf hinein, was wir werden müssen und woran wir leiden sollen? Ich weiß es nicht,—vielleicht ist es auch weder eines Zufalls noch eines Wundervögelchens Stimme, die es uns zuraunt, sondern längst vergangener Jahrhunderte Gewohnheiten, längst verstorbener Frauen Sklavenseligkeiten raunen und flüstern dabei in uns selber nach: in einer Sprache, die nicht mehr die unsre ist und die wir nur in einem Traum, einem Schauer, einem Nervenzittern noch verstehn— (73).

The first possible cause mentioned is the cumulative effect of random violent events on the psyche of the child; in other words, the outside world is held responsible. The second, expressed in sentimental imagery and thus lacking in conviction, suggests predestination of the individual. The third, given privileged last place and dwelt on at length, suggests the power of a tradition of female suffering. This is the theme that Adine develops in the course of the text and this is why Adine, the narrator, is split: she does not want to reject masochism totally, because such a rejection would mean invalidating female experience, including her own, and cutting her ties with other women, in particular her mother.

Adine's experience is implicitly and sometimes explicitly compared to that of other female characters in the text who present a range of responses to the patriarchal structures under which they live. For example, she half-jokingly claims to be envious of both the serving girl in their household and the Baronesse Daniela for the happiness they have found through delusion and servitude of different kinds. The serving girl, an ex-inmate of Benno's asylum, carries out all her duties with exaggerated ceremony and seriousness, her attitude being a leftover from her period of temporary insanity when she experienced the happy delusion of serving the Emperor of China. The Baronesse, though living proof of Benno's new human qualities—he has taught her to accept her physical deformity and is helping her to expand her mind through reading and conversation—is slavishly devoted to him, though apparently unaware of her infatuation and, because of this, deliriously happy. Indeed when Adine paints a portrait entitled "Das Glück," her mother points out that she has, in fact, painted the Baronesse (109). Another female character on whose fate Adine reflects is Mutchen, the younger sister of Adine's friend Gabriele. When Adine discovers that she is having a secret affair with Benno's partner, Dr. Gerold, though at first shocked and a little disapproving of Mutchen's thoughtless and irresponsible behavior, Adine comes to feel that it is less damaging "sich bei oberflächlichen Genüssen zu zerstreuen, als hinabzusinken in allerlei schwüle, dunkle Tiefen alter Gefühlselemente" (114), as she herself is in constant danger of doing. She therefore tacitly approves Mutchen's defiance of social norms in the cause of finding personal happiness, however short-lived it may be.

Gabriele, the proto-feminist, does not, however, meet with Adine's approval at first because of her "sichere Kampfesfreude gegen ihre ganze Umgebung" (79). On Adine's return, Gabriele, though still railing against the old-fashioned attitudes of Brieg men towards women, is no longer desperate to leave because she is now in love with Benno, the most enlightened among the local men. It is in a dialogue between the two women that Adine first defends female subservience. To Gabriele's impatient dismissal of local men for not realizing that the new generation of women is not like their mothers and that "wir mit den alten knechtischen Vorstellungen aufräumen," Adine responds in astonishment, "Ach, tun wir das wirklich?" (95), and goes on to defend the women who have gone before them:

> Unsre armen Urgroßmütter,...die wußten freilich rein gar nichts von solchen Neuerungen. Die einzige Form ihrer Liebe war wohl Unterordnung,—in dies Gefäß schütteten sie alle ihre Zärtlichkeit. Sollte nicht auch

in uns was davon übrig sein? was machen wir dann mit solchem ererbten kostbaren alten Gefäß? (96)

And at the end of her story, reflecting on the split between the successful, artist part of her and the more important, though multilated, part of her, her feminine desire, Adine makes the connection back to this tradition:

> Denn ich kann wohl als Künstlerin entzückt und erregt werden, und zugleich mit tiefster Sympathie nach einem mir teuren Menschenwesen langen,—aber alles, was dem Weib in mir an den Nerv greift, alles, was instinktiv tiefer greift, als Freundschaft und Phantasie zusammen vermögen,—alles das ist dunkel jenem letzten Schauer verwandt, der vielleicht eine lange, unendliche Generationen lange Kette duldender und ihres Duldens seliger Frauen in mir wunderlich und widerspruchsvoll abschließt——.
>
> Auch meine Mutter gehörte ja in irgendeinem Sinne zu diesen Frauen (118–19).

The most prominent role model for female behavior available to Adine is, of course, her mother, who is an archetypal submissive woman and content with her lot. Adine remembers her parents' marriage, in which the mother was subservient, as being exemplary in its harmoniousness, giving the child at the center a feeling of total security: "mein liebes Mütterchen tat alles, was mein Vater wollte, er aber alles, was ich wollte" (73). She is aware that she owes her life as an artist to sacrifices made by her mother who has constantly defended her reputation with the local people, even though, and Adine's own guilt can be heard in this description, she was "weder eine Löwin noch ein moderner Bahnbrecher, sondern ganz einfach eine einsame alte Frau, deren Lebensauffassung himmelweit von der ihres Kindes entfernt war—" (86). At the end of the story Adine is most concerned to affirm her mother's way of life: "'Auf die Länge lieben wir keinen Mann so recht, wie den, er (sic) uns befiehlt—' 'Ach Mama, *das* glaub ich gern'" (119). She is overcome by a desire to regress to infancy where she would be at one with the mother: "und mich überkam heimlich und heiß eine kindische Sehnsucht, mich zur Mutter zurückzuretten und zurück in die erste Jugend, die nicht wiederkam" (121).

The common thread in Adine's narrative is the wish to affirm her own experience and the lives of other women as they have been lived, and to approve of the way they have chosen to invest their desire, whatever the negative effects.

## V

The text, then, shows masochism to be both debilitating and attractive, and Adine simultaneously both deplores and affirms it. A cure is shown to be impossible. I now wish to show that these factors, namely both her ambivalence towards, and the deep-seatedness of, her condition, are given formal expression in her narrative. For the text hovers irresolutely between the desire to attain control over her life (through the labelling of masochism as perverse, the first step towards its banishment) and the masochistic enjoyment of the relived masochistic fantasy; this uncertainty constantly puts the reader into an ambivalent position. An examination of the narrative perspective and an analysis of the final scene of confrontation between Adine and Benno will illuminate this.

Adine writes from a position of non-mastery and non-control of the events related and cannot sustain a constant distance from what she describes, although this is what she seeks. Firstly, it is clear that the past interferes with her present and future happiness. She addresses the account of her life to a male "du," a lover who understands her art well and lives for art, though he is not himself an artist. In her relationship to this narratee she exhibits the old feelings of inferiority: "Wenigstens kommt es mir immer vor, als übte ich mit Kunstmitteln das ein wenig aus, was du mit dem ganzen Leben lebst, in deiner reichen Art, die Dinge voll und ganz zu nehmen und ihnen zu lebendiger Schönheit zu verhelfen." Her reasons for writing are presented as an open-ended question, "warum sitze ich hier am Tisch gebückt, tief gebückt, und schreibe und schreibe, in allen Nerven gebannt vom Rückblick in meine Vergangenheit?" The implicit answer is that she wants to know by what mechanism the past has made her incapable of love: she confesses that "ich nicht mehr kann, was ich so heiß möchte,—nicht mehr mit voller Kraft und Hingebung lieben kann," for "mich hat eine lange Ausschweifung zu ernster und voller Liebe unfähig gemacht" (71). The implication of the opening paragraph is that her preoccupation with the past will probably lose her the beloved "du" as well.

Secondly, she cannot remain detached in her analysis of the past and is still at risk of falling back into her masochistic fantasy. In the first part of her account she is at pains to highlight her present superiority to her past self by diagnosing the causes and cataloguing the course of her illness. She takes care to show that she now has insight into her behavior at the point of her return from Paris. Though she had apparently succeeded in sublimating her desire into artistic activity, she now realizes there was a deep level of her desire that had merely lain dormant:

> Es reute mich nicht mehr, Paris verlassen zu haben, trotzdem ich grade jetzt dort den Winter hatte genießen wollen,—und doch lag in der Stimmung, worin ich diese Reise unternahm, mir unbewußt, ein tieferer Leichtsinn, der von dunkeln Sensationen träumte, als in allen Genüssen, zu denen ich mich dort hätte verleiten lassen können (82).

Though she likes to think that through writing she will overcome the past, this project is endangered. One aspect of her insight is her realization that her masochism does not depend on cruel or sadistic acts committed by Benno, but on her own projection onto him of her fantasies. It was her own weakness and insecurity that made him appear strong: "je untauglicher ich mir selbst für alles vorkam, was er mit mir vorhatte, desto unfehlbarer und autoritativer kam er mir vor, und seine Liebe als etwas nur durch Selbstüberwindung sicher zu Erringendes" (79). After the break with him this trend was exacerbated: "Von jener Stunde aber ging zwingend eine Macht aus, die in meiner Phantasie Bennos Bild übertrieb und fälschte, die ihn hart und grausam, streng und stark bis zur Überlebensgröße erscheinen ließ" (80). In her fantasy she associates her feelings of powerlessness in the face of Benno's "violence" with an etching, Klinger's "Die Zeit den Ruhm vernichtend," a classic image of male violence towards women, which shows a "gepanzerten Jüngling" who "dem vor ihm niedergeworfenen Weibe erbarmungslos mit dem Fuß in die Lende tritt——" (81).

In fact, there is little evidence that Benno mistreated her in the days of their engagement, and he broke off their relationship to save her health, though he seems not to have appreciated her gifts. As a boy and as a young man he stood out from his contemporaries because of his striking physical beauty, his bad eyesight, which caused him to wear glasses, and his capacity and zeal for hard work. The first two of these attributes, particularly the bad eyesight, far from lending support to the image of him as sadist,[4] rather do the opposite, having an emasculating effect that is made much of in the scene of their final confrontation: Benno loses his glasses at the moment when he loses his attractivenesss for Adine. Because of his economic inferiority to Adine, it is she who pursues him, and after the death of her father both she and her mother "warfen alle unsre Hoffnung auf Benno allein" (75). He insists that she overcome her distaste for living near the prison and tries with good intentions to give her some practical tasks to take her mind off her irrational fears, making the mistake though of having these lead her "in die Küche und an die Nähmaschine" rather than to artistic work where she might have exorcized her worries (77). He later realizes his mistake in letting her idolize him rather than seeing their relationship in terms of equality and complementarity: "Anstatt dich durch die Grenzen und Schranken meiner Unerfahrenheit einzuengen, hätt ich mich durch dein reicheres Wesen hinausleiten lassen sollen aus ihnen" (103). Another example of her fantasizing about Benno comes when she visits his new room after her return and is surprised to find it so cozy and pleasant. For a moment she desires to see him in his old, grim surroundings: "Und dennoch tat es mir jetzt fast leid, daß ich ihn hier wiedersehen sollte, und nicht in dem Rahmen, der dort zu ihm gehörte. Ich behandelte ihn in dieser pietätvollen Regung unwillkürlich ganz als Bild—" (89).

So even though the reader has no independent view of Benno, it is clear that he is no monster, except in Adine's fantasies, as she realizes when she starts to write this account. But at one point the narrating consciousness slips into "erlebte Rede," recalling her past thoughts, without signalling the slippage, thus momentarily wiping out the willed distance between past and present. The moment occurs when Adine realizes that what caused Benno to summon her back from Paris was not his moral outrage at her lifestyle, which she finds old-fashioned and ridiculous, but jealousy. The realization makes her desire flood back and she feels that she would have returned much sooner had she known of his love: "Jetzt freilich konnte ich das nicht mehr wollen. Aber auch er sollte es nicht wollen. Nein, auch er soll es nicht, dachte ich, und mein Herz schlug zum Zerspringen. Denn ihm, seinem Willen, diesem harten, engen, bewußten Willen, bin ich schon einmal erlegen" (91). As we have seen, his strong "will" seems on the evidence to be mostly a product of her fantasy, but in reliving this moment the present desire for it makes it seem all too real. The moment is followed by a further fantasy of violence and submission—"da schien es mir gradezu, als käme er mit einer Riesenkeule bewaffnet auf mich zu, um mich niederzustrecken" (91)—and she realizes that she is not dealing with memories but with "eine Lebensgewalt, eine Wirklichkeitsgewalt, die mich selber bedrohte" (92). The unconscious slippage into "erlebte Rede" shows that while she is capable of articulating her problem, she is also still at its mercy.

The final scene between Adine and Benno is also critically poised between control, masochistic enjoyment of the suspense of the moment, and identification. It is a highly dramatic and emotionally charged scene, taking place in the gloomy interior of Benno's room,[5] in which Adine, although she does not utter a single word, manipulates Benno while letting him feel that he is in control. A part of Adine is detached from the scene, not just at the time of writing but also when the action occurs, observing, for example, Benno's egoism when he assumes that because she responds to his caresses, she must feel as he does, and observing her own maternal feelings towards him: "während ich seinen unsinnigen Küssen nachgab, regte sich in mir etwas Wunderliches, ganz Zartes und beinahe Mütterliches,—die Hingebung einer Mutter, die einem weinenden Kinde lächelnd ihre nahrungsschwellende Brust öffnet" (115). It is this part of her that rejects him because of his desire to dominate her and is thus on the way to achieving detachment from her position. The depiction of Benno in this scene shows both that Adine has to some extent overcome her fantasy and that Benno, despite his new, cultivated image, has some negative characteristics that she had previously overlooked, for Adine presents him now in all his human ordinariness: no longer the violent and desirable monster of her fantasy, he is now vulnerable (losing his glasses is a symbol of this), egotistical, clumsily brutal in fact rather than in fantasy ("Er küßte mit einer Gewaltsamkeit und Benommenheit, womit er mich fast brutalisierte, während er mich liebkoste" [114]), passionate, moralistic (in his "Zweifel an der Unberührtheit meines Mädchenlebens" [117]), insensitive, and generally to be pitied. But the other part of Adine is weak and unable to hurt his feelings or make him suffer the humiliation of a rejection, and this makes her choose the way out that leaves the root of her masochistic feelings intact.

While standing outside the masochistic scenario, the reader is thus also constantly invited to identify with it. In this the text approaches what Gaylyn Studlar, in writing about film theory, has termed a masochistic aesthetic. Following Gilles Deleuze, she locates the origins of masochism in the pre-oedipal phase of infancy, where its goal is reunion with the mother (602), as opposed to Freud, who saw the origins of masochism as oedipal. The pre-oedipal origins of masochism mean that it can ground an alternative aesthetic to the prevailing aesthetic of the cinema, which emphasizes "voyeurism aligned with sadism, the male controlling gaze as the only position of spectatorial pleasure, and a polarized notion of sexual difference with the female regarded as 'lack'" (603). In Studlar's view of a masochistic aesthetic, which I would argue can apply just as much to literature as to film, the mother is a figure not of lack but of plenitude and wholeness (608–11), the gaze can also figure masochistic, scopic pleasure, suspense and distance as well as control (611–13), and the spectator is restored to a sense of wholeness by exposure to masochistic fantasy.

## VI

*Eine Ausschweifung* describes a case of feminine masochism as a pathological state; it shows a desire to ascribe positive value to masochism; it sustains a masochistic aesthetic. Bearing these points in mind, it would be helpful now to locate the text within Andreas-Salomé's work as a whole.

I have indicated that the idea of masochism as a feminine perversion was unusual for the time, and that the text stands out among Andreas-Salomé's fictional works because of its sustained treatment of, and ambivalence towards, the theme. The desire to validate masochism may seem odd, but seen in the light of her theoretical work, which tends wholeheartedly to affirm femininity in all its manifestations, it seems less surprising. Indeed those acquainted with Andreas-Salomé's theoretical texts on the nature of woman and on the erotic[6] will find the attempt here to explore and assert the value invested in masochism by women characteristic.

This can be explained by what I see as a crucial distinction between Andreas-Salomé's theoretical texts and some of her fictional works on the one hand, which tend to essentialize and idealize women and femininity and to ignore the social construction of femininity and masculinity, and, on the other, the best of her fiction, which presents a more complex and contradictory picture. To say this is not to devalue her theoretical texts, which, in their affirmation of femininity, fascinatingly anticipate recent debates among French feminist critics. I am thinking in particular of her essays "Gedanken über das Liebesproblem" (1900), which presents a remarkably unromanticized picture of desire as egotistical and rooted in the body, and "Der Mensch als Weib" (1899), which celebrates woman for her closeness to nature and urges women to rejoice in their femininity. While her essays perhaps make what for current tastes is the mistake of positing an idea of 'Weib' that is anchored in 'Natur,' she nevertheless recognizes "die Gefahr der Affirmation einer männlich ausgelegten Lebenswelt" (Salber 98), and insists on the legitimacy of woman as a sex in her own right, and on the value of female experience, all of which links her strongly to much feminist thought in the 1970s and 1980s.[7]

*Eine Ausschweifung* and the story published with it, *Fenitschka*,[8] on the other hand, are more subtle texts because they show the social construction of femininity and deal with the problem that the essays skirt, namely how a woman can be herself and organize her desire in a world that is patriarchally governed. Neither text posits a solution; Biddy Martin's analysis of Fenitschka, namely that "[s]he merely negotiates, she does not resolve the contradictions or completely escape the restraints" (188), applies also to Adine; and Cordula Koepcke makes the point that Adine and Fenitschka both realize the need to leave the men and the institutions that threaten to constrain them, but that it is "ein unscharfes Wissen" (270). It is true that neither text argues clearly for rebellion or change. I would maintain, however, that this is actually the strength of both texts because they avoid the trap of idealizing the oppressed[9] and instead do something much more interesting, which is to explore the subjectivity of the protagonists and to locate their oppression within the construction of that subjectivity. What is thus produced, particularly in the case of *Eine Ausschweifung*, is what was called for by Sigrid Weigel in an article on heroines in literature, namely "eine nachdenkliche Literatur, die den eigenen Anteil von Frauen an ihrer Opferrolle, die Verinnerlichung der Gebenden, erforscht" (150).

### VII

In its exploration of feminine subjectivity and its location of masochism within that subjectivity, the text strikingly foreshadows debate among feminist and psychoanalytic theorists about masochism and can usefully be compared to other literary treatments of the theme. For example, Adine's case can be seen as validating *both* Freud's and Deleuze's contradictory theories about the origins of masochism. Insofar as she is turning her aggression, her pent-up sexuality, and her thwarted ambition as an artist against herself and replacing the beloved, lost father with Benno, her masochism could be said to be oedipal in origin. Of Freud's two possible ways of resolving the Oedipus complex she has not taken the active, sadistic, masculine way, by seeking to supplant the father, but rather "de[n] passive[n], masochistische[n] Weg, bei dem das Kind den Platz der Mutter erstrebt, um vom Vater geliebt zu werden" (Deleuze 212). This would furnish one explanation for her strong identification with her mother's subservient role and with images of female degradation. This would also make her masochism, in Freud's terms, passive and, effectively, "normal" female behavior. It would be the sign that she has accepted her (castrated) place in the Symbolic Order and has internalized oedipal structures.

However, her desire to regress to infantile union with the mother (121) is more in line with Deleuze's theory of the pre-oedipal origin of masochism expressed in his essay on the novels of Sacher-Masoch. In this theory the mother is not a figure of lack with which the weak, masochistic individual identifies, but is glorified as a symbol of pre-oedipal plenitude and wholeness. The masochist seeks a return to the Imaginary, to union with the mother who is posited as "lacking nothing" (Studlar 606), and who represents a state of pre-genitally organized desire where pleasure and pain are inseparable (Studlar 606). For Deleuze the masochist is active rather than passive and exerts a measure of control, for, according to Deleuze, masochism never exists without some kind of contract, even if the contract is only in the masochist's head (227). Deleuze thus provides a less passive, more empowering model than Freud's, a model that may be seen as part of Deleuze and Guattari's wider project to resist the oedipal apparatus as a repressive, capitalist construction (Wright 164). This element of resistance may be of use in an analysis of feminine masochism, and when we bear in mind the strong will exhibited by Adine as a child ("mein liebes Mütterchen tat alles, was mein Vater wollte, er aber alles, was ich wollte" [73]), Deleuze's theory seems to offer the better explanation.

However, neither Freud nor Deleuze focuses on the problems that masochism can bring for women specifically, since both are primarily interested in its manifestation as a masculine perversion (albeit one that means that the men affected behave in a "feminine" way). For an approach focusing on women, attention must be paid to the links between masochism and patriarchal power. As a recent article on Sacher-Masoch's novel *Venus im Pelz* has pointed out, the sexual politics of this work can be read as radical (O'Pecko). The hero of Sacher-Masoch's novel, Severin, before he is cured of his perversion, desires to be abused by a woman because "[i]ch will ein Weib anbeten können, und das kann ich nur dann, wenn es grausam gegen mich ist" (38). When explaining his "cure" he declares that in the world he inhabits, power relations between men and women are unequal, which means (and he quotes Goethe here): "Jetzt haben wir nur die Wahl, Hammer oder Amboß zu sein" (138). His "cure" is signalled by his choosing to adopt again the masculine role of "Hammer," but the point is surely that the work implicitly posits an emancipatory synthesis between the sexes (O'Pecko 8) which would change the present state of affairs where:

> das Weib, wie es die Natur geschaffen und wie es der Mann gegenwärtig heranzieht, sein Feind ist und nur seine Sklavin oder seine Despotin sein kann, *nie aber seine Gefährtin*. Dies wird sie erst dann sein können, wenn sie ihm gleich steht an Rechten, wenn sie ihm ebenbürtig ist durch Bildung und Arbeit (Sacher-Masoch 138).

While Sacher-Masoch's novel, however, makes light of the serious issues it raises,[10] the most puzzling facet of Andreas-Salomé's text is its deep ambivalence about masochism: the insistence on its mutilating effects and the contradictory desire to validate it. To use Deleuze's terms, while *Venus im Pelz* ends with a restoration of the Symbolic Order with the entry of the Greek who takes over Wandla's role and thrashes Severin, thus bringing about his cure, *Eine Ausschweifung* does not see the Symbolic Order restored, and thus no cure is effected.

Adine's refusal to reject masochism despite its mutilating effects seems less surprising if related to the work done by Foucault in analyzing the functioning of power. In an interview entitled "Truth and Power" for instance, Foucault described how he came to realize that power cannot simply be equated with repression, but that its workings are also associated both with pleasure and with creativity:

> If power were never anything but repressive, if it never did anything but to say no, do you really think one would be brought to obey it? What makes power hold good, what makes it accepted, is simply the fact that it doesn't only weigh on us as a force that says no, but that it traverses and produces things, it induces pleasure, forms knowledge, produces discourse (119).

Power is therefore enjoyed by those over whom it is exercised and without whose acquiescence it could not prevail. As Jessica Benjamin puts it, power prevails "not by denying our desire but by forming it, converting it into a willing retainer, its servant or representative" (4). And for women there is no shortage of female role models of suffering. As Angela Carter has pointed out, the idea of "the blameless suffering of women" is a very seductive one (101). Julia Kristeva, in an essay on the iconography of the Virgin Mary and its powerful hold over popular consciousness as valorizer of female pain,[11] demonstrates that the perpetuation of feminine masochism, particularly through motherhood, by successive generations of women, is necessary for the preservation of the patriarchal social order. She describes

[a] suffering lined with jubilation—ambivalence of masochism—on account of which a woman, rather refractory to perversion, in fact allows herself a coded, fundamental, perverse behaviour, ultimate guarantee of society, without which society will not reproduce and will not maintain a constancy of standardized household.... Feminine perversion [*père-version*] is coiled up in the desire for law as desire for reproduction and continuity, it promotes feminine masochism to the rank of structure stabilizer (against its deviations; trans.); by assuring the mother that she may thus enter into an order that is above that of human will it gives her her reward of pleasure (183).

Interestingly this essay contains, as well as its critique of patriarchally produced feminine masochism, passages endorsing the quasi-mystical aspects of motherhood which, in their lyricism, are very much in tune with some of Andreas-Salomé's own writing: Kristeva too seeks to underwrite female experience.

It should be noted, however, that to locate masochism within feminine subjectivity is to go against the work of some recent feminist writers and thinkers who have taken the view that to talk of feminine masochism at all is to shift the focus onto women when the real issue is that of male violence. For example Jenny Diski's novel *Nothing Natural*, after a sensitive exploration of feminine masochism, ends with the masochistic female staging the arrest of her sadistic lover when she becomes convinced that he has committed a sex attack on an innocent victim. The dramatic dénouement shakes her out of her passive dependency and presumably brings relief as she shifts the focus from self-examination to blaming the sadistic, criminal man. In a recent book of essays, *Leiden macht keine Lust: der Mythos vom weiblichen Masochismus,* the very existence of feminine masochism as anything more than a myth has been questioned, in particular in three essays whose titles are self-explanatory: Ulrike Popp's "Vom männlichen zum weiblichen Masochismus: Zur Geschlechtsumwandlung eines psychologischen Deutungskonzeptes," Birgit Rommelspacher's "Der weibliche Masochismus: Ein Mythos?" and Roswitha Burgard's "Weiblicher Masochismus legitimiert Männergewalt." The volume also contains an essay by Maria Marcus, a self-confessed ex-masochist, whose confessional book *Die furchtbare Wahrheit: Frauen und Masochismus* caused a stir when it was published in 1974. In her later essay, however, Marcus has come to the view that her masochism was a sickness that she had to overcome in order to lead a fulfilling life in both sexual and general terms.

While it is clearly politically desirable to draw attention to abuses of power under patriarchy, the full possibilities for resisting this power will, however, not be understood until what is for some feminists the taboo of feminine masochism is explored. In its attempt to do this, Andreas-Salomé's text may be read as anticipating Elfriede Jelinek's powerful and bleak novel *Die Klavierspielerin,* whose heroine has also interiorized "the structures of masculine dominance" (Fiddler 224), and seeks relief in self-mutilation and an unsuccessful sado-masochistic relationship. Jelinek's novel is clearly feminist in intent for, as Fiddler has suggested, it invites the reader to understand the sado-masochistic relationship as an exaggerated microcosm of "normal" sexual relations (239). Andreas-Salomé's text, by contrast, may seem not to progress beyond an extended exploration of the apparent paradox of the simultaneous recognition and embracing of perversion. However, the reader will see that what may have worked for previous generations cannot bring satisfaction to Adine and, as at the end of Jelinek's text, is forced to see patriarchal power structures as the root of her problem. That these structures are internalized is a measure of their strength; the text's simultaneous confession of perverse pleasure, however, also offers the reader possibilities of resistance to oedipal conditioning. Herein lies the significance of this unusual text: in Deleuze and Guattari's terms, it is only by bursting apart the oedipal yoke and disseminating the effects of power that "a radical politics of desire" (Seem xxi) freed from all beliefs can be initiated.

## Notes

[1] Since I am sympathetic to the view that masochism in women is a result of the construction of femininity under patriarchy and not something innate, I shall use the term feminine masochism rather than the alternatives female masochism or masochism in women.

[2] For a brief introduction to her fiction see Livingstone (204–20).

[3] For a reading of *Menschenkinder* see Haines (1991–92).

[4] Proof of sadistic tendencies in Benno would anyway not advance the diagnosis of Adine's condition, since Deleuze has argued convincingly that sadism and masochism cannot be complementary states, for they are "in sich geschlossene, eigenständige Formen" (219).

[5] This is a suitable setting: Deleuze has pointed out that while de Sade's settings depend on the contrast of bright light and shadow, Sacher-Masoch's decors on the other hand "lassen mit ihren schweren Vorhängen, ihrer intimen Überladenheit, ihren Boudoirs und Garderoben ein Halbdunkel herrschen, in dem sich nur verhaltene Gesten und Qualen abheben" (189).

[6] I refer here primarily to the essays contained in the volume *Die Erotik,* and also to her later essays on psychoanalysis, recently published together as a volume with the title *Das zweideutige Lächeln der Erotik.*

[7] For an elaboration of this link see Haines (1991–92).

[8] For a discussion of this text see Haines (1991).

[9] See Benjamin: "this has been a weakness of radical politics: to idealize the oppressed, as if their politics and culture were untouched by the system of domination, as if people did not participate in their own submission" (9).

[10] O'Pecko makes the point that Sacher-Masoch structured the work as a comedy, "treating his hero's malady as a problem whose resolution restores the natural order of things" (2).

[11] Severin, in Sacher-Masoch's *Venus im Pelz,* also finds a source of erotic excitement in the Christian tradition that molds his own masochism. He reads "mit einem Grauen, das eigentlich Entzücken war" how the martyrs "im Kerker schmachteten, auf den Rost gelegt, mit Pfeilen durchschossen, in Pech gesotten, wilden Tieren vorgeworfen, an das Kreuz geschlagen wurden, und das Entsetzlichste mit einer Art Freude litten. Leiden, grausame Qualen erdulden, erschien mir fortan als ein Genuß" (45).

## Works Cited

Adorno, Theodor W. *Minima Moralia: Reflexionen aus dem beschädigten Leben.* Frankfurt a.M.: Suhrkamp, 1951.

Andreas-Salomé, Lou. *Amor. Jutta. Die Tarnkappe: Drei Dichtungen.* Frankfurt a.M.: Insel, 1981.

──── . *Die Erotik: Vier Aufsätze.* Ed. Ernst Pfeiffer. Frankfurt a.M.: Ullstein, 1986.

──── . *Fenitschka. Eine Ausschweifung: Zwei Erzählungen.* Ed. Ernst Pfeiffer. 1898. Frankfurt a.M.: Ullstein, 1983.

──── . *Das Haus: Familiengeschichte vom Ende vorigen Jahrhunderts.* 1921. Frankfurt a.M.: Ullstein, 1987.

──── . *Ma: Ein Porträt.* Stuttgart: Cotta, 1921.

──── . *Menschenkinder: Novellencyklus.* Stuttgart: Cotta, 1899.

──── . *Das zweideutige Lächeln der Erotik: Texte zur Psychoanalyse.* Ed. Inge Weber and Brigitte Rempp. Freiburg i.B.: Kore, 1990.

Benjamin, Jessica. *The Bonds of Love: Psychoanalysis, Feminism, and the Problem of Domination.* London: Virago, 1988.

Carter, Angela. *The Sadeian Woman: An Exercise in Cultural History.* London: Virago, 1979.

Deleuze, Gilles. "Sacher-Masoch und der Masochismus." *Venus im Pelz.* By Leopold von Sacher-Masoch. 1869. Frankfurt a.M.: Insel, 1980.

Deleuze, Gilles, and Felix Guattari. *Anti-Oedipus: Capitalism and Schizophrenia.* Minneapolis: U of Minnesota P, 1983.

Diski, Jenny. *Nothing Natural.* 1986. London: Minerva, 1990.

Fiddler, Allyson. "Rewriting Reality: Elfriede Jelinek and the Politics of Representation." Diss. U of Southampton, 1989. Published in revised form as *Rewriting Reality: An Introduction to Elfriede Jelinek.* Oxford: Berg, 1994.

Forel, August. *Die sexuelle Frage: Eine naturwissenschaftliche, psychologische, hygienische und soziologische Studie für Gebildete.* Munich: Reinhardt, 1905.

Foucault, Michel. "Truth and Power." *Power/Knowledge: Selected Interviews and Other Writings 1972-1977.* Ed. Colin Gordon. Brighton: Harvester, 1980.

Freud, Sigmund. "Das ökonomische Problem des Masochismus." *Gesammelte Werke.* 18 Vols. Frankfurt a.M.: Fischer, 1940. Vol. 13. 369-83.

Haines, Brigid. "'Ja, so würde ich es auch heute noch sagen': Reading Lou Andreas-Salomé in the 1990s." *Publications of the English Goethe Society* 62 (1992): 77-95.

———. "Lou Andreas-Salomé's *Fenitschka*: A Feminist Reading." *German Life and Letters* 44 (1991): 416-25.

Jelinek, Elfriede. *Die Klavierspielerin: Roman.* 1983. Reinbek bei Hamburg: Rowohlt, 1986.

Koepcke, Cordula. *Lou Andreas-Salomé.* Frankfurt a.M.: Insel, 1986.

Krafft-Ebing, Richard von. *Psychopathia sexualis.* 1940. Munich: Matthes, 1986.

Kristeva, Julia. "Stabat Mater." *The Kristeva Reader.* Ed. Toril Moi. Oxford: Blackwell, 1986. 160-86.

*Leiden macht keine Lust: der Mythos vom weiblichen Masochismus.* Ed. Roswitha Burgard and Birgit Rommelspacher. Frankfurt a.M.: Fischer, 1992.

Livingstone, Angela. *Lou Andreas-Salomé.* London: Gordon Fraser Gallery, 1984.

Marcus, Maria. *Die furchtbare Wahrheit: Frauen und Masochismus.* Reinbek bei Hamburg: Rowohlt, 1982.

Martin, Biddy. *Woman and Modernity: The (Life)Styles of Lou Andreas-Salomé.* Ithaca: Cornell UP, 1991.

O'Pecko, Michael T. "Comedy and Didactic in Leopold von Sacher-Masoch's *Venus im Pelz.*" *Modern Austrian Literature* 25.2 (1992): 1-13.

Sacher-Masoch, Leopold von. *Venus im Pelz.* 1869. Frankfurt a.M.: Insel, 1980.

Salber, Linde. *Lou Andreas-Salomé mit Selbstzeugnissen und Bilddokumenten.* Reinbek bei Hamburg: Rowohlt, 1990.

Seem, Mark. Introduction. *Anti-Oedipus.* Gilles Deleuze and Félix Guattari.

Studlar, Gaylyn. "Masochism and the Perverse Pleasures of the Cinema." *Movies and Methods: An Anthology.* Ed. Bill Nichols. Berkeley: U of California P, 1985. Vol. 2. 602-21.

Weigel, Sigrid. "Die geopferte Heldin und das Opfer als Heldin: Zum Entwurf weiblicher Helden in der Literatur von Männern und Frauen." *Die verborgene Frau: Sechs Beiträge zu einer feministischen Literaturwissenschaft.* Ed. Inge Stephan and Sigrid Weigel. Berlin: Argument, 1988. 138-52.

Wright, Elizabeth. *Psychoanalytic Criticism: Theory in Practice.* London: Routledge, 1984.

# Irmtraud Morgner's Postmodern Feminism: A Question of Politics

## Silke von der Emde

Taking the contradictory reception of Irmtraud Morgner's novel *Life and Adventures of Troubadoura Beatriz, As Chronicled by Her Minstrel Laura* as a starting point, this essay examines Morgner's novel in the context of feminist debates on the political nature of postmodernist texts. Unlike other feminists in the early seventies, Morgner uses postmodernist strategies in order to promote feminist goals. Morgner discusses questions of representation and the status of the subject, topics that have become key issues in postmodernist texts. In reading Morgner's novel from today's perspective, we can gain important insights into the current debate about the differences between, and the intersections of, postmodernist and feminist theories. (SvdE)

The appearance of Irmtraud Morgner's novel *Life and Adventures of Troubadoura Beatriz, As Chronicled by Her Minstrel Laura* (GDR 1974 and FRG 1976) sparked controversy in both East and West Germany. Critical responses to the work were bewilderingly varied from the beginning. Neither in the East nor in the West did critics wish to reject the novel completely, emphasizing Morgner's great narrative talent. But a storm of objections underscored the uncertainty of many critics as they were confronted with the complex and extraordinary structure of this novel. While attempts to de-emphasize or ignore all elements of the text that challenged the official aesthetic doctrine of the GDR at the time—especially feminist topics and what I will define as postmodern tendencies—were to be expected from the "official" Marxist critics of the GDR, the strong reaction to certain formal elements in Morgner's novel by "traditional," mostly male, Western critics came as somewhat of a surprise. Martin Gregor-Dellin expressed "deep disappointment in the novel," which he called a "disaster" and an "epic monster"; Fritz Raddatz denounced the text's "downpour of horror and wit" and its "inflation of ideas," which he saw as "based on a misunderstanding of the picaresque novel."

Among feminists, too, the reaction to Morgner's novel has been mixed, even contradictory. After an initial enthusiastic reception of *Life and Adventures,* the debate focused on the tension in the text between a feminist and a Marxist discourse. Critics, disappointed by Morgner's refusal to define the feminist discourse in her novel as the most important one, dismissed her intention as failed and closed the debate for some time. Biddy Martin articulated her criticism most directly. While she argued that Morgner's text could be read "as a textual field of struggle between oppositional knowledge and the theoretical and unitary discourse of traditional Marxism" (60), she maintained that the text does not keep its promises: it "constrains the emancipatory possibilities which it opens up" by giving in to "the discursive limitations of orthodox Marxist rhetoric and the supposed historical necessities that govern the development of GDR society" (61). Martin criticized the novel's "final domesticity," arguing that the author refuses "to conceptualize the body and sexuality as privileged bases of political power" (73).[1] By the time of Morgner's premature death in March of 1990, the lively discussion among feminist critics from the early phases of reception had almost come to a stop.[2] Although there was some general praise of Morgner's works as important for the development of a feminist literature, the earlier debate about the tensions in Morgner's text between supposedly contradictory political tendencies was not continued.[3] Only during the last few years can a renewed interest in Morgner's texts be observed.[4] A volume edited by Marlis Gerhardt, *Irmtraud Morgner: Texte, Daten, Bilder,* appeared in 1990, followed by several articles from the early nineties analyzing specific aspects of Morgner's texts. In 1992 Gabriela Scherer published the first book-length study of the development of Morgner's narrative techniques.

The contradictory early reaction to Morgner's novel and the belated new interest in her work can be explained, I would argue, if we understand the significant differences between *Life and Adventures* and the majority of other feminist texts of the time. Unlike other feminists in the early seventies, Morgner used postmodern strategies in order to promote feminist goals. On the one hand, *Life and Adventures* takes part in a debate on how to define "woman," a debate that has been going on since the emergence of the women's movement. On the other hand, the text discusses questions of representation and the status of the subject, topics that have become key issues in postmodernist texts. In its combination of feminist and postmodernist strategies, Morgner's novel anticipates many arguments of today's debate about the differences between, and intersections of, postmodernist and feminist theories. As a text that is concerned with the possibility and usefulness of a definition of woman and the consequences of such a definition for political practice, *Life and Adventures* makes important contributions to the debate on the political nature of postmodernism.

In this paper, I will read Morgner's *Life and Adventures* as a "feminist" and a "postmodernist" as well as a "political" text, with each of these terms in quotation marks, to indicate that the combination of these elements in the novel encourages a reexamination of certain narrow definitions of feminism, postmodernism, and politics. The result will force us to abandon the simple, polarized pigeonholing of texts and theories as either historical or ahistorical, essentialist or anti-essentialist, political or non-political, emancipatory or reactionary. A discussion of Morgner's novel in the context of the debate on postmodernism is useful because it can point to certain textual elements that were overlooked in the early critical responses. It can also explain in part why this text has been discussed in such contradictory terms.[5]

I distinguish between postmodernism as a cultural and aesthetic designation and postmodernity as the designation of a social and historical period or "condition." In this sense, postmodernism can be understood as a *response* to postmodernity, a historical condition with economic, political, and social determinations (Schulte-Sasse 6). Postmodernity corresponds in the most general terms to a situation that can be characterized by the West's loss of unqualified faith in the "project of modernity," a modernity that starts at the latest with the Enlightenment and the Industrial Revolution in the eighteenth century. Linda Hutcheon points out that such diverse theoretical positions as Derrida's challenges to the western metaphysics of presence, Foucault's investigation of the complicities of discourse, knowledge, and power, Vattimo's paradoxically potent "weak thought," and Lyotard's questioning of the validity of the metanarratives of legitimation and emancipation have all been used to define the term postmodernity in philosophical circles (24). While there can be, as Andreas Huyssen asserts, as many postmodernisms as there are "modernisms," each of which must be understood in terms of historical developments, there does seem to be some agreement concerning several specific characteristics of postmodernism. Many theorists point to postmodernism's self-reflexivity, its emphasis on investigation of the social and ideological production of meaning and the effects of representation, its attempt to move beyond a certain binary "either/or" logic in favor of a logic of the "both/and" (McCormick's phrasing), its use of parody and what some critics (Charles Jencks and Linda Hutcheon, for example) have called "double-coding" in postmodernist texts. More specifically, postmodernist fiction has come to contest the modernist ideology of artistic autonomy and individual expression, as well as the deliberate separation of high art from mass culture and everyday life (Huyssen 53–54). Many of these characteristics are present in Morgner's novel *Life and Adventures* from 1974. Today, we can identify many elements of Morgner's texts as typically postmodernist: the extended use of intertextual connections, for example, and the recurring attempts to parody and rewrite whole parts of the text, thereby consciously correcting and reformulating earlier statements, which undermine the clear presentation of her message and her authority as author.[6] These features were very different from other feminist projects of the early seventies.

It is difficult to read early feminist texts from the former GDR in conjunction with those from the West, since in the early seventies a feminist movement did not exist in the same way in East Germany as it did in the West. In Morgner's case, however, a comparison can be fruitful, not only because her texts articulate a consciousness that is unmistakably feminist, but because her novels, together with those by Christa Wolf and other GDR women writers, were widely read in the West and influenced the development of feminist literature in West Germany.[7] In the case of Morgner's novel, a comparison with other feminist texts of the time helps to contextualize the early feminist critique of the novel.

In the early seventies, at the time Morgner's novel was published, the agitative impulses of the contemporary feminist movement in West Germany, which had grown out of the activism of the 1960s (partly influenced by the American Civil Rights movement, the anti-war movement in the Vietnam era, and the student movement), could still be felt. The large number of feminist publications that appeared during the early seventies and women authors' preference for documentary literature demonstrate the need feminists felt to make their voices heard in order to change history.[8] Feminists tried to "set the record straight" by publishing accounts of "realistic," "authentic" representations of women's experiences. While the realist bias of the early phase of feminist writing shows up most clearly in the great amount of documentary literature at this time, it can also be observed in a different manner in the so-called "I"-texts (texts that also have been labeled as "Identifikationsliteratur"), the most popular of which were Verena Stefan's *Häutungen* (*Shedding*) from 1975 and Karin Struck's *Klassenliebe* (*Class Love*) from 1973. Written in a confessional or thinly disguised autobiographical mode, texts such as these tend to emphasize the supposed sameness of women's experience and thematize variants of the dominant motif of "woman-as-victim."[9]

In contrast, Morgner's different "postmodern" feminism stresses women's need to enter history. In the afterword to her 1972 novel *Die wundersamen Reisen Gustavs des Weltfahrers: Lügenhafter Roman mit Kommentaren,* she quotes from the letter of the novel's fictional author Bele H.:

> In einem anderen Brief behauptete die Verfasserin, Frauen hätten ein schwach entwickeltes Geschichtsbewußtsein, weil sie wesentlich noch nicht in die Geschichte eingetreten wären. Um als Menschen zu leben, das heißt

in die Historie einzutreten, müßten sie aus der Historie austreten: sich Natur aneignen. Zuerst ihre eigne (155).

This passage has been read as Morgner's commitment to the feminist movement and to the discovery of a female essence ("die eigene Natur") that was repressed by a male-dominated history. Looking at the quotation more closely, we find a strange wording that seems to be typical for Morgner's texts. Bele H. talks about "entering history" ("in die Geschichte eintreten") as if she were entering into a building, i.e., something constructed rather than given and unchangeable. Her paradoxical wording of "having to exit history in order to be able to enter it" presupposes an understanding of history as something contrived. Morgner emphasizes the constructedness of history in which women have not been present as subjects. The ability to produce history, she goes on to say, defines human beings as gendered and determines their status. As Morgner lets her character claim: "women have an underdeveloped historical consciousness, since they have not entered history as subjects." But to enter history means for women to appropriate their own nature ("sich Natur aneignen. Zuerst ihre eigne"). Again Morgner uses an unusual verb when she talks about women's "nature." For Bele H., "sich Natur aneignen" does not seem to involve the simple task of *rediscovering* a natural femaleness that is given and easily available; instead, women have to "appropriate" nature. "Aneignen" means to make something one's own as well as to assert power over something or someone. The statement that it is women's task to "appropriate" their own nature points out that women's nature has not been their own so far. Morgner's strange wording unmasks the concept of "nature" in patriarchal societies as something artificial, constructed by human beings or, more specifically in the context of the quote, constructed by men in order to define women and thereby prevent them from assuming the status of subjects.

In fact, the "author" Bele H. creates a highly ironic game with the conception of nature versus civilization/history in this passage. In the tradition of the Enlightenment and German Idealism, "Menschsein," being human, means to assume one's historicity, a process that implies change and progress. Paradoxically, to be a female "Mensch," Bele H. claims, means to become "nature" first, to assume one's "natural" identity. Upon first reading it seems that Bele H. assumes a Rousseauean position of going back to nature. Her unusual wording, however, throws this position into question since it is not clear what women's "natural" identity is. The irony in Bele H.'s words distances the reader from familiar conceptions and models of "nature" and "history," and we are forced to reconsider core ideas of Western culture. In fact, unlike most West German feminists of the time, Morgner deconstructs many such core ideas of Western culture in her texts: through a simple but highly artistic play with words and linguistic structures, she probes the ground that supports concepts and ideas. She questions the mechanisms operative in the construction of certain concepts, thereby rendering them insecure and open for renegotiation.

In addition to deconstructing familiar conceptions of "nature" and "history," Morgner plays with the concept of the author. *Die wundersamen Reisen* has at least four "authors": Irmtraud Morgner, whose name is on the cover of the book; Bele H., who is the fictional "author" ("Verfasserin") and the author of the letter quoted at the end of the book; Dr. phil. Beate Heidenreich, the fictional editor of the text and a friend of Bele H.; and Gustav, Bele H.'s grandfather, who actually tells the "mendacious" stories of the novel. This strategy of creating a chain of voices instead of speaking as one individual, autonomous author is continued in *Life and Adventures*. Not only does Beatriz meet Bele H. on her journey to Split (bk. 8, ch. 22), but Irmtraud Morgner, the intrusive and manipulative author, appears in the novel as a fictional character who discusses writing strategies and the conditions for production of a text with her own character Laura Salman. Morgner thus creates a multiplicity of authors in the text, for Laura, as the chronicler of Beatriz's life, is also an "author." In fact, the chain of voices includes not only Laura, Beatriz, and Irmtraud Morgner, but all the female characters of the novel. They are connected through texts that they write and read *with each other, for each other,* and *in each other's name.* The intermezzos in *Life and Adventures,* for example, are parts of *Rumba auf einen Herbst,* an earlier novel by Irmtraud Morgner that the beautiful Melusine copies into her own Melusinian notebooks.[10] Laura writes stories using Beatriz's name, Beatriz writes stories in "Laura's style" (for example the story "Berta vom blühenden Bett" in bk. 8, ch. 10). In Book 8 we find a letter from Beatriz asking Laura to find an author who can write a poem for Wenzel Morolf in Beatriz's name (198). At Beatriz's funeral, Laura reads as Beatriz's last will Valeska's "Gute Botschaft" ("Gospel"), which Beatriz had received from a man she had met in Hades "when he was still a woman" (421). Valeska's "Gute Botschaft," however, contains among other citations Bele H.'s words from *Die wundersamen Reisen* spoken by Shenja, Valeska's friend and lover. Moreover, Beatriz had also repeated Bele H.'s words from *Die wundersamen Reisen* almost verbatim as her own when she first met Laura. Many passages consist of quotations from different characters in the novel. Sometimes the quotations are slightly changed, sometimes they are repeated verbatim.[11] All of these postmodern devices, which include a proliferation of beginnings, endings, and narrated actions, the parodic thematization of the author, a complex play with multiple coding through allusion and allusive commentary, citation, playfully distorted or invented reference, recasting, transposition, deliberate anachronism, and the mixing of two or more historical and stylistic modes, help to undermine the notion of a stable female identity.

The texts in the novel do not have one single author but contain a multiplicity of voices. Thus, the individual autonomous author who has control over her own text does not exist in Morgner's novel. Speaking, writing, and even experiencing are not forms of individual expression but always occur in dialogue with other voices (other people's as well as other texts'). The subject is not simply split into more than one voice as in other modernist texts, but it constitutes itself only in exchange with other subjects and texts.

In addition to Morgner's refusal to define a stable female subject based on a positive "female essence" that is different from men's, her texts consciously destroy the concept of difference as such. Her main techniques are mimesis and masquerade. In fact, *Life and Adventures* is full of people who cross-dress and exchange gender roles: the "feminine" man Benno, who turns into a male Scheherazade figure at the end of the novel; the "masculine" woman Laura, who ironically behaves like a typical male in the story "Kaffee verkehrt"; Beatriz herself, who when she enters the GDR thinks that she has awakened at a time when conditions for women have improved and acts accordingly, which is perceived as typical macho behavior by the men whom she meets; or Valeska, the woman who pretends to be and looks like a man after having gone through a sudden sex change, and who from that time on oscillates between the sexes. All these figures defy the notion of gender difference as sexual difference. In fact, the story of Valeska Kantus proves that sexual differences are not natural, but are instead constructed by various cultural "technologies of gender" (De Lauretis's term), which include the power to control social meaning and to produce representations of gender. The penis, Valeska finds out, is a "scepter of power" and a "privileging uniform" (428, 429). Her new male prerogatives are based on a political interpretation of a little difference between men and women rather than a natural superiority of the male sex. The difference between man and woman is unmasked as an artificial distinction between two arbitrary categories (those of man and woman) that operates in patriarchal societies to lock women into the position of objects of male desire. The text shows that definitions of gender difference are a matter of societal negotiations rather than essential differences; they *de*fine and *con*fine people. With our traditional gender categories shown to be arbitrary, the concept of difference itself is criticized or at least questioned. In the last instance, the notion of difference only makes sense when it is defined in relation to a specific historic and political situation.

Morgner does not deny the existence of differences between men and women and between individual persons, but she shows that these differences are always operative in specific political situations and can never be locked into fixed categories. Although she has learned how to switch back and forth between the sexes, Valeska Kantus, for example, decides to keep her male body without giving up her female past, since in her specific historical situation (the GDR of the seventies), this strategy allows her to gain experiences she can reveal to other women as her "gospel."[12] Since Valeska believes that it is time for women to question the supposedly natural subordination of the category "woman" under the category "man," she makes the "pragmatic" decision to write down her story in order to encourage women to develop "faith in themselves" and to try out similar "temporary sex changes" (111). In view of women's lack of "spiritual fanaticism" ("geistigem Fanatismus") (164), this is the appropriate strategy for Valeska, since her experiences might help women to question and redefine their female identity. Valeska's statement that she would also have herself crucified if that would convince women to act indicates that Valeska understands her "gospel" as a pragmatic political strategy fit for the present historic and political circumstances, not as another fixed and universal truth (444). In fact, she calls her actions "means for extorting peace" ("friedenserpresserische Mittel") that are appropriate in a time "when there is danger that humanity will destroy itself through wars" (444). It is Valeska's goal to encourage women to try out a similar sex change in order to understand how the concept of difference operates. She does not set out to define the concept of difference abstractly in order to affirm and celebrate some kind of feminine essence, a kind of "difference from." Instead, she insists on difference as a relative category and an ideological construct that needs to be analyzed and put to political use in a specific political situation.

In Morgner's text "reality" itself becomes a network of different discourses. In her important article "Die Frau und das Phantastische in der neueren DDR-Literatur: Der Fall Irmtraud Morgner" from 1979, Patricia Herminghouse points out that Morgner uses the fantastic as a subversive strategy. But even more radically, Morgner forces her readers to accept the fact that the opposition between reality and fiction does not work for her text at all. Fantastic figures like the mermaid Melusine work together with "realistic" figures like East German working woman Laura Salman; fantastic events like movements through time and history or sex changes occur consecutively with realistic descriptions of everyday events; and texts on radically different levels of realism are treated equally. Fairy tales, legends, and myths acquire the same reality in *Life and Adventures* as legal and historical documents or interviews and "factual documents." Texts that are prominently designated as "documents," "witness reports," or "true stories" are shown to be something different. For example, in "Laura's Faithful Record of the Troubadoura's Memories of the Real Raimbaut d'Aurenga Who Does Not Correspond to Reality" ("Sinngemäß von Laura protokollierte Erinnerungen der Trobadora an den wirklichen Raimbaut d'Aurenga, der nicht der Wirklichkeit entspricht") the "real Raimbaut d'Aurenga" turns out to be an ideal model of the non-patriarchal man. "Real" thus represents an ideal that makes sense to Beatriz rather than designating actuality. The borderline between "truth" and "fiction" is consciously brought into flux. Moreover, the same words that Beatriz had put into the mouth of her ideal lover Raimbaut in Book 1 are repeated by Benno when he introduces himself to Laura during his "third information visit" (bk. 10, ch. 17). Thus, it becomes impossible to distinguish fact from fiction, truth from lies, original from imitation, and the reader is constantly made aware of this impossibility. Our so-called "facts" are in the last instance nothing but parts of different texts. Reality as a pre-textual concept is constantly put into doubt.

The deconstructive strategies in the quoted passage from *Die wundersamen Reisen* from 1972, the artistic play with intertexts in *Life and Adventures,* and the radical questioning of prevailing notions of the stable and unified subject or a given reality "out there" make Morgner's discourse markedly different from many other feminist texts of the seventies. While other feminist texts defined gender difference as sexual difference in order to criticize the male practice of excluding the feminine perspective, to define a distinct female tradition, and to create social spaces in which sexual difference itself could be affirmed, Morgner does not rely on the notion of sexual difference or "authentic experience." On the contrary, Morgner's texts deconstruct the metaphysical grounds of concepts like "Nature," the "Subject," the "Author," "History," and "Reality" writ large; Morgner's close affinity to postmodernism is evident.

As a postmodernist text, Morgner's 1974 novel ties in to key questions about the differences and intersections between postmodernist and feminist theories, questions that were not debated until the early eighties. The contribution of a text like *Life and Adventures* to the debate on postmodernism is surprising, since Morgner's novel was written at a time when GDR literature was supposedly just starting to catch up with literary modernism (Emmerich 284). No wonder, then, that the postmodernist elements were overlooked in the early responses to the novel. While there was little doubt in the secondary literature on *Life and Adventures* that Morgner's text displayed a feminist consciousness (even if Morgner did not agree with the definition "feminist" for herself[13]), the question of whether her aesthetic strategies succeeded in making a political impact led to disagreement among critics. And in the debate about postmodernism, questions about the critical potential of postmodernist texts, the political nature of postmodernism itself, and the usefulness of an alliance of postmodernism and feminism have been at the center of interest.[14] Let me now suggest some ways in which a text like Morgner's *Life and Adventures* has unwittingly contributed to this debate.

The connection between postmodernism and feminism has provoked much discussion. One of the main charges made against postmodernism by such critics in the tradition of Frankfurt School critical theory as Jürgen Habermas and Fredric Jameson—although for different reasons—has been that postmodernism as a cultural phenomenon does not preserve a critical potential and as such is politically irrelevant or even dangerously neoconservative.[15] The charges of a lack of historical consciousness and political relevance cannot be made against feminism, a movement that by definition is political with its goal of improving the position and status of women in society. Moreover, from the beginning, the reexamination of history from a feminist perspective has been of utmost importance for feminist critics. Feminism, unlike *post*modernism, is said to have its foundations in the discourses of modernity, and is usually defined as part of modernity's more general emancipatory project. If one looks at the terms of the debate on postmodernism, then, there seems to be a myriad of differences between the two movements.

These basic differences between feminism and postmodernism have been challenged, however, not only by artistic practices that use postmodern strategies in order to support feminist goals, but also by theorists who began to examine the political implications of the intersection of a "feminist critique of patriarchy and a poststructuralist critique of representation" (Owens 59). Critics like Craig Owens, Hal Foster, Andreas Huyssen, or more recently Linda Hutcheon, have all placed feminist issues at the center of the debate on postmodernism and emphasized the common interests of both movements. Andreas Huyssen spoke of a new "postmodernism of resistance" created by the women's movement, the ecology movement, anti-imperialism, and a growing awareness of "other, non-European, non-Western cultures" (219–21). Linda Hutcheon pointed to the overlapping agendas between postmodernism and feminism (ch. 6). In fact, it seems to me that the debate on postmodernism has been greatly enriched by the discussions about the possible usefulness of postmodernist strategies for the political purposes of different marginalized groups. These discussions have allowed for a reevaluation of the critical potential of many postmodernist texts.

While the tendency to point to common interests between postmodernism and feminism seems unusually harmonious in the debate on postmodernism, there have also been warning voices in the camp of feminist critics that underscore the complexity and problematic nature of the argument. For many feminists, the main concern with the connection between postmodernism and feminism is the political status of the "decentered subject" in postmodern texts, a concept that seems to question a theory of personal agency.[16] Such a theory of agency, however, is necessary for feminism (and any other political movement) to guarantee the possibility of political change. Although interested in a deconstruction of (mis)representations, feminists cannot stop there. They need to develop a theory of positive action, create spaces of discourse, rewrite cultural narratives, and define the terms of a different perspective—a view from "elsewhere." What de Lauretis calls the "twofold pull in contrary directions" of feminist theory becomes visible precisely at the intersection between postmodernism and feminism. She calls this tension "the critical negativity of its theory, and the affirmative positivity of its politics" (26). That is, feminist theory has to be interested in a radical critique of dominant discourses on gender, but on the other hand, it also has to develop a theory of positive political action, thereby itself necessarily having to rely on restricting definitions.

The tension between a critical deconstructive impulse and the need for a positive theory of political action noted by de Lauretis is already present in Morgner's texts. *Life and Adventures* explores the contradictions between these two tendencies in feminism and offers suggestions for a political practice that takes this dilemma into account. Morgner's parody of the discourses of different feminist groups—not only in East Germany, but also in the West where feminist debates could take place more openly—proves her interest in the definition of woman and the consequences such a definition might have for the political strategy of different feminist groups.

The first feminist position depicted in *Life and Adventures* is represented by Persephone and Demeter, who have been dethroned by God and the devil and spend their life in a bunker singing matriarchal revenge songs. These two goddesses, who are the first women to give Beatriz advice, represent a separatist wing of feminism whose goal is to overturn patriarchy so that women can assume power. Persephone's radical separatist feminism is quickly rejected by Beatriz as a strategy that only reverses power structures rather than questioning them:

> Aber ebenso wie vor achthundert Jahren fiel ihr [Beatriz] plötzlich ein Bunker vor die Füße. Er war aus Beton gefertigt, würfelförmig und etwa acht Kubikmeter groß.... Aus den Löchern ertönte zweistimmiger Gesang. Beatriz hob wie einst anweisungsgemäß die Eisenstangen aus den Haken. Die Tür wurde von innen aufgestoßen—auch wie einst. Und schon schwoll der Gesang an zu jener eifernden Entschiedenheit, die Beatriz sogleich wieder unangenehm berührte. Sie verbarg aber ihre Abneigung und hörte sich einige programmatische Lieder an. Die erste Stimme wurde von der göttlichen Tochter gesungen, die zweite von der göttlichen Mutter. Gesperrte Münder, einwärts gerichtete Blicke, Persephone und Demeter beschrieben tatsächlich immer noch in den gleichen Rache- und Zukunftsgesängen die Wiedereinführung des Matriarchats.... Beatriz wurde von der Schwägerin hypnopädisch von den reaktionären Bestrebungen unterrichtet und entschied sich auch schnell für die dritte Ordnung. Die weder patriarchalisch noch matriarchalisch sein sollte, sondern menschlich (19-20).

The bunker and the goddesses' "inward view" are indications of their inability to look beyond their immediate political goals. By focusing only on their own agenda and on women, they merely replace one center (men) with another (women), without being able to analyze the mechanisms and structures that lead to the marginalization of different groups in society. Because this strategy leads to a reversal of power structures rather than a questioning of these very structures, Beatriz decides to support the "third order," which is neither patriarchal nor matriarchal, but human.

Beatriz's cousin, the mermaid Melusine, who believes the primary goal for women to be the overthrow of capitalism, represents a second group of feminists for whom the first step is a socialist revolution after which women's struggle for equality will be easier, if not automatic:

> Die Agitpropkunst soll für kapitalistische Verhältnisse gefertigt sein, auf deren Sturz Melusine ihre illegale Tätigkeit konzentriert. Tendenz der benötigten Protestsongs: Eine Frau, die sich heute Charakter leisten will, kann nur Sozialistin sein (104).

Melusine and Laura, a GDR working woman who is also a loyal socialist (although she is the first to admit that reforms of "real existing socialism" in the GDR are overdue), are convinced that Beatriz lacks pragmatism, without which political change will be impossible. They scold her for her absolutism and for her seemingly naive belief in fantasy, poetry, and magic as the only means to change society truly. Although Beatriz's position constantly challenges the customs and "normal" beliefs of the people whom she meets, Laura wants her to become more politically active. She suggests that Beatriz move to Berlin, become the editor of a women's magazine, and work practically toward the emancipation of women.

Since Laura advocates a feminism that allows women to act and make political decisions, she is convinced that magic, subversive as it may be, is a private solution for cowards. Laura emphasizes that women cannot escape personal responsibility for their actions and need to develop a practical and realistic political strategy. She says:

> Die Gegebenheiten akzeptieren, müßte ja nicht heißen, sie samt und sonders bejahen. Jedenfalls verlange der Vorgang Leben Stolz, Realpolitik, Improvisationstalent. Und bestünde in der Fähigkeit, sich durchzubeißen. Wunder ja, aber keine privaten für Drückeberger (112).

Beatriz, on the other hand, argues that in a "hopeless condition" miracles can be necessary for women to gain a subject position from which to speak. Women might have to leave history temporarily in order to analyze the foundations of our concepts of history and reality "from the outside." While Beatriz knows of course that such a movement is only possible with the help of miracles, she nevertheless pleads for a critical analysis of the foundations of our culture:

> Beatriz bezeichnete Laura als zimperlich. Sich Gegebenheiten zu stellen, wäre nur mit Chance [sic] als Zeichen von Stärke zu bewerten. "Wer zum Beispiel zu lebenslänglichem Kerker verurteilt wurde und keine Ausbruchspläne macht, ist nicht stolz, sondern feige. Beklagtest du nicht ebenfalls den Mangel an Solidarität unter Frauen? Er ist natürlich bei Wesen, die jahrtausendelang erniedrigt waren. Ihre Hoffnung, aus hoffnungsloser Lage zu entkommen, konnte sich nur auf Wundern gründen: das heißt auf Einzelaktionen. Ich bin aus der Historie ausgetreten, weil ich in die Historie eintreten wollte. Mir Natur aneignen. Zuerst meine eigne: die Menschwerdung in Angriff nehmen. Dieser Zweck heiligt alle Zaubermittel. Prost" (113).

Just like Bele H. in *Die wundersamen Reisen,* whose words Beatriz repeats almost verbatim, Beatriz points out that the metaphysical grounds of core concepts of our Western culture are really part of a male ideology that excludes women. In this sense, Beatriz represents the view from "elsewhere," a third feminist position. In fact, Beatriz's strategies are very similar to deconstructive reading practices. Yet, from Beatriz's position, any *practical* political action seems difficult, since these actions require different concepts and definitions that again would be subject to deconstructive readings.

On the one hand, the depiction of these different women is a parody of the debates that took place among feminist groups in the two Germanys at the time. It reveals the closed-mindedness of certain groups of feminists who fought each other rather than the circumstances that led to their oppression. On the other hand, the depiction of different camps of feminists is not only humorous but also philosophical and political in nature. On her journey through time and history, Beatriz oscillates between these last two positions: Laura's pragmatism that seeks concrete political results based on a fixed subject position and Beatriz's own more deconstructive mode that radically questions its foundations. Since a deconstruction of feminine identity is included in this process, any concrete positive political action is difficult. Through the debates between the women that include multiple switches in positions, overlappings, and contradictions, the reader understands that it is not only the definitions of men and patriarchal society that have serious consequences for women's position and status in society, but also self-definitions of different women and feminist groups. These definitions are necessary to be able to act politically, but they are also restricting and exclusive.

The text never makes clear what the definition of woman should finally be. At first it seems that Beatriz, after returning from her unsuccessful attempt to find the unicorn Anaximander whose horn could save the world and solve all problems, resigns herself to existing conditions and adopts Laura's pragmatism. But the assimilation of the two women is depicted as problematic and full of contradictions. When Laura realizes that Beatriz is becoming more and more like herself, she warns her: "[W]illst du mich doubeln? Willst du mich überflüssig machen?" (397). Laura, having tried to educate Beatriz to become more realistic, understands that Beatriz's position is an important element in the struggle of women to gain subject status. Both of these roles are needed: the pragmatism *and* the miracles that serve as a deconstructive element challenging the foundations of what we call "reality."[17] In fact, Laura and Beatriz seem to switch roles: while Beatriz becomes concerned with everyday life (and dies from it while cleaning windows!), Laura falls sick with *Fernweh* and is finally elected to the Round Table of the Queen of Sheba in Beatriz's place. Laura finds the utopian man Benno in the end, but instead of engaging in a traditional heterosexual marriage, they switch gender roles in their partnership. While Laura mourns the loss of her friend and alter ego Beatriz, Benno assumes the role of Scheherazade, telling nightly stories in Beatriz's style to save, i.e., justify, his existence. While it seems at first that the Beatrizian element is dropped in the end, the irony of the ending, together with Benno's repetition of the very first words of the novel, "of course this land is a place of wonders," encourages the readers to begin the dialogue anew, a task that Morgner herself took on in *Amanda,* the second part of her Salman-trilogy.[18] Neither Laura nor Beatriz is ever confined to fixed roles; they travel between ideologies, trying out possible roles and definitions like costumes, without complying with definitions of their own subject position once and for all. The attempt to define one's own role and become a subject turns out to be a never-ending *process* rather than a teleological path with a fixed ending. Although the attempt to define oneself is necessary for women, any definition can only be a temporary one based on concrete political needs at a specific time in history.

Much like Teresa de Lauretis's suggestion of a new "subject of feminism," a subject whose definition or conception is in progress, a subject that is "at the same time inside *and* outside the ideology of gender," the text's subject(s) are both inside *and* outside the ideology of gender, "and conscious of being so, conscious of that twofold pull, of that division, that doubled vision" (9-10). While the text demonstrates how dominant representations of women affect all of the figures, new subjects are constructed through the process of moving inside and outside of different discourses, showing that women are more than ideology. These characters move from the male-dominated representations of women to those spaces that this representation leaves out, spaces at the margins of the official discourse, unrepresentable in its dominant images, but nevertheless implied by it.

If Beatriz's quest is for self-definition and, ultimately, a definition of woman, then her journey demonstrates how this quest can only lead to a definition in the "space-off" of discourse. This "space-off," a term borrowed from film theory, designates the space not visible in the frame but inferable from what the frame makes visible (De Lauretis 26). In *Life and Adventures,* these spaces include utopian and fantastic possibilities—Vera Hill's technique of tightrope walking, Valeska's strategy of changing her sex at will, or Laura's fantastic election to the Round Table of the Queen of Sheba. These also include more "realistic" options at the margins of society—female communes, women's friendships, joint artistic projects of women, and women's laughter.[19] Through a constant effort to rewrite and reexamine these options, they are shown to be *possibilities* for women, with none offering a definite answer or solution. In fact, the movement between discourses, the process of being inside a certain discourse and constantly moving outside it at the same time, is the movement that Beatriz and Laura demonstrate in their quest. In the last interview before her death in 1990, Morgner stated:

> Man muß sich selber beobachten können. Sich selbst und die Sprache. Ihre Möglichkeiten. Die Mehrdeutigkeit eines Wortes gleicht ja für den Schriftsteller der Mehrdeutigkeit seines Ich. Das Ensemble von Figuren, das ich schaffe—wie ein Dramatiker—ist ja nur eine Aufspaltung dessen, was man Ich nennt. Die tragenden Figuren meiner Romane sind verschiedene Seiten von mir. Man entzündet sich an sich selbst ("Am Ende bleibt das eigene Leben").

What we call "subject" is not a fixed category in Morgner's texts. It is not only ambiguous and in flux, but facets of the subject are also constantly created and recreated through a process of masquerade and self-experiment that rekindles and opens up other possibilities.

The definition of woman advocated in *Life and Adventures* turns out to be a non-definition, a definition that demonstrates the impossibility of such a project without negating the need for it. Morgner's stated intention in *Life and Adventures* was to create a space from which women could enter history and make their voices heard. She described Beatriz's journey as a quest whose goal it is to "free her own voice range" ("die eigene Stimmlage freilegen" 58) and to define herself as a subject in order "to enter history" (113). Although Morgner sharply criticized modern society as a *Frauenhaltergesellschaft,* a society in which women have the status of slaves,[20] she refused to define herself as a feminist or even admit that what she was writing about were exclusively "women's concerns":

> Das Wort "Feministin" gefällt mir nicht, weil es einen modischen, unpolitischen Zug hat für mich, weil es die Vermutung provoziert, daß die Menschwerdung der Frau nur eine Frauensache sein könnte. Da wird aber ein Menschheitsproblem aufgeworfen. Emanzipation der Frauen ist ohne

Emanzipation der Männer unerreichbar und umgekehrt. "Trobadora Beatriz" ist von einer Kommunistin geschrieben ("Produktivkraft" 111).

As a consequence, many feminists were disturbed at what they perceived to be a privileging of a critique of Western capitalism over feminist considerations ("a woman of character can only be a socialist today" [*Life and Adventures* 104, 385]). These differences in perception, I would argue, arose because of Morgner's different understanding of the term feminist in the early seventies. For Morgner, the problem was not to discover women's nature and "authentic" voice, but rather to excavate, like an archeologist, the *voice range* of woman: "die eigene Stimmlage freilegen" (58).[21] The text points out that there is no *one* voice, one subject position for women, but rather a range of possibilities that are unlimited and never fixed.[22] The characters do assume subject positions and different roles that allow them to act, but these definitions can never be fixed once and for all. On the contrary, they are only possible temporarily and constantly need to be redefined in response to concrete political and historical needs.

If it is true that one of Morgner's agendas was to attempt the construction of a new kind of feminist subject, then the notion of agency also needs to be redefined. Morgner's new type of political agency in feminism would no longer be dependent on a relatively unified notion of the social subject "woman," but would instead represent an attempt to take into account the plurality and diversity between women of different cultures as well as within any given culture. Sensitive to the complex nature of different definitions and self-definitions of women, such a new kind of feminist subject would be structured plurally, it would be a subject that promotes a new kind of political agency able to deal out of and with this plurality.

It seems to me that Morgner's radical questioning of the subject is consonant with other more recent attempts of feminist theoreticians such as Teresa de Lauretis, Judith Butler, and Donna Haraway to come to new definitions of feminist subjectivity. Butler argues for a Foucauldian critique of the subject that does not pronounce the subject's death but instead claims that certain versions of the subject are politically insidious. Butler's goal is to reinscribe the subject outside the terms of an epistemological given. She rejects any attempt to assign a universal or specific content to the category woman and use "identity" as a point of departure. Instead, she wants to use the term "women" as a site of "permanent openness and resignifiability" (16). From her point of view, only through releasing the category of women from a fixed referent does something like "agency" become possible. Only such a practice would expand the possibilities of what it means to be a woman.

Donna Haraway's metaphor for a new kind of feminist subject is the cyborg. Haraway argues that what has now become possible is a political practice that embraces a recognition of the multiple, pregnant, and contradictory aspects of both our individual and collective identities. Such a politics no longer requires essential criteria of identification; we are beginning to see instead the formation of political groupings that rest on the conscious negation of such criteria. Haraway gives the identifying phrase "women of color" as an example for a postmodern identity constructed out of a recognition of otherness and difference.

Morgner's texts, it seems to me, display a sensitivity to the complexities of the problems involved in the attempt to arrive at a definition of woman. Her new kind of feminist subject is a concept that constantly needs to be renegotiated and examined. Through her emphasis of the diverse and sometimes conflicting perspectives of the women in the novel, the text acknowledges and also encourages its readers to see that the premises from which Morgner is working as an author also possess a specific location. *Life and Adventures* makes clear that women's writings cannot proclaim another kind of "truth" that would be different from men's, yet somehow more objective and "real." In fact, the alleged accounts of women's "true," "authentic" experiences as portrayed in other feminist texts of the seventies are prominently missing. In this sense, the text takes issue with those feminist positions that describe "a woman's distinct perspective" and thereby postulate aspects of modern Western culture as present in all or most of human history. With its emphasis on the diversity of women's experiences, the text criticizes attempts to come to a universal definition of woman for their tendency to rely on white, middle-class, heterosexist experiences of women who live in Western capitalist states of the twentieth century.[23] Although Morgner is conscious of the fact that we need to define agendas and political goals at different points in history in order to be able to act politically, she promotes an awareness that any of these definitions can only function temporarily and in the context of specific political needs. In this sense, the new feminist subject of *Life and Adventures* operates in close proximity to De Lauretis's "new subject of feminism," Haraway's cyborg, or Butler's category of women as a "place of permanent openness and resignifiability."

In reading *Life and Adventures,* we can gain important insights for the current debate about the political nature of postmodernist texts. The questions that Morgner examines in her novel from 1974 have become key questions in current feminist debates: How can feminists find a definition of female subjectivity that does not exclude differences among individual women? How is it possible to develop a theory of feminist agency and feminist political practice if the "autonomous subject" is supposed to have disappeared? How is it possible to ensure responsibility and accountability if the individual author seems to merge with a web of texts and intertexts? How can feminists use postmodernist textual strategies in order to deconstruct patriarchal traditions without having to give up any kind of positive identification? Much more than portraying the lives of women in the former GDR or providing "authentic" representations of women's experiences as do most other feminist texts of the time, *Life and Adventures* thus raises questions of representation and definition(s) of subjective identity and political agency. Morgner's plea for a dialogic, open-ended text that would be able to incorporate different positive definitions in a nondogmatic and nonprescriptive way is an attempt to think difference not in terms of binary oppositions but as a 'simultaneous-with.' The fantastic game of masquerade that the novel initiates serves author and reader as a tool of criticism and as an instrument to imagine new models of political practice that are then tested and interrogated in the experimental setting of the text.

> Dabei hat Literatur eine Chance, die sie so noch nie gehabt hat: bei dieser Umwandlung der Sitten, die einen Prozeß der Herstellung von Verwunderung über die Zustände erfordert, die menschlich unangemessen sind. Dafür ist am ehesten durch ein intensives Gespräch zwischen Zweien etwas zu machen—hier zwischen einem, der schreibt, und einem der liest ("Weltspitze sein und sich wundern, was noch nicht ist" 98).

In this sense Morgner has actually come close to "creating a state of astonishment" in the reader that might be the first step toward change.

## Notes

Unless otherwise noted, translations are my own.

[1] Unfortunately, Martin's criticism closed the debate on Morgner's novel for some time; her argument was cited by several critics. See for example, Sara Lennox and Rainer Nägele, both in a volume on GDR literature from 1983.

[2] In Germany, Ingeborg Nordmann was the only critic who already in 1981 analyzed the tension between a feminist and an orthodox Marxist discourse in *Life and Adventures* as a tension that never gets resolved in the novel (427). Nordmann, in contrast to Martin, argued that the "ironic gesture" of the "positive ending" in *Life and Adventures* supported the fundamental openness of the novel. Nordmann states: "Die Morgner ist weit entfernt davon, eine harmonische und zu sich gekommene Identität Laura/Trobadora zu konstruieren. Sie hält die Spannung zwischen der vernünftigen Anpassung an die Realitäten der DDR und der Unbedingtheit des Emanzipationsanspruches aufrecht" (442). Although Nordmann's analysis introduced many new arguments into the debate, her article remained almost unnoticed, and the debate on the success or failure of Morgner's combination of new textual strategies with feminist political goals did not continue.

[3] Angelika Bammer discussed the reception of *Life and Adventures* in the U.S. in her article "Trobadora in Amerika." At that time, Bammer still noted the lack of any more detailed studies of Morgner's work. She stated, however, that this situation might be changing at the beginning of the nineties, a prediction that proved to be true.

[4] Several critics focus on the motif of the sex change in Morgner's novel, e.g., Kornelia Hauser in 1991 and Carlotta von Maltzan in 1990. There are articles on the reception of Romantic texts and the "literary heritage" in Morgner's work, for example by Hanne Castein (1990), Elke Liebs (1990), and Synnöve Clason (1990). Some studies focus on the poetic imagination and the fantastic: Angelika Bammer in an important chapter on Morgner in her book *Partial Visions: Feminism and Utopianism in the 1970s* (1991), Agnès Cardinal (1991), and M. Rasboinikowa (1992). Ulrike Sati analyzes the dialogic structure of Morgner's novel (1990). A few critics have also begun to analyze postmodern elements in Morgner's work, e.g., Michaela Grobbel (1987), Petra Reuffer (1988), and Genia Schulz (1988). Alison Lewis analyzes the construction of female subjectivity in 1993.

[5] It is interesting that critics who now (in the late eighties and early nineties) begin to read Morgner's narrative techniques as postmodern textual strategies seem to have different expectations than those critics who gave earlier evaluations of the text. More used to the playfulness of other postmodern texts that have appeared in the meantime, these critics treat conflicting elements and tensions in the text as productive energy rather than claiming that Morgner's novel lacked a coherent concept or was based on a misunderstanding of certain literary rules. Several critics, however, feel compelled to distinguish Morgner's textual strategies from those in other postmodern works that they suspect of being merely "playful" and lacking "seriousness" and political relevance, e.g., Scherer and Grobbel.

[6] Ingeborg Nordmann, in her early article from 1981, had already analyzed Morgner's montage technique as a montage of text parts that criticize one another and undercut each other's authority. Nordmann maintained that the function of this technique was twofold: on the one hand it served to produce a socialist teleology, on the other hand it destroyed any kind of teleological sense through its technique of decomposing all perceptions of reality (461).

[7] Angelika Bammer shows in her study on utopianism in feminist texts from the seventies that "the case of East and West Germany is only one example of the remarkable degree to which feminism (in its first decade at least) was simultaneously national and transnational. As texts and theories crossed borders they not only carried their original feminist formations with them, but were instrumental in the shaping of different feminisms elsewhere" (*Partial Visions* 65).

[8] Sigrid Weigel in her book *Die Stimme der Medusa* points to Erika Runge's *Frauen: Versuche zur Emanzipation* from 1969, Alice Schwarzer's *Frauen gegen den Paragraphen 218* published in 1971, Ulrike Meinhof's *Bambule* from 1971,

Britta Noeske's *Liebe Kollegin: Texte zur Emanzipation* from 1973, and Alice Schwarzer's *Der kleine Unterschied und seine großen Folgen* from 1975. Patricia Herminghouse analyzes a trend similar to documentary literature in the GDR, citing e.g., Sarah Kirsch, *Die Pantherfrau* (1973), and Maxi Wander's *Guten Morgen du Schöne* (1977) ("Legal Equality" 46).

[9] Angelika Bammer states that a great number of these texts "were predicated upon two basic cultural feminist assumptions: (1) that gender difference was given, and (2) that women's 'difference' should be seen as positive.... This affirmation of femaleness as a positive identity was not limited to cultural feminism, however; it was a vital dimension of 1970's feminisms in general" (*Partial Visions* 93). Compare also her more detailed analysis of Stefan's text in *Partial Visions* (67–79).

[10] The novel *Rumba auf einen Herbst* did not receive permission to be published in the GDR and the manuscript was never returned to the author. From memory, Morgner incorporated large parts of this novel into the intermezzos of *Life and Adventures,* which all are parts of chapters in Melusine's books, as the reader is told. These parts of *Rumba auf einen Herbst* are not the only texts that Melusine quotes in her "Melusinische Bücher" ("Melusinian books"), however. Other texts she copies in her notebooks include an interview with the master chess player Dr. Solowjow, an article from a magazine, the memoirs of Krupskaja, quotations from Laura's notebook, a summary of the results of the Vietnam war produced by the Stockholm Institute for International Affairs, a copy of Olga Salman's petition, excerpts from the GDR health book "Mann und Frau Intim," and the copy of a newspaper report from *Neues Deutschland*. The Melusinian books thus form a third text (together with Laura's chronicle of Beatriz's life and *Rumba auf einen Herbst*) inside of *Life and Adventures*.

[11] In the chapter "Benno Pakulat höchstpersönlich," for example, Benno repeats Laura's story "Coffee the Wrong Way Around" with yet another role change (315). On his third "Information Visit," he repeats words that Beatriz before had put into the mouth of her lover Raimbaut d'Aurenga in a chapter called "Laura's Faithful Record of the Troubadoura's Memories of the Real Raimbaut d'Aurenga Who Does not Correspond to Reality" (bk. 1, ch. 18). And in the last chapter, Benno begins to tell Laura 1001 nightly stories in "Beatriz's style" to console his mourning wife. In the first of these stories, he not only retells the story of Beatriz's life in the Middle Ages as Laura had told it to Irmtraud Morgner in the first chapter of Book 1, but he closes his story with the exact same words that Irmtraud Morgner had spoken at the very beginning of the novel in "Vorsätze."

[12] In her "Frohe Botschaft," Valeska's new sexual relationship to her girlfriend Shenja that takes place after she has changed into a man teaches her that heterosexual relationships can function without the subjugation of women. She is astonished to find that "die erstmals erprobte Aparatur ohne herrscherliche Gefühle und Unterwerfungsvorstellungen funktioniert hatte" (434). Because of these experiences she demands from her lover Rudolf a new type of relationship

that is based on true equality. Valeska says that they now can enjoy a relationship that disregards "die Bilder...die sie sich voneinander und die andere für sie gemacht hatten. Da wußten sie, daß sie einander liebten. Persönlich—Wunder über Wunder" (443). Only after Rudolf has loved her without even noticing her new male body does she switch back to her female body during the time of their lovemaking. With tongue in cheek, Morgner comments that Valeska accomplishes this by "intensely" concentrating on the thought of being made from a man's rib. The temporary change pleases Rudolf who would love her to stay female in order to get a break from sharing the household chores, which comes about naturally when Valeska is a man (443). In fact, homosexual or heterosexual love becomes a question of choice for Valeska. She seems to have learned through the experience of her miraculous sex change that the outer appearances of the lovers' bodies are unimportant as long as the structure of their relationship is one that is radically different from oppressive heterosexual relationships in patriarchal society. Again, it seems to me, Morgner insists on pointing out that it is conventions that define gender roles, not natural differences between men and women. In this point I disagree with Angelika Bammer who maintains that "the motivating factor behind Valeska's dutiful metamorphoses (male in public and female in bed) seems to be the need to maintain the family structure at any cost" (*Partial Visions* 114).

[13] While Morgner's reservations about the definition "feminist" for herself arose in part because of the different understanding of the term in East and West, Morgner remained a convinced Marxist throughout her life. It is important to add, however, that Morgner criticized orthodox Marxist ideology by emphasizing Marx's early emancipatory statements, as well as other utopian socialist thinkers like Fourier, over the more economically oriented later Marx (cf. Nordmann 426).

[14] While it is possible to read postmodernism chiefly as a formal category and to oppose it as such to modernism, such an effort is of limited interest, I would argue with Susan Suleiman (113) and Andreas Huyssen (9). A postmodernist practice in the arts has provoked controversy when it was understood as a cultural intervention rather than an object of descriptive poetics. The debate on postmodernism that has been going on since the eighties is a debate about postmodernism as a cultural category.

[15] In a debate with Jean-François Lyotard, Habermas identified the notion of postmodernity with French poststructuralism, which he attacked as the (neo)conservative position of those who believe that modernity has failed and that the utopian impulses it gave rise to should therefore be abandoned. But modernity or "the project of Enlightenment," Habermas argues from the point of view of his own emancipatory philosophy of rational consensus, is not an obsolete project, only an unfinished one. What should be rejected, in Habermas' opinion, is not modernity but the neoconservative ideology of postmodernity (cf. his famous Adorno-Preisrede from 1980, reprinted in *New German Critique*). While Fredric Jameson, unlike Habermas, deals with postmodernism as something that

has to be reckoned with, he similarly comes to a negative evaluation of postmodernism, a term that he equates with postmodernity. Jameson argues that as a typical outgrowth of a late capitalism, postmodernism lacks historical consciousness and is unable to preserve critical distance. He charges that postmodernism does not only replicate the logic of late capitalism but reinforces and intensifies it. Postmodernism's intertextuality, in his view, is "a field of stylistic and discursive heterogeneity without a norm" and "a blank parody, a statue with blind eyeballs" (65). Many critics have pointed out that both Habermas and Jameson have raised important questions, and that the argument of both critics is more complex than has usually been stated in the rather heated debate on postmodernism. I admit to similarly simplifying both of their arguments here for the sake of brevity.

[16] Wolfgang Welsch has recently pointed out that the transformation of our conception of the subject is at the center of the debate on postmodernism. The criticism of the subject has been rejected, he maintains, because it seemed to lead to a weakening of the autonomous subject and the responsible citizen, the basis for any political criticism until today. Welsch argues, however, that the postmodern criticism of the subject does not necessarily lead to the "death of the subject," as has often been maintained, but on the contrary needs to be understood as the criticism of a certain type of subject. For Welsch, the challenge that presents itself to us today is to come to a different conception of the subject, a subject that would be able to deal with the plurality of our modern reality. Welsch calls this new type of subject the "vielheitsfähige[s] Subjekt."

[17] Bammer makes a similar point in her discussion of *Life and Adventures*. She writes: "If the Lauras of this world are not to be stuck forever coping with dirty diapers, polluted cities, and oppressive relationships, they must also be able to imagine that alternatives exist. They must periodically 'step out of history' to prevent the future from being exhausted by its own past.... Beatriz' fantasies are as important as Laura's productivity. Beatriz thus embodies Morgner's challenge to the productivist ideology of a state that denies the usefulness of fantasy even as it acknowledges its power by censoring it" (*Partial Visions* 111).

[18] *Amanda: A Witch Novel* appeared in 1983. Beatriz's story is retold again by Beatriz herself, because the troubadoura who has been resurrected as a siren claims that Irmtraud Morgner made mistakes in her version of the story not only because Morgner did not know all of the facts, but also because her novel smacks of self-censorship. Morgner herself emphasized the irony at the end of the novel in an interview with Doris Berger. To Berger's question why she decided to write a second part to *Life and Adventures* in which she openly "corrected" certain statements in the first novel, Morgner answered: "Nun, also—das Ende, das scheinbare happy end von *Beatriz* war ja verdächtig. Ich meine, das mußte man auflösen, da mußte man ja mal dahinter graben und fragen, was ist dann?... Also diese Sache stand schon im Ende des Romans eigentlich vor der Tür" ("Gespräch mit Irmtraud Morgner" 29).

[19] Friendships and common projects among women repeatedly lead to significant changes and challenges of existing structures in GDR society in *Life and Adventures*. The community of women and children who live together as a new type of family in Valeska's "Hadische Erzählungen" not only leads to a radically new life style for Valeska, but also to a new type of relationship to her parents, her children, and her lover. She says, for example: "Die Liebe verlor ihr dogmatisches System mit Naturereignischarakter, das die Welt mit großen Gesten vergewaltigt. Ereignisse und Gegenstände näherten sich vergleichsweise ihrem Eigenwert. In freundlichem Umgang war Vielfalt, schöne Menschengemeinschaft" (234).

[20] In one of the information visits of Benno Pakulat, Morgner lets her character state: "Große Schriftstellerinnen gibts gar nicht. Kanns nicht geben. Die griechische Kultur hatte die Sklavenordnung zur Grundlage, die moderne Kultur die Frauenhalterordnung" (273). Morgner herself made the same argument in a study group at the VIIth *Schriftstellerkongreß* in 1974.

[21] The first translation of "Stimmlage" in German is "pitch" or "register" of the voice. "Lage" can also mean layer, position, situation, or condition. Together with the verb "freilegen," a verb that is mostly used for the activity of an archeologist, Morgner creates a range of possible meanings and associations here that describes the novelty of the situation for woman. At the same time, Morgner's choice of words alludes to Foucault's concept of historical science as an "archeology of knowledge" (cf. Foucault).

[22] The second chapter of Book 2 is called "Beatrizens Stimmlage wird freigelegt." The narrator tells us: "Schließlich erkannte sie [Beatriz], daß sie keine scholastischen Kanzonen mehr verfassen konnte, diese Nachbildungen mit verstellter Stimme Tenor, Bariton, Baß. Unmerklich, vielleicht auf den brutalen Wegen der Demütigung, war ihre eigene Stimmlage freigelegt worden. Für deren Gebrauch es freilich noch keine Vorlagen gab" (58).

[23] In fact, women with radically different experiences appear in the text: they come from the Middle Ages and modern GDR society, there are working-class women and noble ladies, women from socialist and capitalist societies, old and young women, lesbians and heterosexual women, and women from many different cultures (the United States, France, the Soviet Union, Yugoslavia, and Italy).

## Works Cited

Bammer, Angelika. *Partial Visions: Feminism and Utopianism in the 1970s.* New York: Routledge, 1991.

―――. "Trobadora in Amerika." *Irmtraud Morgner: Texte, Daten, Bilder.* Ed. Marlis Gerhardt. 196-209.

Butler, Judith. "Contingent Foundations: Feminism and the Question of 'Postmodernism.'" *Feminists Theorize the Political*. Ed. Judith Butler and Joan W. Scott. New York: Routledge, 1992. 3-21.

Cardinal, Agnès. "'Be Realistic: Demand the Impossible': On Irmtraud Morgner's Salman Trilogy." *Socialism and the Literary Imagination: Essays on East German Writers*. Ed. Martin Kane. New York: Berg, 1991. 147-61.

Castein, Hanne. "Wundersame Reisen im gelobten Land: Zur Romantikrezeption im Werk Irmtraud Morgners." *Neue Ansichten*. 114-25.

Clason, Synnöve. "Auf den Zauberbergen der Zukunft: Die Sehnsüchte der Irmtraud Morgner." *Text und Kontext* 12.2 (1984): 370-86.

de Lauretis, Teresa. *Technologies of Gender: Essays on Theory, Film, and Fiction*. Bloomington: Indiana UP, 1987.

Emmerich, Wolfgang. *Kleine Literaturgeschichte der DDR: 1945-1988*. Erweiterte Ausgabe. Frankfurt a.M.: Luchterhand, 1989.

Foster, Hal. "(Post)Modern Polemics." *Recodings: Art, Spectacle, Cultural Politics*. Seattle: Bay, 1985.

Foucault, Michel. *The Archeology of Knowledge and the Discourse on Language*. Trans. A. M. Sheridan Smith. New York: Pantheon, 1972.

Gregor-Dellin, Martin. "Trobadora aus der Retorte: Was die Spielfrau Laura der DDR-Autorin Irmtraud Morgner verriet." *Frankfurter Allgemeine Zeitung* 10 March 1975.

Grobbel, Michaela. "Kreativität und Re-Vision in den Werken Irmtraud Morgners von 1968 bis 1972." *New German Review* 3 (1987): 1-16.

Habermas, Jürgen. "Modernity versus Postmodernity." *New German Critique* 22 (Winter 1981): 3-14.

Haraway, Donna. "A Manifesto of Cyborgs: Science, Technology, and Socialist Feminism in the 1980s." *Socialist Review* 80 (1985): 65-107.

Hauser, Kornelia. "Weiblicher Teiresias oder trojanisches Pferd im Patriarchat? Geschlechtertausch bei Christa Wolf und Irmtraud Morgner." *Das Argument* 187 (1991): 373-81.

Herminghouse, Patricia. "Die Frau und das Phantastische in der neueren DDR-Literatur: Der Fall Irmtraud Morgner." *Die Frau als Heldin und Autorin: Neue kritische Ansätze zur deutschen Literatur*. Ed. Wolfgang Paulsen. Bern: Francke, 1979. 248-66.

———. "Legal Equality and Women's Reality in the German Democratic Republic." *German Feminism: Readings in Politics and Literature*. Ed. Edith Hoshino Altbach, Jeanette Clausen, Dagmar Schultz, and Naomi Stephan. Albany: State U of New York P, 1984. 41-46.

Hutcheon, Linda. *The Politics of Postmodernism*. London: Routledge, 1989.

Huyssen, Andreas. "Mapping the Postmodern." *New German Critique* 33 (Fall 1984): 5-52.

*Irmtraud Morgner: Texte, Daten, Bilder*. Ed. Marlis Gerhardt. Darmstadt: Luchterhand, 1990.

Jameson, Fredric. "Postmodernism, or the Cultural Logic of Late Capitalism." *New Left Review* 146 (July–August 1984): 53–92.
Jencks, Charles. "Postmodern versus Late-Modern." *Zeitgeist in Babel.* 4–21.
Lennox, Sara. "'Nun ja! Das nächste Leben geht aber heute an.' Prosa von Frauen und Frauenbefreiung in der DDR." *Literatur der DDR in den 70er Jahren.* Ed. Peter Uwe Hohendahl and Patricia Herminghouse. Frankfurt a.M.: Suhrkamp, 1983. 224–58.
Lewis, Alison. "'Foiling the Censor': Reading and Transference as Feminist Strategies in the Works of Christa Wolf, Irmtraud Morgner, and Christa Moog." *German Quarterly* 66.3 (Summer 1993): 372–86.
Liebs, Elke. "Melusine zum Beispiel: Märchen und Mythenrezeption in der Prosa der DDR." *Neue Ansichten.* 126–41.
Maltzan, Carlotta von. "'Man müßte ein Mann sein': Zur Frage der weiblichen Identität in Erzählungen von Kirsch, Morgner und Wolf." *Acta Germanica* 20 (1990): 141–55.
Martin, Biddy. "Socialist Patriarchy and the Limits of Reform: A Reading of Irmtraud Morgner's *Life and Adventures of Troubadora Beatriz as Chronicled by her Minstrel Laura.*" *Studies in Twentieth Century Literature* 5.1 (Fall 1980): 59–74.
McCormick, Richard W. *Politics of the Self: Feminism and the Postmodern in West German Literature and Film.* Princeton: Princeton UP, 1991.
Morgner, Irmtraud. "Am Ende bleibt das eigene Leben. Ost-Berlin, 1990: Ein Gespräch mit Irmtraud Morgner-kurz vor ihrem Tod." With Synnöve Clason. *Die Zeit* 6 November 1992.
———. *Amanda: Ein Hexenroman.* Darmstadt: Luchterhand, 1983.
———. "Gespräch mit Irmtraud Morgner." Interview with Doris Berger. *GDR Monitor* 12 (Winter 1984/85): 29–37.
———. *Leben und Abenteuer der Trobadora Beatriz nach Zeugnissen ihrer Spielfrau Laura: Roman in dreizehn Büchern und sieben Intermezzos.* Darmstadt: Luchterhand, 1985.
———. "'Produktivkraft Sexualität souverän nutzen': Ein Gespräch mit der DDR-Schriftstellerin Irmtraud Morgner." With Karin Huffzky. *Frankfurter Rundschau* 16 August 1975: 111.
———. "Rede vor dem VII. Schriftstellerkongreß." *VII. Schriftstellerkongreß der Deutschen Demokratischen Republik.* Ed. Schriftstellerverband der Deutschen Demokratischen Republik. Berlin: Aufbau, 1974. 113. Vol. 2.
———. *Rumba auf einen Herbst.* Ed. Rudolf Bussmann. Hamburg: Luchterhand, 1992.
———. "Weltspitze sein und sich wundern, was noch nicht ist." Interview with Oskar Neumann. *Kürbiskern* 1 (1978): 95–99.
———. *Die wundersamen Reisen Gustavs des Weltfahrers: Lügenhafter Roman mit Kommentaren.* Frankfurt a.M.: Luchterhand, 1989.

Nägele, Rainer. "Trauer, Tropen und Phantasmen: Ver-rückte Geschichten aus der DDR." *Literatur der DDR in den 70er Jahren.* Ed. Peter Uwe Hohendahl and Patricia Herminghouse. Frankfurt a.M.: Suhrkamp, 1983. 193-223.

*Neue Ansichten: The Reception of Romanticism in the Literature of the GDR.* Ed. Howard Gaskill, Karin McPherson, and Andrew Barker. GDR Monitor Special Series 6. Amsterdam: Rodopi, 1990.

Nordmann, Ingeborg. "Die halbierte Geschichtsfähigkeit der Frau: Zu Irmtraud Morgners Roman *Leben und Abenteuer der Trobadora Beatriz nach Zeugnissen ihrer Spielfrau Laura.*" *Amsterdamer Beiträge zur Neueren Germanistik* 11-12 (1981): 419-62.

Owens, Craig. "The Discourse of Others: Feminists and Postmodernism." *The Anti-Aesthetic: Essays on Postmodern Culture.* Ed. Hal Foster. Seattle: Bay, 1986. 57-82.

Raddatz, Fritz. "Marx-Sisters statt Marx: Neue Bücher von Morgner, Schlesinger, Köhler." *Die Zeit* 21 May 1976.

Rasboinikowa-Fratewa, Maja Stankowa. "Strukturbildende Funktion des Verhältnisses von Wirklichkeit und dichterischer Phantasie—vorgeführt am Werk von Irmtraud Morgner." *Neophilologus* 76 (Jan. 1992): 101-07.

Reuffer, Petra. *Die unwahrscheinlichen Gewänder der anderen Wahrheit: Zur Wiederentdeckung des Wunderbaren bei G. Grass und I. Morgner.* Essen: Die Blaue Eule, 1988.

Sati, Ulrike. "Figuren im Gespräch: Irmtraud Morgners 'Leben und Abenteuer der Trobadora Beatriz nach Zeugnissen ihrer Spielfrau Laura.'" *Carleton Germanic Papers* 18 (1990): 75-87.

Scherer, Gabriela. *Zwischen "Bitterfeld" und "Orplid": Zum literarischen Werk Irmtraud Morgners.* Bern: Lang, 1992.

Schulte-Sasse, Jochen. "Modernity and Modernism, Postmodernity and Postmodernism: Framing the Issue." *Cultural Critique* 5 (1986-87): 5-21.

Schulz, Genia. "Kein Chorgesang: Neue Schreibweisen bei Autorinnen (aus) der DDR." *Bestandsaufnahme Gegenwartsliteratur.* Ed. Heinz Ludwig Arnold. Special Issue. Munich: edition text und kritik, 1988. 212-25.

Suleiman, Susan Rubin. "Feminism and Postmodernism: A Question of Politics." *Zeitgeist in Babel.* 111-30.

Weigel, Sigrid. *Die Stimme der Medusa: Schreibweisen in der Gegenwartsliteratur von Frauen.* Dülmen-Hiddingsel: tende, 1987.

Welsch, Wolfgang. "Subjektsein heute: Überlegungen zur Transformation des Subjekts." *Deutsche Zeitschrift für Philosophie* 39.4 (1991): 347-65.

*Zeitgeist in Babel: The Postmodern Controversy.* Ed. Ingeborg Hoesterey. Bloomington: Indiana UP, 1991.

# Creativity and Nonconformity in Monika Maron's *Die Überläuferin*

Susan C. Anderson

Maron's novel *Die Überläuferin* represents the disintegration and regeneration of an individual's sense of identity. The narrative traces the process by which its heroine breaks free from her conformist ways of thinking and acknowledges her most feared desires. Fantasy is depicted as a means for recognizing and discarding an authoritarian society's underlying utilitarian principles that can confine and paralyze an individual. The article analyzes the images of walls, death, and rebirth as well as the function of fantasy and memory to demonstrate the destabilizing and self-emancipatory effects of creative action. (SCA)

Much attention has been devoted to German literary works that deal with the Berlin Wall in an attempt to discover anticipations of its opening or assumptions about a "German" national identity.[1] The Wall itself has been ascribed varied functions; in Christa Wolf's *Der geteilte Himmel* (1963) it serves as a protection, but it is an obstruction in Ulrich Plenzdorf's *kein runter kein fern* (1978). It becomes a barrier with no meaning in Peter Schneider's tale *Der Mauerspringer* (1982) and Bodo Morshäuser's *Die Berliner Simulation* (1983). In Peter Schneider's *Paarungen* (1992) it marks difference. In East German literature the difficulty or danger in crossing over to the other (western) side of the Wall is frequently overcome through fantasy, as in Klaus Schlesinger's "Die Spaltung des Erwin Racholl" (1977). However, in *Der geteilte Himmel* and in Helga Schubert's "Das verbotene Zimmer" (1982), the heroines do gain real access to the other side, but, finding the West as decadent as they had been taught to believe, they return home. Endeavors to break down or transcend obstacles, represented by the Wall metaphor, are most often the result of a longing for autonomy. Political unity with West Germany plays a secondary role, if any at all.

East German texts dealing with the Wall since the 1970s frequently depict the debilitating effects of the internalization of an authoritarian political system. In some instances this process results in psychological breakdown. In Schlesinger's short story, for example, the main figure mentally destroys the barriers that he is physically unable to surmount, thereby breaking all ties to the world around him. This crisis occurs after a fantasized trip to the West and is reminiscent of the heroine Rita's collapse in *Der geteilte Himmel,* only Schlesinger offers no hope for a better future. In most of these narratives, what the protagonists discover on the other side of the Wall, whether through fantasy or experience, is not what they had expected. The wall narratives inevitably problematize more general aspects of what it means to be German in either the East or West as well as of how identity is conceived. For example, Schlesinger's character suffers from suppressed guilt for the Holocaust, and Martin Walser's protagonist experiences a personality split while living a double life as an East German spy in *Dorle und Wolf* (1987).

In her novel *Die Überläuferin* (1986), Monika Maron likewise portrays a trip to the western side of the Wall, but presents a different outcome to the crossing of borders. Through retrospection and fantasizing, Maron's protagonist Rosalind Polkowski eventually demolishes all cultural and social barriers between her public conformity and repressed individuality. Her efforts climax in her fantasy of a visit to New York City, where she finds a new self after a symbolic embrace of her most repugnant and forbidden desires. Thus the West, precisely because of its degeneracy, provides the locus for Rosalind's liberation and revitalization. Among the derelicts in the Bowery during her imagined liberation, Rosalind recognizes, acknowledges, and absorbs fragments of her self that she had relegated to the margins of her psyche. In her imagination, she is able to manipulate her interactions with her lover, her friends, and various officials in order to uncover the absurdities of their perceived superiority over her. For example, she resorts to speaking an Eskimo language while debating with her lover and his drinking companion, both of whom claim to be better educated than she. "Und Rosalind: Niune napivâ erdluvdlune" (85). Her apparent knowledge of a language they do not comprehend exposes the hollowness of their rhetoric, which they have employed to impress and silence her rather than to communicate (82–86).[2]

In the figure of Rosalind we are confronted with a woman who through creativity is able to subvert the public discourses of control that entrap her. She takes statements to their most absurd yet logical conclusion, as in the narrative's four satirical *Zwischenspielen* where characters spout clichés and party doctrine in discussing such topics as family and identity. Rosalind's victimization corresponds to the systematic suppression of irrational, affective, sensual, and creative human qualities by dominant norms, by "einer autoritären kleinbürgerlich-feudalen Machtstruktur," as Maron later asserted in reference to the GDR ("Schriftsteller" 70). She posits through her main character an alternative power of private action.

Although Rosalind is unable to break out of her enclosure in this narrative, which was written when the opening of the Wall was only a chimera, the novel itself provides a model of resistance grounded in a non-linear form of expression that has most commonly been associated with the "feminine." Yet such a form of expression is, in the words of Juliet Mitchell, "just what the patriarchal universe defines as the feminine, the intuitive, the religious, the mystical, the playful, all those things that have been assigned to women—the heterogeneous, the notion that women's sexuality is much more one of a whole body, not so genital, not so phallic" (102). My intention is not to determine what Maron's notion of "feminine" is. I rather maintain that her narrative exposes the life-draining effects of the suppression of those qualities that have traditionally been ascribed to the "woman's sphere," such as non goal-oriented patterns of thinking, sensuality, and creativity. The narrative also shows how fantasy can help bring suppressed desires into consciousness, a process similar to Julia Kristeva's concept of the functioning of "poetic" (rhythmic, disruptive, unstable) language.[3]

Through an analysis of the representation and role of fantasy and memory in the protagonist's quest for self-assertion and the related images of walls, death, and rebirth, my article will reveal how *Die Überläuferin* demonstrates a means for inverting an overpowering structure of control. I suggest that the narrative represents the destabilizing and self-emancipatory effects of creative action. The self-knowledge resulting from such action can be achieved only after recognizing the oppressive nature of an unreflected "identity." The main figure's growing awareness of her inferior position in her personal relationships and profession allows her to create new roles for herself. She deserts the self she has been taught to be in order to seek a more liberating one. In the words of Ricarda Schmidt, "[t]he rejection of the concept of a closed identity as part of the status quo is a central part of her desertion" (435).

As Rosalind's sense of self disintegrates, she becomes increasingly alienated from her body. Her limbs become paralyzed; she loses her sense of touch and feels neither hunger nor thirst. She is, in a way, imprisoned in her body, for as we learn later, her physical condition deteriorates as a sign of her increasing self-alienation and in rebellion against it.[4] The less her body moves, however, the more freely her imagination runs. Indeed, during her dreamy states following her frequent operations, she attains a sense of her repressed self (or selves):

> Aber in den Atempausen, die mir durch die Operationen vergönnt waren und die ich vorwiegend benutzte, um zu schlafen, und ich schlief, um zu träumen, verlor sich das fremde Etwas in mir, es verschmolz mit meinem geschwächten, widerstandslosen Körper zu einer Person, die wieder ganz und gar ich war (103).

Her imagination seeks to break its confines, to "live" without the body. Her situation approaches that of the schizophrenic, as defined by Gilles Deleuze and Félix Guattari, who, in a stationary position, crosses over limits in order to set "desiring-production back into motion" (130–31).

Rosalind's body represents the limitations of her existence as a middle-aged, intellectual woman who has obediently accepted all restrictions imposed on her by her parents, lover, employer, and the state, that is, a "Sklavendasein" (99). Her remembered feelings of inadequacy in comparison to her lover Bruno, based in part on his education and family background, lead to the angry recognition that her perceived inferiority derives from her acceptance of certain ideas about her gender,

> über die eigene Unzulänglichkeit, über die Ungerechtigkeit der Natur, die sie mit so verschieden wirkenden Hormonen bedacht hatte, über das ewige Gerede von junger und schöner Weiblichkeit, dem auch sie sich nicht entziehen konnte, wodurch ihre Wut letztlich wieder auf sie selbst gelenkt wurde (81).

Rosalind judges her inchoate desires negatively because she has learned to view them as part of being female, different, and therefore deficient. The narrative traces her process of overcoming her fear of acting out her own inclinations. Her paralysis, a reaction against her socialization into a "useful" member of a collective, initiates a process of self-destruction that concludes with a new self-awareness. Such knowledge comes only after rejecting rational, logical thought patterns for a freely flowing, associative mode of thinking that gradually disengages the protagonist from the world around her, a way of thinking referred to in the narrative as writing by "Damen" (156), as "Wind, Sonnenstrahlen und Wellenschaum" (159). She appears lost in her own fantasies because she is involved in a search for something she cannot yet express but which is partially embodied in Martha and Clairchen, her alter egos.

Maron depicts Rosalind's search as an example of the power of self-creation through reflection. By treating herself as an object of investigation, Rosalind can use her historical skills to unearth the knowledge she needs to heal herself. In re-creating herself in her imagination, Rosalind allows her old self to disintegrate until she sees her image in the person of Martha, the "other woman" she has been pursuing. This creature, consisting of her recollections of a woman she admired, is all she is not. By reinventing herself as this woman towards the end of the narrative, Rosalind in effect dies and becomes a new person, one who is also Martha.[5]

Rosalind's distance from a notion of a complete self is represented formally by the frequent changes between first- and third-person narration, thereby, as Schmidt points out, "preventing a neat separation between the levels of memory, fantasy and reflection" (430). As the narrative voice becomes more confused, so too does the narration, such as the juxtaposition of Rosalind's memory of sorting through her Aunt Ida's possessions and her vision of wounded bodies. Rosalind's jumping from one imagined adventure to another creates a surrealistic disjointedness in the narrative as well as the impression that she is going mad. The increasingly violent scenes in the protagonist's mind serve as a parallel to the violations against humanity in the system of rigid work and gender roles in which she has grown up and to which she has submitted herself.

Several critics have seen the ending of Maron's novel as offering merely a hope for art to alter the oppressive mechanisms of patriarchal society (Hauser, Puhl, Kane). Other analyses have focused on the role of fantasy and remembrance in reconstructing the main figure's image of herself and have emphasized its so-called utopian aspects. Some critics maintain, for example, that Maron offers no real response to an oppressive reality, for they view the world of fantasy as not truly liberating (Franke, Jung). As Ursula Mahlendorf contends:

> Die Sehnsucht nach der Wirklichkeit und die Rückbesinnung auf weibliche Lebenskraft lösen aber wohl das Identitäts- und Wirklichkeitsproblem kaum; eindringlicher und realer als diese Sehnsucht wirkt der Alptraum einer der Frau feindlichen gesellschaftlichen Welt (459).

Other scholars see the novel as more provocative. Schmidt claims that Maron challenges the concept of a "whole" person, for her narrative suggests a plethora of identities lying repressed in Rosalind. Nevertheless, Schmidt finds that Maron's figures are still caught up in conventional forms of sexual desire that prevent a more radical narrative of liberation (435). Martin Kane, on the other hand, regards Maron's depiction of "anarchic fantasy" as more universally disruptive, "as potentially subversive to a capitalist as to a socialist way of ordering things" (233, 234).

In keeping with the latter two readings, I suggest that Maron's novel presents an example of how fantasy can transform the silenced citizen by allowing her to create herself in opposition to her cultural role. Fantasy offers her a site for examining her conformity to cultural norms. Enclosed in her room, but no longer entrapped, Maron's main character is a different person at the end, and she achieves her new identity with the aid of a nonlinear reconstruction of her past that defies her professional training, which she recalls as "ihr verbissener Kampf um eine ihr wichtige These oder Formulierung" (109). Her imagination incites a powerful rush towards freedom that can transcend any external barrier—be it the body of the dreamer, as her paralysis suggests, or the social/political system of repression. Although Rosalind cannot completely overcome the narrowness of her physical world, she can alter her position within it. Strength in the private sphere nurtured by a different manner of thinking, one that is perceived as useless because it does not serve dominant ideological purposes, can undermine the internalized public apparatus of control by revealing opportunities for personal growth. This new way of thinking is what Martha suggests to Rosalind as the way to begin her biography (51) and what Maron's narrative does in its rejection of the tenets of socialist realism.

Maron's protagonist gradually re-evaluates the way she has been viewing the world:

> Sie hatte gelernt, ihr Denken für Wochen oder Monate einem einzigen Thema zuzuordnen, es in eine bestimmte Richtung zu lenken und zu einem konkreten Ergebnis zu führen—zielstrebiges wissenschaftliches Denken nannte Barabas [ihr Chef] das (98).

Martha provides the model for other ways of contemplating: she thought "was sie wollte und wie sie wollte, sprunghaft, verträumt und, wie Rosalind immer öfter bemerkte, geradezu kindlich" (98). Rosalind then makes use of her professional training to speculate about her own immuration (129). She slowly withdraws from contributing to the creation of a history of collective progress, convinced it would only legitimate the status quo, in favor of imagining a past that focuses on desire and its repression. As Rosalind dreams an alternative history, Maron writes one that reveals the daily concessions that individuals in industrialized societies make in their attempts to become useful citizens, such as Rosalind's diligence at accomplishing work projects that do not engage her creatively. Additionally, Rosalind's musings over Martha's description of a future society that promises to instill only automated responses in its members make clear for her the necessity of a persistent focus on personal needs and the refusal to abandon the desire to fulfill them:

> Deinen Kopf bauen sie einer Maschine ein, deine Arme machen sie zu Kränen, deinen Brustkorb zum Karteikasten, deinen Bauch zur Müllhalde. Aber in jedem Menschen gibt es etwas, das sie nicht gebrauchen können, das Besondere, das Unberechenbare, Seele, Poesie, Musik, ich weiß keinen passenden Namen dafür, eben das, was niemand wissen konnte, ehe der Mensch geboren war (51).

One can resist such a robotlike future, Rosalind realizes, by tapping those internal creative resources that defy automation.

Rosalind's playing with her thoughts during her paralysis is analogous to attempts to move freely within the authoritarian socialist system that the narrative alternately satirizes and directly criticizes here.[6] Rosalind's imagination offers her a power that is at first exhilarating. "Es ist unglaublich," she exults, "es ist phantastisch, noch phantastischer, als ich dachte" (58). Within her static confines she has a force that can open the door to a world of unlimited space for movement. She must allow it free rein, however, for it to be effective, because, as her friend Clairchen advises her, "Imädshineischen [sic]...halbjewagt, is janz verloren" (179).

Isolation provides the opportunity for one to nurture a liberating fantasy. In reference to nineteenth-century American women's writing, Judith Lowder Newton asserts that by focusing on the private sphere certain women writers represent how women develop a "power of ability" (771). They use that power to give themselves inner strength rather than attempting to exercise influence over others. Their writing provides a model for action for their readers (Warhol 762). Maron similarly presents a dreamer whose thoughts prepare her to take an active role. In order to succeed in her quest for power over herself, Rosalind must first confront the different forms of authority to which she has been subjected. In Maron's novel, male characters most often represent authority, but Rosalind discovers that even her beloved Aunt Ida has instilled in her a fear that makes her submissive and goal-oriented (176-77).

One type of rebellion against the pressure to submit is a reworking of language. As mentioned above, Bruno, Rosalind's estranged lover, and his friend Baron, a Sinologist nicknamed the Count, as well as the characters in the *Zwischenspielen* represent the alienating effects of a language that no longer communicates. It is used only as a means of exerting control over others through issuing orders or exhibiting "superior" knowledge.[7] However, Rosalind learns from listening to her female alter egos that there is a secret language within the public discourse, composed of the same words, through which one can perceive a different world: "Für die andere Welt bedeuteten das Geheimnis und das Unerklärbare nicht weniger als den unbenennbaren Zusammenhang der Dinge und unserer selbst, die wir uns zwischen ihnen bewegen" (95). This secret language has the potential to challenge the dominant discourses, although its use is fraught with danger: when Martha uses that language in unconventional ways in order to undermine its hierarchical function, she commits a transgression punishable by death. As the male poet/vampire who intends to kill her explains: "Die Sprache ist keine bunte Wiese, Madame, auf der man verliebt spazierengeht. Sie ist eine steile, hochragende Felswand, und die kleinsten Risse muß der Dichter nutzen, um an ihr emporzusteigen" (156). Christine Betzner sees Martha as representative of the semiotic sphere that Rosalind has ignored: "Schwingungen, Ton, Musik und Körpersprache sind die Sprachen, die Martha zugängig sind" (63).

Another direction for revolt is against the concept of utility. Rosalind's longing for the secretive and forbidden as a means of extricating herself from patriarchal control also focuses on Martha's admonition that she find her own "nutzloseste Eigenschaft" and develop it (50-51)—advice that directly contradicts the official counsel she later receives: "Jeder Mensch ist glücklich, wenn er sich nützlich fühlt" (67), where the term "nützlich" is defined by the state. But seizing the initiative would contradict Rosalind's inculcated notion of her social role, a role that makes it difficult for her to accept the solution to her dilemma as represented by

Martha and Clairchen. The latter, as Thomas Beckermann makes clear, are "beyond the reach of representatives of law and order because they do not take reality seriously" (100). Martha is so alluring because she breaks the rules and goes unpunished. The danger to the state of such autonomy is expressed satirically by the Man in the Red Uniform in one of the narrative's *Zwischenspielen*: "Der unidentische Mensch denkt aufrührerisch und strebt Veränderungen an, was ihn zu einem gesellschaftsgefährdenden Subjekt, in Einzelfällen sogar zum Kriminellen macht" (125). Martha is just such an "unidentical" person, one who rejects any notion of self foisted upon her. Rosalind, in contrast, is most alone when she has bought into the ideology of influence over others. In an attempt to steal a sense of control for herself, Rosalind imagines that she instigates a riot at a grocery store and regards it proudly as her "eigene Tat" (63), as "[e]in unerfüllter Traum" (65). However, she undermines her own tentative steps toward freedom by endeavoring to please the Robert Redford-like detective interrogating her. The narrative reveals here a susceptibility to the seduction of masculine virility and power masked as concern, which maintains the conformist in a girlish, docile role.

The images of death, walls, and madness further illustrate the main character's gradual process of self-recognition. In keeping with the theme of (self-)redemption, her rebirth begins on the third night of her immuration (9). Up until then, as Horst Hartmann asserts, she has been living with the feeling "lebendig begraben zu sein" (176). Her internalization of the structures that oppress her has deadened her to the creative, spontaneous parts of herself. Death represents both freedom and the end of it, a synthesizing state that Rosalind desires and fears from her earliest memories: she tried to die before being born, hoping to escape "einen eigenen, kalten, schmerzhaften Tod" (15). Accordingly, death wishes and figures permeate the rest of the narrative (Beckermann 99; Stamer 70), such as her desire for her father's death, her Aunt Ida's feared demise, the landscape of wounded and dying characters, and her own imagined death. As the narrative winds its way toward a conclusion and the images of decay increase, the death Rosalind symbolically endures proves to be instead a process for eradicating malignant patterns of thinking.

The most disgusting harbinger of doom to be exorcised is the conductor and former Nazi with a lame leg and a missing eye, a figure similar to the limping gatekeeper at her place of employment. Both men have regulated her movement, but the former Nazi is the more repulsive representative of oppression. Thus his resemblance to the little piglike dog that suddenly appears:

> Sein Schwanz, der sich steil ringelte, erinnerte an einen Schweineschwanz, stammte aber wahrscheinlich von einem Spitz, wogegen der Kopf sogar einen Schäferhund in der Ahnenreihe vermuten ließ.... Plötzlich spritzte warme Nässe gegen Rosalinds Hand. Der Hund raste kläffend davon,

während der Alte den Rest seiner Pisse auf die Erde laufen ließ.... Rosalind war aufgesprungen, stand vor dem Mann, dessen Schwanz aus der offenen Hose hing wie eine vertrocknete Wurzel. Die Pisse auf ihrer Hand brannte, als hätte sie in Brennesseln gegriffen. Du Sau, sagte Rosalind, du alte mistige Pissau (136-37).

In this episode, we see how Rosalind too is contaminated by the filthy past. The old Nazi exemplifies a fascist mentality that still lingers in her own society. It is a fascism that Michel Foucault described as "the fascism in us all, in our heads and in our everyday behavior, the fascism that causes us to love power, to desire the very thing that dominates and exploits us" (xiii). The phallic symbolism that relates the old man to the dog exposes the beastlike nature of patriarchal power systems. The episode depicts a part of Rosalind that she needs to confront, an aspect that lies in the realm of public depravity. And the episode occurs after she has decided to put her head through the wall, a turning point that marks the beginning of Rosalind's assumption of responsibility for her thinking: "Und jetzt, sagt Rosalind, werde ich mit dem Kopf durch die Wand gehen" (130). Her growing self-awareness at this point allows her to recognize and repulse those aspects embodied by the old man that she had internalized.

Clairchen, an anarchic figure and another alter ego of the main character, is also a portent of death. She illustrates the repressive aspects of love that help maintain Rosalind in a dependent position. Her role as incarnation of Rosalind's fear of sensuality and skepticism towards love becomes clear when Clairchen takes off her head to expose the smaller head of actress and *femme fatale* Greta Garbo (127-28). This surrealistic scene also reveals Clairchen's function of reflecting in an exaggerated manner Rosalind's own split between the rational and sensual. For when Clairchen begins to think, her head reverts back to its familiar form (128). Her search for a loving relationship with another person as an antidote to her identity problems is unsuccessful, for the concept of love has become perverted to mean coercion. For example, Clairchen's insatiable thirst for affection feeds on the emotions of others:

Sobald es ihr [Clairchen] gelungen war, einem Menschen, gleichgültig, ob Mann oder Frau, Gefühle der Liebe zu entlocken, stürzte sie sich mit der gleichen werbenden Hartnäckigkeit, die eben noch dem einen gegolten hatte, auf einen anderen, um auch ihm einen Tropfen Liebe aus dem Leib zu saugen wie eine Mücke einen Tropfen Blut aus einem menschlichen Körper (69).

The above description of Clairchen's exploitative use of love foreshadows the later scene depicting the male poet's/vampire's feeding on women's suffering to obtain material for his poetry. In addition, Martha interprets

Clairchen's suicide as her response to a loveless world and as evidence that "love" is another manipulative device:

> Demzufolge seien die Gefühle liebender Europäer ein nicht entwirrbares Chaos aus Zuneigung, sadistischer Herrschsucht, masochistischer Unterwürfigkeit, und es läge nahe, daß die so Liebenden sich zudem oft erpresserischer Methoden bedienten (71).

By having Rosalind use the subjunctive in reporting Martha's facile summation of Clairchen's troubled life, Maron also problematizes Martha's critique of the abusive nature of love. Not love itself, but the conditions under which love exists are the focus of criticism here. The narrative continues a tradition of women's writing, such as that described by Newton, which illustrates how women develop a power of ability. That power serves as an alternative to a love that exercises influence over others (771).

Rosalind's fantasies become increasingly surrealistic as her conformity becomes clearer and she begins to change. The bleeding bodies lying all over the streets, the memories of Clairchen's and Ida's demise and their unhappy love affairs, the end of Rosalind's relationship with Bruno, the dark, dank streets down which she wanders, all signify a moribund world, the world into which she was born and in which she is mentally trapped. The motif of disproportional heads and bodies, such as Clairchen's Garbo head or the little dog's German shepherd one, suggests further the schizophrenic condition of her public (officially sanctioned) and private identities. Yet it is possible to break out of this world.

The walls surrounding her, however, are also necessary for establishing a sense of identity. She considers the nature of walls until she feels that she can ascertain their functions:

> Eine Wand, die in keiner Beziehung zu einer anderen Wand steht, ist eine Mauer. Ein System aus vier Wänden und einem Fußboden, einzig nach oben mit einer Öffnung versehen, ist ein Loch. Ein Raum aus vier Wänden mit Decke, Fußboden und einer Tür, die durch den Insassen des Raumes nicht zu öffnen ist, ist ein Gefängnis. Ein Raum mit Fenstern und einer Tür, die nach Belieben von beiden Seiten geöffnet und geschlossen werden kann, ist ein Zimmer.... Die Wände um Rosalind trennen sie von dem Nachbarn, vom Hausflur, vom Korridor und von der Straße. Sie hält sie alle für unverzichtbar. Je länger sie ihre Wände betrachtet, um so sicherer wird sie in der Annahme, daß Wände zu den wichtigsten Regulatoren des menschlichen Zusammenlebens gehören (129–30).

This passage expresses the need for a balanced relationship between control and movement, which is lacking in Rosalind's society. A room as defined in this passage would provide a necessary structure for physical and psychological freedom. Walls, or limitations, then, are not negative in themselves. Their relation to openings makes them tolerable or stifling. Rosalind longs to exchange her *Gefängnis* for a *Zimmer*. Oddly enough, theft is one means she sees for doing so, for she would like to take possession of a self that she relinquished at birth. Only by acting against the rules and conventions of her society, such as through stealing food and wine, can she gain access to suppressed aspects of herself, for example, the outrage she feels at being forced to tolerate unnecessarily long lines at a grocery store. She would in effect be reappropriating an identity that she lost the moment she was born into a world of repressive social relations, the moment when she began to die.

The extreme example of such identity loss is Rosalind's futuristic encounter with a clone during her daydreams. The notion that each person has a double, which the state can at any moment substitute for the original, shows the fragility of the human being in a system that controls technology. The clone, who looks like a man, uses fantasy to simulate living. Like Rosalind, he has learned "ganz und gar aus dem Geist zu existieren" (205). But unlike her he lives only to serve science. Here there is no possibility for the suppressed to take charge of their life. The clone has no desire to rebel, similar to Martha's earlier warning of such a fate in store for all who neglect their "useless" qualities (51). With no hope for the future and no comfort in her past, Rosalind continues her pursuit of an identity, but her will becomes stronger as she reviews her life of gradual surrender to the fear instilled by the authoritarian system in which she exists.

She crosses over, indeed puts her head through a wall in her imagination, and experiences the dissolution of her self. By using her head to break out, Rosalind reappropriates a part of herself that she had allowed to be infused with injunctions that kept her docile and ill. Her increasingly violent visions, such as of the struggles near the Berlin Wall, Martha's blood being sucked out by a vampire, and Ida's death, accompany her flight from herself. Her shedding of her old identity exposes a new creature radically different from the image of herself that she has been programmed to accept. It provokes guilt, and later horror. She reacts at first by searching for a cause for her unsettling thoughts and thereby seeks solace in her old pattern of logical reasoning. In the last *Zwischenspiel,* Rosalind hesitates as she imagines the Man in the Red Uniform accusing her of harboring aimless visions and almost allows her desires to be overcome by doubts—"Ich schweige noch immer, und obwohl ich mich dagegen zu wehren suche, schwindet meine Sicherheit, nicht schuldig zu sein" (177)—until an image of Clairchen dancing ballet to her heart's content, despite her lack of talent, strengthens her resolve to probe her private, "useless" longings further (179). But the more she analyzes her feelings, the more her internal system of control strives to suppress her. She envisions a couple approaching her to carry her away and is shocked to see herself in the figure of the woman: "Sie sah, sehr nah, ihr eigenes Gesicht; die kräftigen Finger, die schon nach ihr griffen, gehörten einer Frau, die ihr Gesicht trug" (210). She is cast further into confusion on her flight to the railway station, when she hears someone say "Der Bahnhof ist überall" (211) and recognizes the unfamiliar voice as her own. Encountering Martha at that point is the beginning of her recovery, for she gradually understands that Martha, like the other figures and voices, belongs to a part of herself that has eluded control.

The confusion of pronouns and narrative voice reflects Rosalind's separation from her traditional thought patterns as she identifies with Martha:

> Eine Frau kommt auf mich zu. Ich spreche sie an und bitte sie, mir zu helfen.... Sie will vorübergehen, und in diesem Augenblick erkenne ich sie. Rosalind, sage ich, Rosalind Polkowski. Sie bleibt stehen. Ihre Augen suchen hilflos auf mir herum, bis endlich der erwartete Schrecken in ihnen aufglüht. Martha, bist du Martha, fragt sie. Statt mir aufzuhelfen, setzt sie sich neben mich und weint. Ich habe dich gesucht, sagt sie. Jetzt hast du mich gefunden, sage ich (212).

This is the first time that Rosalind takes on the narrative voice of another figure. By distancing herself from her previous form, she is able to shed the apprehensions that have prevented her from acknowledging her desires. As Rosalind and Martha merge, Rosalind as Martha registers the shock of seeing her former self: "Ihr Entsetzen widert mich an, obwohl ich gleichzeitig den Eindruck habe, ich selbst betrachte mich mit diesen erschrockenen Augen. Oder bin ich Rosalind; oder bin ich eine dritte" (213). She then assumes her Rosalind persona and surrenders to her sexual instincts with a male derelict (while Martha watches), reactivating in her mind her paralyzed body and abandoning her prudish sensibilities.

> Ich lache, ich kreische wie ein Affenweibchen. Ich habe es satt, gewaschen und sauber gekleidet zwischen den Menschen umherzugehen.... Ich finde mich ekelhaft, so gefalle ich mir. Angelockt von meinen Schreien, kommt Billy. Wir wälzen uns auf dem harten Pflaster.... Mich gibt es nicht mehr, ich muß nichts mehr fürchten. So schlafe ich ein (218–19).

The final meeting between Martha and Rosalind in the West, the incarnation of her most forbidden longings, leads to Rosalind's symbolic demise—and rebirth. After realizing her identity with Martha, she reassumes her form as Rosalind, but incorporates Martha. "Wir sind wieder allein, Martha und ich" (219). When she follows Martha into her room she is able to state "Das ist mein Zimmer" (220) because she has found a door out. While the narrative ends where it began, and Rosalind has not really changed her position outwardly, the question remains as to the function of fantasy in a repressive world. Without an outlet it is potentially self-destructive, and on a macro-level a society without creativity is stagnating or even decomposing. The lack of balance for those living in such a world could, according to the narrative, eventually result in brutal self-destruction. But that is only one possibility. A mixture of deeds and dreams, a flexible framework for the imaginary, provides a model for eroding the regulatory forces in society that have deadened its members. The "retreat" to the private sphere does not marginalize the creative individual from the collective. It provides a site for discarding paternalistic oppression and voicing unacknowledged desires.

By embracing her most fearsome dreams Rosalind is able to become a new person—just as she wished when a child. She is the one who creates herself anew, before an imaginary public. Fantasy has enabled her to overcome her status as mere object and become the agent of her own deeds. She has achieved a "power of ability" by withdrawing to a private place. In her solitude she restructures the story of her life so that it encompasses different forms of identity. By this time she has imagined herself calling for help at the sight of wounded people, rejecting her lover's condescension, accepting her own sensuality, and leaving her room. Without bothering to exert influence over others, she has acted to correct inequities in various situations. As she takes stock of herself and her surroundings once she has been able to accept her disparate selves, Rosalind reflects: "Da bin ich also wieder...eher belustigt als verwundert über die Einsicht, daß ihre aufwendigen Bemühungen, sich vom Ausgangspunkt ihres Denkens zu entfernen, sie sicher an ihn zurückgeführt hatten" (220-21). In contrast to her earlier novel *Flugasche,* about which Sigrid Bostock asserts: "Ich-Form als auch innerer Monolog charakterisieren den auf sich selbst geworfenen, von der Gesellschaft isolierten und dadurch kommunikationslosen Menschen" (20), the switch between first-person and third-person narrator signals here a reflective process that enables the protagonist to reconnect herself to her environment, to her room, albeit as a new person.

But is she now able to take charge of her life? Is the "sensual," "feminine" part of her more powerful than the authoritarian system that restrains her? It would appear that it has the potential to be. Suppression of fantasy increases the division between real and fantastical until the imaginary takes on a reality of its own. Rosalind can then imagine different roles for herself in this new "reality." As a reaction to her suppression of the free play of her desires, her creative imagination floods over physical constraints to the point of destroying them, so that when Rosalind reenters her body and looks around, she sees herself in a room instead of a prison (220). She has found a way in and out. Yet it is uncertain how long she will remain in her present condition. For although her physical senses are beginning to function again, she notices that the room is even smaller but more distant from her, "[a]ls würde sie vom falschen Ende durch ein Fernglas sehen" (221). She is outgrowing it. But what kind of person is this who is about to hatch out?

Maron's protagonist may well be completely "mad" by the end of the narrative, but, as Rosalind recalls, "wenn die Welt irre ist, liegt im Irrsinn der Sinn" (29). Her irrational, "feminine" manner of thinking is incompatible with the society that Maron is criticizing, one that is still tainted by the paternalistic totalitarianism of the fascist system that it replaced. But the narrative presents a solution to the seemingly unending cycle of hyperrational tyranny over "useless" human attributes. Rather than imitating one's oppressors, as Rosalind had learned to do at work or as the clone demonstrates, Maron posits a commingling of private reflection and public action that engages creative, "human" potential. Maron thus rejects the hierarchy of public over private sphere that Jane Tompkins, for example, also designates as "a founding condition of female oppression" (1080). Maron's alienated woman figure has learned to embrace those aspects of her persona unsuited to a system centered on purpose and linear logic. By portraying a figure who imagines herself initiating a rebellion at, for example, the absurd circumstances in a grocery store, Maron opens possibilities for real action later on. She presents a biography that retraces the retardation of personal growth, and this biography is inscribed oppositionally within the history of social evolution advanced by the state. For Rosalind was stuck in the role of the child, representing her inferior position.[8] Her mistaken search for her father in her lovers (22-23) and through her alter ego Martha, that is, for someone to guide her, prevented her from attaining adulthood.

In closing the circle of the narration, the narrative has arrived back at the beginning, and we know that this is also the signal for a repetition of the confusion of images that make up the inner narratives. There appears to be no closure in such a structure, no directional motion, no ventilation. It masks a destabilizing force that threatens to burst forth at any moment. And it exhibits the revolutionary nature of desire: "If desire is repressed, it is because every position of desire, no matter how small, is capable of calling into question the established order of a society" (Deleuze and Guattari 116). Rosalind has found a door out of her room, one that promises unlimited freedom of movement. The aperture leads further inside to an inarticulate profusion of desires that can transform her conformity into autonomy. Maron's social critique is an admonition to unseal the doors to emancipatory desires and creative action in order to overcome internalized, stultifying patterns of viewing the world. The narrative demonstrates a means for undermining the entombing effects of a totalitarian mindset and reworking enforced alienation into self-emancipation.

## Notes

I would like to thank Jacqueline Vansant as well as the reviewers and editors of the *Women in German Yearbook* for their helpful comments concerning this essay.

[1] See, for example, Craig (esp. 35–40) and Mews; for analyses of the debates surrounding the role of German intellectuals in foreseeing the opening of the Wall and their reactions to it, see, for example, the clusters of pertinent articles in *New German Critique* (Winter 1991), *Women in German Yearbook 7* (1991), and *German Studies Review* (May 1991); see especially Bathrick.

[2] See also Betzner, who concludes that Rosalind speaks Eskimo to compete with the men for recognition. "Sie kämpft um ihren Platz im Symbolischen, da sie sich dadurch eine neue Identität verspricht, während sie ihren anderen Ort im Semiotischen verdrängt" (69).

[3] For a thorough discussion of Maron's novel as an example of women's writing, see Betzner. For more on Kristeva's concept of language, see *Desire in Language,* the essays in *The Kristeva Reader,* and the overview in Morris.

[4] Maron reveals in an interview that the working title of the book was *Die Lähmung,* "was Ausdruck der psychischen Lähmung sein sollte, weniger Kafka als ein Nachspüren allgemeiner Befindlichkeit" (Richter 4).

[5] See Shari Benstock's essay, in which she examines how certain women's autobiographies challenge the notion of a unified identity.

[6] It is a system that has created a country Maron later describes sarcastically as "ein Land mit einer maroden Wirtschaft, mit verwahrlosten öffentlichen Umgangsformen, mit Städten, deren Altbauviertel den Slums amerikanischer Städte immer ähnlicher werden, und mit einer Verlogenheit in den öffentlichen Verlautbarungen, die den Grad zur Lächerlichkeit längst überschritten hat" ("Warum?" 23).

[7] For a discussion of "women's language" and "men's language," see Baym; Shoshana Felman also articulates the problem of a woman's discourse when she states: "If, in our culture, the woman is by definition associated with madness, her problem is how to break out of this (cultural) imposition of madness *without* taking up the critical and therapeutic positions of reason: how to avoid speaking both as *mad* and as *not mad.* The challenge facing the woman today is nothing less than to "re-invent" language, to *re-learn how to speak*: to speak not only against, but outside of the specular phallocentric structure, to establish a discourse the status of which would no longer be defined by the phallacy of masculine meaning" (152–53).

[8] See Vallance, who asserts: "Throughout Maron's work the central characters find themselves in situations of impotence vis-à-vis a fatherly authority" (62).

## Works Cited

Bathrick, David. "The End of the Wall before the End of the Wall." *German Studies Review* 14 (May 1991): 297-311.

Baym, Nina. "The Madwoman and Her Languages: Why I Don't Do Feminist Literary Theory." *Feminisms*. 154-67.

Beckermann, Thomas. "Die Diktatur repräsentiert das Abwesende nicht." *German Literature at a Time of Change 1989-1990: German Unity and German Identity in Literary Perspective*. Ed. Arthur Williams et al. Frankfurt a.M.: Lang, 1991. 97-116.

Benstock, Shari. "Authorizing the Autobiographical." *Feminisms*. 1040-57.

Betzner, Christine. "Mit dem Kopf durch die Wand: Monika Marons Erzählung *Die Überläuferin* als Ausdruck weiblicher Schreibweise." Master's Thesis, University of Oregon, 1992.

Bostock, Sigrid. "Ich- und Sie-Erzählung: Rede und Handlung in Monika Marons Roman 'Flugasche.'" *Carleton Germanic Papers* 18 (1990): 9-21.

Craig, Gordon A. "The Big Apfel." *The New York Review of Books* 7 November 1991: 31-40.

Deleuze, Gilles, and Félix Guattari. *Anti-Oedipus: Capitalism and Schizophrenia*. Trans. Robert Hurley, Mark Seem, and Helen R. Lane. Minneapolis: U of Minnesota P, 1983.

Felman, Shoshana. "Women and Madness: The Critical Phallacy." *The Feminist Reader: Essays in Gender and the Politics of Literary Criticism*. Ed. Catherine Belsey and Jane Moore. New York: Blackwell, 1989. 133-53.

*Feminisms: An Anthology of Literary Theory and Criticism*. Ed. Robyn R. Warhol and Diane Price Herndl. New Brunswick: Rutgers UP, 1991.

Foucault, Michel. "Preface." *Anti-Oedipus*. Gilles Deleuze and Félix Guattari. xi-xiv.

Franke, Eckhard. "Monika Maron." *KLG-Textdienst* 31 (1989): 1-6; A-D.

Hartmann, Horst. "Monika Maron: Die Überläuferin: Roman." *L'80* 41-43 (1987): 175-77.

Hauser, Kornelia. "Monika Maron: *Die Überläuferin*." *Das Argument* 169 (1988): 424-26.

Jung, Werner. "Die Anstrengung des Erinnerns." *Neue Deutsche Hefte* 35 (1988): 96-104.

Kane, Martin. "Culpabilities of the Imagination: The Novels of Monika Maron." *Literature on the Threshold: The German Novel of the 1980's*. Ed. Arthur Williams, Stuart Parkes, and Roland Smith. Providence, RI: Berg, 1990.

Kristeva, Julia. *Desire in Language: A Semiotic Approach to Literature and Art*. Ed. Leon S. Roudiez. Trans. Thomas Gora, Alice Jardine, and Leon S. Roudiez. New York: Columbia UP, 1980.

———. *The Kristeva Reader*. Ed. Toril Moi. New York: Columbia UP, 1986.

Mahlendorf, Ursula. "Der weiße Rabe fliegt: Zum Künstlerinnenroman im 20. Jahrhundert." *Deutsche Literatur von Frauen*. 2 vols. Ed. Gisela Brinker-Gabler. Munich: Beck, 1988. Vol. 2: 445-59.

Maron, Monika. "Die Schriftsteller und das Volk." *Der Spiegel* 12 February 1990: 68-70; the essay was translated and reprinted as "Writers and the People" in *New German Critique* 18 (Winter 1991): 36-41.

———. *Die Überläuferin*. Frankfurt a.M.: Fischer Taschenbuch, 1988.

———. "'Warum bin ich selbst gegangen?'" *Der Spiegel* 14 May 1990: 22-23.

Mews, Siegfried. "Political Boundaries and the Boundaries of Politics: The Berlin Wall in Recent Fiction." *Proceedings of the XIIth Congress of the International Comparative Literature Association, München 1988*. Ed. Roger Bauer, Douwe Fokkema, and Michael de Graat. Munich: iudicium, 1990. 260-65.

Mitchell, Juliet. "'Femininity, Narrative and Psychoanalysis.'" *Feminist Literary Theory: A Reader*. Ed. Mary Eagleton. New York: Blackwell, 1986. 100-03.

Morris, Pam. "Identities in Process: Poststructuralism, Julia Kristeva and Intertextuality." *Literature and Feminism: An Introduction*. Cambridge, MA: Blackwell, 1993.

Morshäuser, Bodo. *Die Berliner Simulation*. Frankfurt a.M.: Suhrkamp, 1983.

Newton, Judith Lowder. "Power and the Ideology of 'Woman's Sphere.'" *Feminisms*. 765-80.

Plenzdorf, Ulrich. *kein runter kein fern*. Frankfurt a.M.: Suhrkamp, 1984.

Puhl, Widmar. "Eine läuft über: Monika Marons Roman." *Die Zeit* 7 November 1986: Literaturbeilage 5.

Richter, Gerhard. "Verschüttete Kultur: Ein Gespräch mit Monika Maron." *GDR Bulletin* 18 (Spring 1992): 2-7.

Schlesinger, Klaus. "Die Spaltung des Erwin Racholl." *Berliner Traum: Fünf Geschichten*. Frankfurt a.M.: Fischer, 1977.

Schmidt, Ricarda. "The Concept of Identity in Recent East and West German Women's Writing." *German Literature at a Time of Change 1989-1990: German Unity and German Identity in Literary Perspective*. Ed. Arthur Williams et al. Frankfurt a.M.: Lang, 1991. 429-47.

Schneider, Peter. *Der Mauerspringer*. Darmstadt: Luchterhand, 1982.

———. *Paarungen*. Berlin: Rowohlt, 1992.

Schubert, Helga. "Das verbotene Zimmer." *Das verbotene Zimmer: Geschichten*. Darmstadt: Luchterhand, 1982.

Stamer, Uwe. "Monika Maron—'Die Überläuferin': Muße zum Nachdenken." *Beiträge zur Literaturkritik*. Ed. Uwe Stamer. Stuttgart: Heinz, 1989. 70-72.

Tompkins, Jane. "Me and My Shadow." *Feminisms*. 1079-92.

Vallance, Margaret. "Monika Maron: Harbinger of Surrealism in the GDR?" *GDR Monitor* special series (1988/89): 57-64.

Warhol, Robyn R. Introduction. *Feminisms*. 761-64.

Walser, Martin. *Dorle und Wolf: Eine Novelle*. Frankfurt a.M.: Suhrkamp, 1987.

Wolf, Christa. *Der geteilte Himmel*. Halle: Mitteldeutscher Verlag, 1963.

# Dankrede zum Grimmelshausen-Preis

Ruth Klüger

The following is the text of a speech given by Ruth Klüger on her acceptance of the 1993 Grimmelshausen prize, awarded for her autobiographical account *weiter leben: Eine Jugend* (1992). Her prefatory remarks are addressed to Marcel Reich-Ranicki, who wrote about her award in the *Frankfurter Allgemeine Zeitung* (16 October 1993).

Lieber Herr MRR: "Trotz und Stil" sagten Sie. Den Trotz bestätige ich Ihnen gern, den Stil, den Sie mir beglaubigten, glaube ich Ihnen, nachdem ich Ihnen zugehört habe. Wenn das Buch Sie zu diesen Worten inspirieren konnte, dann darf ich glauben, daß ich es richtig gemacht habe.

Meine sehr geehrten Herren und Damen,
   Es liegt mir auf der Zunge, und so kann ich nicht umhin, Ihnen zunächst ein gesegnetes Neujahr zu wünschen. Der jüdischen Religion zufolge, mit ihrem unverwüstlichen, erinnerungsträchtigen Zutrauen zur Vergangenheit, besteht die Welt nämlich schon seit fünftausend siebenhundert und dreiundfünfzig Jahren. Heute ab Sonnenuntergang hat sie Geburtstag und wir beginnen ihr fünftausend siebenhundert und vierundfünfzigstes Jahr. Und da die Juden erfahrungsgemäß—wer will es ihnen verdenken?—ihr Zutrauen zur Vergangenheit durch ihr Mißtrauen vor der Zukunft ausgleichen, und daher ein kosmisches "Fortsetzung folgt" nicht ohne Weiteres hinnehmen, so ist ihnen der Geburtstag alles Bestehenden der höchste Feiertag. Wo immer eine jüdische Gemeinde sich so was leisten kann, stößt ein Mann heute in ein schön geschwungenes Widderhorn, genannt Schofer, um den Menschen die Freude am Seienden zu verkünden. Es ist eine unsinnige Freude, diese Freude am Selbstverständlichen. Goethes Faust drückt dieses Gefühl aus, wenn er dankbar sagt: "Du Erde warst auch diese Nacht beständig / Und atmest neu erquickt zu meinen Füßen." Auch den Ungläubigen und den Abergläubischen unter uns weht an diesem Abend die Begeisterung über die Ursprünge ins Gesicht.
   Abergläubisch und ungläubig, wie ich nun einmal bin, kann mir das Datum nicht gleichgültig sein. Man muß die Feste feiern, wie sie fallen,

heißt es, und wenn zwei auf denselben Tag fallen, so darf man wohl gleich doppelt feiern. Dazu brauchen wir eine Bereitwilligkeit für Perspektivenwechsel und Zeitverschiebung. Als Sie, sehr geehrter Herr Bürgermeister, mich vor ein paar Monaten mit Ihrem erstaunlichen Anruf bei meinem kalifornischen Morgenkaffee überraschten war es bei Ihnen schon Abend. Daß zwei Menschen miteinander reden, während vor ihren Fenstern die Sonne ihnen zwei ganz unterschiedliche Tageszeiten vorspielt, daran haben wir uns dank transatlantischer Telephongespräche gewöhnt, und doch kommt es uns so ungewöhnlich vor, daß wir unvermittelt sagen: "Bei dir ist es doch schon..." "Bei Ihnen est es ja erst..." Wir müssen uns sozusagen verbal vergewissern, daß der Gesprächspartner am anderen Ende der Leitung Gleichberechtigung genießt für seine verschobene, verschrobene Uhrzeit.

Nur mit dieser Bereitwilligkeit werden Sie eine Brücke schlagen können zwischen Grimmelshausen und der ersten Grimmelshausenpreisträgerin. Das meine ich so: wenn Sie zum Beispiel sagen, Grimmelshausen habe im Jahre unseres Herrn 1676 das Zeitliche gesegnet, so ist das eine Feststellung, die unanfechtbar scheint. Wenn ich auf meine Weise nun sage, der Tod habe den Dichter im Jahre 5437 nach der Erschaffung der Welt ereilt, so stelle ich damit, ohne es besonders zu beabsichtigen, die Sachlichkeit der ersten Mitteilung in Frage. Es ist ja nicht gleichgültig, mit welchem Maßstab man die Zeit mißt. Wer in einer fertig interpretierten Welt leben will, wird selbst einen *Gruß* in fremder Sprache als Zumutung empfinden. Sie hingegen, die Sie sich eben meine Neujahrswünsche gefallen ließen, werden mir sicher noch weitere Zeit- und Raumwechsel zubilligen. Und da wäre ja noch dieser: Die Hoffnung auf ein gutes Neues Jahr gründet sich heute ausnahmsweise auf die Tatsachen im Nahen Osten, und wer diese Woche von Krieg oder, wie hier, von Kriegsbüchern, redet, darf und soll getrost hinzufügen: Aber diese Woche ist der Frieden ausgebrochen. Ein *mehr* als dreißigjähriger Krieg geht zu Ende. Das passendste Datum ist es auch für unsere Feier, auch hier in Deutschland.

Ja, lieber Herr Bürgermeister, nach Ihrem Anruf ließ ich, wie Sie sich denken können, zunächst besagten Kaffee kalt werden. Die Freude, einen Preis zu bekommen, versteht sich von selbst. Meine Genugtuung mit einem *solchen* Buch einen *deutschen* Preis zu erhalten, ist wohl auch verständlich. Aber einen Grimmelshausen-Preis! Was würde er selbst dazu sagen?

Seit fast fünfzig Jahren, seit ich vierzehn bin, hat er mich zum Lachen und zum Gruseln gebracht, denn er hat ja über Lebenssituationen geschrieben, die ich auch ohne ihn oft kannte, wenn sie in seinen Seiten auch seltsam kostümiert vorlagen. Entsetzt habe ich mich oft über seine Roheit und Direktheit und habe ihn beiseite gelegt, denn ich mochte es damals nicht, daß er so leichtfertig, wie mir schien, über Gewalt und

Folter, über Vergewaltigung und Tod schrieb. Aber später, wenn ich mich satt gelesen hatte an dem Schönheits- und Hoheitsgetue in anderen Klassikern, war ich begeistert von seiner Roheit und Direktheit. Und als ich schließlich noch später am anderen Ende der Welt, im kalifornischen Berkeley, mit einem barocken Thema promovierte, da hatte ich schon gelernt, daß er nicht nach Belieben roh und direkt sondern in literarischen Traditionen verwurzelt und somit leider doch kein Achtundsechziger des siebzehnten Jahrhunderts war.

So grüble ich vor mich hin, was er denn zu diesem Preis sagen würde, während ich meinen erkalteten Kaffee zum Aufwärmen in den Mikrowellenherd stelle. Und wie ich mich umdrehe, siehe, da sitzt er. Ein wenig im Schatten, denn sein Gesicht kann ich mir nicht recht vorstellen, seine Stimme viel eher. Ich bin nicht erstaunt. Wenn ich Probleme mit Autoren habe, fange ich an, mit ihnen zu diskutieren, und bevor man sich's versieht, ist aus der einseitigen Auseinandersetzung eine Beschwörung geworden, und die Dichter sitzen bei dir am Küchentisch und lassen sich auf deine Reden ein. Allerdings nur, wenn man ihre Werke schätzt. Auch im Tode sind sie noch so eitel, nicht zu ihren Kritikern, sondern nur zu ihren Bewunderern zu kommen. Damit hat es hier ja keine Not. Er ist bei einer treuen, langjährigen Leserin eingekehrt.

Ich erkläre ihm also, es wird einen Preis geben und ein großes Treffen, wo viel von ihm die Rede sein wird. "Ein Treffen in Telgte?" fragt er hoffnungsvoll, um mir zu beweisen, daß er nicht unbedarft ist in unserer Literatur und ihren Rückschaubedürfnissen und daß auch er die Zeit hin- und herschieben kann. In Telgte, das stimmt, da war er ein Mittelpunkt, und das war ein schönes Treffen, gebe ich zu, aber kein echtes, nur ein erdachtes, und dieses hier wird echt sein und in Renchen stattfinden. Er verbessert meine Aussprache des Stadtnamens. Den kennt er besser als ich.

Und der Preisträger, wer ist das, fragt er höflich, welcher wackere Mann wird für seine Schreibtüchtigkeit geehrt? Ich gestehe ihm betreten, das sei eine Preisträgerin, von Schreibtüchtigkeit könne nicht die Rede sein, eher von Schreibfaulheit, und kurz und gut, ich selber sei's, und erwarte nun Ablehnung, Enttäuschung, Entrüstung. Hat er doch immer nur die passiven Tugenden bei Frauen anerkannt, vor allem die Keuschheit, eine Unterlassungstugend, für die man keinen Preis kriegt. Aber er hat angefangen zu lachen: Er hätte doch selber ein weibliches Ich, behauptet er. Verunsichert durch seine Heiterkeit verweise ich ihm dieses, wie mir scheint, sarkastische Gerede. Das mit dem weiblichen Ich im Mann, dazu sei er zu früh geboren, meine ich, das sei was für die Jung'schen Psychologen, mit ihrer verstiegenen Idee von der Anima, der weiblichen Seele im männlichen Geist und er möge mich damit verschonen, die C.G. Jung- samt der Hermann-Hesse-Welle sei längst vorüber. Er versichert mir, leicht pikiert, von C.G. Jung hätte er auch wahrlich nie etwas gehört und auch von Hermann Hesse garantiert nicht. Bertolt Brecht schon, der hätte sich an seinen Werken vergriffen und Günter Grass sei sowieso sein Ururgroßenkel. Wenn ich mich übrigens zu meinen Bücherregalen bemühen möchte, sagt er, so würde ich ja herausfinden, was es mit seinem weiblichen Ich für eine Bewandtnis habe.

Da finde ich sie auch ohne Schwierigkeit, die alternde Frau (sie ist fast genau mein Alter), die ihre Lebensgeschichte erzählt, vor allem die Geschichte ihrer Jugend, die Landstörtzerin, diese Ausländerin, denn das ist sie, von heutiger Pespektive, sie ist keine Deutsche, sondern eine Böhmin, mit dem zärtlichen slawischen Kosenamen Lebuschka, die sich Courage (oder Courasche) nannte, ein Name, der, wie uns ihr Buch anvertraut, eine kindisch-obszöne Bedeutung für sie hatte. Ich lese stundenlang, wie ihr Krieg und Wanderungen arg zusetzen, versunken in diese tollen Episoden, diese Verkleidungen und Schlägereien, diese Zoten und Schlachten, diese Liebschaften und die Ehen, die im gewaltsamen Tod enden. Sie erzählt und erzählt: mit demselben Scharfsinn erzählt sie, was sie alles angestellt hat und was ihr alles angetan wurde. Sie behauptet sich. Ihre Skrupellosigkeit wirkt befreiend, ihr Witz macht das Schlimme erträglich. Am Ende ist sie unbekehrt, will von Pfaffen und der Reue nichts hören, überläßt die Askese und die Gewissensbisse den Jüngeren, die noch Zeit haben, sich zu bessern, und steht zu ihrem Leben, Charakter, Fehlern. Und setzt sich dadurch scharf ab von ihrem berühmteren Gegenspieler, dem Simplex, der uns alle, gestehen wir's nur, als reuiger Einsiedler am Mummelsee ein wenig langweilt.

Es ist spät geworden, er, der Schöpfer der Courage, sitzt noch immer als Geist in meiner Küche. Anders als in den Morgenstunden, kann ich jetzt auch seine Gesichtszüge schattenrißartig erkennen. Was ich von seinem weiblichen Ich halte, will er wissen, mit leisem Spott. Ich zögere ihm zu sagen, wie sympathisch mir seine Lebuschka ist, denn die Literaturwissenschaft kann einem solchen subjektiven Urteile madig machen und einem den Geschmack am eigenen Geschmack verderben. Ich weiß, daß sie mir unsympathisch zu sein hat. Als Protagonistin, antworte ich, das heißt als Heldin, als Mensch, als Gestalt, ist sie unmöglich, eine Vettel, eine Hure, ein unverläßliches Weib, die Freunde und Liebhaber hereinlegt. Aber sie ist ja noch etwas anderes, sie ist Berichterstatterin in bittern Zeiten, und als solche ist sie unvergleichlich, deine Maske, mein großer Gast, und wenn du dir eine solche aufstülptest, so wirst du auch meinem Jugendbericht über Krieg und Not und Gefangenschaft und Vagabundieren etwas abgewinnen, zumal ich es unternahm, ihn nicht ganz witzlos hinzukritzeln. Und in diesem Sinne bitte ich ihn um sein Wohlwollen, wenn ich hier vor Ihnen in seinem langen Schatten stehe. Denn den wirft er noch immer, und nicht nur in Renchen.

Diese Bitte scheint er gutmütig zu gewähren. Er klatscht sogar Beifall. Allerdings nur mit einer Hand, wie die Zen-Mystiker es zur Übung des

Geistes, zum kreisrunden Grübeln, tun. Wie man mit einer Hand Beifall klatscht, ist ein Rätsel, über dessen Lösung man bis zur Verzückung, beziehungsweise Erleuchtung, grübeln darf. Lautloses Klatschen selbstverständlich. Weiteren Fragen entzieht er sich lachend, auch das lautlos, und löst sich auf in eben das Gespensterlachen, das seit nunmehr einem Drittel Jahrtausend den Staub von seinen Büchern bläst.

# Gender Identities and the Remembrance of the Holocaust

## Karen Remmler

In light of current debates about the construction and formation of female identities, this article raises questions about the continued dearth of critical writing on the significance of gender differences for both the remembrance and representation of the Holocaust. Focusing on the relationship between structures of memory and the portrayal of female bodies, the author analyzes Mali Fritz's account of her experiences as a survivor of Auschwitz-Birkenau, *Essig gegen den Durst,* and Marie Nurowska's novel *Postscriptum für Anna und Miriam.* She argues that both works undermine the public memory of their respective social context by writing against universalized images of suffering. (KR)

Soon the survivors, witnesses, and perpetrators of the Holocaust will no longer be alive to give account of their experiences. Many have recorded their memories in testimonials, diaries, essays, fictional renditions, and on video, while others have chosen to remain silent. At the same time, the remembrance of the Holocaust "has shifted from being an issue of motivation (the willingness to remember) to an issue of representation (how to construct the presence of the past)."[1] In light of current debates about the construction and formation of identities, I would like to address this shift by raising questions about the continued dearth of critical writing on the significance of gender differences for both the remembrance and representation of the Holocaust. As the critical reception of Judy Chicago's controversial "Holocaust Project" has shown, attempts to represent the specificity of women's suffering in the concentration camps often lead to essentialist reinscriptions of femininity instead of insights into the structures that constitute gender difference in situations of utter dehumanization.[2] Accordingly, my essay questions the feasibility of relying on single categories of difference for describing the way that women writers in particular remember and represent the experience of the Holocaust. And finally, I suggest that we can read texts on the Holocaust not as universal examples of suffering, but as examples of how, even in moments of utter destruction and dehumanization, Holocaust survivors reclaim agency through a gendered recollection of painful memories.

In 1943, the Austrian anti-fascist Mali Fritz was deported to Auschwitz-Birkenau. More than forty years later she wrote *Essig gegen den Durst: 565 Tage in Auschwitz-Birkenau,* an autobiographical account of her experiences in the concentration camp. In 1989, Marie Nurowska, a Polish writer born in 1944, published *Postscriptum für Anna und Miriam: Roman*. The novel depicts the events and consequences surrounding the decision of the male protagonist Witold Łazarski to take home a Jewish infant whom he finds wrapped in rags outside of the Warsaw ghetto in the year 1943. Fritz's account of her survival bears witness to the atrocities of the Holocaust and, just as powerfully, pleads for its remembrance in an Austria that elected suspected war criminal Kurt Waldheim its president. Nurowska's novel renders the aftershock of the extermination of the Jewish population in Poland by depicting the fictional identity crisis of a woman who discovers at age forty that she is not a Polish Catholic, but a Jew. Both texts depict the past infliction of physical and psychological pain upon female survivors of the Holocaust by representing the social and historical context in the present that denies access to the painful memories in the public sphere.[3] In both texts, the female body becomes the site and conveyor of images that have been repressed by a practice of public memory that not only suppresses the suffering of millions of people, but also marginalizes the personal experience of female survivors and ignores their differences as gendered subjects of diverse class, racial, and ethnic identities.

Whereas Fritz transforms her lived experience as a survivor into a painful journey through her past, Nurowska draws on historical data in order to represent the dilemma of female and Jewish identity in present-day Poland. Reading the two works side by side does not diminish the impact or integrity of the difference between experience and imagination. By choosing to compare an autobiographical account with a fictionalized version of the consequences of the Holocaust within their respective historical circumstances, I question the separation imposed between imagination and reality in retrospect, not in the moment of experience. Reading the texts in terms of gender and the multiple representations of the female body will not collapse the distinction between Fritz's experience and Nurowska's narrative, but rather shed light on the importance of understanding how history is filtered through actual experience and imagination. Both texts attest to the struggle of women to maintain a sense of self that is not subsumed under non-differentiated notions of history and of pain that ignore the meaning of gender in forming identities. By tracing the role of the female body in each text as both a catalyst and site of remembrance, I hope to contribute to an understanding of the relationship between gender identity and the remembrance of the Holocaust as well as its representation in fictional renditions.

Fritz's autobiographical account and Nurowska's literary construction cannot be separated from the contexts in which they were written. Both texts counter a gender-neutral remembrance by avoiding metaphorical images of the female gender that diffuse the difference among and between women faced with remembering the physical and psychological pain inflicted upon them during the Holocaust. Fritz and Nurowska not only portray the singularity of oppression against women under the Nazis. They also document the suppression of female experiences by collective processes of public memory that ignore the intersection between, for example, class and gender differences or, in the case of Nurowska's narrative, cultural identity and gender. The texts explored here subvert the repressive public memory of their respective social context by portraying the continuing suppression of personal memories and experiences of Holocaust survivors in the present. The two texts by Fritz and Nurowska counter a public memory that obscures the suffering of the victims in the present for the sake of national harmony by exposing modes of misremembering in their respective public spheres. Frequent references to attitudes and events that affect relations between Jews and non-Jews in Austria and in Poland form the backdrop in each text. Poland and to some extent Austria have as nations perceived themselves to be victims of the German Nazis. In fact, the Allies deemed Austria a victim of German Nazi aggression as early as 1943 (cf. Whitnah and Erickson 43-44). It is no coincidence that Mali Fritz, a former Communist and social critic, published her account in 1986, the year in which Austria lost its self-perceived victim status due to Waldheim's election and the ensuing internal and external protest and debates about his wartime activities in former Yugoslavia.[4] Many Austrians continue to silence their own anti-Semitism and collaboration in the killing of Jews during the Holocaust. Poland, on the other hand, was invaded by the Germans in 1939 and had the largest number of people interned in camps. As Iwona Irwin-Zarecka insists in her book on memory in postwar Poland, however, critically remembering the Holocaust entails recalling the treatment of Polish Jews or Jews living in Poland before the Holocaust as well as during and after it. The ambiguous status of many Poles as victims of the Nazis and as collaborators or, at the very least, passive bystanders in the annihilation of their Jewish neighbors continues to counteract a simplistic assessment of recent Polish history. In postwar Poland, for example, Jews were killed after the Holocaust in a series of pogroms, of which the 1946 killing of over forty Jews in Kielce is the best-known example.[5]

Given the marginal status of Jews in both Poland and Austria and the public reluctance to take responsibility for continued discrimination against them, the two texts at hand can be read as counter-memories. As such, they seek to uncover lies and silences that have prevented exposure of the myth of victimization in Austria and a more differentiated self-perception by Poles of their roles as victims, though they themselves may have been collaborators or passive bystanders.[6]

Numerous studies on the representation of the Holocaust in memoirs, novels, films, and in interviews with survivors discuss the dilemma of interpreting texts about an event seemingly beyond imagination in its brutality.[7] Few studies, however, specifically address the particular experience of women in the Holocaust as survivors and as victims. Consequently gender difference rarely functions as an analytical category for distinguishing the multiple perceptions and experiences of the survivors. Studies on women and the Holocaust by Marlene Heinemann, Joan Ringelheim, Ellen Fine and, most recently, Carole Rittner and John K. Roth emphasize the specific attributes of female identity that shaped not only the experiences of women differently from those of men in the German concentration camps but also their rate of survival. Heinemann locates the major difference in the biological roles assigned the female body and in the conventional socialization of women to nurture (14). The former was frequently fatal, since pregnant women were sent directly to the gas chambers. The latter made it possible for women to form supportive bonds despite the inhumane conditions of the camps. Whereas Fine addresses the social conventions that typically equipped female survivors with "spiritual resistance" (87), Ringelheim warns against an inadvertent tendency to glorify oppression of women by attributing a positive result of survival to the necessity of struggling against the oppression (758–59).

Although these studies have raised important issues about how gender differences shape the experience of the Holocaust, they only implicitly consider the problematic metaphorical function of the female gender as a sign of suffering, absence, and vulnerability in Holocaust memoirs and narratives.[8] As Robertson argues in her reading of *The White Hotel,* the representation of Holocaust victims and "woman" functions as a metaphor for marginalization, absence, and "culture unrepresentativeness":

> How to make the fate of a woman or a camp inmate significant in the terms of the mainstream of civilization? For contemporary culture the oppression of women in history might seem cognate with the oppression of ethnic groups in the twentieth century; certainly there is often even a common psychological and physical brutality. But even if the Jews were more brutally treated in the holocaust than is the fate of woman, the important thing both share is the attempt by dominant patriarchal cultures to make their sufferings seem marginal to the history of the human race, to make their historically and materially particular fates seem unrepresentative of the wider culture's depraved condition (465).

In other words, female experiences—like those of Holocaust victims—do not easily enter public discourse. Their representation relies heavily on writers and witnesses willing to name the institutions and perpetrators who continue to marginalize the experiences of victims as exceptional cases or to subsume different experiences under single categories. Yet, since positing the experience of Holocaust survivors as beyond representation is just as ethically problematic as the demand that victims represent their experiences, Robertson's initial comparison begs further exemplification.[9] For example, the symbolic absence with which Mali Fritz contends in Austria as a survivor of the Holocaust bears a resemblance to her actual experience of marginalization in postwar Austria. In order for her experience to become part of the history represented by the official public memory, she must remember both the experience of disembodiment common among concentration camp prisoners and the process of embodiment as an agent of her own narrative.[10] How does Fritz's portrayal of her body reveal the complex identity of herself as a female survivor in a culture that marginalizes both her and her body in flesh and metaphor? How does Nurowska construct a similar phenomenon in her novel by having her female protagonist discover her hidden identity as a Jew? In *Essig gegen den Durst* and *Postscriptum,* the portrayal of the female body plays a central role in determining the remembering process and its content. The staccato dialogues and the constant interchange between tenses and narrative structures in Fritz's account and Nurowska's novel suggest the fragility of remembrances that are both stored in and conveyed by the bodies of the rememberers. The embodiment of their experience through narrative reveals the semiotic meaning assigned to female bodies, while at the same time showing how this meaning is embedded in the perceptions and actions of the members of their society. In the two texts, the references to the female body and to the intersection of that body with categories of class and race determine not only the form of suffering, but also the process of recalling the suffering in order to condemn it.

By reclaiming her body, the female Holocaust victim transforms her personal experience into history. Yet the relationship to their female identity itself is filtered through other identities that have shaped the experience of being alienated and/or marginalized not only as survivors of the Holocaust, but also as women. For example, in recalling her suffering in the concentration camp and the subsequent absence of a public forum about this suffering in postwar Austria, Fritz, in explaining her decision to write about her experiences, draws attention to the plight of working-class women who are marginalized in Austrian society. In a different vein, the female protagonist in *Postscriptum* struggles to integrate her new-found knowledge of her Jewish heritage with her memories of growing up as the daughter of a Polish Catholic. Her attempts to piece together the fragments of information about her family of origin are intertwined with accounts of anti-Semitic outbursts and incidents in postwar Polish history and her own memories of feeling alienated from the man she thought was her father.

By portraying the state of the female body as fragmented, dismembered, incomplete, or absent, the texts represent female subjectivity as an identity that exists within a continuum of history rather than in a metaphor of femaleness. The remembering processes and images in the texts intersect with the historical context of a public memory, thus demonstrating how societal and cultural conventions determine the way Mali Fritz remembers her survival just as it determines the dual identity of the female protagonist in Nurowska's novel. The texts counter the monolithic inscription of survivor experiences into monuments and memorials prevalent in the Austrian and Polish postwar environment that collapse many experiences into one. Instead, the texts reveal the complexity of gendered experience, a complexity that is often obscured by the assumption that the suffering experienced by both male and female victims and survivors of the Holocaust was not mediated by gender and/or other differences, such as class, race, ethnic background, and sexual orientation.[11] The works by Fritz and Nurowksa are only two examples of how women writers in particular bear witness as mourners who resist the consolidation of the suffering under the Holocaust into universalized images.

In *Essig gegen den Durst* Mali Fritz narrates her experience as a member of the resistance. She tells her own story in a language that Elfriede Jelinek has described as sober, not dramatic.[12] Mali Fritz fled Austria in 1938. A member of the Communist party, she had fought against the fascists in Spain during the Spanish Civil War. She continued her resistance to the Nazis in France until her arrest in 1941 after being denounced by Josef Pasternak, a former resistance fighter who became an informant for the Gestapo. She escaped from the "reception" camp in Brens, only to be recognized once more by Pasternak and handed over to the Gestapo in 1942. Subsequently, she was transferred to Vienna and interrogated for nine months in a Viennese prison before her deportation to Auschwitz-Birkenau in 1943.[13] She was later interned in the concentration camp at Ravensbrück until the end of April 1945. Her previous book *Es lebe das Leben! Tage nach Ravensbrück,* coedited with Hermine Jursa, describes her six-week trek from Ravensbrück to Vienna following her liberation from the camp at the end of the war.

After many years of silence, Fritz was motivated to write about her struggle for survival in the concentration camp by her disgust with Austrians' acceptance of Waldheim, with promoters of the so-called "Auschwitz Lie," and with a growing disregard for marginalized working-class women in Austrian society.

> Aber im Lauf der Jahre verloren manche Ewiggestrigen wieder ihre Scheu
> und traten offen auf, unterstützten und finanzierten eine Flut von Druckerzeugnissen, um nachzuweisen, daß das Dritte Reich verleumdet wurde, daß
> der Widerstand damals Hochverrat war, und die Greuel nur einfach Härten
> im Krieg gewesen wären, wie man sie seit eh and je und überall in der Welt
> erleben mußte und erleben kann, und daß überhaupt bezüglich der sogenannten Vernichtungslager alles erstunken und erlogen wäre. Und da es ja
> Überlebende gibt, wären sie der Beweis, daß es keine systematische Vernichtung gegeben hätte (138).

Fritz expresses her dismay towards the resurgence of fascist tendencies by using the subjunctive mood, thus leaving the words of the promoters of the "Auschwitz Lie" to stand for themselves. Further, she depicts the continued humiliation that the survivor is forced to bear in a social sphere in which many Austrians prefer to forget their complicity in the Holocaust rather than commemorate the victims of the Holocaust. Fritz demonstrates the continuity of attitudes and actions that perpetuate the abstract rendering of the Holocaust into a faint recollection separate from the present. She illustrates this point by describing her encounter after the war with a doctor who asks her why she has a number on her arm:

> Ich erzählte ihm, daß die Gefangenen, die im KZ Birkenau über nacht
> gestorben waren, nicht nach ihrem Namen gefragt werden konnten. Aber der
> Name zählte gar nicht, die Nummern der Toten wurden auf den Listen der
> Lagerleitung abgehakerlt, und die Essensration für den Block wurde gekürzt.
> Daraufhin sagt mir der Arzt: "Soo schlimm wird's schon nicht gewesen
> sein, sonst wären Sie ja nicht hier." Wenn ein Mediziner so daherredet, was
> hatte ich da von Ämtern und Behörden zu erwarten—und zu hören bekommen. Dafür war ich zu erschöpft. So habe ich mir die Nummer herausschneiden lassen, um nicht mehr deswegen befragt zu werden. Darüber
> waren manche ehemaligen Auschwitz-Häftlinge empört, und die machten mir
> Vorwürfe (136).

Fritz captures the irony of the survivor having to vouch for her existence. She testifies to the society's denial of her experience.

Moving between past and present tenses in her recounting of total dehumanization and displacement, Fritz deconstructs any historical approach to the Holocaust that would have it extracted from the present and neatly compartmentalized into the past. Her account consists of one- to five-page passages, each marked by a title that signifies a particular event, experience, or emotion from the time of her capture in France to her everyday confrontation with Holocaust denial in present-day Austria. As she moves chronologically through the narrative of her internment, Fritz intersperses ironical commentary about the hypocrisy of her non-survivor contemporaries with blunt renditions of unspeakable brutality. In her account of her internment in Auschwitz-Birkenau, Fritz remembers not only the control over her body by her interrogators and incarcerators, but also their denial of an identity based on her subjective relation to her body: "Ich hatte nur mit, was ich auf dem Leibe hatte, aber nicht einmal meine Haare haben sie mir gelassen, alles wurde weggeschoren, und dann wurde ich tätowiert. Sie markieten mich am linken Unterarm. Es kann die Nummer 46333 gewesen sein, die Dreierserie ist mir aufgefallen" (12). The inscribed number textualizes her body as the property of the Nazis. Years later, after having the number surgically removed, Fritz defies the displacement of her body into forgetfulness by speaking in public about her experiences and giving them body in writing. In the Austrian public sphere, she is shunned because she reminds her fellow citizens of the atrocities committed by the Nazis and their collaborators, and thus causes discomfort among those who would rather forget. After speaking about her experiences in the concentration camp to a group of high school students, she is faced with one young pupil's accusation that she had been "brainwashed" into believing the Holocaust took place.

Fritz's sense of identity is closely tied to survival despite the pain and humiliation of being reduced to a "body in pain."[14] Fritz vividly describes the unsanitary conditions and intentional neglect in the camps that reduce her body and the bodies of her fellow female inmates to pus-ridden, swollen, emaciated living corpses. By vividly describing the physical hardship and pain she experienced in the concentration camp, Fritz invokes bodily images that leave no doubt about the primacy of the body for remembering: "Den Mist schwingen und manchmal auch Kloacken ausschaufeln, im dampfenden Durchfallkot stehen, der mir zu kochen scheint. Ihn ausschaufeln, aber nur nicht vor Ekel ersticken und zusammenklappen, das ist das einzige, woran ich denke" (28). Survival depends on masking illness and exhaustion in order to remain invisible to the camp commanders and guards who send the weak to their death. Food becomes poison. Contaminated tea is the only remedy for quenching thirst after a day shoveling under the hot sun, despite the danger of developing fatal diarrhea. Fritz portrays her struggle to avoid being reduced to body not only by the dehumanizing conditions of the camps, but also by the whims of concentration camp commanders who both randomly and systematically "select" prisoners for death in the gas chambers:

> "Nackt ausziehen", sich reihenweise auf dem Boden, im Freien hinhocken. Wenn einem dann wieder Kleider gegeben wurden, dann war es also doch vorbei, für dieses Mal....Ein andermal: ab in die Dusche. Und was sollte daraus werden—wer wußte das schon? Es konnte eine Kontrolle dort lauern. Gefährlich waren Phlegmone, eitriger Brustfraß, überhaupt Wunden, schwere Erschöpfung und die Krätze, sogar Ansätze, die auf Krätze schließen ließen (61).

Fritz describes the disintegration of her body and the constant knowledge that she is surrounded by the ashes of the dead: "Immer diese Vorstellung, ich trage auf den Schultern Schlamm- und Staubschichten und obenauf die Asche derer, die nicht mehr mitmarschieren" (22). The concentration camp thus reveals itself as a place of excess that transforms human beings into nothing but bodies. The excessive violence of the guards and of the killing in the gas chambers and the burning of corpses in the ovens cruelly accentuates the lack of sustenance, dignity, and human rights:

> Massives Verbrechen geht hier vor, sodaß zusätzliches Töten durch harte Arbeit, Schikane, Hunger, Quälereien, Läuse und Milben, Dreck und Eiter und galoppierende Seuchen für die Lagerleitung eine Hilfe bedeuten.... Hier braucht keiner einen Vorwand für Exzesse, das Lager ist Exzess (15).

By writing about her experience and by focusing on the reduction of her self to body in the concentration camp and the invisibility of her pain in postwar Austria, Fritz refuses to allow her body to become merely a monument of pain, inscribed by the Nazis. She writes about her body as it is, scarred, but not totally defeated. In the remembering, Fritz peels the accusations of her torturers and her interrogators off her skin and transcribes them onto a blank page in order to defy the dehumanizing effect they were meant to have upon their victims and their memories. But what makes her experience different from that of male survivors and of other female survivors who suffered similar pain? Although Fritz does not explicitly distinguish her experience according to gender difference, the narrative of remembrance and the description of the pain locates her marginalization in postwar Austria as a combination of her status as a former member of the Communist party, a concentration camp survivor, and a woman. It is not the so-called essentialism of female nurturance that gets her through the ordeal of the camp, but the realization that her behavior and that of her fellow women prisoners is neither predictable nor "female" per se. Rather, the structures of violence and oppression affect individual women differently depending on their previous affiliations and backgrounds. Only with the help of particular women does Fritz survive. The physicality of relationships between inmates is accentuated, whether it be to make more room for another on the narrow wooden slats in the barrack or to share a piece of bread or hold one another up to prevent the guards from sending an inmate to her death. Her remembrance of contact with other women is intertwined with the memory of pain and the mercy of others who reduce the pain at the risk of their own lives.

The physical scars left by the nightmare of the concentration camp absorb the memories. Later, remembering the conditions in the concentration camp, Fritz touches a small lump on her body, a remnant of her bout with typhoid in the camp. By touching the lump she reassures herself that she is alive and that she has survived indescribable pain and humiliation.

Her body keeps the painful memories alive not to torment her, but to bear witness to the disruption of her life. Fritz re-writes the memories as her body becomes the site of both the dislocation and relocation of female identity in a present social climate that would have the experience of the Holocaust either negated altogether or reduced to one example of universal suffering.

The representation of the female body as both a site of utter humiliation and, conversely, as a place that resists the loss of identity forced upon it by the oppressive conditions created by the Nazis and their supporters is also the implicit subject of Nurowska's novel *Postscriptum für Anna und Miriam*. Unlike Fritz's first-hand account of the concentration camp, Nurowska's text is apparently not based on personal experience.[15] Nevertheless, the frequent references to the relations between Jews and Poles in postwar Polish history imply that the primary narrative is based on actual accounts of Poles who have recently discovered that they were born Jews.[16] *Postscriptum* imitates the common form of the Holocaust memoir in that it interweaves diary entries, letters, and interviews into what Barbara Foley calls the "pseudofactual mode" of representation:

> In the pseudofactual novel, "reality" is restricted to the point of view of a single character/witness—not in order to suggest the inherently subjective nature of perception and interpretations, but to guarantee that we do not incorporate Holocaust experience into abstract generalizations or draw from it the ethical solace that routinely accompanies even the most concretely immediate "fictitious" fiction. The pseudofactual mode provides the unified image of a fictive realm but challenges the autonomy of this realm. While it projects an imagined world in its totality, in its local effects it substitutes historical probabilities for literary ones, and thus insistently reminds the reader of the text's relations to the historical world (351).

Thus, Nurowska's novel juxtaposes historical accounts of anti-Semitic purges and sentiments in postwar Poland with the identity crisis of the female protagonist Anna who tries to come to terms with her previously unknown double identity as a Jew and as the "daughter" of a Polish Catholic named Witold Łazarski. After having spent close to forty years as Łazarski's daughter, thinking he was her father, Anna is confronted with her other identity as Miriam, the daughter of Jewish parents who did not survive the Holocaust. She discovers her Jewish heritage accidentally while paging through Łazarski's diary after he has taken deathly ill. The discovery leads her to a reassessment of her past. Looking back, Anna recalls feeling alienated in Polish society for no apparent reason and realizes the uncanny presence of her previously unknown origin in her life. She remembers situations in which she was called a Jew and a love affair with a Jewish American virtuoso that failed due to her being a "gentile." She also questions her noncommittal stance towards political events in Poland where anti-Semitism was officially promoted, leading to the expulsion of Jewish student leaders and others during the student protests in 1968.

Anna reviews the events that affected her only indirectly, but which were recorded by the man who raised her and whom she had assumed was her biological father. She reconstructs her adoptive father's motives for taking her in and for harboring a Jewish infant in German-occupied Poland, despite the risk. The pressure of bringing two apparently irreconcilable identities into focus causes Anna (and Miriam) only anguish. Anna struggles with her inability to accept her new-found identity as Miriam, while at the same time she loses her sense of self as Anna. The conflict between the two identities is played out against the backdrop of Polish and German society in which Jewishness occupies the realm of otherness. Ironically, Anna, who grew up feeling alienated from her surroundings, does not find a way to integrate her newly discovered Jewish heritage into her present self-identity even though it provides her with an explanation for her feelings of alienation. It is her body that becomes the site of the struggle as she begins to interact with the surviving members of her Jewish family.

In a series of informal interviews with the German Hans Benek, a newspaper correspondent for Polish affairs, Anna tells the story of her sudden discovery that she, a Polish Catholic, is actually Miriam Zarg, the daughter of the Jewish couple Samuel and Ewa Zarg. Anna tells her story to Benek in Cologne, Germany, where she has decided to stop on her way to the United States to meet her only remaining biological sister, Ewa. She chooses Cologne for no other reason than that it was a place she visited with Łazarski, her "father," when she was sixteen. "Vielleicht bin ich deshalb hergekommen. Vielleicht wollte ich mich wiederfinden, jenes Mädchen von damals. Und ihn wiederfinden..." (14). After Anna commits suicide, Benek continues the reconstruction of her life story by bringing together different pieces of her history as recounted in letters from surviving members of her Jewish family, Łazarski's diary, and tape recordings of interviews with her. The piecemeal uncovering of information about Anna/Miriam's life illuminates both the content and the form of the interaction between historical and subjective remembering that shapes Anna/Miriam's own identity formation.

In the course of the interviews and in notes she writes in the intervals between the interviews, Anna/Miriam retells the accidental discovery of her past. At a particularly difficult moment—her father's dependence upon her due to his terminal illness has exhausted her—Anna opens a drawer and begins to read the first passages of his diary.

> Ich hatte geglaubt, recht gut zu wissen, wer ich sei, bis zu dem Moment, als ich in der Schreibtischschublade seine Notizen fand.... Welches Kind, dachte ich damals, warum hat er mir nie davon erzählt? Ich blätterte ein paar

> Seiten zurück und stieß auf die Beschreibung, wie er es gefunden hatte. Mich beschlich die Ahnung, daß dieses jämmerliche Leben, das er in den Falten einer alten Jacke entdeckt hatte, mein Leben sein könnte. Entsetzt verwarf ich diesen Gedanken (12–13).

As Anna reads the diary she is shocked to learn that she is the "kleine Jüdin" (12) whom her father found in "einem dreckigen, modrig stinkenden Lumpen" (17). Though she tries to resist this knowledge, she ultimately tries to accept her identity as Miriam, a Jewish infant, left outside the ghetto walls by her Jewish father shortly before the ghetto was "liquidated." Faced with her new-found identity, Anna undergoes a crisis from which she does not recover:

> Was tat ich, als mir endlich klar wurde, daß ich diese kleine Jüdin war? Ich glaube, ich ging zum Spiegel und schaute in mein Gesicht. Ja, ich schaute es an, schaute tief hinein wie in etwas, das ich zum erstenmal sah. Mein Gesicht.... Ich hatte mich daran gewöhnt, hatte es als ausgemachte Sache genommen, und jetzt sollte sich plötzlich herausstellen, daß es nicht mir gehörte. Selbst als ich ein Kind gewesen war, da hatte jene vor dem Spiegel Grimassen geschnitten, wenn niemand zuschaute, und ihr Gesicht verzogen, da hatte sie Schleifen in meine Zöpfe geflochten. Aber wo war ich in dieser Zeit gewesen? (17)

Anna begins to feel alienated from her body, as though she had been temporarily inhabiting someone else's without knowing that the rightful owner would some day return and lay claim to it. Anna's relationship to Łazarski becomes complicated as she learns about the fates of the female members of her Jewish family through encounters with her maternal grandfather (who survived and who had known of her identity all along) and in letters from her Jewish sister Ewa, who writes her from the USA. The female members of her Jewish family were raped, beaten, and killed by Germans and Poles. The brutality of the German invasion of Poland, the anti-Semitic acts committed by Catholic Poles against Polish Jews, and the post World War II pogroms in Polish cities against surviving Jews are interwoven into Anna/Miriam's failure to come to terms with different identities.[17]

Parallel to her excavations into her past identity as Miriam, Anna explores her relationship to Łazarski. She recalls the reserved manner in which he treated her and his refusal to call her "daughter." She remembers him lovingly and has pangs of guilt for leaving him on his deathbed without revealing to him that she has read his diary. In her uncovering of her past Anna also attempts to find out Łazarski's motives for saving Miriam's life. She concludes that she will never know if he raised her to allay his own guilt for forcing his lover (who happens to be his wife's sister) to have an abortion or to make up for his own lack of political engagement against the German invaders of Poland. By taking on the persona of Miriam, she fears she has lost the right to be Anna and to see Lazarski as her father. "Aber dieser menschliche Schatten war jemand überaus Reales in meinem ganzen Leben gewesen. Dieser Mensch von fremden Blut war meine Familie. Fremdes Blut, kann es eine Trennung zwischen Menschen geben, die grausamer ist?"(8).

Anna's inability to reconcile her origin with her present identity not only represents the historical and cultural conflicts between Jews and non-Jewish Poles in Poland, but also raises questions about the assumption that Anna's discovery implies: namely, that her origin as the biological daughter of a Jewish couple determines her identity more than her lived experience as a Polish gentile. Given the current discussion in feminist theory and post-colonial discourse on the constructedness and permeability of identities and the danger of essentializing "Jewishness" especially within the context of the Holocaust, I read Nurowska's text as an attempt to demonstrate the pitfalls of relying on single categories of identity.

Anna's trauma of remembering is complicated by having to reconstruct her Jewish past. Remembrance of her first identity as Miriam takes place through the narratives of other family members who survived the Holocaust, family members whom Anna knew nothing about and to whom she develops an extremely ambiguous relationship. Anna slowly weaves the devastating and brutal history of her family's suffering under the Nazis with the help of letters from Ewa and in conversations with her maternal grandfather. Anna meets her (Miriam's) grandfather when she brings a tattered scrap of newspaper that Lazarski found in the pocket of the jacket in which Miriam was wrapped as an infant to a Yiddish-speaking writer in her neighborhood. Surprisingly, the writer recognizes Anna as Miriam. Aware of her Jewish identity, due to her resemblance to her biological father, he has followed her career as a concert violinist and tells her he expected her to show up someday with the scrap of paper, a review of a concert in the ghetto played by the violinist Samuel Zarg and his second daughter Chaja. Anna only later learns that the Yiddish writer is her grandfather.

Anna's genealogical remembering is dependent on the words and remembrances of others who knew her as the infant Miriam. They help her reconstruct Miriam's origin. At the same time she deconstructs her past as Anna, a past familiar to her, in order to re-remember the instances when being Jewish would have made a difference in her perception of an event or in her interaction with other people. Anna gathers bits of information more out of desperation than out of duty. Frightened by the prospect of being alone after Lazarski dies, she struggles to reclaim an identity denied her by the legacy of the Holocaust. As Anna grows more conscious of the physical resemblances to the Miriam she could have become, her body exhibits symptoms of disorientation and anxiety as she attempts to merge both identities. Her body is the site where the two conflicting identities are represented. Yet, there is no return to "original" identity. As Michel Foucault has theorized, "[t]he body manifests the stigmata of past experience and also gives rise to desires, failings and errors. These elements may join in a body where they achieve a sudden expression, but as often, their encounter is an engagement in which they efface each other, where the body becomes the pretext of their insurmountable conflict" (148). In her search for her second identity, Anna experiences the dissociation of her self as her body becomes the "inscribed surface of events" she herself did not experience, but to which she is bound through history (Foucault 148). In order to reconnect with the female line of her Jewish family, she reenacts the trauma of her separation from this family in the most empathetic and affective way possible: returning in her mind and through her body to the day on which she was left outside the ghetto wall, she commits suicide as her biological mother had on that same day. Anna/Miriam jumps to her death from a ninth-story window. She chooses the ninth floor based on her sister's description of her mother's suicide.

In the process of mourning the loss of both identities—for Anna cannot exist once she has accepted her connection to Miriam—Anna's body becomes foreign to her. Yet, her identity as Anna is in part dictated by her identity as Miriam. Her musical talent links her to her biological father Samuel Zarg and to her sister, both of whom played violin brilliantly.

> Ich fühlte mich schuldig, und folglich war mir in meiner neuen Rolle plötzlich unwohl. Dazu kam, daß meine Geige nicht mein Eigentum sein sollte.... Irgendwie, dachte ich, ist es zuviel von mir verlangt, Jüdin zu sein. Ich konnte die Last des ganzen Leidens und Sterbens nicht so einfach auf mich nehmen (41-42).

Anna finds herself living as a "divided self," a psychological phenomenon common among Holocaust survivors who live in the present with the shadow of their past lives, which were destroyed.[18] Her sister's letter describes the individual suffering of different family members, their deaths and survival. Anna lives in two spaces simultaneously—the site of the Holocaust as it is recorded in her sister's letter and the once familiar space of her identity as a Polish woman in postwar Poland.

As her sister's memories are imparted to her, Anna/Miriam finds herself taking on physical attributes of the suffering. For example, Ewa's letter describes how she witnessed the death of her other sister Chaja. The Zargs had sent the two sisters out of the ghetto in the hopes that they would be hidden by a Polish family. Instead they are sent away by this family and forced to fend for themselves in a forest. As they approach a road, Chaja is stopped by a German gendarme who happens to be riding by on a bicycle:

> Er hatte es überhaupt nicht eilig. Er hob ihr Kinn hoch und fragte: "Jude?" Unsere Schwester erwiderte nichts, sie fing nur leise an zu weinen. Und da riß er ihr die Augen aus. Ich habe das gesehen. Seine gekrümmten Finger, die nachher ganz blutig waren. Sie hat so schrill geschrien, und dann ist sie zusammengesackt. Mit den Händen fuhr sie über die Erde, als suchte sie etwas und könnte es nicht finden. Der Gendarm nahm seinen Karabiner von der Schulter und schoß auf sie. Dann stieg er auf sein Fahrrad. Chaja fiel auf die Seite und bewegte sich nicht (39).[19]

Ewa's letter also tells of other acts of random brutality and of her own survival in a Polish farmer's potato storage crib. The farmer rapes her night after night, impregnates her, and buries her stillborn baby. After reading the letter, Anna begins to imagine an identity that could function as Miriam.

When asked to play at a dinner reception for German bank directors while in Cologne, Anna furiously plays a passage from Wagner's *Lohengrin*. Playing the violin creates a bridge between her and her biological father. The bridge transports her to a fit of rage directed at the Germans assembled around her. She begins screaming at the German guests in Polish. The journalist, who had invited her to the social gathering with good intentions, is the only one present who understands the Polish words she screams: "Ihretwegen habe ich kein Trommelfell, Sie haben zu Ihrem Vergnügen herumgeschossen.... Sie haben mich blind gemacht! Sie haben mir die Augen ausgestochen, dort, auf jenem Weg, ich erkenne Sie wieder..." (124). The first accusation refers to an incident that Ewa describes in her letter. Miriam's Aunt Sara is forced to sing by a German officer, who then shoots his pistol next to her ear causing her eardrum to rupture. Anna takes on the persona of her dead and living relatives through her body. The mutilation of their senses represents the destruction of memory, sight, and sound. Her body becomes the vehicle through which her dead relatives, maimed and killed by brutal acts of individual German soldiers, can regain their senses and face the perpetrators. Though the Germans gathered at the dinner party may or may not have been involved in the atrocities, they serve as the receivers of Anna's rage as her persona Miriam gains an identity, albeit not an individual one. She takes on the agency denied her family.

Just as the victims are differentiated and given individual identity and memories, so are the perpetrators and their descendants given agency and responsibility for their deeds, good and bad. It is Benek, the German journalist, who records Anna's voice and collects her papers after her suicide. He secures Ewa's permission to publish the collection, but his search for a German publisher fails. The date is 1982, shortly after the clash between Solidarity and the Polish government under Jaruzelski. Rather than reveal the conditions that led to Anna's suicide and to see it as a result of the Holocaust, publishers prefer to stage Anna's suicide as an act of despair in light of the present-day political situation in Poland. Benek eventually publishes the book in the United States.

Anna/Miriam is simultaneously the daughter of her biological parents and of the Polish man who took her in. Before jumping to her death in Germany, she regains a voice that accuses all of humanity for committing the atrocities and individual acts of brutality against both her families:

> Ich klage die Menschen des Märtyrertodes meiner Schwester Chaja an.... Ich klage sie an, daß mir die Chance einer würdigen Kindheit verwehrt wurde.... Ich klage sie an, daß ich an dem guten Menschen Witold Łazarski gezweifelt habe, daß ich ihn in seinem Leid und seiner Krankheit verlassen habe.... Ich klage sie an, daß mich der Krieg nach vierzig Jahren eingeholt hat.... Mit meinem Tod warne ich alle Menschen (142).

Anna/Miriam's suicide note ends with two signatures preceded by the statement attesting to her identity as the daughter of Ewa and Samuel Zarg and of Witold Łazarski. Anna's quest for Miriam ends in the death of both.

In addition to the attempt to reclaim her Jewish identity, Anna also establishes a fateful connection to her female identity—one that is formed, in part, by the violence committed against the women in her family of origin. Her body becomes the site to remember the particular pain of rape and humiliation directed towards these women. Nurowska portrays the relations between men and women in the differentiated light of a prism that reflects the actual circumstances that have pitted the two against one another. Mali Fritz's account alludes to a similar differentiation. She does not stereotype, but describes people within the context of the concentration camp that did not erase difference in gender. The issue of gender may seem less central once the stories have been told. Yet, the experiences remembered by Mali Fritz and constructed by Maria Nurowska depict the infliction of pain upon the female body in ways that are signified by the extreme codes of behavior between men and women in the camp. It is the female bodies in the texts that bear the pain and carry the memories that name the inflictors of the pain.

In the episodes of brutality depicted in Ewa's letters to Anna and in her conversation with a Jewish woman whom she follows home from the Jewish cemetery in Warsaw, Anna/Miriam is exposed for the first time to the extreme brutality of the German soldiers against Jewish women. By having individual German soldiers commit acts of atrocity that include poking the eyes out of a child before shooting her, throwing a Polish baby into a burning kitchen oven, and repeatedly raping a woman who is dependent upon her rapist for survival, the author transfers the responsibility of the Holocaust from the abstract collection of Nazis to individuals who kill at random or, as in the cases described by Mali Fritz, commit acts of violence and humiliation against women.

Despite their differences, the texts are similar in their treatment of memory and in their representations of the female body. Both texts bear witness to the victimization of women during the Holocaust and its consequences for their lives in the present. Both texts recall the horrors by embodying human suffering within specific historical and social contexts. Memory images and historical events are depicted through the body. It is through the body, for example, that Fritz recalls both pain and the unresolved continuation of pain. Whereas Fritz continues to speak, the female protagonist in Nurowska's novel finds herself unable to inhabit her body as Anna or as Miriam. In the text, the female body represents the expression of the painful simultaneity of the destruction of her Jewish family and remembrance of her life as Łazarski's daughter. By drawing attention to the failure of universalized images of suffering to account for the complexity and specificity of gender for shaping the remembrance and representation of the Holocaust, the two texts at hand demonstrate the repression of the different contexts and historical constellations in which suffering takes place.

## Notes

I would like to thank Leslie Adelson and an anonymous reader for their rigorous and thoughtful comments on an early version of this essay. I am also much indebted to the editors of this volume for their superb editing skills and to the members of the "Reading Group" in the valley for their feedback.

[1] Geyer and Hansen discuss this shift at length (177). The debate about the dilemma of representation and remembrance of the Holocaust has become a major topic in the humanities in the United States, especially in response to German unification and to the opening of the Holocaust Museum in Washington, DC in 1993. See works by Friedländer, Hartmann, and Young (*The Texture of Memory*).

[2] See Zemel's review of Chicago's book *Holocaust Project*.

[3] In this essay, "public sphere" denotes the forum in which national history and public memory converge in everyday life. Public memory signifies the conventional and/or normative recollection of the past as portrayed and communicated through mass media and other institutions responsible for information dissemination. Personal memory, on the other hand, often has the distinct function of undermining public memory, while at the same time being formed by it. For further reading on this subject see Halbwachs, Hutton, and Young (*The Texture of Memory*). Surprisingly, few scholars have explored the relationship between gender and memory.

[4] Beckermann points out that this status was, in part, allocated to the Austrians by the Allies, who officially declared Austria the first country occupied

by the German Nazis (39). She also documents the refusal of Austria both officially and in the society at large to welcome exiled Jews back to Austria. Frequently, the bureaucratic regulations have also made it difficult for Jews to reclaim property that had been taken from them in 1938 after the annexation. See also Vansant's informative essay on the factors that motivated Austrians involved in the resistance movement against the Nazis to write about their experiences late in life.

[5] For a critical reading of how memory has been "neutralized" in Poland, see Irwin-Zarecka. Compare Beckermann's discussion of a similar phenomenon of suppression, the "Irrealisierung" of Nazism in Austria, and Vansant's article on Austrian personal narratives.

[6] The particular dilemma of remembering in Poland is thoroughly discussed in Irwin-Zarecka's *Neutralizing Memory*. In many ways Nurowska's book parallels Irwin-Zarecka's by exposing the process of repression that accompanies the apparent interest in remembering things Jewish during the past decade in Poland. Despite the move for the "Jewish memory project" in which the opponents of the government, the government, and the church have participated, Irwin-Zarecka classifies much of the remembering as nostalgic and as crucial for bolstering Poland's public image (8).

[7] More recent studies have, in particular, concentrated on the dilemma of interpreting representations of the Holocaust in light of postmodern definitions of history, truth, and memory. See the anthologies and works by Felman and Laub, Friedländer, Hartman, Hayes, Langer, and Young.

[8] In general, the studies have shown how the experience of Jewish women in the Nazi camps has been subsumed under "the Jewish experience," which was actually based on the experience of Jewish men (cf. Addelson 831). Robertson's approach differs from the above-mentioned scholars in that she focuses on the transformation of the manifest experience into a trope.

[9] The symbolic proximity between Jews and women is a topic also considered in Gilman's work on sexuality.

[10] Adelson, in her book on the construction of identity in works by Duden, Torkan, and Lander, reminds us that "historical consciousness is perforce mediated first and foremost through sentient bodies." Thus "historical processes and relationships are rooted in concrete, sentient experience, while narratives of history comprise *interpretations* of bodily experience" (23). It is the body where conflicting power relations, metaphors of difference and deviance, and structures of remembering and pain are expressed.

[11] This is not to say that the oppressive conditions did not harm men in an equally inhumane manner. Accounts by the male survivor Jean Améry, for example of his torture under the Gestapo and subsequent internment in Auschwitz, attest to extreme bodily pain and humiliation. In one instance, Améry describes the violation of his body as rape, an act more commonly associated with violence against women.

[12] Jelinek made these comments at a reading by Mali Fritz of her work at the *Alte Schmiede* in Vienna in 1987.

[13] Fritz's book is also the subject of my forthcoming article "Sheltering Battered Bodies in Language: Imprisonment Once More?"

[14] The term is taken from Scarry's book *The Body in Pain*, in which she explores the relationship between language and the body in extreme situations of torture and nuclear war.

[15] Attempts on my part to track down biographical information on Nurowska have been unsuccessful, but would certainly add another dimension to the reading of her novel.

[16] Kempe reports on the recent discovery by a number of Polish citizens that they are actually Jewish. As many as 1,000 Poles may be unaware that their Jewish identity has been kept a secret from them by Polish foster parents who took them in during the Holocaust for noble or not-so-noble reasons.

[17] The critical treatment of the relationship between Jews and Poles depicted in the novel reflects, in part, the growing interest in Poland in the "Jewish memory project" analyzed in Irwin-Zadecka's book on memory. The proliferation of events, books, meetings, and monuments about Jewish history and their role in Polish history only serves to neutralize the memory when it does not include the process of repression in its reevaluation of how anti-Semitism was manifested in twentieth-century Poland. The publicizing of direct acts of anti-Semitism—most notably the 1946 Kielce pogrom and the official denouncing of countless Jews in 1968 for instigating student protests, as well as evidence of anti-Semitism in the Solidarity movement—all appear in Nurowska's book through the eyes of Anna as she is confronted with her Jewish identity in a state that has been traditionally anti-Semitic (cf. Kempe).

[18] For a discussion on the "divided self" and the experience of the Holocaust see Langer.

[19] Although there is no explanation for the act of violence, a passage in *Essig gegen den Durst* throws light on the significance of the eyes: "Man hat immer schon Geschichten von Augen und vom Schauen erzählt: Der Geknechtete darf den Herrn nicht einfach anschauen. Hier wird mir klar, warum das so ist. Der Mächtige fürchtet die Augen des Erniedrigten. Deshalb muß dieser sich dem Herrn in gebeugter Haltung nähern, und der Mächtige wird nicht zu bedenken haben, daß ein Mensch vor ihm steht. In Birkenau dürfen Häftlinge nicht 'schauen.' Augen haben ihre geheime Sprache. 'Das Miststück glotzt!' Und klatsch, schon hat man den Schlag mitten ins Gesicht. Ein Peitschenhieb, ein Fußtritt und das gemartete Menschenbündel duckt sich" (21).

## Works Cited

Addelson, Kathryn Pyne. "Comment on Ringelheim's 'Women and the Holocaust: A Reconsideration of Research.'" *Signs* 12.4 (1987): 830-33.

Adelson, Leslie. *Making Bodies, Making History: Feminism and German Identity*. Nebraska: U of Nebraska P, 1993.

Améry, Jean. *At the Mind's Limits: Contemplations by a Survivor on Auschwitz and its Realities*. Trans. Sidney Rosenfeld and Stella P. Rosenfeld. Bloomington: Indiana UP, 1980.

Beckermann, Ruth. *Unzugehörig: Österreicher und Juden nach 1945*. Vienna: Loecker, 1989.

Felman, Shoshana, and Dori Laub, eds. *Testimony: Crisis of Witnessing in Literature, Psychoanalysis, and History*. New York: Routledge, 1992.

Fine, Eileen. "Women Writers and the Holocaust: Strategies for Survival." *Reflections of the Holocaust in Art and Literature*. Ed. Randolph C. Braham. New York: Columbia UP, 1990. 79-95.

Foley, Barbara. "Fact, Fiction, Fascism: Testimony and Mimesis in Holocaust Narratives." *Comparative Literature* 34.4 (Fall 1982): 330-60.

Foucault, Michel. "Nietzsche, Genealogy, History." *Michel Foucault: Language, Counter-Memory, Practice: Selected Essays and Interviews*. Ed. Donald F. Bouchard. Ithaca: Cornell UP, 1977. 139-64.

Friedländer, Saul, ed. *Probing the Limits of Representation: Nazism and the "Final Solution."* Cambridge: Harvard UP, 1992.

Fritz, Mali. *Essig gegen den Durst: 565 Tage in Auschwitz-Birkenau*. Vienna: Verlag für Gesellschaftskritik, 1986.

Fritz, Mali, and Hermine Jursa. *Es lebe das Leben! Tage nach Ravensbrück*. Vienna: Verlag für Gesellschaftskritik, 1984.

Geyer, Michael, and Miriam Hansen. "German-Jewish Memory and National Consciousness." *Holocaust Remembrance: The Shapes of Memory*. Hartman. 175-90.

Gilman, Sander. *The Jew's Body*. New York: Routledge, 1991.

Halbwachs, Maurice. *The Collective Memory*. Trans. Francis J. Ditter and Vida Yazdi Ditter. New York: Harper, 1980.

Hartman, Geoffrey, ed. *Holocaust Remembrance: The Shapes of Memory*. Oxford, UK: Blackwell, 1994.

Hayes, Peter, ed. *Lessons and Legacies: The Meaning of the Holocaust in a Changing World*. Evanston, IL: Northwestern UP, 1991.

Heinemann, Marlene E. *Gender and Destiny: Women Writers and the Holocaust*. Contributions in Women's Studies, Number 72. New York: Greenwood, 1986.

Hutton, Patrick H. *History as an Art of Memory*. Hanover, NH: U of Vermont P, 1993.

Irwin-Zarecka, Iwona. *Neutralizing Memory: The Jew in Contemporary Poland*. New Brunswick: Transaction, 1989.

Kempe, Frederick. "Hidden Heritage: Some Older Poles Now Discover That They Were Born Jewish." *Wall Street Journal* 14 February 1991: A1, col 1.

Langer, Lawrence L. *Holocaust Testimonies: The Ruins of Memory*. New Haven: Yale UP, 1991.

Nurowska, Maria. *Postscriptum für Anna und Miriam: Roman*. Trans. Albrecht Lempp. Frankfurt a.M.: Fischer, 1991.

Remmler, Karen. "Sheltering Battered Bodies in Language: Imprisonment Once More?" *Displacements: Cultural Identities in Question*. Ed. Angelika Bammer. Bloomington: Indiana UP, forthcoming.

Ringelheim, Joan Miriam. "Women and the Holocaust: A Reconsideration of Research." *Signs* 10.4 (Summer 1985): 741-61.

Rittner, Carole, and John K. Roth, eds. *Different Voices: Women and the Holocaust*. New York: Paragon, 1993.

Robertson, Mary F. "Hystery, Herstory, History: 'Imagining the Real' in Thomas's *The White Hotel*." *Contemporary Literature* 25.4 (Winter 1984): 452-77.

Scarry, Elaine. *The Body in Pain: The Making and Unmaking of the World*. New York: Oxford UP, 1985.

Vansant, Jacqueline. "Challenging Austria's Victim Status: National Socialism and Austrian Personal Narratives." *German Quarterly* 67.1 (Winter 1994): 38-57.

Whitnah, Donald R., and Edgar C. Erickson, eds. *The American Occupation of Austria: Planning and Early Years*. Westport, CT: Greenwood, 1985.

Young, James E. *The Texture of Memory: Holocaust Memorials and Meaning*. New Haven: Yale UP, 1993.

———. *Writing and Rewriting the Holocaust: Narrative and the Consequences of Interpretation*. Bloomington: Indiana UP, 1988.

Zemel, Carol. "Beyond the Reach of Art?" *The Women's Review of Books* 11.7 (April 1994): 6-7.

# From the Prater to Central Park: Finding a Self in Exile

Suzanne Shipley

This study introduces the autobiographical writings of two Austrian Jewish women, Franzi Ascher-Nash and Stella Hershan, who left Vienna during the Hitler period and settled in New York. Five stages in their emigration experience emerge: astonishment at the rejection of Jews by Austrian society; a sense of losing a homeland; an attitude of discovery upon arrival in America; concern for the safety of family members left behind; and a redefinition of home in exile. It is hypothesized that these stages may be indicative of a broader response to exile, one perhaps shared by other female emigrants of this period for whom arrival in and assimilation to America was the decisive element in finding a self. (JC)

*I, H.D., am amazingly young. I only came into the world in 1951. Crying, as does everyone coming into this world. It wasn't in Germany, even though German is my mother tongue. Spanish was spoken and the front lawn was full of coconut palms.* —Hilde Domin 21[1]

When does losing a home mean finding a self? For women who left Germany during the Hitler period, their outcast status could come to hold a positively transformative power. The boundaries crossed in their exodus to new homelands were not just geographical: uprooted from cultural heritages, they were also able to loosen restrictive stereotypes attached to their gender, their race, and/or their class. Hilde Domin's exile metamorphosis into a world-famous author is well-known (see D. Stern and G. Stern). Less widespread is the awareness of many other women's lives touched by the muse of uprootedness. This study concerns two little-known female authors, their exodus and consequent rebirth, and the differences that being female brought to their exile experience. Although their stories embody the joyfulness of survival, it was still the Holocaust that catapulted them into change. Joan Ringelheim has warned us that "[t]he Holocaust is a story of loss, not gain" (747). In looking at these women's experiences and those of other exiles, we must be on guard not to glorify oppression in the celebration of their survival. As Ringelheim further warns, we must guard against suggesting that, among Jews, women survived more easily than men:

> To suggest that among those Jews who lived through the Holocaust, women rather than men survived better is to move toward acceptance or valorization of oppression, even if one uses a cultural and not a biological argument. Oppression does not make people better; oppression makes people oppressed (757).

Nevertheless, the circumstances that propelled German and Austrian women into exile, their expulsion or voluntary departure from a racist society, legitimized their emigrant status in their new homes and led to an unprecedented plethora of life stories. Andreas Lixl-Purcell, who has researched over three hundred autobiographical narratives by women who fled Hitler's Germany, explains their motivation to record their stories as "the wish to universalize political convictions, the urge to propagate individual truths, and the memory of their personal sufferings, disillusionments, and achievements" (*Women* 2). Ellen S. Fine equates the role of writing by women victims and survivors of the Holocaust with a mission: the "mission of memory has become the survivors' principal strategy of survival and ultimately, the justification for their existence" (94). More generally, Sidonie Smith observes that "voices from the margins are louder at the moment of cultural instability" (197). Smith, who traces a prevalence in women autobiographers to rely upon a prescriptive status as wife or daughter in order to place themselves historically, notes that this can be replaced by a "confidence in the importance of [their] individual destiny derived from the culture's ideological preoccupation" (124). This indeed proved to be the case in the two lives examined here. Humanity's need to know about the Holocaust may well have freed these and other women to record their individual fates, although they might otherwise not have done so.

Unlike nineteenth-century women immigrants from German-speaking countries who settled in America, emigrant women from Nazi Germany were not viewed as potentially radical or suspect for having immigrated (cf. Stuecher). Whereas earlier women settlers were urged by their emigrant culture to protect the German home and to shelter German heritage against an invasive dominant American culture, twentieth-century exiles would succeed based upon their degree of assimilation into the American way of life. Even the nomenclature differs: I would like to suggest that, while earlier German-American settlers are designated "immigrants" because their entry into the United States was so pivotal, Hitler's exiles be referred to as "emigrants." Due to the conditions surrounding their exit, their undetermined destinations or length of absence from their homelands, and their possible unwillingness to depart, leaving becomes the decisive act for the latter, while arriving in America assumed greater importance for the former.

Additionally, emigration allowed women to escape narrowly prescribed roles that Nazi myths of "die *deutsche* Frau" were reawakening in Hitler's Germany (cf. Koonz). Straddling two cultures, home and host, women's emigrant status, their place as outsider, could thus help to liberate them from the confining ideologies of gender emerging in their lost homes. Their hard-won exile abilities to adjust, survive, and possibly even thrive as cultural outsiders were similar to coping strategies known already to well-educated, socially well-situated Jewish women in German and Austrian society. Since emigration already made them anomalies, their self-reporting did not seem so idiosyncratic in their host country. Rather, their irrevocably altered attitudes toward home and their search for a place among their host cultures would expand their views of themselves as individuals and inspire them to write autobiographically and publicly. Thus losing a home really could mean finding and documenting the discovery of a self.

The two women whose autobiographical writings are considered here have much in common: Franzi Ascher-Nash and Stella Hershan were Jewish, from financially stable families well assimilated into Austrian culture, and in their twenties at the time of their emigration to the United States. Neither was a writer before exile, both became writers in exile.[2] Both left Vienna in the late thirties and settled in New York. Of course, there are differences: Ascher-Nash's family had observed Jewish holidays and attended temple regularly in Vienna; the day of Hershan's marriage was only the second time in her life she had been in temple. Ascher-Nash published primarily in German and Hershan exclusively in English, with works subsequently translated (by someone else) into German. Ascher-Nash, five years older than Hershan, had completed a college education before exile; Hershan was to complete hers two decades after coming to New York. Their commonalities and differences combine to present an anomaly in the study of exile writers: while recognized writers were viewed as vulnerable in the exile situation, their lives severed from the language and culture on which their work depended, Ascher-Nash and Hershan found their writing careers in exile and even established permanent homes in their new cultures. Even more distinctively, both indicate that they only came to understand and integrate the loss of Austria into their present lives in America through the act of writing. Whether or not they might have become writers without the exile experience would be difficult to determine, but it is clear that writing became their mode of return, and perhaps for this reason, they considered America their rightful destiny.

Franzi Ascher was born in Vienna in 1910; her father, Leo Ascher, was famous for composing numerous operettas. She received her *Matura* in 1928 and studied singing at the University of Vienna until 1932, when she became a student performer with the *Volksoper* in Vienna. In November 1938 she emigrated to America. There she wrote one-act radio plays for the German American Writers' Association (GAWA) and offered a program series "A Viennese Sees New York" for Station WLTH in New York for twenty-five dollars per broadcast. After her father's death in 1942, Nash worked at three part-time jobs, one in a Wall Street office. Her lecture series for the Women's Club of the *New York Tribune and Herald* included topics like "Mutual Misconceptions," "Dangers and Benefits of Translation," and "Vivid Personalities of Various Countries." She received fifteen dollars for each lecture given within a 120-mile radius of New York City. From 1941-49 she served as music critic and essayist for several German-American newspapers, also publishing one poetry collection and two collections of essays. She married Edgar Nash, also an emigrant. Her unpublished autobiography "Lauf, lauf, Lebenslauf...Der rote Faden einer Autobiographie" ("Run, run, Life's Course...The Thread of an Autobiography") was completed in 1978, when she was sixty-eight years old. Ascher-Nash died in 1991 in Elmhurst, New York.

Stella Hershan was also born in Vienna, five years after Ascher-Nash, in 1915. After completing a Montessori School, she first attended a *Gymnasium,* where she did poorly, and then a girls' finishing school, which better suited her creative talents and her special interest in writing. At age seventeen she married, and by the time of her 1939 emigration to New York, she was the mother of a year-old daughter. Hershan held a variety of part-time positions; she was learning English from *True Confessions Magazine* when Elizabeth Arden cosmetics dealers hired her, sure that her European accent would underscore the elegance of the cosmetics line. Like Ascher-Nash, she became a broadcast personality, giving interviews and lectures for lunch groups and television or radio stations. Hershan served as the editor of *Talent,* a quarterly published by the American Council for Emigres in the Professions. In 1970, she published her first book, *A Woman of Quality: Eleanor Roosevelt,* followed by the best-selling novel *The Naked Angel,* now translated into seven languages.

Hershan earned a Certificate of Liberal Arts from New York University in 1962 and a Certificate of Human Relations from the New School of Social Research in 1968, where she has also been an instructor. She received the Golden Medal of Merit from the City of Vienna in 1986. Neither Ascher-Nash nor Hershan returned to Austria to live—although Hershan did visit the country several times.

I would like to explore the stages that emerge in Ascher-Nash's and Hershan's writings, stages I believe indicative of a broader response to exile, one perhaps shared by many other women in a similar situation. These stages form a template that might organize their common experiences and open our eyes to differences. Specifically, Hershan and Ascher-Nash describe growing astonishment at the rejection of Jews by Austrian society, loss at departure from their homeland, an attitude of discovery toward first foreign experiences, concern about the safety of family members still in Europe, and a redefinition of home as life in exile unfolds.[3]

Astonishment at Rejection

The first stage in Hershan's and Ascher-Nash's exile is marked by the surprise of having their class and educational status, which had placed them in the mainstream of Viennese society, brought into question by Hitler's racist legislation. Not used to seeing themselves as "Jewish," but instead as "Austrian," rejection on such artificially racial terms came as a shock. Although it was difficult for Ascher-Nash to be specific, symbols of rejection gradually emerged: "In a scarcely noticeable way, nothing about our lives was the same as it had always been for as long as I could remember. My father's activities continued, but in a puzzlingly different and distorted way" (*Faden* 105). In fact, many diaries[4] cite exactly the same turning point as do here first Ascher-Nash and then Hershan:

> Spring 1938 was gorgeous in Vienna. The city parks were overflowing with lilac, its scent perfuming the air. Flower beds burst out in reds, blues, and yellows, and the chestnut trees put on their pink blossoms. The newly painted park benches carried black signs: "Jews not permitted to sit here." Signs like that sprang up all over the city. On movie houses, on restaurants, on stores (*Memoir* 188).

In 1938, Ascher-Nash writes: "Strolling through the Prater was still permissible for Jews, but not sitting on park benches there" (*Faden* 185). As does Hershan, she notes the loss of domestic support caused by anti-Jewish legislation: "March, April, May, the seasons changed, nature went her way, yet we Jews were excluded from all the usual things.... We sat down to lunch at midday without household help, since they were no longer allowed to breathe the air of Jewish households" (*Faden* 106). The oppression was cumulative. From not being able to sit on park benches, to being unable to employ household help, to losing one's individual freedom through arrest, the free spaces became ever smaller until the surprise became the desperation that would eventually motivate exile. After the arrest of her father Leo Ascher, who was only detained for one day, Franzi felt herself a part of other lives that were affected by the loss of male relatives to Hitler's terrorism. But she records an inability to imagine the truly serious terrors lurking:

I was often in the kitchen. I would hear tentative steps approaching and stopping at the open kitchen window. It was the women who belonged to the men who were arrested at the same time as my father. They were seeking even the most delicate thread to cling to, knocking at our door to ask if my father had seen their husband, their brother, their son, and if we had anything, any news at all to pass on. The thought of a concentration camp had no meaning for me at that time. Arrest, imprisonment—I couldn't go any further than that in my thoughts (*Faden* 114).

## Loss of a Homeland

From the moment of her father's release, Franzi joined the Ascher efforts to secure affidavits for exile to America. Like others in their situation, they searched the telephone books of New York to find addresses of other Aschers to write to for help. Finally, a successfully fabricated relative emerged, Albert Ascher, whose response, "Go see my lawyer!," resulted in their being the fifteenth such affidavit he had signed.

Despite their relief in escaping, leaving Austria meant severe loss. As Ascher-Nash expressed it: "When it is finally time to leave your homeland, you no long carefully consider each action. You pack your bags and for the last time it is evening. You vacate the apartment and don't listen as the door is pulled shut for the very last time" (*Faden* 120). The final leave-taking from Austria was almost physically painful for her—although she knew she must go, she longed to stay.

> Day dawned, and the country lay before us, carrying no traces of its people's actions and miseries. All at once my heart rose up and cried out the words least fitting for this day into which I was travelling: Yes! Yes! Yes! This is where I belong! Here and nowhere else! (*Bilderbuch* 22).

Hershan's sense of loss was more tempered than was Ascher-Nash's. She knew that Austria had changed, and that she would only be safe by leaving it behind. With her husband and young daughter, she left the very day her passport was stamped for departure.

> We took the trolley car home. It was January and very cold. Snow was on the branches of the trees on the Ringstrasse. I looked at the white edifices, the Parliament, the State Opera House. Was I never to see all this again? Never again? But I barely saw it now. Enormous red flags with black swastikas were fluttering everywhere....
> I think the first thing I did when the train gathered speed was to put on some lipstick. In Nazi Vienna one did not dare to draw attention to oneself. My gray face looked at me in the mirror. How did I feed the baby? Change her? I can't remember. "We are safe!" I said to my husband. "We really are safe!" (*Memoir* 190–91).

Here, in the drama of an intensely emotional moment, the artistic force of these writings emerges. Ascher-Nash's juxtaposition of present moment and dreaded future, Hershan's depiction of snow-white buildings swathed in red and black heighten the symbolic nature of their departures.

Attitude of Discovery

The relief at being safely in New York softened the loss of homeland. In addition, they were receptive to the experiences a new culture might bring. "Things were different here," Hershan writes of New York City:

> Jews were not ashamed of being Jewish, as they were in Vienna. Delicatessens had Hebrew letters on their windows. The first time I had seen Hebrew letters in Vienna was when the Nazis forced them onto Jewish stores. We tried to tell everyone what was happening in Europe. We were convinced that there would be a war. They laughed at us. What was happening in Europe had nothing to do with America. Except that all those refugees were taking jobs away from American people (*Memoir* 194).

Ascher-Nash's first impressions were of the need to find financial support. With her father, she took responsibility for their financial security.

> Technically speaking, how does one start a new life? with telephone calls that lead to appointments that bring something new and productive....
> The three years from the beginning of 1939 until the sudden death of my father in February 1943 went by in one hectic pace. My father and I, partly together, partly separately, circulated without interruption. My mother remained in the apartment and created a new home for us (*Faden* 137–38).

Rather than identifying with her mother, who stayed home, Ascher-Nash considered herself responsible for the family's financial stability. It could have been her abilities in the language or her father's age that made her take on a professional identity she had previously lacked, except for her role in student operatic productions. She well understood the seriousness of her father's loss of status and did all she could to reestablish him professionally. Hershan also, who had never had a career before moving to New York, sought one out, but not until her husband was established in his work.

> While the country went to war, I went to work. My daughter was four years old and she needed other children to play with. The Children's Colony was a Montessori school run by an Austrian educator for children whose émigré mothers worked. I registered my daughter there and found a job selling cosmetics for Elizabeth Arden at a store on Thirty-fourth Street called McCrory's. Now I earned $15 a week. My own paycheck! I think that never before in my life had I been so happy (*Memoir* 196).

Her work brought her into the mainstream of American life, but it was not until a meeting of the National Council of Jewish Women, where Hershan heard Eleanor Roosevelt speak, that she found a way to establish herself in America:

> From then on I read her newspaper column "My Day" religiously. She taught me about democracy and freedom, what it meant and how every citizen had to work for it. She made me feel like a respected human being again, and she gave me the courage to go on (*Memoir* 194).

Eleanor Roosevelt thus became a role model for Hershan. Hershan closely identified with the woman and her work; it was Roosevelt she chose as the subject for her first book.

Concerns for Family

Much of Hershan's and Ascher-Nash's early concerns centered around the rescue of family. Both were able to secure affidavits to bring their remaining relatives to New York. Ascher-Nash writes of her uncle's arrival: "Uncle Viktor brought along a wine-red shawl of tulle with wine-red satin flowers on it. That was typical of Uncle Viktor. He had to bring Franzi something, no matter where he came from. Even if he came from hell" (*Faden* 170). Hershan writes:

> A letter came from my parents. They had been transported from Nice to a detention camp in Gurs in the Pyrenees. My neighbor asked her parents to issue an affidavit for my mother and father. Somehow, even thought it was wartime, through the help of a Jewish organization we managed to bring them to America. My mother went to work sewing in a factory. My father, quite old and ill with a heart condition, became a traveling salesman.... All agreed that Vienna was a place to which they would never return (*Memoir* 196).

In countless other diaries,[5] family concerns dominate for women in exile, whether it is their family with whom they emigrated and whom they must now sustain, or those loved ones left behind.

Redefining Home

It would be the death of loved ones that would occasion a second wave of change in the two women's lives and establish them firmly in America. With the death of her father in 1943, Ascher-Nash found she could not align the two parts of her persona, the Austrian and the American.

> I realized that it was the breadth and depth of Austria around which and in which my life had been constructed.

> The multiplicity of images in a small space, with their soft transitions from one to the other, that is Austria, and it suits me better than anywhere else on earth.... The life that I lead in America is "too big" for me. Too big the variety, too big the format of everything around me, too big these things of value, that now dangle by a single thread in these years of war. I can neither ban nor bind it with my writing (*Bilderbuch* 74-79).

Ascher-Nash's part-time office employment led to more and more disillusionment with her life until finally, by admitting her love of Austria, she came to terms with America. On the banks of the Hudson River one day in 1949, she saw a vision of Austria rising from the waters: "...Others could claim that this Austria was a dream. Fine: it was a dream that had grasped me and shown me its way, the way back into my own life" (*Bilderbuch* 79). The integration of past and present, of the roles of Austria and America in her life, led Ascher-Nash to a fuller appreciation of America. She began to teach art appreciation in Elmhurst, New York, and, by 1975 could write:

> The train approached Manhattan Island and nothing in me rejected this approach. On the contrary. There was a dark, nameless, inexplicably warm feeling of being drawn in, the first premonition of a homecoming—coming home to New York.
>
> How New York accomplished this, without ethics or esthetics, without the least support on my part, without my slightest feeling of appreciation or approval—this will forever remain the secret of this unique city (*Bilderbuch* 74).

Like Ascher-Nash, Hershan felt the double identity of her emigrant nature. When her husband died, she made major changes in her life, no longer selling cosmetics but instead enrolling in courses at New York University, where she studied writing. She turned her sense of aloneness with her own language and past into a topic for her writing, which focused more and more on Vienna.

> And then, through an odd chance of circumstances, my first novel was published in translation in Vienna. I had to see it in the stores. I just had to. And so I planned a trip to Vienna. How can you do this? I asked myself through sleepless nights. Are you just like those others who went back? Have you too no shame? No character? The German translation of my book seemed more mine than my English original. I was split in two and I could not get the two parts together (*Memoir* 198).

So, whereas Ascher-Nash would only imagine her postwar Austria, Hershan was to experience it firsthand. In 1972 she returned to Vienna, and a simple experience there cemented her gratefulness for the changes emigration had brought to her life. She writes of eavesdropping on two women of her generation seated at a nearby table in a sidewalk cafe.

Their conversation began and ended with descriptions of the schnitzel they would prepare for dinner. Hershan realized that this could have been her conversation, her day, her lackluster life: "What would have happened to me if there had never been a Hitler and I had lived out my life in the city of my birth? Had I been able to stay in Vienna until I grew old, would I be sitting there now just like them? Perhaps—" (*Memoir* 206). With this realization, Hershan becomes more positive about emigration, aware that her status as an American refugee has been invaluable to her personal growth. Although she acknowleges that she will always miss Vienna, she concludes: "I think the most important thing that has happened to me is that I no longer hate. And I no longer blame everyone" (*Memoir* 203). For both Ascher-Nash and Hershan, then, action preceded emotion in their integration into life in America. Expelled from their former homeland, both felt called to provide security for their families, called to position themselves firmly in this new society. Even as they accepted the call, they were struggling for peace within themselves. The peace came with time and with their acceptance of America as their destiny.

Some Conclusions

At a recent conference in Mexico City, people from Europe and North and South America met to discuss the many aspects of German-speaking exile in Mexico. A number of exiles attended the conference, their comments on the papers giving a constant and valuable "reality check." The women exiles there, as other women exiles' work substantiates, said that the issue of gender was a non-issue in their exile experiences. "Did you have a job before exile?" they were asked. No, they did not. Yet they came to have not only jobs, but actual careers in exile, a result that had far-reaching effects on not just their professional, but also their personal development. "Did you meet with other women, for instance in Jewish women's groups, or for luncheon meetings?" Yes, they did. And those meetings brought about a collaboration that they might overlook, but that we today know to have been valuable. In the overriding aloneness of exile there were communities and group support efforts, yet separation from families and country often left exiles with an impression of themselves as outsiders in their host environments. Such experiences as these bound them in special ways to other women.

Similarly, although the excerpts presented here rarely uncover women's views of themselves as women, these are indeed gendered writings.[6] In Stella Hershan's case, gendered symbols emerge repeatedly: from her acceptance of Eleanor Roosevelt as a model and the subject of her first book, to her startling identification with the two women who never left Vienna, Hershan's work presents a consciousness emerging from a self-abnegating identity to self-realization. Ascher-Nash, on the other hand, symbolizes the difficulties inherent in loss of status and illuminates the role of the daughter shaped by a powerful father's influences. Her "autobiography" is actually more the story of her father's life than of her own, even concluding with his death, which occurred when she was not yet forty. As such, Ascher-Nash exemplifies many of the traits common to women's autobiography, most particularly the usurpation of her own life story by that of another.[7]

For both writers, however, the force of events so strongly shaping their lives overshadowed concerns of gender, race, and class. Their lives were otherwise directed when exile rendered them directionless. In two distinct ways, in the living of their lives and in the recording of their personal stories, exile made them different from their counterparts who stayed home. Their reactions to exile may well provide a valuable connection between race and gender: with Hitler's advent to power, for the first time in their lives, their Jewishness was the most significant aspect of their identity. Not only did this racial distinction seem artificial to them, it could have proven deadly. Rejected for racial reasons that made no sense to them (as assimilated Jews in German-speaking cultures), they extrapolated to other layers of their experience, freeing themselves from societal strictures they came to view as irrelevant. This anomalous identity led many women to grow away from previously accepted stereotypes of gender, race, and class. Many carved out new lives for themselves. Thus losing a home really could mean finding a self and, in the process, recording for future generations the metamorphosis occasioned by exile.

## Notes

[1] All translations from the German presented here are my own.

[2] The scattered nature of women's works from any historical period brings out the detective in its researchers: Stella Hershan's autobiography was unpublished when I read it in the Austrian Institute in 1991. Its literary merit convinced me to meet her, and when I encouraged her to have it published, she gave it to me for that purpose. The Ascher-Nash biography, still an unpublished manuscript, was donated by the author to the German-American collection of the University of Cincinnati. In the seventies, Ascher-Nash visited the Department of Germanic Languages and Literatures where she lectured and held poetry readings.

[3] Similar concerns are, for example, found in the writings of Margot Block-Wresinski and Else Meyring as documented in Lixl-Purcell's *Erinnerungen*.

[4] Primary collections presenting personal documentation are found at the Leo Baeck Institute in New York.

[5] See also Toliver and Lixl-Purcell (*Women* 91–102).

[6] In addition to Sidonie Smith's work, Bateson and Heilbrun effectively delineate the gendered aspects of autobiographical writing.

[7] Qualities inherent in Ascher-Nash's work are common to other women's writings, such as those explored in Friedrichsmeyer, Kord, and Weigel.

## Works Cited

Ascher-Nash, Franzi. *Bilderbuch aus der Fremde*. Vienna: Wiener, 1948.

———. *Essays aus jüngster Zeit, 1974-75*. Saarbrücken: Literarische Union, 1976.

———. "Lauf, lauf, Lebenslauf...Der rote Faden einer Autobiographie." Unpublished MS, 1978.

Bateson, Mary Catherine. *Composing a Life*. New York: Penguin, 1990.

Domin, Hilde. "Unter Akrobaten und Vögeln: Fast ein Lebenslauf." *Gesammelte autobiographische Schriften*. Munich: Piper, 1992.

Felstiner, Mary Lowenthal. "Engendering an Autobiography in Art: Charlotte Salomon's 'Life? or Theater?'" *Revealing Lives: Autobiography, Biography and Gender*. Albany: State U of New York P, 1990. 183-92.

Fine, Ellen S. "Women Writers and the Holocaust: Strategies for Survival." *Reflections of the Holocaust in Art and Literature*. Ed. Randolph L. Braham. New York: Columbia UP, 1990.

Friedrichsmeyer, Sara. "Paula Modersohn-Becker and the Fictions of Artistic Self-Representation." *German Studies Review* 14.3 (1991): 490-510.

Heilbrun, Carolyn. *Reinventing Womanhood*. New York: Norton, 1979.

Hershan, Stella. *A Woman of Quality: Eleanor Roosevelt*. New York: Crown, 1970.

———. *The Naked Angel*. New York: Pinnacle, 1972.

———. "A Memoir of Nazi Austria and the Jewish Refugee Experience in America." *The American Jewish Archives Journal* 48. Ed. Abraham Peck. Cincinnati: American Jewish Archives (1991): 181-206.

Koonz, Claudia. *Mothers in the Fatherland: Women, the Family, and Nazi Politics*. New York: St. Martin's, 1987.

Kord, Susanne. "'Und drinnen waltet die züchtige Hausfrau'? Caroline Pichler's Fictional Auto/Biographies." *Women in German Yearbook 8*. Ed. Jeanette Clausen and Sara Friedrichsmeyer. Lincoln: U of Nebraska P, 1992. 141-58.

Lixl-Purcell, Andreas. *Women of Exile: German-Jewish Autobiographies Since 1933*. New York: Greenwood, 1988.

———. *Stimmen eines Jahrhunderts 1888-1990: Deutsche Autobiographien, Tagebücher, Bilder und Briefe*. Fort Worth: Holt, 1990.

Ringelheim, Joan. "Women and the Holocaust." *Signs* 10.4 (1985): 741-61.

Smith, Sidonie. *A Poetics of Women's Autobiography: Marginality and the Fictions of Self-Representation*. Bloomington: Indiana, 1987.

Stern, Dagmar C. *Hilde Domin: From Exile to Ideal*. Bern: Lang, 1979.
Stern, Guy. "In Quest of a Regional Paradise: The Theme of Return in the Works of Hilde Domin." *Germanic Review* 52.3 (1987): 136–42.
Stuecher, Dorothea. *Twice Removed: The Experience of German-American Woman Writers in the Nineteenth Century*. New York: Lang, 1990.
Toliver, Suzanne Shipley. "In Exile: The Latin American Diaries of Katja Hayek-Arendt." *American Jewish Archives Journal* 39.2 (1987): 157–88.
Weigel, Sigrid. "Der schielende Blick: Thesen zur Geschichte weiblicher Schreibpraxis." *Die verborgene Frau: Sechs Beiträge zu einer feministischen Literaturwissenschaft*. Ed. Inge Stephan and Sigrid Weigel. Berlin: Argument, 1988. 83–137.

# Dokument und Fiktion: Marie-Thérèse Kerschbaumers *Der weibliche Name des Widerstands*

Sigrid Lange

This essay introduces Marie-Thérèse Kerschbaumer's *Der weibliche Name des Widerstands* to American audiences. Thematically this collection of portraits of women who died in the Holocaust is discussed as a contribution to the literature of women's antifascist resistance; at the same time the article examines the poetics of the work as distinct from documentary prose. With reference to Kerschbaumer's linguistic studies as well as her feminist and political intentions, the article develops a specific semiotic of the female. (SL)

*Es ist nicht wahr, daß die Opfer mahnen, bezeugen, Zeugenschaft für etwas ablegen, das ist eine der furchtbarsten, schwächsten Poetisierungen.... Auf das Opfer darf sich keiner berufen. Es ist Mißbrauch. Kein Land und keine Gruppe, keine Idee, darf sich auf ihre Toten berufen.*—Bachmann 335

Die österreichische Dichterin Marie-Thérèse Kerschbaumer veröffentlichte 1980 eine Sammlung von Porträts weiblicher Opfer des Nationalsozialismus unter dem Titel *Der weibliche Name des Widerstands*. In einem dieser Porträts, Helene und Elise, fällt folgender paradoxer Dialog auf:

> Lebten wir damals schon? Wir lebten, sagte Elise, wir lebten, sagte Helene. Wir sind Zeugen der Geschichte, unsere kurze Existenz ist Zeugnis dieser oder jener Geschichte. Dann muß das Ende kommen, aber du hast noch gar nicht begonnen (*Widerstand* 18).

Paradox ist dieses leitmotivisch wiederholte Gespräch zum ersten durch die Redesituation: Die hier ihre Lebensgeschichte bilanzierenden beiden Frauen befinden sich im Oktober 1942 auf dem Transport von Wien nach Theresienstadt. Sie fuhren in den Tod. Dieser Kontext wirft zum zweiten ein Zwielicht auf die Übereinstimmung von individuellem Leben und Geschichte suggerierende Redewendung von der "Zeugenschaft", verkehrt sie in ihren Gegensinn, wenn die Auslöschung von Individualität "Zeugnis ablegt" vom Gang der Geschichte: "Dann muß das Ende kommen, aber du hast noch gar nicht begonnen." Zum dritten spielt die stilistische Unterwanderung des Pathos von "dieser und jener Geschichte" in den Doppelsinn von Historie und Narration im Begriff Geschichte hinüber.

In vier fast beiläufigen Sätzen formuliert Kerschbaumer ein literarisches, genauer: sprachphilosophisches Problem von einem moralischen Standort aus. Wie bringt man Opfer zum Sprechen, ohne sie, als Objekt der Sprache, noch einmal zu töten? Wie widerspricht man dem scheinbar Authentischsten, dem "Zeugnis" der Geschichte, in seiner Macht des Faktischen? Was hat die "Geschichte" als im Nachhinein sinnträchtiger Prozeß menschlichen Handelns, der Opfer fordert, zu tun mit dem sprachlichen Prozeß dieser Sinnstiftung, genannt "Geschichtsschreibung", die sich auf Faktisches, auf "Zeugnisse" beruft? Wie stellt sich die literarische Fiktion mit dem Impetus des Gegensinns dazu?

Das Verdikt der Passage über die Zeugnisse steht, analog dem eingangs angeführten Bachmann-Zitat, vorerst konträr zu Kerschbaumers erklärter Absicht, mit ihrem Buch "starke Mütter für die heutige Frauenbewegung" zu präsentieren, denn "um vernichtet zu werden, braucht es Stärke" (Vansant 114). Es steht desgleichen konträr zum Kontext des Kerschbaumerschen Buches. In den achtziger Jahren entstanden in drei deutschsprachigen Ländern, in Österreich, der BRD und der DDR, eine ganze Reihe von dokumentarischen Büchern über weibliche Opfer und den weiblichen Widerstand gegen den Faschismus, sie alle erst im Gefolge der Frauenbewegung. Beispielhaft können genannt werden: *Der Himmel ist blau. Kann sein. Frauen im Widerstand Österreich 1938–1945* (Berger et al.), *Jeden Moment war dieser Tod. Interviews mit jüdischen Frauen, die Auschwitz überlebten* (Fürstenberg), *Kreuzweg Ravensbrück. Lebensbilder antifaschistischer Widerstandskämpferinnen* (Jacobeit und Thoms-Heinrich), *Sag nie, du gehst den letzten Weg. Frauen im bewaffneten Widerstand gegen Faschismus und deutsche Besatzung* (Strobl). Ihnen analog trägt Kerschbaumers *Der weibliche Name des Widerstands* den Untertitel *Sieben Berichte,* geschrieben auf der Grundlage dokumentarischen Materials größtenteils aus dem Wiener Archiv zur Geschichte des Nationalsozialismus. Das Ergebnis ist jedoch keine Dokumentation, vielmehr entstanden stark poetische Texte in dialogischem Gestus, assoziativ, die Zeitebenen wechselnd, die Figuren vervielfachend, konstrastierend, mit fragmentarisch eingesetzten Dokumenten aus Briefen, Prozeßberichten, Flugblättern, aktuellen Nachrichten über Verfolgung und Gewalt, Opfer und Täter in aller Welt. Dennoch gewinnen sieben Porträts Konturen: einer jüdischen Schriftstellerin; der beiden genannten Schwestern Elise und Helene, jüdische Sprach- bzw. Literaturforscherinnen in Wien; einer katholischen Nonne, die sich zu individuellem Widerstand entschloß; einer Arbeiterin, eines Lehrmädchens, einer Lehrerin, die zum organisierten Widerstand gehörten.

Die Opfer zum Sprechen bringen, sie zu verlebendigen und damit ihren durch Geschichte und "Zeugnisse" besiegelten Tod aufzuhalten, das ist Kerschbaumers Thema. Anders formuliert: Es geht ihr um den Widerstand der Sprache, den sie als Dichterin gegen die Zeugnisse und deren paradoxen Charakter zu leisten hat. Diese Arbeit des Schreibens will ich im folgenden am Beispiel der Erzählung von Elise und Helene analysieren. Die Interpretation greift den bei Kerschbaumer entwickelten Begriff von Geschichte und seinen Bezug zum Problem des Erzählens auf, das hier von ihr auf das Dokumentieren zugeschnitten ist, untersucht Aspekte des poetischen Verfahrens, geht auf ihre Auffassung von Sprache und Literatur ein und ihr politisch-feministisches Selbstverständnis als Dichterin.

Jedem der sieben Porträts ist ein Vorspann vorangestellt, in dem die gesicherten Fakten der ausgewählten Biographien jeweils auf die unverrückbaren Daten von Name, Beruf, Geburtstag und -ort sowie Todestag und -ort reduziert erscheinen:

RICHTER, ELISE
österreichische Phonetikerin,
erste österreichische Hochschullehrerin
geboren: 2.3.1865 in Wien
verschleppt: 9.10.1942 (KZ Theresienstadt)
verschollen: seit 1944

RICHTER, HELENE
Schwester von Elise,
österreichische Anglistin,
schrieb über die englische Romantik
und zur Geschichte des Burgtheaters
geboren: 4.8.1861 in Wien
verschleppt: 9.10.1942 (KZ Theresienstadt)
verschollen: seit 1944

Das Schriftbild setzt bis hin zum Vermerk "verschollen" mangels eines eindeutigen, aber gewissen Todesdatums ein Zeichen—das einer Grabinschrift—und metaphorisiert die im Text verbalisierte Ambivalenz von Zeugnis und Zeugenschaft. Zum mahnenden Gedenken für die Nachgeborenen zeugen die Opfer von der Geschichte ihrer Vernichtung und besiegeln sie damit endgültig. Das Tatsachengedächtnis paßt die Biographie der Opfer in die Geschichte ein und bestätigt sie darin. Von dieser Macht des Faktums hebt nun jeweils die folgende Geschichte in Kerschbaumers Buch ab, indem sie deren Logik hinterfragt. Die Erzählung von Helene und Elise beginnt und endet fast identisch mit derselben Passage:

> Am Anfang, sagte sie, war alles ganz anders. Am Anfang war das Andere..
> Am Anfang, sagte Helene, am Anfang warst du noch gar nicht da. Wo war
> ich, sagte Elise. Bei mir, sagte der Vater, noch in mir bist du gewesen,
> bevor du in ihr warst. Dann bist du gewachsen und groß geworden. Wie
> groß, na so groß, eben so (*Widerstand* 17, 39 f.).

Die erzählerische Kreisbewegung beinhaltet den Versuch, einen biographischen Ursprung in der väterlichen Genealogie zu finden, der dann abbricht und in die kontradiktorische, lakonische und kursiv von der Erzählung abgehobene Notiz mündet: "(Am 9.10. 1942 um 20 Uhr 25' ist vom Wiener Aspangbahnhof der 45. Judentransport [13. Tagestransport nach Theresienstadt] mit 1322 Köpfen abgegangen" (*Widerstand* 40). Wie dieser Versuch, durch das Feststellen eines Anfangs eine Kontinuität für ihre Biographie zu setzen, verschmelzen alle anderen aufgegriffenen "Geschichtsfäden" in der Erzählung immer wieder mit der Reise in den Tod. Die Geschichte ihrer Geburtsstadt Split, die Geschichte Dalmatiens, die Geschichte der Juden ihrer Stadt, die Vorgeschichte ihrer beruflichen Karriere, schließlich gar die Natur- und Menschheitsgeschichte—"...als die Natur (Schnitt) das Bewußtsein (Schnitt) ihrer selbst (Schnitt)..." (*Widerstand* 39)—werden auf ihren "Anfang" hin befragt, um eine historische Struktur für ihre individuelle Lebensgeschichte zu finden. Alle diese "Geschichtsfäden" werden verworfen, denn sie besiegeln eine Kausalität mit dem Ende als Opfer, gegen die die Erzählung immer wieder anhebt: "Aber das war nicht das Ende." Die hier präsentierte Auffassung von Geschichte läßt sich, beabsichtigt, so leicht nicht auf einen Nenner bringen. Kontinuität unterliegt ihr insofern, als Kerschbaumer das Paradigma von Opfern und Tätern durchaus mit politisch-moralischem Gestus bis in die Gegenwart führt bzw. von der Gegenwart aus schreibt. Explizit ist die Erzählung *Die Zigeunerin* in der Mitte des Bandes plaziert, nennt keinen individuellen Namen und berichtet über die zeitgenössischen Erfahrungen der Erzählerin im eigenen und beobachteten Umgang mit Zigeunern:

> Warum hast du keinen Namen unter zweitausendsiebenhundert ermordeten
> österreichischen Zigeunern gefunden, keine Geburtsdaten, Verschleppungs-
> oder Vernichtungsdaten gefunden? Warum behauptest du, in deiner Ge-
> schichte seien alle Daten enthalten, auch gute und böse, ja auch gute? sagst
> du. Warum sprichst du ausgerechnet bei den Zigeunern von den Lebenden
> und nicht von den Toten? (*Widerstand* 121)

Die Antwort scheint der Frage eingeschrieben, und sie wird ergänzt durch aktuelle Einblendungen etwa aus dem Vietnamkrieg, dem faschistischen Putsch in Chile, dem Antisemitismus in der Sowjetunion einerseits und dem antipalästinensischen Zionismus in Israel andererseits, Rassenverfolgung und Gewalt in beinahe beliebigen Beispielen. Der Fortführung der Diskriminierungs- und Vernichtungspraxis korrespondiert die anhaltende Verdrängung der Mittäterschaft am Holocaust. Damit beginnt das Buch überhaupt: "Aber du sagst, sie sei wiedergekommen, Alma Johanna zurück von einer langen Reise..." (*Widerstand* 7)—eine fiktive Zeugin der Deportation der Wiener Juden spricht sich frei von Mitwissen, euphemistisch die Verschleppung als "Reise" apostrophierend, die Wiederkehr des Opfers suggerierend, sich gleichzeitig widersprechend, wenn sie sich zur Begründung ihres Schweigens auf die gefährlichen Bedingungen nationalsozialistischer Realität beruft. Immer wieder auch finden sich die symptomatischen Zitate über das unerwünscht "Unzeitgemäße" von Kerschbaumers Buchprojekt im gegenwärtigen Österreich:

...ich finde das reichlich geschmacklos, ich finde das reichlich naiv. Beinahe opportunistisch. Ja, und auch so schrecklich verspätet. Bei uns ist das schon alles vorbei. Bei uns kräht kein Hahn mehr danach. Wir haben die Theorie empfindlich gekürzt. Wir haben das Verlagsprogramm entscheidend vereinfacht. Wir sind ein bißchen realistischer geworden (*Widerstand* 36).

Das hier von Kerschbaumer präsentierte Geschichtsbild hat drei Zuschreibungen: es ist das *aufklärerische*—die im Menschen zum Bewußtsein ihrer selbst gekommene Natur zitiert Friedrich Engels (22)—, fortgetrieben bis zur Dialektik der Aufklärung im Kontinuum eines Opfer-Täter-Paradigmas; insofern hat es eine *zeitliche Kategorie,* die sich in der Kreisbewegung als Progreß wiederum selbst ad absurdum führt, und sie ist *patriarchalisch*—ausgerechnet der Vater reklamiert den natürlichen Ursprung der Töchter für sich. Damit repräsentiert sie den Text der symbolischen Ordnung schlechthin:

Die symbolische Ordnung—Ordnung der verbalen Kommunikation, väterliche Ordnung der Kindesgenealogie—ist eine zeitliche Ordnung.... Ohne Rede gibt es keine Zeit. Also gibt es keine Zeit ohne den Vater. Der Vater, das ist übrigens das folgende: Zeichen und Zeit (Kristeva 262 f.).

Diese Ordnung des geschichtlichen Textes eliminiert, was das umschließende Zitat vom Anfang in Kerschbaumers Erzählung auch postuliert: "das Andere."

Kerschbaumers Porträts, könnte man in diesem Verständnis formulieren, sind Ein-Sprüche in das Symbolische, um "das Andere" hervorzubringen. Das entscheidende Stichwort in bezug auf Geschichte heißt "Schnitt", ein Terminus aus der Filmtechnik, der die Unterbrechung der vor dem Betrachter ablaufenden Bildfolge bezeichnet. Es zerlegt die Dokumentation des historischen Textes, sprengt die Zeit und bringt Subjektives in die Geschlossenheit der vorgeblichen Objektivität der Tatsachen:

Die Geschlossenheit einer Erzählung, das heißt immer derselbe bleiben während der Erzählung, das heißt die Zeit aufheben im Ablauf der

Handlung, eine Unmöglichkeit. Also keine Geschlossenheit, es sei denn, was ich erzähle, geschieht nebeneinander. Die Gleichzeitigkeit im Ablauf einer Erzählung, ein Ding der Unmöglichkeit, sagt der Reporter. Wenn ich erzähle, verändere ich mich, ich bin nicht derselbe, also ist die Erzählung am Ende nicht mehr dieselbe wie am Anfang, verstehst du? (*Widerstand* 28 f.)

Diese Bemerkung hebt auf die Unangemessenheit der geschlossenen Geschichte im Sinne von Narration ab, und nicht umsonst verneint der Reporter, der Berichterstatter "objektiver" Ereignisse, die Möglichkeit der Differenzierung. Das Dokumentarische, der "Film", setzt den selektierenden Blick auf das voraus, was vorab zum Wesentlichen erklärt wurde und einen "Sinn" ergibt, der sich im Kontinuum der Bilder präsentiert. Die Kategorie Zeit hingegen, so die weitere Argumentation, bringt die Subjektivität des/der Erzählenden ins Spiel und verändert damit den Text. Kerschbaumer spiegelt dabei Geschichte(n)erzählen als Narration und Historie unmittelbar in der Metapher des Films ineinander:

Ich liebe dich, sagt der Mann auf dem Bildschirm. Ich danke dir, sagt die Frau auf dem Bildschirm. Ein Bild auf das andere. Schnitt. Segmente, abgetrennte Teile eines Kontinuums, eine semiotische Kette, gibts die, fragte Elise. Wenn du die Geschichte als semiotisches Corpus bezeichnest, als eine konventionelle Kette von Zeichen betrachtest, ist das Fehlen von Solidarität unter den Frauen ein Zeichen, verstehst du? Wofür oder wovon, fragte Elise. Ihrer Unterdrückung, wie bei Malern, Schriftstellern, Unselbständigen, Lohnempfängern, Abhängigen einfach, wie bei den Opfern dieser Erzählung, in der Geschichte (*Widerstand* 30).

Diese programmatischen Äußerungen sind zwei Sprachwissenschaftlerinnen unterlegt. Kerschbaumer, selbst promovierte Linguistin, formuliert hier den Kern ihrer Poetik, die aus zwei Quellen gespeist ist—einer politischen Intention und einer strukturalistisch fundierten Auffassung von Sprache einschließlich der poetischen. Ihr erster Roman, *Der Schwimmer* (1976), thematisiert die Positionierung eines Ich im "Code" eines Zeichensystems, von dem es sowohl beherrscht als auch ausgegrenzt wird und dessen einzige Identitätsstiftung dennoch darin besteht, ein "Wesen [zu sein] dessen mentale Struktur so geschaffen ist Sprache zu besitzen" (*Schwimmer* 104). Der Schwimmer, politischer Gefangener auf der Flucht von einer Insel zum rettenden Schiff, steht gleichzeitig als Allegorie des Dichters auf der Suche nach der Sprache am "Ende jeder Kollaboration (Bewußtsein für andere)" (*Lesen* 68), d.i. der Komplizenschaft mit dem Mechanismus der Gewalt. Nach Kerschbaumers Darstellung stellt sie sich her durch die Verselbständigung der Zeichen, ihr Abheben vom ursprünglichen Signifikat in der kommerziellen Vereinnahmung. "Wortzeichen" werden zu "ikonische[n] Zeichen" (*Lesen* 69), die jedem Mißbrauch offenstehen. Damit verliert die Sprache ihre Funktion als menschliches Kommunikationsmittel. Sie neu zu finden, gilt Kerschbaumer als Aufgabe des Dichters. Zu diesem Zweck unternimmt sie es im *Schwimmer*, in endlosen semiotischen Verschiebungen der Funktionsweise einer textlichen/kulturellen Struktur auf den Grund zu gehen:

> ...da gibt es keine Koordiniertheit der zeitlichen Handlungsabläufe keine Konsequenz in bezug auf die Identität eines Ich da verweigert sich jede Logik der objektiven Sprache (über Dinge) die Einstellung auf den Kontext ist verschoben zugunsten einer Einstellung auf den Code (über Sprache)... (*Lesen* 67).

Kerschbaumers Selbstkommentar zum *Schwimmer* fällt deutlicher aus als die Erläuterungen zum *Weiblichen Namen des Widerstands*, die Textstruktur aber ist bei beiden Büchern dieselbe. Die Dekonstruktion des Symbolischen erfolgt über die Demontage der Zeitstruktur, des sprachlichen Zeichens, und eines doppelten Ichs: der dargestellten Figur und der Erzählerin. Wie Kerschbaumer darin ihre politisch-moralische Intention realisiert, "das Fehlen von Solidarität unter den Frauen", den Unterdrückten im allgemeinen festzumachen, will ich an einem längeren Textbeispiel aus der Erzählung von Elise und Helene erklären:

> Ich meine, wenn die Geschichte es will, erwischt es dich halt. Da gibt es kein Pardon für den einzelnen. Ach so, sagt Helene. Es gibt also keine Entschlossenheit in dieser Geschichte. Nein, es gibt keine Geschlossenheit in der Geschichte, denn sie ist Menschenwerk. Geschichte ist Menschenwerk und daher veränderbar. Zumindest erzählbar, sagte Helene. Dann erzähle endlich, erzähle, erzähle. Wie kann ich, wenn ich hier stehe und lese. Ein Wettlesen, ein Wettstreit, ein Wettkampf, ein Rutenlauf. Die Zeit, sagt Elise. Das Einhängen des Hörers, das Klicken am anderen Ende der Leitung und die Reaktion darauf. Bis man die Nummer gewählt, die Verbindung hergestellt und nach dem Gesprächspartner rückgefragt hat, ist jener aus dem Zimmer gegangen, drei Stockwerke tiefer, über den Hof, an den Mahnmalen der Nationen vorbei, an den Delegationen vorbei, an den Besuchern vorbei, hinaus aus der Richtstätte, der Gedenkstätte, dem Todeslager. Unsere Verbindung konnte nicht hergestellt werden, zwischen dem Klicken in meinem Telephonhörer und meinem nochmaligen Drehen der Wählscheibe ist Zeit vergangen, die sich für den so abspielt und für den so. Und dann ist alles unwiederbringlich vorbei, irreversibel, sagt Elise, ohne Umkehr, murmelt Helene. Ich bin nicht derselbe, der Mensch ist nicht derselbe, nein, diese Einheitlichkeit ist nicht mehr gegeben (*Widerstand* 29).

Gegen die gesicherte Faktizität eines Vorgangs ist dieser Text als etwas "Fließendes" konstruiert, das sich über die metonymische Verschiebung von Metaphern herstellt. Das sprachliche Mittel entlehnt Kerschbaumer der Theorie ihres sprachwissenschaftlichen Lehrmeisters, Roman Jakobson, gleichermaßen wie ihrem poetischen Umfeld, der Wiener Konkreten Poesie. Die Aphasie, der Versprecher—medizinisch der Ausdruck mangelnder Sprachbeherrschung—fungiert als gestisches Mittel, die Funktionsweise der Sprache zu befragen. Auf die "Geschlossenheit der Geschichte", in der es "dich dann halt erwischt", trifft die scheinbar sprachspielerische Korrektur der nicht vorhandenen "Entschlossenheit"—wessen?—, den Mechanismus aufzuhalten. Im Kommentar zum *Schwimmer* heißt es in der Fortsetzung des angeführten Zitats:

> ...da gibt es keine Konsequenz in bezug auf die Identität eines Ich da verweigert sich jede Logik der objektiven Sprache (über Dinge) die Einstellung auf den Kontext ist verschoben zugunsten einer Einstellung auf den Code (über Sprache) die Möglichkeit des Verlusts ist in Traum Ausnahmezuständen Halluzinationen und unter Drogen oder in vollkommener Isolation gegeben und dem Schwimmer nicht unbekannt *wer dahinter Sprachspiele vermutet mißversteht die Situation*... (Lesen 67, Hervorhebung von mir).

Die "Logik der objektiven Sprache" wird, im Bild gesprochen, auch im *Weiblichen Namen des Widerstands* ins Schwimmen gebracht durch die Aphasien Geschlossenheit/Entschlossenheit, Wettlesen/Wettstreit/Wettkampf/Rutenlauf und Richtstätte/Gedenkstätte/Todeslager. Jedesmal wechselt die lautlich assoziative Verschiebung, die kein Sprachspiel ist, politisch-moralische Kategorien mit solchen der Texttheorie. Desgleichen kann die Metapher vom mißlingenden Telefongespräch, das hier auf die Absenz des anderen Menschen, der seine Solidarität und damit die mögliche Rettung verweigert, als Bild eines Grundtheorems der strukturalistischen Sprachtheorie gelesen werden. In ihren Wiener Vorlesungen (To honour Roman Jakobson), abgedruckt in *Für mich hat Lesen etwas mit Fließen zu tun* (23–112), hat sie ausführlich das Problem der Übertragung einer Botschaft zwischen Absender und Empfänger mittels eines gemeinsamen Codes erläutert. Der Code garantiert die Möglichkeit der Verständigung. In der zitierten Textpassage fällt der Hilferuf aus dem Code heraus. Gleichzeitig bezeichnet der Code in weitester Bedeutung jenes verselbständigte Zeichensystem, das zur Konvention der Herrschenden geworden ist und das der Poststrukturalismus mit dem Begriff des Symbolischen besetzt. Das Benennen der Leerstelle als "Zeichen" jedoch löst die Struktur aus ihrer Festigkeit. Die Konstruktion vom Kontinuum der Zeit, das von der mangelnden Solidarität über die Vernichtung der Opfer selbstberuhigend zu ihrer Ehrung als Tote führt, wird in ihrer moralischen Fragwürdigkeit deutlich durch die Bewegung der Sprache. Am Ende ruft Kerschbaumer mit den Mahnmalen die Grabtafeln auf, die ihre Erzählungen einleiten.

Das Bild der Zeit allerdings ist doppeldeutig. Kerschbaumers durch die Verschiebung von Bedeutungen segmentierte Sinnproduktion impliziert im sprachtheoretischen Verständnis den Prozeß der Symbolisierung in seiner potentiellen Mehrdeutigkeit: Die Zeit, die beim Drehen der Wählscheibe des Telephons bis zum Auslösen des Rufes vergeht, spielt sich für verschiedene Personen ganz anders ab. Es gibt keine semantisch einheitlich verifizierbare Zeit. Am Ende der Passage stehen zwei konträre Aussagen: die der potentiellen Differenzierung der Zeit und die der geschlossenen, linearen Chronologie: "Dann ist alles unwiederbringlich vorbei, irreversibel." Dieser Doppelheit entsprechen zwei Möglichkeiten des Erzählens—das Dokumentieren in der gesetzten Linearität des Prozesses, das der Techniker und der Reporter benutzen, und die Erzählung, die die Autorin letztlich selbst produziert: "Wenn ich erzähle, verändere ich mich, ich bin nicht derselbe, also ist die Erzählung am Ende nicht dieselbe wie am Anfang, verstehst du?" (*Schwimmer* 28 f.). Das Einbringen des sprechenden Subjekts verändert den Text der symbolischen Narration oder, in Kerschbaumers moralischer Explikation des Sprachtheoretischen: Als politisch verantwortliche Zeitgenossin hebt sie die zeitliche Differenz zwischen dem historischen Gegenstand und der Gegenwart als nicht abgegoltene Frage der Verantwortung auf. Als Erzählerin, die sich nicht auf die Opfer berufen will, weil sie sie in der Dokumentation noch einmal tötet, zum Objekt der Narration macht, baut sie ein dialogisches Verhältnis zu ihren Figuren auf. Die Erzählinstanz wechselt in verschiedenen Figurenperspektiven, entwirft Parallelfiguren, nimmt die Rolle des Verhörers, Zeugen, Richters, Interviewers ein. Sie bleibt darin sowenig homogen wie die vorgestellte Person selbst.

Gegen das "Irreversible" der Vernichtung stellt Kerschbaumer schließlich eine sprachliche Umkehr:

Und was soll Franca in dieser Geschichte? Nichts, außer daß sie hundertzwanzig Jahre nach Adolfo, dem Sohn des Rabbiners, nach Wien kam, in das Wien nach unserem Tode, sagte Elise. In das Wien nach unserem Leben, murmelte Helene (*Widerstand* 20).

Das Wien nach unserem Tode/nach unserem Leben: der Perspektivwechsel in scheinbar derselben Aussage verändert ihre Bedeutung. Er verkehrt sie im Sinne des Themas, die Logik des Todes aufzuheben. In einem weiteren, philosophischen Verständnis der rhetorischen Figur kann man diese Überkreuzstellung der Aussage als Chiasmus bezeichnen. Nach Eva Meyers Darstellung, auf die ich mich hier berufe, hat die klassische Logik von der Antike an diese Stilfigur als inadäquat aus ihrem System ausgegrenzt, weil sie mit den Gesetzen der Rationalität nicht beschreibbar ist. Die Vertauschung von Subjekt und Prädikat einer Aussage führt nicht zu ihrer spiegelbildlichen Negation. Eva Meyer verdeutlicht den Mechanismus der logischen Setzung an dem Satz "Die Frau ist weiblich", eine Subjekt-Prädikat-Relation, die in der Umkehrung die fatale Identität von Weiblichkeit und Frau behaupten würde, eine Definition, die mit der Qualifizierung "essentialistisch" zurückzuweisen wäre. Meyer will auf das sprachtheoretische Problem hinaus, daß dieser Satz und seine Umkehrung den verständlichen Wunsch eines sprechenden Subjekts artikulieren, dem

Phänomen—als semiotischer Begriff verstanden—Weiblichkeit einen Platz in der Realität des Logos zuzuweisen. Damit findet eine Vereinfachung statt. Ein Allgemeines, "das Weibliche", wird in der Logik dieses Aussagens, die die Umkehrung bereits potentiell impliziert, auf etwas Konkretes, "die Frau", reduziert. Der entscheidende Punkt in der Argumentation liegt in der Beziehung des sprechenden Subjekts und seiner Aussage. Sie trifft eine Setzung, und zwar grammatikalisch die einer hierarchischen Struktur von Subjekt und Prädikat und logisch die einer chronologischen Kausalität. Ein Phänomen wird auf einen Ursprung zurückgeführt. Solcher Text kann als ein selbständiges rationales Konstrukt von seinem Sprecher abgetrennt werden. Die chiastische Umkehrung des Satzes "Die Frau ist weiblich" aber würde in einer Verschiebung bestehen: "Das Weibliche ist komplex." In dieser sprachphilosophischen Interpretation eignet der Stilfigur des Chiasmus damit die Eigenschaft, der die poststrukturalistische Sprachtheorie hinsichtlich der Sprache/der Schrift im ganzen auf die Spur zu kommen sucht: den Prozeß der Bedeutungsgebung in seiner vielfachen Bedingtheit und Potentialität zu beschreiben. Die Dynamik der sprachlichen Symbolisierung freizulegen schließt ein, das sprechende Subjekt in seiner Aussage wiederzufinden, die nichtsymbolischen, d.h. psychischen, unbewußten, körperlichen Elemente der Sprache/Schrift einschließlich ihrer phonetischen Materialität im Akt des Sprechens mitzuteilen.

Damit scheinen in Hinblick auf Kerschbaumers Text eine ganze Reihe von Entsprechungen auf, die der Klärung bedürfen. Kerschbaumer formuliert nicht nur im Text die Veränderung der Erzählung durch das Einbringen des Sprechenden als ein Postulat, sondern sie realisiert es im Gestus ihres Schreibens—oder auch: Sprechens. In ihrem Interview hat sie auf den Charakter ihrer Prosa als Sprechtexte ausdrücklich hingewiesen. Die Bedeutung des/der Erzählenden, der/die als Instanz oder Figur immer wieder präsent ist, wird somit zusätzlich durch die Stimme unterstrichen, die im Vortrag das stark Rhythmische dieser Texte zur Geltung bringt. Gleichzeitig haben die Porträts die Struktur des Erinnerns, das gerade nicht auf faktisch Verfügbarem beruht. Vielmehr sucht es Spuren von Ereignissen in der Psyche, in Emotionen, in im Unbewußten gespeicherten Bildern auf, die zu einem Gegentext zusammengefügt werden.

Der Argumentation zum Chiastischen weiter folgend, erkennt man in der Umkehrung der Logik des Symbolischen—"das Wien nach unserem Tode/nach unserem Leben"—die Frage nach dem "Anderen" als dem Nicht-Eindeutigen, der Differenzierung in die Komplexität des Potentiellen. Im gegenständlichen Sinn des Kerschbaumerschen Textes bedeutet dies, die zur Vernichtung bestimmten Frauen dem Leben zurückzugeben. Gesucht wird der andere Text der Geschichte. Im semiotischen

Verständnis heißt das, dem männlich-symbolischen Text in der Literatur einen weiblich-poetischen entgegenzusetzen.

Damit bin ich bei einer problematischen, aber unverzichtbaren Gender-Charakteristik des Sprachlichen angelangt, die in den psychoanalytisch fundierten Texttheorien entwickelt worden ist und darunter Positionen innerhalb des Symbolischen versteht. Das Problematische besteht in der durch die Begriffe intendierten potentiellen Identifizierung mit sozial und/oder sexuell konnotierten konkreten Termini von "männlich" und "weiblich". Die Begrifflichkeit rührt in der Tat aus der Kulturgeschichte, aus der sie in die Textsemiotik eingegangen ist, ohne daß beide Deutungsmuster ineinander aufgehen.

Aus zwei Gründen greife ich dennoch darauf zurück. Kerschbaumer, die nach eigener Auskunft in ihrem Interview die feministisch-poststrukturalistischen Theorien nicht rezipiert hat, verfolgt dennoch deren Intention. Sie besetzt im *Schwimmer* und im *Weiblichen Namen des Widerstands* das semiotische Gender-Raster mit konkreten Geschlechtertypologien. In diesen poetischen Ausführungen verfährt sie damit analog den Texttheoretikern, die mit mythologischen Beispielen arbeiten und darin die Beziehung männlicher und weiblicher Figuren als Fallbeispiele interpretieren. Einen solchen paradigmatischen Mythos greift Kerschbaumer selbst auf—den Mythos von Orpheus und Euridike. Für seinen hier interessierenden Kern—der Sänger Orpheus will seine Geliebte Euridike aus dem Totenreich zurückholen, was ihm potentiell gewährt wird unter der Bedingung, sich nicht umzuschauen; er erfüllt die Bedingung nicht und kann am Ende nur schmerzvoll ein letztes Mal ihren Namen rufen—, hat Hélène Cixous in einem frühen Text eine treffende Interpretation anhand des 13. Rilkeschen Sonnettes an Orpheus geliefert:

> …ich werde die Struktur Orpheus-Euridike als Metapher für das poetische Vorgehen lesen, um über die Stellungen der beiden Körper die symbolischen Stellungen zu befragen: da ist eine Frau hinter dem Rücken eines Mannes, der singend aufsteigt (Cixous 59).

Die Lesart ergibt die Produktion der Schrift auf dem verdrängten Weiblichen, das über die Nennung des Namens—Euridike—als abwesend gekennzeichnet und fixiert wird. Es wird in der Schrift getötet und "konserviert"—Kerschbaumers Metapher von der Grabtafel trifft zu. Das Nennen des Namens bedeutet die Chiffre für die abwesend bleibende Frau, ihr Tod umgekehrt die Bedingung für den Gesang—die endlose Variation auf den Namen Euridike. Die so produzierte Poesie ist, in Cixous' Terminologie, identisch mit dem männlich-symbolischen Text. Eine sozialgeschichtlich fundierte semiotische Auslegung dieser mythischen Konfiguration Orpheus-Euridike als einer Beziehung von Kunst, Macht und Geschlechterhierarchie kann man auf 1200 Seiten in Klaus Theweleits *Orpheus und Euridike* nachlesen. Kerschbaumer formuliert sie, in gleichem Verständnis, im *Schwimmer*. In der von Cixous beschriebenen Körperkonstellation durchzieht die Figuration "Orfeo und Rike ein Paar" (*Schwimmer* 34) den gesamten Roman. Dafür kann eines unter mehreren Textbeispielen zitiert werden, das gerade nur die Konstellation nachvollzieht, ohne die Namen zu erwähnen:

> ...wenn das die Sonne ist habe ich meine Richtung verfehlt ich habe mich nicht umgedreht obwohl die Frau mich ansah obwohl das das Wichtigste ist ein solcher Blick aber ich bleib nicht stehn noch weniger drehte ich mich um wenn du plötzlich vor dem Fenster der Straßenbahn ein bekanntes Gesicht siehst was tust du steigst du aus und beginnst ein neues Leben nein du bist keine Station du bist eine Kraft wenn du die Stufen hinaufeilst und oben steht einer in der Tür und winkt oder du gehst denselben Weg aber langsamer zurück und wieder steht einer in der Tür und winkt läufst du zurück in der Zeit hinunter geht man mit anderen Schritten als hinauf das ist bekannt... (*Schwimmer* 9).

Die Figurenkonstellation "Orfeo"—die italienische Form von Orpheus—und "Rike" ist bei Kerschbaumer, anders als in der Eindeutigkeit Cixous', in ihrer Vielfalt kaum auszumachen. Für Orfeo, den "kontextbeladenen Typ" (*Schwimmer* 86) lassen sich vielleicht drei Grundversionen ausmachen. Er repräsentiert einmal den Dichter, der mit den Herrschenden paktiert und als Voyeur, "die Hände in den Taschen", das Elend der Welt beschaut und besingt. Dagegen steht Orfeo als Stimme der Unterdrückten—zitiert wird Victor Jara, der ermordete chilenische Sänger, dem die Hände abgehackt wurden: "und doch bedeutet Victor Sieg" (51), und gleich darauf "Orfeo der Arbeiter mit den schwieligen Händen, die kein Instrument spielen lernten" (58). Dann wieder ist er der tanzende Dichter auf dem Mondstrahl, der "die Richtung" gibt. Die räumlichen Koordinaten, bei Cixous klar fixiert in der Konstellation "da ist eine Frau hinter dem Rücken eines Mannes, der singend aufsteigt", weichen bei Kerschbaumer der unbestimmten Richtung des Mondstrahls, der allerdings symbolisch weiblich konnotiert ist. Doch wie die Figuration unterschiedlich bewertet wird, so fließen selbst die Geschlechtergrenzen: "Orfeo diese weibliche Variante des längst in die Literatur eingegangenen Unaussprechlichen" (*Schwimmer* 120).

Wenn *Der Schwimmer* in den Strukturen der Sprache nach der Position des Dichters fragt, der mittels der Sprache nicht mit ihren Symbolisierungen kollaboriert, so wird sie im *Weiblichen Namen des Widerstands* faßbarer. Das in der letzten Sequenz der Orfeo-Euridike-Konstellation angesprochene Chiastische—"...läufst du zurück in der Zeit hinunter geht man mit anderen Schritten als hinauf"—kann als poetisches Verfahren Kerschbaumers hier konkretisiert werden. Es muß einen anderen Text ergeben als den in der "Wirklichkeit" der Historie fixierten:

Alle Wege führen plötzlich nach Minsk, sagt Helene. Aber in Wirklichkeit weiß sie gar nicht, daß es nach Minsk geht, daß es nach Theresienstadt geht. In Wirklichkeit wird eine alte Frau einfach verschleppt, natürlich geht sie freiwillig, hat freiwillig dieser Aufforderung Folge geleistet (*Widerstand* 35).

Beides, geschichtlicher Text und poetischer Gegentext, bilden die Struktur der Porträts im *Weiblichen Namen des Widerstands*—als chiastische Umkehrung der Grabtafeln in einem offenen Entwurf weiblicher Biographien. Das ist meine These zur poetischen Struktur dieses Buches.

Für Kerschbaumer bedeutet dies nicht die Realisierung eines Programms "Weibliches Schreiben", sondern schlicht die Produktion von "Poesie pure" als engagierter Literatur. Ihr Selbstverständnis als Dichterin rührt aus der Verweigerung des immer wieder konstruierten Gegensatzes von Politik und Literatur. Bei ihrem Thema von weiblichen Opfern und weiblichem Widerstand im Nationalsozialismus läßt sie sich gerade deshalb nicht auf ein realistisches Schreibkonzept ein, weil es die ideologische Intention, die Opfer zu ehren, in ihr Gegenteil verkehren würde. "Auf die Opfer darf sich keiner berufen...", hatte Ingeborg Bachmann formuliert. Der Kontext des kurzen Fragments dieses Titels begründet den Satz damit, daß die Berufung auf die Opfer sich aus jenen fatalen Sinnstiftungen ergibt, die der Selbstverständlichkeit des Lebens eine tiefere Bedeutung zu geben bestrebt sind. Erst dies legitimiert die Opfer mit der Weihe des Transzendentalen als einer "Wahrheit", der sich Bachmann verweigert.

Diese Argumentation geht, bei Bachmann und bei Kerschbaumer, über direkt artikulierte feministische Interessen hinaus, und doch hat sich Kerschbaumer dazu bekannt. Auf ihr Verhältnis zur Frauenbewegung befragt, äußerte sie: "...mich interessiert Literatur, und die wollte ich für die Frauen schreiben, aber doch nicht einzig über Hausfrauenschmerzen" (Vansant 111). In der Einleitung zu ihrer Essaysammlung *Für mich hat Lesen etwas mit Fließen zu tun* (1989) spricht sie sich noch deutlicher aus. Sie erklärt, daß sie ohne die Kenntnis grundlegender Bücher des Feminismus aus der frühen, unmittelbar politischen Phase—sie nennt Simone de Beauvoir, Kate Millett, Phyllis Chesler—ihre Vorlesungen über Linguistics and Poetics so nicht hätte halten können. Die Aussage verblüfft, weil es in diesen schulmäßig den Strukturalismus abhandelnden Vorträgen keinen einzigen Hinweis auf geschlechterspezifische Funktionsweise oder auch nur geschlechterspezifischen Gebrauch von Sprache und Literatur gibt. Die Irritation klärt sich auf bei der Lektüre ihrer Interpretation von Jakobson selbst. Immer wieder betont sie das von ihm herausgestellte soziale Moment in der Semiotik der Sprache einschließlich der poetischen. Die Sprache steht nicht neben der politischen, sozialen, ideologischen Wirklichkeit, sondern sie ist selbst soziale Realität. Sie ist nicht Form einer "eigentlichen" Wahrheit des Lebens, sondern deren Repräsentation selbst. Die kulturelle Symbolik der Geschlechter, kann man schlußfolgern, ist ihrer Struktur eingeschrieben. Im Vertrauen auf die allgemein formulierte Einsicht hat Kerschbaumer im Gespräch einmal bekannt, die Auseinandersetzung mit dem sprachwissenschaftlichen Strukturalismus habe sie politisiert. Darauf hat sie ihr schriftstellerisches Werk gegründet. Neben Gedichtbänden und einem Schauspiel sind vor allem ihre fünf hochpoetischen Prosawerke zu nennen: nach dem *Schwimmer* und dem *Weiblichen Namen des Widerstands* die Romane *Die Schwestern, Versuchung* und *Die Fremde*.

Für den *Weiblichen Namen des Widerstands* fasse ich zusammen:

Erstens: Kerschbaumers Porträtsammlung steht im Kontext der von der Frauenbewegung inspirierten, seit den achtziger Jahren in den deutschsprachigen Ländern veröffentlichten Dokumentarliteratur über weiblichen Widerstand gegen den Faschismus. Sie teilt deren Intention, eine verschwiegene und verdrängte Seite der neueren Geschichte aufzuarbeiten, und überschreitet gleichzeitig deren formelle Möglichkeiten, indem sie die Textsorte Dokument aus einer sprachphilosophischen bzw. poetologischen Perspektive problematisiert. In seinem Authentizitätsanspruch als "Zeugnis" behandelt sie das Dokument als ein Element des Symbolischen. Das bedeutet, daß es die Präsentation des Nichtsymbolischen explizit ausgrenzt. In einem textsemiotischen Verständnis des Begriffs kann dieses als "Weibliches" verstanden werden, das, metaphorisch, als Opfer zu Grabe getragen und in Grabtafeln textlich manifestiert wird.

Zweitens: Dieses semiotische Textverständnis besetzt Kerschbaumer mit dem konkreten historischen Tatbestand der massenhaften Tötung von Frauen durch die Faschisten. Der Widerstand gegen diese Gewalt ist bei ihr sowohl Thema als auch Schreibprinzip—letzteres, indem *Der weibliche Name des Widerstands* in seiner poetischen Realisierung den Text des Symbolischen aufbricht. Semantisch bedeutet das, gegen den Status der Opfer als notwendige, inhärente Sinngebung der Geschichte der Sieger anzuschreiben. Kerschbaumer dekonstruiert insbesondere den Geschichts- bzw. Zeitbegriff der patriarchalischen abendländischen Kultur und seine adäquate Struktur der "großen Narration".

Drittens: Dazu gehört die Dekonstruktion des Erzählers als ein integres Subjekt außerhalb seines Textes—bei Kerschbaumer in das Bild des Reporters, der vorgeblich objektive Tatsachen berichtet, gefaßt. Der/die Erzählende in ihrem Buch bringt sich in den Text ein und so seine Potentialität zum Sprechen. Im texttheoretischen Sinn heißt das, die manifeste Struktur des Symbolischen zu unterlaufen.

Viertens: Auf semantischer Ebene entsteht damit ein Text, der sich mit dem Opfer der Frauen als Tribut an die Geschichte nicht abfindet, sondern sie als lebendige Menschen auferstehen läßt. Ihrer soll nicht einfach auf Grabtafeln gedacht werden, vielmehr intendiert Kerschbaumers poetische Schreibweise des Fragmentierens, Erinnerns, Entwerfens, die "andere" Geschichte schlechthin. Gleichzeitig überschreiten die Porträts in ihrer ausgestellten Potentialität und Fiktionalität das herkömmliche Verständnis der möglichst authentischen Wiedergabe eines fremden Lebens.

Fünftens: Dem historischen Gegenstand des weiblichen Widerstands gegen den Faschismus und seiner poetischen Umsetzung, die sich in geschlechtertypologischen texttheoretischen Kategorien beschreiben läßt, korrespondiert eine mythologische Besetzung des poetischen Verfahrens in der Mythe von Orpheus und Euridike. Die Interpretation beinhaltet die Auffassung des symbolischen Textes als Prozeß der Tötung des Weiblichen. Im gleichen Sinn wie Cixous und Theweleit verwendet Kerschbaumer die Mythe als semiotische Figur von Macht, Sprache/Kunst und Geschlechterbeziehungen zum ersten Mal in ihrem Roman *Der Schwimmer*. Im Anschluß an Eva Meyer habe ich diese Figur als Chiasmus gelesen und als Grundstruktur in der Poetik des *Weiblichen Namen des Widerstands* aufgefaßt: die Zweiteilung der Porträts in dokumentarische Grabtafeln und fiktive Erzählungen kann als chiastische Umkehrung des symbolischen Textes verstanden werden. Der "weibliche Widerstand" wird darin semantisch und poetologisch eingelöst.

## Zitierte Literatur

Bachmann, Ingeborg. *Werke*. Ed. Christine Koschel, Inge von Weidenbaum, and Clemens Münster. 4 vols. München: Piper, 1978. Vol. 4.

Berger, Karin, Elisabeth Holzinger, Lotte Podgornik, and Lisbeth N. Trallori, eds. *Der Himmel ist blau. Kann sein: Frauen im Widerstand Österreich 1938–1945*. Wien: Promedia, 1985.

Cixous, Hélène. "Wer singt? Wer veranlaßt zu singen?" *Weiblichkeit in der Schrift*. Berlin: Merve, 1980.

Engels, Friedrich. *Dialektik der Natur*. Berlin: Dietz, 1973.

Fürstenberg, Doris. *Jeden Moment war dieser Tod: Interviews mit jüdischen Frauen, die Auschwitz überlebten*. Düsseldorf: Schwann, 1986.

Jacobeit, Sigrid, and Lieselotte Thoms-Heinrich. *Kreuzweg Ravensbrück: Lebensbilder antifaschistischer Widerstandskämpferinnen*. Leipzig: Verlag für die Frau, 1987.

Kerschbaumer, Marie-Thérèse. *Die Fremde*. Klagenfurt: Wieser, 1992.

———. *Für mich hat Lesen etwas mit Fließen zu tun: Gedanken zum Lesen und Schreiben*. Wien: Wiener Frauenverlag, 1989.

———. *Schwestern: Roman*. Olten: Walter, 1982.

———. *Der Schwimmer: Roman*. Salzburg: Winter, 1976.

———. *Versuchung: Roman*. Berlin: Aufbau, 1990.

———. *Der weibliche Name des Widerstands: Sieben Berichte*. Olten: Walter, 1980; hier zitiert nach: Berlin: Aufbau, 1986.

Kristeva, Julia. *Die Chinesin: Die Rolle der Frau in China*. Frankfurt a.M.: Ullstein, 1976.

Meyer, Eva. *Zählen und Erzählen: Für eine Semiotik des Weiblichen*. Wien: Medusa, 1983.

Strobl, Ingrid. *Sag nie, du gehst den letzten Weg: Frauen im bewaffneten Widerstand gegen Faschismus und deutsche Besatzung*. Frankfurt a.M.: Fischer, 1989.

Theweleit, Klaus. *Orpheus & Euridike*. Basel: Stroemfeld/Roter Stern, 1990.

Vansant, Jacqueline. "Interview mit Marie-Thérèse Kerschbaumer." *Modern Austrian Literature* 22.1 (1989): 107–20.

# Lesbian Life and Literature: A Survey of Recent German-Language Publications

Miriam Frank

The article discusses similarities and differences of Lesbian/Gay politics and culture in German-speaking countries and in the USA and surveys recent non-fiction German-language publications, documenting widespread cultural borrowing and a keen interest in historical research. A new genre, the "merged anthology," juxtaposes the pioneering work of non-German writers/activists in translation with original German contributions on related themes. Recent scholarly works provide a historical survey of Lesbian literature and document the existence of Lesbian subcultures in the GDR, in Switzerland in the 1930s and 1940s, and in Germany during the Third Reich. Analysis of the specifically German situation demonstrates the intrinsic connection between homophobia, racism, and institutionalized violence by the State. (JC)

## I. Lesbian Politics, Lesbian Discourse

Throughout the world, the movement for Lesbian/Gay liberation has transformed how we think of sexuality, difference, and political change. In 1994, massive demonstrations celebrated the twenty-fifth anniversary of the New York City Stonewall rebellion, while a clause protecting civil rights regardless of sexual orientation became a part of the new national constitution of the Republic of South Africa. Homosexual marriage is a reality in Norway, while in the USA numerous municipalities and corporations provide employment benefits for homosexual domestic partners.

Gay/Lesbian politics and culture have a long history in Germany as elsewhere; the heyday of the homosexual movement in the Weimar Republic, for example, has been well documented.[1] Limited though it was, that era's tolerance for Lesbian/Gay lifestyles was a serious threat to the sexual politics of National Socialism. Despite intense policy debates and some resistance, Nazi repression effectively destroyed the integrity of Gay/Lesbian communities. In the post-war period, Gay/Lesbian activism re-emerged slowly. It was the world-wide feminist movement as well as the watershed of the USA Stonewall Rebellion that pushed Gay/Lesbian legal issues and cultural change into public prominence, both in the FRG and GDR.

Now, in the 1990s, Germany's unification has had a powerful impact on the evolution of its Lesbian and Gay communities. Between the old FRG and GDR there had been substantial differences in Gay/Lesbian lifestyles and official policies. Changes in the laws and cultural climate affect the everyday lives of all German Lesbians and Gay men—minimally ten percent of Germany's people. How then are Germans reconciling their history, their personal issues, their laws, and their lifestyles with the problems and possibilities of the new society?

A brief review of the names of movement organizations and community institutions in the USA shows that the political agendas of Lesbians and Gay men are often joined. In the 1990s younger activists have proudly revived and reclaimed the old pejorative "Queer," a term that refers to both men and women. Their defiant, coalition-driven discourse reflects political pressures and successes that have emerged here since Stonewall—most importantly in recent years the devastation wreaked on our communities by the AIDS epidemic, paralleled by substantial civil reforms.

In Germany neither the Lesbian/Gay nor the Queer discourse is so significant. Men are *schwul* and women are *lesbisch,* and political agendas and cultural activities are located, for the most part, in separate spheres.[2] While Lesbians are sometimes concerned with issues such as civil rights that also affect Gay men, Lesbian activists firmly accept Lesbian-feminism as the most appropriate and viable contemporary theory. The Gay male culture is rarely self-critical of how it habitually ignores female participation, while the feminist community has focused on nurturing its Lesbian denizens.[3] To that end, much Lesbian discourse in Germany is emphatically feminist in political tone and subject.

Because feminism is so essential to the thriving of Lesbian culture and community in Germany, the year 1994, so important in Lesbian and Gay world history, should also be understood as an important year for the German feminist community. In 1994 two important German feminist publishing enterprises celebrated their twentieth anniversaries: Munich's Frauenoffensive and Berlin's Orlanda Frauenverlag (née Sub Rosa, née Frauenselbstverlag). Since 1974 both of these institutions have integrated Lesbian-feminist topics and consciousness into their programs. Indeed, the topics of three Orlanda anthologies to be discussed below—one on motherhood, another on psychology and sexuality, and a third on domestic violence—all have their origins in feminist discourse.

In the 1990s, German Lesbian writers who are not adapting themes that have originated with the women's movement turn most eagerly to history. Feminist history and the Lesbian exploration of heritage are certainly firmly bound to one another; however, the discussion of Lesbian difference has demanded that writers who are reflecting on tradition look more closely at the larger topic of homosexuality. Thus Germany's Gay males—*die Schwulen*—and the communities they have created with or without Lesbian participation have become a part of the Lesbian historical discourse. The results vary as the freedom of *Schwulen* and *Lesben* to find and be of support to one another has changed over the decades. The Lesbian-feminist analysis certainly informs the record of cooperation and tensions between Lesbian and Gay historical subjects, but without feminism, the record of Lesbian participation in history would be meager indeed.[4]

In the five original monographs discussed in this essay, history is a major concern. Madeleine Marti's *Hinterlegte Botschaften: Die Darstellung lesbischer Frauen in der deutschsprachigen Literatur seit 1945* is structured as a historical review of themes, authors, and literary politics. Ursula Sillge's *Un-Sichtbare Frauen: Lesben und ihre Emanzipation in der DDR* contains fifty pages of documents relating to the eleven-year struggle of Lesbians to organize as an officially recognized social entity in the former GDR. Ilse Kokula and Ulrike Böhmer write about Lesbian organizing and culture in the German-speaking regions of Switzerland in the 1930s in *Die Welt gehört uns doch! Zusammenschluß lesbischer Frauen in der Schweiz in der 30er Jahre*. Finally, both of Claudia Schoppmann's books, *Nationalsozialistische Sexualpolitik und weibliche Homosexualität* and *Zeit der Maskierung: Lebensgeschichten lesbischer Frauen im "Dritten Reich"* are concerned with the history of Lesbians under National Socialism.

While German Lesbian heritage is a subject that has long interested Lesbian researchers—German and non-German scholars alike[5]—the methods, passions, and resources marshalled by each of the German language writers discussed here highlight the personal stake each has in the exploration of themes. Marti writes about literature from the vantage point of her scholarly expertise as well as from her personal familiarity with the Lesbian literary scene. Sillge has been a tireless activist in the East Berlin Lesbian community. Kokula has dedicated at least fifteen years of intense work in the Lesbian community to the rescue of Lesbian history through collecting and publishing interviews and other documents.[6] The forward to her Swiss Lesbian history, coauthored with the Swiss historian Ulrike Böhmer, tells a story of dogged fundraising and the difficult road to achieving special access to rare archival materials.

Both of Schoppmann's two volumes study the same historical phase but from very different vantage points: in one book, Schoppman develops a scholarly foundation and in the other she gives voice to individual historical participants. *Nationalsozialistische Sexualpolitik* is a traditional university dissertation on the history of Lesbians in the Third Reich, while *Zeit der Maskierung* gathers the voices of the witnesses and survivors of that history. Indeed, all the writers considered here are consciously reporting and rescuing traditions that are their own. Each takes advantage of her own insights as a participant in the Lesbian scene today to sharpen her use of historical documents, novels, and interviews.

## II. Literary Production and Translation

Like much of the German reading public, German-speaking readers of books by or about Lesbian life form an enthusiastic market for translated texts. Imported from countries with thriving Lesbian cultures and communities (e.g., Denmark, the Netherlands, the UK, the USA), translated publications form a powerful intellectual base for the literary life of Germany's Lesbian communities. Offerings from establishment publishers range from Djuna Barnes's classic 1936 American expatriate novel *Nightwood* (*Nachtgewächs*) to Danish anthropologist Karin Lützen's 1986 review of European/American Lesbian lifestyles and history *Hvad Hjertet Begaerer* (*Frauen Lieben Frauen*).

But more important than the mainstream publishers have been the alternative presses, especially feminist publishing houses. For over twenty years, they have been central in creating and maintaining an international list of accessible Lesbian texts. Their editorial independence has enabled the development of strong political programs implicit in their translation choices. For example, in the mid-1970s, Tomyrisverlag published the separatist *Clit Manifesto* (*Rufe alle Lesben, bitte kommen!*), while in the past decade writings by Audre Lorde such as the *Cancer Journals* (*Auf Leben und Tod*) and a collection of poems and essays (*Lichtflut*) were featured in the anti-racist program of Orlanda Frauenverlag.

Rowohlt may boast multiple printings of the translation of a popular Lesbian novel like Rita Mae Brown's *Rubyfruit Jungle* (*Rubinroter Dschungel*), but there are several other Lesbian titles that would never have been translated were it not for feminist publishers. Nevertheless, while the promotion and distribution networks of feminist publishers have necessarily become more sophisticated in the 1990s, many Lesbian titles from the independent houses—both translated and original German—are still hard to come by. Finances have become tighter, and many of the smaller alternative presses find they cannot match the money offered to authors by mass houses nor, with alternative bookstores failing, reach a wider German reading audience. Still, translations provide some financial security for alternative publishers. Titles that have proven themselves in the authors' home countries are often more successful than many original German texts.

There is a long tradition of feminist internationalism implicit in the presence of so many translations on the German Lesbian reading list.

German readers often appropriate such literature as their own, freely incorporating feminist research, terminology, and insights (not to mention heroines and anniversaries) from half a dozen countries and languages into their own texts and ideas.[7] The themes and concerns of the discourse are thus distinctly cosmopolitan, and even if the voices are not originally German, only *GermanistInnen* seeking specifically German texts might find it disturbing that so many reading sources began in another language.

Still, there is another issue implicit in the popularity of translations, and that is the short supply of German language literary fiction by or about Lesbians. Does the easy availability of Lesbian novels in translation stifle the production of homegrown fiction? The popularity of Orlanda Frauenverlag's USA, British, Canadian, and Dutch Lesbian detective novels indicates some readership for fiction. However, excluding reprints (Ilse Frapan's 1899 *Wir Frauen Haben Kein Vaterland,* reprinted in 1983, and Christa Winsloe's 1930 *Mädchen in Uniform,* reprinted in 1983) the catalogue of Madeleine Marti's *Hinterlegte Botschaften* lists only sixteen German-language novels published between 1980 and 1991 with a Lesbian central theme or central figure. Short stories and life story narratives (biography, autobiography, protocol collections) are slightly better represented. Given publishing house programs (both mainstream and alternative) and the tastes of the reading public for nonfiction, few writers have committed themselves to the fictional representation of Lesbian experience.

Certainly the strengthening of German Lesbian communities and the development of Lesbian literary clubs, writing circles, journals, and prizes[8] will enable more Lesbian novels to be created from the "real life" situations that are so well depicted in documentary literature. Still, new ventures are not very secure. A writer with any reputation is not tempted by an enterprise that may publish a few titles and then disappear (like the short-lived Lesbenverlag Ätna), even if the center of its program is original German Lesbian fiction and drama. The easy availability of translated fiction probably has some effect on the readers' tastes and on authors' willingness to attempt novels. But ultimately a stronger German Lesbian literary infrastructure—the book reviews, the longevity of publishing ventures, the successful merchandising venues—is what is needed to support new authors and their efforts.

III. Three Merged Anthologies

Three recent non-fiction Lesbian anthologies from Orlanda provide an interesting challenge to the traditional publication of translated works. Uli Streib's 1991 *Von nun an nannten sie sich Mütter: Lesben und Kinder,* JoAnn Loulan, Margaret Nichols, and Monica Streit's 1992 *Lesben Liebe Leidenschaft: Texte zur feministischen Psychologie,* and Constance Ohms's 1993 *Mehr als das Herz gebrochen: Gewalt in lesbischen*

*Beziehungen,* all probe lifestyles and problems in Lesbian communities. In each of these collections the pioneering work of non-German writer/activists is not only translated but is also newly contextualized with original German texts on related topics. I call this form a "merged anthology." It is rarely attempted by publishers who specialize in translation because it adds expenses to the translators' fees—the commissioning of new articles by German language authors. However, it is a valuable strategy because it establishes an explicit relationship between the original country's culture and the situation in Germany.

*Von nun an nannten sie sich Mütter,* the earliest of these merged anthologies, is the broadest in scope. The discourse on Lesbian motherhood joins German, American, French, British, Danish, Turkish, Canadian, and Dutch voices in letters, poetry, literary criticism, personal testimony, reports, and argumentative essays. The German authors are especially strongly represented in the debates presented by Uli Streib, Christiane Quadflieg, and Cornelia Burgert, which problematize Lesbian motherhood as a choice (19–42, 55–70).[9] There is also a useful review by Gisela Leppers of German law regarding child custody and the absence of a father/husband ("illegitimacy") (200–14). Hilde Heringer has contributed a sketch about foster mothering (192–97) and "Aki Berg" (a pseudonym) writes a touching sketch about the failure of a co-mothering relationship (178–82).

*Lesben Liebe Leidenschaft* makes available to German readers the work of two American streams of Lesbian psychology and psychotherapy. Articles by JoAnn Loulan of San Francisco and members of the Boston Lesbian Psychology Collective explore common psychotherapeutic issues such as sexual passions, internalized homophobia, alcoholism, eating disorders, and the consequences of sexual abuse. This volume contains only four contributions by German writers, and while they are substantial, they are not as well synthesized into the overall plan of the anthology as we saw in *Von nun an nannten sie sich Mütter.* Nevertheless, both of the essays by Monica Streit, on Lesbian merging ("Symbiotische Beziehungen") (10–32) and on Lesbian autonomy and singlehood (316–32), provide practical directions for the therapeutic setting and are compatible with other theoretical viewpoints in the volume.

The American writers in *Lesben Liebe Leidenschaft* are all rather sanguine about the liberating potential of Lesbian psychotherapy. Yet even when the practitioner is a Lesbian, psychotherapy can fail because there are so many specific differences among women that are not necessarily anchored in sexual identity. Two German writers raise such criticisms of therapeutic practice. Ika Hügel demonstrates in a short collection of personal statements how Black Lesbians have suffered from the racist assumptions of their Lesbian therapists (298–307), and Ahima Beerlage reports on the overall discrimination against chronically ill women prevalent in the Lesbian community. Her decision to work with a heterosexual feminist practitioner was based on that therapist's sensitivity to her condition rather than on similarities in the two women's identities (308-15).

*Mehr als das Herz gebrochen* probes intensively a previously well-kept secret of the Lesbian community: partner violence in relationships. This anthology includes translations from important American writers on the topic, e.g., Barbara Hart's influential 1986 essay "Lesbian Battering," but it is predominantly a German-language publication, with the editor, Constance Ohms, also the chief author.[10]

In two essays at the beginning of the book, Ohms, herself a survivor of a battering relationship, develops theory and definitions of Lesbian violence, including issues of racism both in her analysis and in the interviews with other Lesbians that follow. Ohms's inclusion of S/M sex in her definitions of violence and abuse is echoed by translated writers throughout the anthology (26-27). She later briefly studies the psychological aspects of sexual abuse and revictimization, the tendency of battered women to return to battering relationships (131-36). Her passionately thorough essay on ending the violence integrates psychological profiles of victims and abusers with ethical challenges. She argues that battered women's shelters must be willing to act responsibly when Lesbians seeking help present themselves (146-49), and she also sees anti-racism work among Lesbians as an essential step towards strengthening and widening communities' existing support networks (150).

*Mehr als das Herz gebrochen* concludes with three pithy and practical articles. Ohms's review of the legal parameters affecting cases of Lesbian domestic violence includes information on lodging a criminal or private complaint (173-80). Vera Schwenk's discussion on crisis intervention suggests how psychotherapists should handle such cases and outlines how health insurance regulations limit resources available to Lesbians seeking counseling referrals (160-72). The final translated article by Sunny Graff concerns self-defense training for abused Lesbians and is an especially interesting merging of German and American influences. Along with pragmatic advice on how to handle escalating confrontations, there is also encouragement and support to overcome victimization synthesized with legal information culled from Graff's knowledge of German statutes (183-92).[11]

## IV. Recent German-Language Works on Lesbian Life and Literature

Cultural borrowing is rampant in the German Lesbian book world, but as mentioned earlier, Lesbian historical consciousness has been the important theme of several original contributions. Madeleine Marti's survey of Lesbian literature, *Hinterlegte Botschaften: Die Darstellung lesbischer Frauen in der deutschsprachigen Literatur seit 1945*, is a well-researched, sharply argued, and intellectually useful doctoral dissertation that reviews how Lesbian themes, characters, and authors have developed in German literature over a period of forty-five years. For its historical survey, literary analysis, and bibliography alone *Hinterlegte Botschaften* is an invaluable aid to all scholars of contemporary German women's literature. But Marti does more than that; she powerfully advances the discourse on Lesbian culture with a feminist vision evident in all her many discussions of the women's movement, Lesbian life, and the wider world of German literature.

As a traditional dissertation, *Hinterlegte Botschaften* moves through the decades with descriptions in each chapter of the social context of Lesbian life accompanied by reviews of literary representation and production. Each decade is then completed by a lengthy discussion of an exemplary author and her texts, for example, Marlen Haushofer's *Eine Handvoll Leben* for the 1950s, Johanna Moosdorf's *Die Freundinnen* for the 1970s. As the decades roll, the expansion of locations, personalities, plot variations, and characterizations, both of authors and their fictional characters, indicates the growing openness of the Lesbian subculture in German-speaking societies.

A more clarified Lesbian literary discourse is central to Marti's purpose. Academic categories are enriched by her highlighting the emergence of a more open Lesbian presence in society as a whole, while the panorama of a Lesbian literary tradition provides fresh perspectives on classic themes. For example, she reads Haushofer's depiction of a Lesbian suicide both as a psychologically meaningful moment and as a plot element common in earlier German Lesbian novels (58–59). Then, in the following 1960s chapter, the inevitable Ingeborg Bachmann story "Ein Schritt Nach Gomorrha" prompts her to a thematic comparison on the possibility of open Lesbian relationships in Bachmann and Haushofer (107–09).

In defining a German Lesbian literary continuum Marti goes beyond the academic project. The discussions of literary production, informed by Marti's access to authors' correspondence files, are especially rich. Her investigation of the politics of the mainstream publishing houses reveals the suppression of Lesbian themes. Suhrkamp, for example, long championed "classical" Gay male authors in translation such as Marcel Proust and Oscar Wilde, but Barnes's *Nachtgewächs* was their only Lesbian title. A proposed volume on Lesbian life never saw print in Suhrkamp's social outsiders series because not enough "authentic reports" were available. A novel and a story collection by Johanna Moosdorf were published by Suhrkamp in the early 1960s, but her overtly Lesbian *Die Freundinnen* was rejected in 1969 by Siegfried Unseld because the house had already published Lesbian novels; as "proof" he named Barnes's *Nachtgewächs* and Bachmann's *Malina* (!) (114–16). Luchterhand's treatment of their author Marlene Stenten was not much different. Her *Puppe Else* received good in-house reviews, but was ultimately rejected. Later at Suhrkamp, Hans Magnus Enzensberger read Stenten's manuscript and recommended self-publication (118–19).

It is fascinating to see what then happened to Lesbian novels rejected by the mainstream companies. When they have been published, either by smaller experimental houses, women's presses, or through self-publication, they have often been quite successful. Factoring in the problems that these independent venues have—accessibility of reviewers, bookstore distribution, and advertising—it is quite surprising to see a publication figure of 5,000 for Stenten's 1977 self-published novel.[12] In the 1980s the S. Fischer *Frauenreihe* began to publish Lesbian fiction and took over some of the more successful independently published titles. A ready market responded. In 1990 *Puppe Else* had sold 13,000 copies (Marti 120).

The special topics in Marti's survey—a lengthy review of the life and work of Christa Reinig, a chapter on the historical development of Swiss Lesbian literature with a focus on authors of the 1970s—provide valuable information. The *schwul/lesbisch* dialectic is thematic in Marti's discussions of discrimination in the publishing industry. Her criticisms of Gay male involvement in perpetuating Lesbian invisibility are also explicitly sharp when directed at her fellow Germanists: "Selbst in wissenschaftlichen Studien werden *lesbische Frauen* als Unterkategorie zur Oberkategorie *schwule Männer* subsumiert" (28–29).

In the excellent chapter on GDR Lesbian life and literary themes there is an especially intriguing analysis of the reception of Waldtraut Lewin's work. Most reviewers either hesitated to identify her Lesbian themes or wrote in coded language about their sensitivity to the topic (275–78). Nevertheless, these themes in Lewin's work, especially her story "Dich hat Amor gewiß" (written in 1974, first published in 1983) clearly touched her GDR readership. Lesbians using the personal ad columns often made literary references such as "Sappho" or "Manuela" their passwords, but one woman used the term "Waldtraut Lewin" to signify her search (278).

Very little has been published on Lesbian life in the former GDR; Ursula Sillge's *Un-Sichtbare Frauen: Lesben und ihre Emanzipation in der DDR* is the first book we have by a member of that community.[13] Still, without official sanction, Lesbian love did exist and informal discrete friendship circles provided some succor to women whose marriages, divorces, and children masked their homosexual desires. As Sillge documents, in the 1980s open social groups began forming; years before the wall fell, a movement was active. The Evangelical church, which does not ordain openly Gay ministers, nevertheless offered shelter to homophile associations. Covertly grinding out flyers with a mimeograph machine, the Sonntags-Club of Berlin became the first independent Lesbian group (96–103).

*Un-Sichtbare Frauen* outlines important issues such as the ideological and social constructions of Lesbian identity and sexuality; coming out in the workplace, the family, and the community; lifestyles of Lesbian couples; and the situations of Lesbian mothers. But ultimately Sillge's book is frustrating. It is too brief, too general, and too impersonal to provide the palpable sense of what life was like for Lesbians before 1989.

The book's strength lies in Sillge's descriptions of the campaign for Lesbian rights and the fifty pages of bureaucratic materials she appends to her descriptive text. Reflecting eleven years of Lesbian and Gay organizing, these papers document how the system was challenged by homophile initiatives in the church, by university study groups, and by social groups. Even the small but meaningful privilege of having access to personal contact advertisements was officially rejected in 1984 as "gegen die sozialistische Moral und Ethik gerichtet" (133). In this section Sillge's own intrepid work as a movement leader is revealed in police documents, position papers, and correspondence with SED district leaders.

Sillge is also a confident polemicist and *Un-Sichtbare Frauen* often has the ring of a campaign pamphlet. Her angry discussion of Lesbian invisibility in the Gay community (16) comes as no great surprise but it also reveals a powerful split in consciousness with Gay men who, as many of the documents reveal, are otherwise effective political allies. Her call for a coalition of feminist, Lesbian, and Gay forces ("Lesben, Schwule, Heteras in einem Boot") challenges the values of all three communities (114–19). Nevertheless, it is clear from the 1990 *Unabhängiger Frauenverband* program (the final document in the collection) that feminists have made a substantial commitment to Gay and Lesbian issues (178–79).

Sillge's arguments with the theories of GDR endocrinologist Günther Dörner are also politically articulated. The scientist's late-1980s experiments with pregnant rats and his subsequent interviews with Gay men about the stresses their mothers experienced during pregnancy "proved" that male homosexuality was an inborn hormonal trait. The Lesbian corollary to this theory also posits a hormonal marker (66). Although Sillge acknowledges that this scientifically constructed essentialism was a factor in the 1980s campaign to decriminalize male homosexuality,[14] she also rightly worries that such a physiological definition of homosexuality is not "eine wirkliche Akzeptanz.... Daß sie gegenüber Homosexualität zugenommen hat, ist den Bemühungen von Lesben, Schwulen und heterosexuellen MitstreiterInnen zu verdanken, ihrer unermüdlichen Öffentlichkeitsarbeit" (67).

*Un-Sichtbare Frauen* defines the GDR Lesbian community on the cusp of the old and new Germany. When it expresses the precarious balance of consciousness, it is an exciting and immediate documentation. But much remains to be revealed. An in-depth and comprehensive discussion of how

GDR Lesbians coped with their closed society and closeted lifestyles would be immensely valuable. The lengthy appendix of urban and provincial contacts (e.g., "Lesbengruppe der Aufbau" in Gera or "Courage" in Berlin) certainly indicates that rich material is available.

*Die Welt gehört uns doch! Zusammenschluß lesbischer Frauen in der Schweiz der 30er Jahre*—the title of this history of Swiss Lesbians of the 1930s indicates the grand ambitions of a small subculture. And yet, Ilse Kokula and Ulrike Böhmer show how the women and men who organized social clubs, newspapers, and parties, and who also maintained their relationships did achieve what no other continental European Lesbian and Gay community was able to accomplish in the 1930s and 1940s: simple survival. While fascism thoroughly suffocated the once-active cosmopolitan communities of Berlin and Paris, Lesbians in Zurich and Basel continued to work publicly until at least 1942.[15]

While much of the volume provides a detailed analysis of the organizational development of the social groups that formed, flourished, and retrenched during the 1930s, the club history is supplemented by discussions of Lesbian lives in earlier years when Lesbian consciousness in Switzerland was part of the Zurich student *Frauenbewegung* scene: e.g., Aimée Duc (pseudonym of Minna von Wettstein-Adelt) wrote *Sind es Frauen* and Ilse Frapan wrote *Wir Frauen haben kein Vaterland* (21–25). And after 1933, many prominent German Lesbians lived in exile in Switzerland, among them Christa Winsloe and the couple Lida Gustava Heymann and Anita Augspurg (35–36).

Kokula and Böhmer are clearly committed to Lesbian history as community preservation. To that end they have lovingly rescued the accomplishments of otherwise obscure Lesbian foremothers like Laura Thoma and Anna Vock who organized under pseudonyms and made their livings as clerical workers (100). A rare collection of minutes of the *Schweizer Freundschaft-Verband* describes how these women were constantly organizing educational evenings, plenary meetings, group excursions, seasonal parties, and balls. Together with a core group of Gay men, they wrote and edited the organization's newspaper, battled police interference in their social activities, and tried to protect members from defamation in the fascist press (105–27). And finally, they were deeply involved in the inevitable in-fights that plagued the organization (143–58).

For all their careful reading of police reports, minutes books, and old newspapers, Kokula and Böhmer never let their readers forget that this movement was about the recognition of love in people's lives. A special pleasure of this history is the collection of original documents scattered among the pages. From the newspaper there is a facsimile of a personal ad section (166) and a reprint of a tender Lesbian fantasy: "Frauenliebe, welche Fülle von Harmonien und Glück birgst du in dir.—Nur du kannst uns restlos glücklich machen" (90). Particularly poignant is a formal family photograph of Laura Thoma's brother's wedding: She and her longtime companion Anneli are both included in the bridal party (74).

Since the early 1980s, feminist historians and Gay historians have been substantially researching the sexual politics of the Third Reich. Employing bureaucratic archives and oral histories, court records and contemporary theoretical studies, they have found women living the lives of victims, collaborators, and perpetrators, and Gay men wearing SA uniforms as well as pink triangles.[16] *Nationalsozialistische Sexualpolitik und weibliche Homosexualität,* Claudia Schoppmann's exhaustive dissertation-based study widens that scholarly discourse by examining the particular construction and destruction of Lesbian lives in fascist Germany. Schoppmann analyzes Nazi propaganda and ideology, "racial hygiene" policies of the state, literature published by and for the medical and psychiatric communities, and legal theory, penal codes, and court records.

While the book in its entirety is necessarily chilling, the chapters on the persecution of Lesbians and on concentration camp culture are especially grim. That Schoppmann is able to cull any information from her scanty sources is admirable. Like all the writers considered here, she understands the importance of making visible Lesbian lives in history, and it is history, not glory that interests her. Thus, the modern Gay Liberation slogan "we are everywhere" has a particularly mordant ring to it when we read Schoppmann's accounts of Lesbian prisoners, Kapos, and camp guards (223–44).

One of the greatest contributions of *Nationalsozialistische Sexualpolitik* is Schoppmann's lengthy analysis of the legal debate over the exclusion of female homosexuality as a criminal act under Paragraph 175 (86–95). Lesbian sexuality was never legally proscribed, but Schoppmann demonstrates that while this legal invisibility protected Lesbians from being criminalized in the same way that Gay men were, Nazi eugenicists, legal scholars, and psychiatrists did create a substantial body of anti-Lesbian theory. Some of it included racial theory (104), some of it was inherited from antifeminist ideology of earlier generations (57–61), and some of it was entirely original. For example, in a section on Nazi population policy she shows how Lesbians were not seen in the same threatening way that Gay men were with this quote by Minister of Justice Thierack: "Die Frau ist—anders als der Mann—stets geschlechtsbereit" (23). And a 1936 commission considering the criminalization of Lesbian seduction also saw a minimal threat because "eine verführte Frau [werde] dadurch nicht dauernd dem normalen Geschlechtsverkehr entzogen... sondern bevölkerungspolitisch nach wie vor nutzbar... " (99).

Lesbians were persecuted viciously in the Third Reich, but it was not a direct legal attack that was employed to destroy them and their cosmopolitan culture; instead, eugenic policy came into play. Along with people who were male homosexuals, mentally impaired, physically handicapped, or obviously non-Aryan, Lesbians, considered dangerous to the genetic future of the Aryan race ("Gesetz zur Verhütung erbkranken Nachwuchs"), endured forced sterilizations. Their numbers are not known because their "defects" were not specifically identified as homosexual (66-71). It is also not known how many of the tens of thousands of non-Jewish Germans who were sent to concentration camps as "asozial" were Lesbians, because that term also covered pimps, prostitutes, and other deviants (208-14).[17]

In *Nationalistische Sexualpolitik* Schoppmann has chronicled an important moment of German Lesbian heritage and has produced the best kind of history: her book is exact, comprehensive, and powerfully principled. By scrutinizing the particularly German situation she has demonstrated the intrinsic connections between homophobia, racism, and the state's capacity for violence.

Whereas *Nationalsozialistische Sexualpolitik* is a significant scholarly achievement, Schoppmann's *Zeit der Maskierung: Lebensgeschichten lesbischer Frauen im "Dritten Reich,"* a much slimmer volume consisting of short, intimate biographies, is "etwas für das Herz." But *Zeit der Maskierung* is certainly not a light work. The chronicling of individual Lesbian lives—in the best of circumstances a difficult reconstruction—has been severely hindered by the policies of the Third Reich, which destroyed and denied women's independence in general and any sort of sexual autonomy in particular. But that is what makes so compelling the stories that can be told. The remembering and telling themselves constitute resistance to historic dispossession.

Schoppmann's introduction to the collection summarizes much of the scholarship found in *Nationalistische Sexualpolitik*. Most of the ten witnesses whose testimonies compose this book were the subjects of oral histories that Schoppmann conducted while she was researching her dissertation. Others left behind memoirs, letters, and biographies. Those who have shared their memories with Schoppmann and her readers are not only rescuing their own pasts but memorializing long-dead lovers and friends whose support sometimes meant the difference between survival and capture. In her search for Lesbian survivors Schoppmann also reviews the meager documentation culled from concentration camp lists (11) and records of the war crime tribunals (24).

Aware of the oppression of official policy and avoiding—sometimes through sheer luck—annihilation, individual Lesbians did live their lives, though often masked, as the title of the book indicates. As these sketches show, survival was successful only if the mask—be it marriage (often, for mutual protection, to a Gay man), social withdrawal, or hiding—was successful. "Instinktiv hat man sich geschützt," remembers Elisabeth Zimmermann (114). Although there were certainly Lesbians among Nazi functionaries and wives,[18] the women of *Zeit der Maskierung* are more likely to be Jews, resistance operatives, and exiles.

What is truly remarkable about this small sample is the variety of Lesbian fates. Before the Third Reich some of the women had been notorious denizens of Berlin's night life while others were simply young women coming to terms with Lesbian identity within their families and friendship circles. Their responses to National Socialism were indicative of their characters and their situations. There were heroes and there were apologists: Hilde Radusch, a Berlin Communist, survived arrests and harrassment, worked with the party underground, and was job-blacklisted. Her lover Eddy, with whom she lived throughout the war, supported them both. In her seventies Radusch got involved with the new feminist movement; in 1974 she co-founded the L74, a group for older Lesbians (32–41). On the other hand there was Ruth Roellig who, before 1933, wrote Lesbian fiction as well as the popular *Berlins lesbische Frauen*,[19] a jolly guide to the clubs of Weimar. In the Third Reich she continued to write, but her themes changed: anti-Semitism in one novel, and elsewhere a declaration of herself in an autobiographical note as a "durch und durch deutsch fühlender Mensch" (139–41).

*Zeit der Maskierung* supplements the interviews with then-and-now photos. It is moving to see the changes in a woman like Elisabeth Leithauser. Her resistance was both personal and political. The deep dreamy gaze in a youthful photograph is transformed over the years to a craggy proud mask (123–24). Weimar-era drawings by artist Gertrude Sandmann, whose sketches used to illustrate the 1970s Lesbian feminist journal *UKZ (Unsere Kleine Zeitung)*, show the talent and erotic sensitivity of this Lesbian artist. She survived the war in hiding in Berlin, masking her art as well as her Jewish and Lesbian identities.

Of all the German Lesbian books reviewed here, Schoppmann's *Zeit der Maskierung* is the most capable of attracting a popular readership. The language is simple and accessible, the stories are economically edited and forcefully narrated, and the topic—Lesbian existence and everyday life during a dangerous time—is gripping. This book could provide Lesbian content to reading-level German courses and it will also be a valuable addition to Holocaust studies or to twentieth-century Lesbian/Gay history studies.[20]

Conclusions

In the 1990s German Lesbian writers consolidated their grip on the past. Historical resources flourished in documentary collections, in protocol books, and in academic studies. Knowledge of this history could provide some direction to those seeking resolutions to the theoretical and practical problems facing Lesbian communities today, for example, the relationship of the Gay male community and its culture and issues to German Lesbian-feminism.

A mainstay of the German Lesbian reading list remains, however, translation. Some original German works are being published, especially nonfiction, but there has been little growth in original literary offerings. The comparative plethora of excellent historical and documentary resources indicates that material is available, but few publishing projects have remained viable long enough to offer German Lesbian fiction writers the distribution, continuity, and financial backing that would support the growth of Lesbian fiction.

Clearly, the flux apparent in the German Lesbian literary scene is not greatly different from the changes in the German Lesbian community in particular and Germany in general. As the words of writers and the tastes of readers from the former GDR join with those of the former FRG feminists, and as the multicultural discourse gives greater urgency to the Lesbian and Gay dialogue, we will certainly be seeing a new Lesbian sensibility emerging in German-language literature. It is likely that that consciousness will carry the polemical Lesbian-feminist toughness, the intellectual precision, and the warm compassion of the best of Lesbian literature of the early 1990s.

## Notes

[1] Basic information is available in Steakley. For materials on Lesbian nightclubs see *Lila Nächte*.

[2] In recent years Berlin's Gay men and Lesbians have cooperated in celebrating Gay pride with an end-of-June "Christopher Street" parade/demonstration, named after the Greenwich Village neighborhood where the Stonewall riots took place.

[3] While Lesbians have long been integrated into German feminist culture, the community is much less comfortable with women from racial minorities, whether they are Lesbian or not. See Dagmar Schultz.

[4] In her forward to *Nationalsozialistische Sexualpolitik und weibliche Homosexualität*, Claudia Schoppmann comments on the state of knowledge about Lesbians in "Faschismusforschung" and in historical research overall: "Im Unterschied zu ihrem männlichen Pendant muß sich die historische Forschung zur weiblichen Homosexualität häufiger die Frage nach der Existenz und nach Beweisen für die Existenz ihres 'Forschungsgegenstands' stellen (lassen).... Andererseits stehen homosexuelle Männer aufgrund ihrer Geschlechtszugehörigkeit meist im Mittelpunkt der Diskussionen und des 'öffentlichen Interesses.' Spuren weiblicher Homosexualität sind dagegen kaum in die Männergeschichtsschreibung eingegangen" (3).

[5] USA authors Jeannette Foster and Lillian Faderman have given special attention to German Lesbian subjects.

[6] See, for example, her protocol/document collection *Jahre des Glücks, Jahre des Leids: Gespräche mit älteren lesbischen Frauen*.

[7] See the very title of the feminist literary review *Virginia—Frauenbuchkritik*. It appears twice a year and is distributed free through bookstores. See also the biographies, quotations, historical sketches, and literary resource lists in the *Frauenkalender* series, the *Lesbenkalender* series or in the *Berühmte Frauen: Kalendar* series.

[8] The *Lesbenliteraturpreis,* established in Hamburg in 1987, rewards German Lesbian fiction and journalism.

[9] Artificial/alternative insemination ("künstliche Befruchtung") is not common in the German Lesbian community and there is much more curiosity and theorizing about its possibilities than actual practical experience. Indeed, new German legislation stipulates that it should only be made available to heterosexual (married) couples. German Lesbians who want to avail themselves of sperm banks in order to conceive do travel to Holland. This is reminiscent of the trips to Holland German women undertook in the early seventies to obtain abortions.

[10] Ruston, one-third of the separatist triad that contributed the translated essay "S/M = Sadismus & Masochismus = Heterosexism" is a New Zealander.

[11] The American author is not only a psychologist and attorney but also a Tae Kwon Do artist and self-defense teacher whose Frankfurt martial arts school *Frauen in Bewegung* has been an important center for the German anti-violence movement. See *Schlagfertige Frauen*.

[12] Indeed, considering such obstacles, Verena Stefan's *Häutungen* is a breathtaking phenomenon. By 1984 it had sold 250,000 copies. Stefan and Frauenoffensive have steadfastly refused to sell the title to a mainstream publisher.

[13] In *"Wir leiden nicht mehr, sondern sind gelitten!"* Ilse Kokula briefly describes GDR Lesbian social life and outlines the official position of Lesbian and Gay groups of the mid-1980s. This is complemented by summaries of conversations with two participants in the Berlin Lesbian scene. Sillge's colleague Christine Schenk covers Lesbian politics until 1992 in *Gender, Politics and Post-Communism*.

[14] Paragraph 175, the law against male homosexuality, was abolished in the GDR in 1968; in its place Paragraph 151, penalizing homosexual relations between adults and minors, held as law until late 1988. In the FRG Paragraph 175 continued as law and was only abolished in 1994.

[15] The continuity of the work of the Lesbian and Gay community can be read in its publications. The newsletter *Freundschafts-Banner* (1932–37) had a women's section. It became the politically toned journal *Menschenrecht* and had Lesbian and Gay male subscribers from 1937–42. The title changed in 1943 when it became a men's cultural newspaper, *Der Kreis*, with a French

supplement, *Le Cercle*; after the war it acquired an English-language supplement, *The Circle*. In this format it continued publication until 1967 (*Die Welt gehört uns doch*).

[16] The pink triangle, a symbol of today's Gay Liberation movement, commemorates the concentration camp emblem for the crime of male homosexuality. The pink triangle did not designate women. The "asocial" Lesbians wore black and occasionally green triangles.

[17] We have a better idea of the numbers and fates of Gay men—many of whom were stigmatized and punished as a specific group. See Plant.

[18] Schoppmann quotes SS correspondence concerning a Lesbian affair of the wife of Gruppenführer Herbert Becker in *Nationalsozialistische Sexualpolitik*.

[19] Later reprinted as *Lila Nächte*.

[20] A translation is being prepared by Columbia University Press and is due for publication in Spring 1996.

## Works Cited

Bachmann, Ingeborg. *Werke*. Ed. Christine Koschel, Inge von Weidenbaum, and Clemens Münster. 4 vols. Munich: Piper, 1982.

Barnes, Djuna. *Nachtgewächs*. Trans. Wolfgang Hildesheimer. Pfüllingen: Neske, 1959; reprint, Frankfurt a.M.: Suhrkamp, 1971.

*Berühmte Frauen: Kalendar*. Ed. Luise F. Pusch. Frankfurt a.M.: Suhrkamp, 1988–.

Brown, Rita Mae. *Rubinroter Dschungel*. Trans. Barbara Scriba-Sethe. Hamburg: Rowohlt, 1980.

CLIT. *Rufe alle Lesben, bitte kommen!* Berlin/W: Tomyris, 1977.

Duc, Aimée. *Sind es Frauen? Roman über das dritte Geschlecht*. 1901; reprint, Berlin/W: Amazonen, 1976.

Faderman, Lillian, and Brigitte Eriksson, eds. *Lesbian-Feminism in Turn-of-the-Century Germany*. Weatherby Lake, FL: Naiad, 1980.

Foster, Jeannette H. *Sex Variant Women in Literature*. Vantage, 1956; reprint, Baltimore: Diana, 1976.

Frapan, Ilse. *Wir Frauen haben kein Vaterland*. Berlin, 1899; reprint, Berlin/W: Courage, 1983.

*Frauenkalendar*. Berlin: Frauenkalendar Selbstverlag, 1975–.

Haushofer, Marlen. *Eine Handvoll Leben*. Vienna: Zsolnay, 1955; reprint, Knaur, n.d.

Kokula, Ilse. *Jahre des Glücks, Jahre des Leids: Gespräche mit älteren lesbischen Frauen: Dokumente*. Kiel: Frühlings Erwachen, 1986.

———. *"Wir leiden nicht mehr, sondern sind gelitten!" Lesbisch leben in Deutschland*. Cologne: Kiepenheuer, 1987; reprint, Munich: Knaur, 1990.

Kokula, Ilse, and Ulrike Böhmer. *Die Welt gehört uns doch! Zusammenschluß lesbischer Frauen in der Schweiz der 30er Jahre.* Zürich: Verein Feministische Wissenschaft, 1991.

*Lesbenkalendar.* Ed. Anke Schäfer. Wiesbaden: Selbstverlag Anke Schäfer, 1986–.

Lewin, Waltraud. *Dich hat Amor gewiss.* Berlin: Neues Leben, 1983.

*Lila Nächte: Die Damenklubs der 20er Jahre.* Ed. Adele Meyer. Cologne: Zitronenpresse, 1981.

Lorde, Audre. *Auf Leben und Tod: Krebstagebuch.* Trans. Renate Stendhal. Berlin: Orlanda Frauenverlag, 1984. 2nd expanded edition 1994.

———. *Lichtflut: Neue Texte.* Trans. Margarete Längsfeld. Berlin: Orlanda Frauenverlag, 1988.

Loulan, JoAnn, Margaret Nichols, and Monica Streit, eds. *Lesben, Liebe, Leidenschaft: Texte zur feministischen Psychologie.* Berlin: Orlanda Frauenverlag, 1992.

Lützen, Karin. *Frauen lieben Frauen: Freundschaft und Begehren.* Trans. Gabriele Haefs. Munich: Piper, 1992.

Marti, Madeleine. *Hinterlegte Botschaften: Die Darstellung lesbischer Frauen in der deutschsprachigen Literatur seit 1945.* Stuttgart: Metzler, 1992.

Moosdorf, Johanna. *Freundinnen.* Munich: Nymphenburger, 1977; reprint, Frankfurt a.M.: Fischer, 1988.

Ohms, Constance, ed. *Mehr als das Herz gebrochen: Gewalt in lesbischen Beziehungen.* Berlin: Orlanda Frauenverlag, 1993.

Plant, Richard. *The Pink Triangle: The Nazi War Against Homosexuals.* New York: Holt, 1986.

Schenk, Christine, "Lesbians and their Emancipation in the former German Democratic Republic: Past and Future." *Gender, Politics and Post-Communism: Reflections from Eastern Europe and the former Soviet Union.* Ed. Nanette Funk and Magda Mueller. New York: Routledge, 1993. 160–67.

*Schlagfertige Frauen: Erfolgreich wider die alltägliche Gewalt.* Ed. Denise Caignon and Gail Groves. Berlin: Orlanda Frauenverlag, 1990.

Schoppmann, Claudia. *Nationalsozialistische Sexualpolitik und weibliche Homosexualität.* Pfaffenweiler: Centaurus, 1991.

———. *Zeit der Maskierung: Lebensgeschichten lesbischer Frauen im "Dritten Reich."* Berlin: Orlanda Frauenverlag, 1993.

Schultz, Dagmar. "Racism in the New Germany and the Reaction of White Women." *Women in German Yearbook 9: Feminist Studies in German Literature and Culture.* Ed. Jeanette Clausen and Sara Friedrichsmeyer. Lincoln: U of Nebraska P, 1994. 241–51.

Sillge, Ursula. *Un-Sichtbare Frauen: Lesben und ihre Emanzipation in der DDR.* Berlin: LinksDruck, 1991.

Steakley, James. *The Homosexual Rights Movement in Germany.* New York: Arno, 1975.

Stefan, Verena. *Häutungen.* Munich: Frauenoffensive, 1975.

Stenten, Marlene. *Puppe Else*. Berlin/W: Sudelbuch (Selbstverlag), 1977; reprint, Frankfurt a.M.: Fischer, 1984.

*Virginia Frauenbuchkritik*. Ed. Hinrike Gronewald and Anke Schäfer. Wiesbaden: Frauenliteratur, 1986–.

*Von nun an nannten sie sich Mütter: Lesben und Kinder*. Ed. Uli Streib. Berlin: Orlanda Frauenverlag, 1991.

Winsloe, Christa. *Mädchen in Uniform*. 1930; reprint, Munich: Frauenoffensive, 1983.

# Ein Streit um Worte?
# Eine Lesbe macht Skandal
# im Deutschen Bundestag[1]

Luise F. Pusch

In 1988-89 the German *Bundestag* was the scene of a bizarre and illuminating case of language censorship: The leadership and majority parties attempted to prohibit the use of the words *Lesben* and *Schwule* in their official documents, and insisted that the Green Party use *Lesbierinnen* and *Homosexuelle* in their motions instead. The Greens argued for and finally won the right to use the terms preferred by Lesbians and Gay men themselves. This case provides the basis for my linguistic analysis of the social mechanisms by which words become "dirty" or acceptable and for reflections concerning homophobia and language, such as information management in homophobic societies and the act of coming out as a complex and widely misunderstood speech act. (LFP)

>...*if you live in this world expecting appreciation, you would do better to look in the dictionary for it.*—Evander Smith, schwuler Anwalt für Schwule, zitiert in Marcus 159
>
> *Wovon man nicht sprechen kann, darüber muß man schweigen.*—Ludwig Wittgenstein, schwuler Philosoph, 1921[2]

1. Überblick

Ich bringe einen Bericht über einen Fall von Sprachzensur im Deutschen Bundestag aus dem Jahr 1988-89. Die Auseinandersetzung geht darum, wie Lesben und Schwule bzw. "Homosexuelle" genannt werden sollen. Die politisch aktive, organisierte Avantgarde der Lesben und Schwulen in Deutschland favorisiert die Bezeichnungen Lesben und Schwule. Der Bundestag hielt diese Bezeichnungen für "Ausdrücke aus der Gosse" und wollte sie in offiziellen Verlautbarungen nicht zulassen.

Ein großer Teil der linguistisch-politischen Analyse dieses Lehrstücks wurde von den Zensierten—hauptsächlich von der offen lesbischen Abgeordneten der Grünen, Jutta Oesterle-Schwerin—bereits geleistet und ging in die Dokumente ein, die insofern weitgehend für sich selbst sprechen. Kaum artikulationsfähig scheinen die Offiziellen im Bundestag. Ihre Position bleibt verschwommen; deshalb versuche ich im Anschluß an die Präsentation der Dokumente klar herauszupräparieren, was diese Abgeordneten—und sicher auch die durch sie vertretene schweigende Mehrheit "draußen im Lande"—im Innersten dumpf bewegt.

Der Vorgang ermöglicht einen tiefen Einblick in die deutsche Bürokraten-Mentalität, die "Untermenschen" schon immer gerne auf anmaßend-bürokratische Art ihren Platz zuwies. Deshalb habe ich die Dokumente auch nur behutsam gekürzt; es war mir wichtig, die selbstzufriedene Arroganz "meiner" VolksvertreterInnen und anderer Amtsorgane und die Scheinheiligkeit, mit der sie unter dem Vorwand, Lesben und Schwule vor Diskriminierung schützen zu wollen, genau dies tun (nämlich diskriminieren), in voller Länge öffentlich zu machen. Die heroische Standfestigkeit der ersten offen lesbischen Bundestagsabgeordneten, Jutta Oesterle-Schwerin, verdient es ohnehin, ungekürzt in die Annalen der Lesben- und Schwulengeschichte einzugehen.

Wichtig ist der Vorfall natürlich auch für die (Emanzipations-) Geschichte der Lesben und Schwulen in Deutschland und somit als Gegenstand einer *Queer Theory,* die im und für den deutschsprachigen Raum erst noch rezipiert und entwickelt werden muß.

2. Sprache und Homophobie
2.1 Das Thema "Sprache und Homophobie" als Forschungsgegenstand in Deutschland und in den USA
2.1.1 Persönliches

Die Probleme von Lesben und Schwulen waren und sind, von Anfang an bis heute, immer auch Sprach- und Kommunikationsprobleme. Aber Sprach- und KommunikationswissenschaftlerInnen haben sich aus Berührungsangst kaum um diesen Forschungsgegenstand gekümmert. Ich wollte im Jahr 1980 meine Antrittsvorlesung an der Universität Konstanz über das Thema "Verschweigen, Leugnen, Verschleiern: Sprache und Homosexualität" halten. Ich hatte auch viele Ideen dazu, aber ich habe mich schließlich doch nicht getraut. Das Aufgreifen dieses Themas hätte damals beruflichen Selbstmord bedeutet.

Inzwischen ist "mein" damals ängstlich vermiedenes Thema "gesellschaftsfähig" geworden, vgl. etwa Buchtitel aus dem Jahre 1994 wie: *Queer Words, Queer Images: Communication and the Construction of Homosexuality* (Ringer). Wir leben im Zeitalter von Aids; das Leben ist zu kurz und zu kostbar, um es im Versteck zu verbringen. Allenthalben haben sich Lesben und Schwule organisiert und—angesichts der Untätigkeit der Regierungen—zunehmend radikalisiert. Sie haben nichts mehr zu verlieren, wenn sie aus dem "Closet" herauskommen, um endlich auch ihre BürgerInnenrechte zu fordern wie alle anderen diskriminierten

Gruppen: "Lesbian and Gay people are the last remaining group against which public displays of bigotry are respectable, from the high school locker room to the floor of the U.S. senate. We are a group whose right to love as we choose is criminalized in half the states of the union, and we are officially discriminated against by our government," schreibt Larry Gross in *Contested Closets: The Politics and Ethics of Outing* (172 f.).

Beruflichen Selbstmord habe ich damals dann doch noch begangen durch mein Engagement in der feministischen Linguistik.[3] Also kann ich nun getrost noch einen Schritt weitergehen und mich dem öffentlichen Nachdenken über die vielschichtigen Zusammenhänge zwischen meinem Fachgebiet Sprache und meiner politischen Situation als Lesbe widmen.

2.1.2 Methodisches

Es geht in diesem Artikel unter anderem darum, wie die "Homosexuellen" genannt werden sollen. Und welche Ausdrücke wähle ich nun für meine Darstellung dieses "Streits um Worte"? Ich benutze—je nach Mitteilungszusammenhang—alle drei Bezeichnungen, *Lesben, Schwule* und *Homosexuelle,* nicht jedoch das Wort *Lesbierin,* das vom Bundestag ebenfalls empfohlen wurde. Dieses Wort ist in der deutschen Lesbenbewegung völlig "out".

Für die Zwecke dieser Untersuchung einer Gesellschaft im Übergang unterscheide ich zwischen den beiden Entwicklungsstufen "homophobische Gesellschaft (HPG)" und "tolerante Gesellschaft". Eine emanzipierte Gesellschaft ist das Ziel, aber soweit sind wir noch nicht. Wir können uns eine solche Gesellschaft aber ausmalen, auch zu Modellzwecken.

2.2 Inwiefern ist Homosexualität auch ein Sprachproblem?
2.2.1 Homosexuelles Stigma-Management ist weitgehend Informationsmanagement

Da Homosexuelle in homophobischen Gesellschaften geächtet sind und verfolgt werden[4] und, anders als etwa Schwarze in einer Mehrheit von Weißen, ihr Stigma auch verbergen können, leben die meisten im Versteck, hinter einer Fassade der größtmöglichen Unauffälligkeit/Angepaßtheit.[5] Aus der Diskrepanz zwischen subjektiver schwuler Wirklichkeit und vorgetäuschter bürgerlicher "Normalität" ergeben sich vielfältige Informations- und Kodierungsprobleme im Alltag—also: Sprachprobleme. Ob ich es will oder nicht, meine Mitmenschen gehen davon aus, daß ich heterosexuell bin, solange ich nichts anderes mitteile und mich "unauffällig/normal" benehme. Ich selbst gehe übrigens ebenfalls davon aus, daß meine Mitmenschen heterosexuell sind, solange sie mir nichts anderes zu verstehen geben.

Wie gebe ich mich als Lesbe oder Schwuler in der HPG einer Frau oder einem Mann zu erkennen, von denen ich nur vermute, daß sie ebenfalls lesbisch oder schwul sind? Hier ein Beispiel:

> We began the hinting process, which usually occupied two or three letters. The way you hinted was by saying that you were interested in philosophy, poetry, and biographies, but not very interested in sports, except walking and swimming. You could mention tennis or ping pong or miniature golf. So then you named a few recent biographies or poets that you'd read. You didn't start with people like Wilde or Whitman, but you could include Bacon or some of the ones who were less specifically identified. And then you brought it up (Marcus 46).

### 2.2.2 Das Sprechen über Homosexualität ist kein normaler Sprechakt
#### 2.2.2.1 Abwehrstrategien gegen den Verdacht der Homosexualität

Eigentlich spricht man ja "darüber" am besten überhaupt nicht. Und wenn man "darüber" spricht, läuft man Gefahr, sich zu verraten und, ob zu Recht oder Unrecht, als lesbisch oder schwul angesehen zu werden. Denn da "darüber" nicht geradeheraus gesprochen werden kann wie über andere Themen, kommt das Sprechen über Homosexualität—auch ohne reguläres "Bekenntnis"—bereits einem Bekenntnis gleich, denn der "normale Mensch" hat ja gar kein Bedürfnis, kein Interesse und keinen Anlaß, "darüber" zu sprechen.[6]

Komme ich dennoch in die Verlegenheit, Homo- oder Heterosexualität thematisieren zu müssen, so muß ich in der HPG, um meinem Publikum keine unliebsamen Schlüsse nahezulegen, geeignete Vorkehrungen treffen. Ich muß mich von der Homosexualität überzeugend distanzieren und meine Heterosexualität dezent unter Beweis stellen. Die vulgäre Art der Distanzierung ist die Beschimpfung oder sonstige Herabsetzung der Homosexualität und der Lesben und Schwulen, an der sich oft sogar Lesben und Schwule selbst beteiligen, um nicht entlarvt zu werden. Die HPG hat ein wirkungsvolles Beschimpfungs-Vokabular für Schwule und Lesben entwickelt. Die feinere Art der Distanzierung—die der Bundestag in unserem "Streit um Worte" mit allen Mitteln gewahrt sehen will—ist die Benutzung eines Fachvokabulars.

Sogar wenn ich nur das Wort *heterosexuell* verwende, mache ich mich des Lesbischseins verdächtig, riskiere ich ein ungewolltes Coming Out.[7] Denn der "normale Mensch" in der HPG hat keinen Anlaß, Heterosexualität zu thematisieren. Sexualität ja, aber Heterosexualität ergibt nur dann als Thema einen Sinn, wenn ich zugleich Homosexualität im Sinn habe. Und wie könnte ich das, wenn ich nicht selber—? Undsoweiter.

Was für eine Art Sprechakt ist dann meine Verwendung des Wortes *heterosexuell*?

Wie spreche ich über Homosexualität, ohne die "eindeutigen" Wörter *schwul, lesbisch, homosexuell* etc. zu verwenden? Hier ein Beispiel—Jim Kepner berichtet, unter welchen Bedingungen er in den fünfziger Jahren für das Schwulenmagazin *One* recherchierte:

> You could read most papers for a year without finding any gay news unless you learned how to read between the lines. They might not have mentioned the raid of a homosexual or queer bar, but they'd mention a "house of ill repute". And if several men were arrested and no women were mentioned as present, you assumed it was not a whorehouse. In the article they might mention one man was dressed in a "womanish" manner. When *Time* magazine mentioned the subject, they usually used words like *epicene* to describe someone. When they reviewed—holding their noses—Tennessee Williams or Carson McCullers, they would use the term *decadent*. You looked for those words and then read the whole thing carefully. Then you would go and investigate. So I would write to one of our subscribers in the place from where the story was reported and ask, "Is this a gay story?" (Marcus 51)

### 2.2.2.2 Der erzwungene Exhibitionismus beim Coming Out

Viele Lesben und Schwule machen die niederschmetternde Erfahrung, daß ihr heroisches Coming Out von den anderen trivialisiert und verkehrt wird zu einem Akt unerwünschter, peinlicher Vertraulichkeit oder gar exhibitionistischer Belästigung. Wie oft hören wir Reaktionen folgender Art: "Warum erzählst du mir das? Was du im Bett machst, ist doch deine Privatsache, interessiert doch sowieso niemanden. Ich belästige dich doch auch nicht mit meinen Bettgeschichten." Man wirft uns vor, wir "gingen mit unserer 'Sexualität' hausieren", auf Englisch: "we are flaunting our sexuality". Wie kommt es zu dieser gängigen Mißinterpretation heroischer Sprechakte?

Die ganz ungewöhnlichen Bedingungen des Sprechakts "Coming Out" werden von den Nichtbetroffenen, den Heterosexuellen, in der Regel nicht verstanden. Vor allem wird übersehen, daß es sich nicht um eine "unmotivierte" und daher peinlich aufdringliche Mitteilung über meinen "Intimbereich" handelt, sondern um eine *Korrektur* irriger Annahmen über meine *Identität*. Da alle meine Mitmenschen dieselben irrigen Annahmen über mich hegen, solange ich sie nicht korrigiere, muß ich bei jeder neuen Begegnung entscheiden, ob sich die Quälerei des Coming Out lohnt.

Zum Teil liegt die Mißinterpretation auch an dem hybriden Wort *homosexuell* und seinen Derivaten selbst mitsamt seinen Problemen der Polysemie. *Homosexuell* von griechisch *homoios* 'gleich' und lateinisch *sexus* 'Geschlecht' bedeutet eigentlich: 'Angehörigen des gleichen bzw. eigenen Geschlechts zugeneigt'. Von Sexualität ist also eigentlich keine Rede, nur von den beiden Geschlechtern. In der deutschen

Umgangssprache ist aber das Wort *sexuell* weniger assoziiert mit den beiden Geschlechtern als vielmehr mit genitaler Sexualität.

Sexualität ist aber in unserer Kultur tabu. Die meisten tun "es" zwar gerne und denken viel daran, aber das *Reden* darüber unterliegt vielfältigen Beschränkungen. Ein Code der Umschreibungen hat sich herausgebildet.

Da angenommen wird, daß der Mensch heterosexuell ist, es sei denn, das Gegenteil stellt sich heraus, braucht über die Sexualität der Heterosexuellen weiter kein Wort verloren zu werden. Eve Kosofsky Sedgwick knüpft daran die berechtigte Frage, ob Heterosexualität überhaupt etwas mit Sexualität zu tun habe:

> ...if we are receptive to Foucault's understanding of modern sexuality as the most intensive site of the demand for, and detection or discursive production of, the Truth of individual identity, it seems as though this silent, normative, uninterrogated 'regular' heterosexuality may not function as a sexuality at all. Think of how a culturally central concept like public/private is organized so as to preserve for heterosexuality the unproblematicalness, the apparent naturalness, of its discretionary choice between display and concealment: 'public' names the space where cross-sex couples may, whenever they feel like it, display affection freely, while same-sex couples must always conceal it.... Thus, heterosexuality is consolidated as the opposite of the "sex" whose secret, Foucault says "the obligation to conceal...was but another aspect of the duty to admit to (*Tendencies*: 10; zitiert wird Foucault 38–40).

Die peinliche Assoziation des Fickens, um einmal einen "schockierend bildhaften" Ausdruck zu gebrauchen, kommt daher im Alltag nicht auf, wenn von Menschen-Kategorien die Rede ist, sogar dann nicht, wenn, wie in toleranten Gesellschaften zunehmend üblich, Heterosexualität thematisiert und nicht einfach vorausgesetzt wird. Nur bei der Kategorie *homosexuell* denken alle an Sex, obendrein an "widernatürliche" Geschlechtsakte wie Anal- oder Oralverkehr.[8]

Lesben und Schwule, die nur ihre Identität klarstellen wollen, sehen sich daher zu einem exhibitionistischen Akt gezwungen. Wenn sie politisch verantwortlich handeln und aus ihrem Versteck herauskommen wollen, *müssen* sie sich bloßstellen. Diese unselige Kopplung des einen an das andere ist für Außenstehende/Heterosexuelle schwerlich nachvollziehbar. Im Englischen wurde, wegen der verwirrenden Doppeldeutigkeit des Wortes *sex* ('Geschlecht' und 'Geschlechtsverkehr', wie in *the female sex* vs. *oral sex*) das Wort *gender* eingeführt, das wir mit *soziales Geschlecht* übersetzen oder oft auch unübersetzt lassen.

Nach meinem Selbstverständnis als Lesbe, und nach meiner Kenntnis anderer Lesben, verlieben wir uns in Angehörige des eigenen "gender", des eigenen "sozialen Geschlechts".

2.2.2.3 "The love that dare not speak its name"⁹ und die Zweiteilung der Linguistik

Üblicherweise unterscheiden wir in der Sprachwissenschaft zwischen der "reinen" oder Systemlinguistik, die sich mit Grammatik und Wortschatz befaßt, auf der einen und der Pragmalinguistik/Gesprächsanalyse auf der anderen Seite, deren Gegenstand das sprachliche Handeln ist. Der "Problemkomplex" Homosexualität in homophobischer Gesellschaft fällt in beide linguistische Disziplinen—ja er läßt diese Zweiteilung recht künstlich aussehen, denn "the love that dare not speak its name" hat nicht nur Probleme mit dem *"Nennen/Aussprechen des Namens"*, das in die Zuständigkeit der Pragmalinguistik fällt. Die Schwierigkeit des *Nennens/Aussprechens* liegt an dem oder den *Namen* selbst, für die Lexikologie und Semantik—Unterabteilungen der Systemlinguistik—zuständig sind. Das Aussprechen des Wortes *schwul* zum Beispiel ist schwer—für viele unmöglich—eben wegen der ungewöhnlichen Geschichte und semantischen und pragmatischen Eigenschaften des Wortes *schwul*.

2.2.3 Die Bezeichnungen für Homosexuelle sind linguistisch nicht "normal" hinsichtlich ihrer Denotation, Konnotation, Intension und Extension, von ihrer Geschichte ganz zu schweigen

2.2.3.1 Konnotationen: Wir sind wie häßliche kleine Entlein, nur andersrum

Eve K. Sedgwick schreibt in ihrem Aufsatz "Queer and Now": "A word so fraught as 'queer' is—fraught with so many social and personal histories of exclusion, violence, defiance, excitement, never can only denote; nor even can it only connote..." (*Tendencies* 9). Es kommt hinzu, daß das, was diese Wörter "denotieren" sollen, selbst fraglich und umstritten ist. Ich beziehe mich hier auf die Auseinandersetzung zwischen den sogenannten "essentialists" und den "social constructionists" über die Frage, ob es Homosexualität und Homosexuelle schon immer gegeben hat oder erst seit es diese Begriffe gibt.[10]

Die "history of exclusion and violence" macht die Identifikation mit Bezeichnungen, die einmal Schimpfwörter waren (*Schwule, queer*) und von vielen noch heute so verstanden und/oder gebraucht werden, psychisch quälend. Bevor eine "Lesbe" oder ein "Schwuler" überhaupt erkennen und akzeptieren kann, daß sie/er der Gruppe der Lesben und Schwulen angehört, hat die HPG ihnen in aller Regel beigebracht, daß Homosexuelle das Letzte sind, der Inbegriff des Abartigen, Unanständigen und Perversen. Mit einem Wort: menschlicher Abschaum, weit schlimmer als Kapitalverbrecher, "lower than the animals, than the snakes that crawl...on the earth" (Marcus 137). So galten etwa bei den Gefangenen der Konzentrationslager die Homosexuellen als unterste Kategorie: "...the antihomosexual prejudice, so carefully nurtured in Western civilization over so many centuries, proved its strength even among the condemned, and the hypocrisy, which is inevitably part of it, triumphed even in this modern, man-made hell" (Haeberle 377). Kein Wunder, daß viele Lesben und Schwule Mühe haben, sich "eigenhändig" unter dieser Rubrik einzuordnen, selbst wenn sie wissen, daß es politisch sinnvoll, ja lebensnotwendig ist.

2.2.3.2   Extension
2.2.3.2.1 Geschichtliche Dimension

Sexualgeschichtlich und soziologisch interessant sind die Probleme der Definition: Wie Halperin (482 f.) ausführt, wurde das Wort *Homosexualität* 1869 von K.M. Kertbeny erfunden und 1892 ins Englische eingeführt. "Before 1892", so Halperin (in einer leicht anglozentrischen Version von Nominalismus) "there was no homosexuality, only sexual inversion" (482). Die Frage ist also, ob der Homosexuelle und die Homosexuelle auch Erfindungen des vorigen Jahrhunderts sind, oder ob es sie schon früher gegeben hat. Oder gab es vielleicht nur "homosexuelle Akte" von Personen, die aber nicht aufgrund solcher Akte als Sondergruppe definiert und behandelt wurden? Der Seigneur de Brantôme (1540-1614) etwa berichtet in seinem *Leben der galanten Damen,* die lesbische Liebe sei eine "Methode" (162), von einer Italienerin nach Frankreich eingeführt. Bisweilen nennt er sie auch "eine Leibesübung" (160). Wie auch immer—beides klingt nicht gerade nach "Veranlagung" oder "angeboren", auch nicht nach "Sünde" oder "Krankheit"—Begriffe, mit denen lesbische Liebe später konzeptualisiert wurde.

War die "romantische Freundschaft" zwischen so vielen Frauen der Mittelschicht im achtzehnten und neunzehnten Jahrhundert "lesbische Liebe" oder nicht? Die historische Lesbenforschung, besonders natürlich Carroll Smith-Rosenberg und Lillian Faderman in ihren bahnbrechenden Studien, hat zur Klärung dieser Frage Wesentliches beigetragen.

2.2.3.2.2 Geschlechterdimension

Sexualwissenschaftlich und feministisch interessant ist auch die Frage, was Lesben und Schwule miteinander gemeinsam haben, abgesehen von der "Eigenschaft", das eigene Geschlecht zu lieben und deshalb gesellschaftlich verfolgt und geächtet zu werden. Mit anderen Worten: Faßt der Begriff "Homosexuelle" vielleicht Individuen zusammen, die nichts miteinander gemeinsam haben—außer eben, daß sie wegen ihrer "sexuellen Orientierung" verfolgt werden? Unter meinem Pseudonym Judith Offenbach habe ich dazu 1983 folgendes verkündet:

> Unsere Vorstellungen über "normale" Heterosexualität und "abweichende" Homosexualität sind, genau wie die über "Weiblichkeit" und "Männlichkeit", Produkte von Männern und auf männliche Bedürfnisse zugeschnitten:

voreilige Verallgemeinerungen einer rein männlichen Weltsicht, die sich, soweit sie weibliche Belange "mit erfassen" wollen, zunehmend als unhaltbar erweisen.... Weibliche Heterosexualität ist etwas ganz anderes als männliche: Sie ist in dem Maße abwählbar, wie ihre Unvereinbarkeit mit genuin weiblichen Interessen erkannt wird. Weibliche Homosexualität ist etwas ganz anderes als männliche: Sie ist wählbar in dem Maße, wie sie als der Ausweg, als konsequente Absage an patriarchalische Herrschaftsansprüche erkannt wird (213).

Diese Sicht scheint mir heute noch ziemlich plausibel,[11] u.a. als Erklärung für das häufige problemlose Wechseln der Frauen von der Heterosexualität zur lesbischen Lebensweise. Julia T. Wood stellt in einer empirischen Untersuchung über Krisenmanagement in lesbischen und in schwulen Beziehungen fest, daß zumindest in dieser Hinsicht kaum Gemeinsamkeiten der beiden Gruppen feststellbar sind, im Gegenteil: die "männlichen" Verhaltensweisen potenzieren sich bei schwulen Paaren sozusagen, ähnlich wie die "weiblichen" bei lesbischen Paaren.

Viele assoziieren *Homosexualität* und *Homosexuelle* sowieso nur mit Männern—wofür der ehemalige Bundestagspräsident Jenninger ein schönes Beispiel abgibt. Das allgemeine Strukturgesetz patriarchalischer Sprachen—MAN = Male As Norm—gilt also auch im "subkulturellen" Bereich: Bezeichnungen für den männlichen Teil der Subkultur können den weiblichen mit einschließen, aber nicht umgekehrt. Wir haben weibliche und männliche Homosexuelle und Schwule, aber nicht weibliche und männliche Lesben. Im Englischen ebenso: *Gay(s)* und *homosexual(s)* referieren auf Frauen und Männer, *lesbian(s)* referiert nur auf Frauen. Dabei wurde laut Judy Grahn (24 f.) das Wort *gay* 1922 von Gertrude Stein für Lesben umgemünzt. In ihrer Erzählung "Miss Furr and Miss Skeene" benutzte Stein *gay* als Code- oder Deckwort, um lesbische Inhalte an der Zensur vorbeizuschmuggeln, was ihr auch gelang.

2.2.4 Teil-Zusammenfassung

Der Terminus *homosexuell* ist also irreführend in vieler Hinsicht insofern er

- an Geschlechtsverkehr denken läßt
- an das biologische Geschlecht der "Liebesobjekte" denken läßt statt an das soziale Geschlecht (*gender*)
- wegen der Prototypizität des Mannes, auch des schwulen Mannes, in unserer Kultur sowieso eher an Männer denken läßt
- an *homo* = Mann denken läßt
- Individuen in eine konzeptuelle Gruppe zwängt, die eher aufgrund äußerlicher als inhärenter Merkmale in eine Gruppe gehören. Wäre es sinnvoll, ZeugInnen Jehovas und "Homosexuelle" in einem Wort

zusammenzufassen, etwa als "Jehosexuelle", weil beide Gruppen von den Nazis verfolgt wurden?

Kommen wir damit nun zu jener Auseinandersetzung zwischen Lesben und Schwulen auf der einen und dem Deutschen Bundestag auf der anderen Seite, in dem Lesben und Schwule gezwungen werden sollten, sich als Homosexuelle zu bezeichnen.

## 3. Ein Streit um Worte: Ein deutsches Lehrstück
### 3.1 Vorspiel

Im Frühjahr 1988 wies die Deutsche Postreklame GmbH eine Anzeige des Feministischen Frauengesundheitszentrums in Berlin (FFGZ) zurück. Der Text lautete: "Feministisches Frauengesundheitszentrum: Beratung und Kurse zu allen Fragen der Frauengesundheit, u.a. zu: Blasen- und vaginalen Infektionen, Verhütung, Ernährung, Menstruation, Wechseljahre. Kurse auch für Mädchen und Lesben."

Die Deutsche Postreklame begründete die Ablehnung mit dem Hinweis, daß das Wort *Lesbe* in einer Postreklame einen Verstoß gegen die "guten Sitten" darstelle. Wenn ich mich in das gesunde Volksempfinden hineinversetze, in dem ich ja sehr gut unterrichtet worden bin, so finde ich schon allein die öffentliche Erwähnung der Wörter *Vagina, Blase und Menstruation* unanständig. Solche "schmutzigen" Dinge erwähnt man nicht in der Öffentlichkeit—Tabu! Aber es läßt sich nicht leugnen, daß diese Dinge zur Gesundheit von Frauen gehören. Also braucht es einen anderen Grund zur Ablehnung. Dieser nun ist in dem Wort *Lesbe,* das ohnehin den Gipfel des Obszönen darstellt, gegeben.

Eine Klage des FFGZ gegen die Deutsche Postreklame GmbH wurde vom Amtsgericht Frankfurt abgewiesen. Ich zitiere aus der Urteilsbegründung[12]:

> Der Text...verstößt...durch die Verwendung der an der Grenze zwischen Jargon- und Vulgärsprache angesiedelten saloppen Formulierung "Lesbe" gegen das...als Grundrecht deklarierte Recht auf freie Persönlichkeitsentfaltung derjenigen Frauen, die in ihrem erotischen Empfinden sich zu weiblichen Partnern hingezogen fühlen.
>
> Die Zahl dieser Frauen ist nach durchaus ernstzunehmenden Schätzungen relativ hoch [es werden Kinsey und Hite zitiert].
>
> Dieser erhebliche Anteil erwachsener Frauen hat...einen Anspruch auf entsprechende Achtung in der Öffentlichkeit. Dieses Grundrecht wird hier durch die Formulierung "Lesbe" verletzt.
>
> Die "lesbische Liebe" mit der bislang üblichen Bezeichnung "Lesbierin" für eine Frau mit gleichgeschlechtlichem Empfinden ist von der griechischen Insel Lesbos abgeleitet. Die Formulierung "Lesbierin" hat eine sehr

ernstzunehmende und achtbare Herkunft. Wegen des zu geringen Streitwerts ist eine Revision nicht zugelassen.

Die deutsche Gerichtsbarkeit als Streiterin für Lesbenrecht und Lesbenwürde? Gegen das Feministische Frauengesundheitszentrum Berlin?? Die Welt scheint auf den Kopf gestellt, und die selbstgerechte Gerichtsbarkeit scheint es nicht einmal zu merken, denn sie ist lesbenpolitisch ignorant—und sie kann es sich leisten.

Am 14. Januar hatte das Landgericht Rottweil per Beschluß festgestellt, daß das Wort *schwul* nicht gegen die guten Sitten verstoße und widersprach damit der Auffassung des Amtsgerichts Freudenstadt, das mit dieser Begründung eine Eintragung der "Schwulengruppe Freudenstadt" abgelehnt hatte.

Das Landgericht Rottweil hatte sich dabei auf ein Gutachten der Duden-Redaktion gestützt, die sich wiederum auf Wiedemann berief, der wie folgt argumentiert:

> Das Wort "schwul" ist das alte niederdeutsche Wort für "schwül" und wurde unter dem Diktat der Rollenfixierungen (männlich = hart, kühl; weiblich = weich, warm) im 19. Jahrhundert umgangssprachlich für homosexuell gebräuchlich (vgl. warmer Bruder). Es ist in weiten Kreisen bis in die Schule hinein ein diskriminierendes Schimpfwort, wird aber heute allgemein in emanzipatorischen Gruppen verwendet, um es in seiner Wertung umzukehren. Das ist auch zum Teil gelungen und hat zahlreiche Vorbilder (vgl. "black" in der Parole "black is beautiful")... (21).

Die linguistische Auseinandersetzung der Lesben- und Schwulengruppen mit dem deutschen Amtsschimmel bringen die Abgeordneten Oesterle-Schwerin, Briefs und Hoss und die Fraktion der Grünen in einer "Kleinen Anfrage" dem Bundestag zur Kenntnis. Nach Unterbreitung der Fakten folgt ein Katalog von neunzehn Fragen, von denen ich die linguistisch relevanten zitiere:

1. Wird die Bundesregierung ihren Einfluß bei der Deutschen Postreklame geltend machen, um ein Erscheinen der Anzeige zu ermöglichen? Falls nein, warum nicht?
2. Kann die Anzeige erscheinen, wenn das Wort "Lesbe" durch "lesbische Frau" oder "Lesbierin" ersetzt würde? Wenn nicht, warum nicht?
3. Das Wort "Lesbierin" ist...die weibliche Form von Lesbier,[13] männlicher Bewohner von Lesbos. Wie beurteilt die Bundesregierung die Verwendung des Wortes "Lesbe" von Seiten der Frauenbewegung und ihrer Institutionen vor dem Hintergrund...der..."männlichen Provenienz" des Wortes "Lesbierin"?
4. Ist der Bundesregierung bekannt, daß die lesbischen Selbsthilfegruppen das Wort "Lesbe" im Namen führen?

5. Ist der Bundesregierung bekannt, daß der bundesweite Dachverband der bundesdeutschen Lesbenbewegung der Lesbenring e.V. ist?
6. Ist die Bundesregierung bereit,...das Recht auf Selbstbezeichnung im Sinne einer emanzipatorischen Meinungsäußerung für Schwule und Lesben ggf. zu garantieren?

Die Grünen verfolgen das Ziel, die Diskriminierenden als solche dingfest zu machen. Wenn sie emanzipationsfördernde Maßnahmen ablehnen, sollen sie sagen, warum. Die Grünen vermuten, daß die Beanstandung des Wortes nur ein Vorwand ist. Beanstandet wird eigentlich die "Dreistigkeit", mit der die FFGZ-Frauen so tun, als seien Lesben etwas ganz Normales und nicht Menschen, die sich zu verstecken haben. Wenn sie aus dem Versteck herauskommen, erregen sie öffentliches Ärgernis. Denn dann muß man sie zur Kenntnis nehmen, mit ihnen irgendwie umgehen, und das wollte man durch das Tabu ja gerade vermeiden.

3.2 Hauptakt

Etwa zur gleichen Zeit, am 1. Juli 1988, schreibt der Präsident des Deutschen Bundestages, Jenninger, an die "sehr verehrte Frau Kollegin Oesterle-Schwerin", daß er ihren Antrag zum Thema "Beeinträchtigung der Menschen- und Bürgerrechte von Schwulen und Lesben durch die 'Clause 28' in Großbritannien nur in "etwas geänderter Fassung zulassen kann. In der Überschrift muß die Wendung 'Schwulen und Lesben'...durch die Wendung 'Homosexuellen und Lesbierinnen' ersetzt werden." Seine Begründung:

> Nach ständiger Übung des Bundestages sind Überschriften und Themen, die wie die Überschrift dieses Antrags in die Tagesordnung des Plenums übernommen und damit dem ganzen Parlament zugerechnet werden können, so zu fassen, daß sie von allen Mitgliedern des Hauses akzeptiert werden können. Mir ist bekannt, daß die Begriffe "Schwule" und "Lesben" von nicht wenigen Kolleginnen und Kollegen nicht als Bestandteile der Hochsprache, in der die Tagesordnung des Plenums abgefaßt wird, anerkannt werden.

Hier ist besonders das "anerkannt" bzw. "akzeptiert werden" interessant. Wann sind die Mitglieder des Hauses bereit, die Formulierungen zu akzeptieren? Gibt es u.U. eine Möglichkeit, sie zum Akzeptieren zu zwingen? Etwa, wenn die umstrittenen Ausdrücke von berufener Seite als "Bestandteile der Hochsprache" eingestuft werden? Und wer entscheidet, welche zur Entscheidungshilfe eventuell herangezogenen Sachverständigen "akzeptabel" sind? Interessant ist auch, daß Jenninger sich das Recht zu einer Sprachzensur anmaßt, obwohl er die Sprache nicht beherrscht. Er weiß nicht, daß "die Hochsprache" den Begriff "Lesbierin" als Unterbegriff von "Homosexuelle" einordnet.

Oesterle-Schwerin, die als Jüdin noch einer weiteren diskriminierten Gruppe angehört, gibt Jenninger in einem langen Antwortbrief vom 12. Juli 1988 linguistische Nachhilfe:

> Die Worte "Lesbe" und "schwul" sind die Bezeichnungen, unter denen sich der größte Teil der homosexuellen Frauen und Männer in der Bundesrepublik selbst definiert. Der Dachverband der homosexuellen Frauen...heißt nicht "Lesbierinnenring", sondern "Lesbenring". Die homosexuellen Männergruppen, die es heute fast in jeder Stadt gibt, tragen mehrheitlich die Bezeichnung "schwul" in ihren Vereinsnamen. Der Bundesverband "Homosexualität" hat das Wort "schwul" nur deswegen nicht in seinem Vereinsnamen integriert, weil zur Zeit seiner Gründung versucht wurde, einen gemeinsamen Verband für Schwule und Lesben ins Leben zu rufen und weil heute auch einige gemischte Gruppen von Lesben und Schwulen in diesem Verband sind.
> Ihr Vorschlag, anstelle der Wendung "Schwulen und Lesben" die Wendung "Homosexuellen und Lesbierinnen" zu verwenden, ist völlig unakzeptabel. Erstens weil das Wort "Homosexuelle" sowohl Lesben als auch Schwule umfaßt—unser Antrag würde Ihrem Vorschlag entsprechend sinngemäß heißen "Beeinträchtigung der Menschen- und Bürgerrechte von Schwulen und Lesben und Lesbierinnen..." und zweitens weil das Wort "Lesbierin" von den meisten Lesben als altmodisch empfunden wird und sie sich in ihm nicht wiederfinden.[14]
> Aber auch die Beschränkung auf das Wort "homosexuell"...kommt für uns nicht in Frage.
> Die Abneigung gegen die Worte "Lesbe" und "schwul", die Sie bei einem Teil der Mitglieder des Bundestags vermuten, beruht darauf, daß diese Begriffe mitunter als Schimpfwörter[15] gelten und zur Beleidigung betroffener oder auch nichtbetroffener Personen verwendet werden. Es gehört jedoch zu der Politik von Lesben- und Schwulen-Organisationen, die negative Befrachtung dieser Begriffe abzulegen und sie als Bestandteil der Emanzipation von Lesben und Schwulen offensiv und stolz zu verwenden.
> Ihr Verbot, die Worte "Lesbe" und "schwul" in den Überschriften unserer Anträge erscheinen zu lassen, empfinde ich als Teil einer permanenten Diskriminierung von Lesben und Schwulen. Wenn die Bezeichnungen "schwul" und "Lesbe" für die Bundestagsdrucksachen nicht gut genug sind, wie ungemein schlecht [i.e. widerlich für Sie und Ihre Gesinnungsgenossen, LFP] muß es dann erst sein, als Schwuler oder als Lesbe zu leben.... Es sind nicht die Worte, an denen Sie und ein Teil der Kollegen sich stören, sondern eine bestimmte Lebensform, die abgelehnt wird und die an ihren offensiven Emanzipationsbestrebungen gehindert werden soll....
> Eines werden Sie aber auf jeden Fall nicht erreichen: Ich werde im Hohen Haus weiterhin von Lesben und Schwulen und nicht von homosexuellen Mitbürgern und Mitbürgerinnen reden.

Ich wurde später, auf dem Höhepunkt der Debatte im Spätherbst 1988, von etlichen Zeitungen, Zeitschriften und Rundfunkstationen gebeten, als feministische Linguistin meinen Kommentar zu der Sprachgroteske im Bundestag abzugeben. Ich habe jeweils auf diesen Brief von Oesterle-Schwerin an Jenninger verwiesen, der alles Notwendige dazu enthält. Besser konnte ich den Standpunkt der Lesben und Schwulen damals auch nicht begründen. Heute interessieren mich darüberhinaus vor allem die wohl weitgehend unbewußten Motive der homophobischen Mehrheit. Schließlich geht es doch "nur" um Wörter! Was ist es, das diese Wörter für manche so schrecklich macht?

Aber die Groteske geht noch weiter. Jetzt wird es erst richtig lustig. Am 12. Oktober schreibt Oesterle-Schwerin erneut an den Bundestagspräsidenten.

> ...Da die Begriffe "homosexuell" und "Homosexueller" bzw. "Homosexuelle" einen wissenschaftlich-pathologisierenden Charakter haben, lehnen wir diese Ausdrücke in bestimmten Zusammenhängen als Bezeichnungen für Schwule und Lesben ab. Wir bitten Sie daher erneut, unseren Antrag in der vorgelegten Form zuzulassen, sind jedoch bereit, um eine baldige Befassung unseres Antrags zu ermöglichen, folgende hochsprachliche Fassung als Antragsüberschrift zu akzeptieren: "Beeinträchtigung der Menschen- und Bürgerrechte von homosexuellen Menschen durch die 'Clause 28' in Großbritannien sowie vergleichbare Angriffe auf die Emanzipationsbestrebungen der Schwulen- und Lesbenbewegung in Bayern". Die Wortbildungen "Schwulenbewegung" und "Lesbenbewegung" sind nach Duden, das große Wörterbuch der deutschen Sprache (6 Bde., 1976, siehe unter Schwulen-Bewegung) hochsprachliche Ausdrücke. Da das Wort "schwul" von der Umgangssprache in die Hochsprache überwechselt, ist bereits die Mehrzahl der Wortbildungen mit dem Begriff "schwul" hochsprachlich. Ausnahmen hiervon bilden allein die Begriffe "Schwulenszene", "Schwulentreff".[16]

Auf diesen Brief antwortet am 21. November die amtierende Bundestagspräsidentin Renger. Der ursprüngliche Adressat Jenninger hatte nämlich in der Zwischenzeit selbst durch unbedachte Äußerungen in einer Bundestagsrede zum 50. Jahrestag der sogenannten Kristallnacht einen Skandal verursacht und mußte sein Amt niederlegen. Die skandalösen Äußerungen wären übrigens dem "Hohen Hause" nicht weiter aufgefallen, wenn die Jüdin Oesterle-Schwerin nicht durch einen Zwischenruf ihre Empörung geäußert hätte.

Renger schreibt noch eine Spur kühler und herablassender als Jenninger, finde ich:

> Für die Zulassung des Betreffs in seiner Ursprungsfassung besteht kein Anlaß. Seit seiner Zurückweisung am 1. Juli 1988 haben sich keine neuen Umstände ergeben, die eine Überprüfung der damaligen Entscheidung nahelegen würden.

Nach einer weiteren Erörterung dieser Angelegenheit im Präsidium kann ich auch den hilfsweise vorgeschlagenen Betreff nicht zulassen. Die Begriffe "Schwulen-" und "Lesbenbewegung" mögen zwar inzwischen von der Umgangs- in die Hochsprache übergegangen sein, sie können aber trotzdem nicht von allen Mitgliedern des Hauses akzeptiert werden. Ich darf daran erinnern, daß sich auch der Ältestenrat[17] am 29. September mit breiter Mehrheit dagegen ausgesprochen hat, die Verwendung derartiger Begriffe zuzulassen.

Jenninger hatte sich noch genötigt gesehen, einen Grund für das Mißfallen einiger Bundestagsmitglieder anzugeben: Die beanstandeten Wörter gehörten nicht der Hochsprache an. Nachdem Oesterle-Schwerin nun als Kompromiß Ausdrücke verwenden will, die laut Duden der Hochsprache angehören, wird dies Argument nicht mehr benutzt. Es genügt jetzt die Behauptung, die Ausdrücke könnten nicht von allen Mitgliedern des Hauses akzeptiert werden.

"Nicht von allen"—das bedeutet, einer genügt. Und einer, der CSU-Abgeordnete Wittmann, hatte sich in der Tat schon im Mai in einem Protestschreiben an Jenninger heftig über die "Verwilderung der Sprachkultur" entrüstet, für die die Abgeordnete Oesterle-Schwerin verantwortlich sei, die in mehreren Anfragen an die Regierung betreffs der rechtlichen Behandlung homosexueller Paare "der Gosse zugehörige Vokabeln" wie *Lesben* und *Schwule* "genüßlich ausgewalzt" habe. Beide Vokabeln seien daraufhin nicht nur in die offizielle Bundestagsdrucksache, sondern "zu allem Überfluß" auch noch in die Parlamentsberichterstattung aufgenommen worden, obwohl sie "des Hohen Hauses unwürdig" seien (Nordpresse). —Frau beachte das enorme Gefälle zwischen einer Gosse und dem Hohen Hause!

Wir kommen nunmehr zum Höhepunkt und Eklat unserer linguistischen Horror-Story: Oesterle-Schwerin und einige Getreue gegen den Deutschen Bundestag, so geschehen am 24. November 1988. Ich zitiere aus dem Protokoll der 110. Sitzung der 11. Wahlperiode.

**Oesterle-Schwerin:** ...Ich möchte hier zwei Anträge verlesen, die leider noch nicht schriftlich vorliegen. Erster Antrag: ...In der Abteilung "Familie und Soziales" soll eine Dienststelle "Schwulenreferat" eingerichtet werden.
(Zuruf von der CDU/CSU: Was ist denn das?)
Im Arbeitsstab "Frauenpolitik" soll eine Dienststelle "Lesbenreferat" eingerichtet werden.
(Dr. Hoffacker, CDU/CSU: Das ist ja wohl nicht wahr!)
...Begründung: Im Bereich Lesben- und Schwulenpolitik zeichnet sich die Bundesregierung durch völlige Untätigkeit aus.
(Heiterkeit und Beifall bei der CDU/CSU—Dr. Rose, CDU/CSU: Gott sei Dank!)

…Es wäre gar nicht notwendig gewesen, das hier zu verlesen, wenn das Präsidium diesen Antrag wegen der kleinen Wörtchen "Lesbe" und "schwul" nicht abgelehnt hätte. Aber ich mache das ja gerne. Wie der Herr Wittman von der CDU ja schon sagte: Die Wörter "Lesbe" und "schwul" werden von mir gerade in diesem Hause immer wieder genüßlich ausgewalzt.

**Vizepräsidentin Frau Renger:** Meine Damen und Herren, ich darf dazu vielleicht eine Bemerkung machen, die die Angelegenheit dann klärt.
In den Anträgen, die eben begründet wurden, werden *Begriffe* verwendet, die sprachlich von der überwiegenden Mehrheit der Mitglieder des Hauses nicht akzeptiert werden können.
  (Beifall bei der CDU/CSU).
[Bisher hieß es immer nur "nicht von allen Mitgliedern des Hauses", jetzt ist es plötzlich "die überwiegende Mehrheit"—also mindestens 60-70%. Eine Umfrage wurde m.W. nicht durchgeführt. Der Ausgang der Abstimmung gibt Renger dann allerdings insofern recht, als die Mehrheit der zu dem Zeitpunkt Anwesenden gegen die Wörter *Lesbe* und *Schwule* stimmte. Renger weiter:]
Die Anträge sind deshalb nach ständiger Parlamentspraxis unzulässig. Würden sie angenommen, würde ihr Text…nicht nur der Fraktion DIE GRÜNEN, sondern dem ganzen Deutschen Bundestag zugerechnet werden.
  (Frau Schoppe, GRÜNE: Das ist doch mittelalterlich, was sich hier abspielt!)
Ich darf daran erinnern, daß sich der Ältestenrat am 29. September 1988 mit breiter Mehrheit dagegen ausgesprochen hat, die Verwendung derartiger Begriffe zuzulassen....
[Die Bundestagsvizepräsidentin schreibt zwar die Wörter *Lesben* und *Schwule,* aber sie nimmt sie nicht in den Mund. Sie sagt nur *diese* bzw. *derartige Begriffe.* Renger weiter:]
Selbstverständlich werden die Anträge zugelassen, wenn statt der von den Antragstellern verwendeten Begriffe die Begriffe "Homosexuellenbewegung" und "Homosexuellenreferat" verwendet werden. Kann sich der Antragsteller damit einverstanden erklären?
[*Der* Antragsteller ist Jutta Oesterle-Schwerin bzw. die Partei DIE GRÜNEN.]
**Oesterle-Schwerin:** Nein, natürlich nicht!
**Renger:** Bitte Herr Kleinert, zur Geschäftsordnung.
**Kleinert** (GRÜNE): …Wir sehen uns nicht imstande, diesem Vorschlag des Präsidiums zu entsprechen. Es geht nicht darum, daß hier die Gefühle irgendeiner Seite des Hauses verletzt werden sollen, aber es kann umgekehrt auch nicht darum gehen, daß die Gefühle von anderen durch eine bestimmte Wortwahl verletzt werden.... Ich beantrage deshalb,…darüber abzustimmen, ob diese Anträge in der vorliegenden Form hier zur Abstimmung gestellt werden oder nicht.

...

**Becker** (SPD): ...Ich glaube, es gibt eine breite Übereinstimmung in diesem Hause, daß wir es bei den Homosexuellen mit einer Gruppe in der Bevölkerung zu tun haben, mit der wir uns auseinanderzusetzen und der wir auch zu helfen haben. Aber es kann doch nicht darum gehen, daß hier jetzt ein Streit über Worte entfacht wird, die man im Parlament gebrauchen will oder nicht. Wir sind in der Sache völlig einverstanden damit, daß man sich gründlich mit diesem Thema beschäftigt. Aber dann geben Sie doch bitte zu—nicht um der Schau willen—daß Sie Begriffe verwenden, die eine breite Mehrheit nicht will,...die selbst Mitglieder der Szene, dieser Bevölkerungsgruppe nicht wollen. Das ist doch ein Streit um Worte.

(Frau Beck-Oberndorf, GRÜNE: Worte haben ihre Bedeutung. Die stehen doch für Tabuisierung. Das kann jeder Sprachwissenschaftler [*sic*] erklären!)

Nun noch ein Zweites: Warum machen Sie denn nicht von dem nach der Geschäftsordnung vorgesehenen Verfahren Gebrauch?

(Kleinert, GRÜNE: Das machen wir doch!)

...Warum machen Sie denn formal schon alles falsch?...Warum wollen sie einen solchen Schaueffekt hier im Hause?

(Zuruf von der CDU/CSU: Hysterie!)

Aus diesem Grunde können wir ihnen bei dem, was Sie vorhaben, leider nicht helfen....

(Beifall bei...der SPD sowie bei der CDU/CSU und der FDP).

**Bohl** (CDU/CSU): ...Ich glaube, Frau Präsidentin, daß es völlig richtig ist, wie Sie hier entschieden haben: Ich möchte nur in Ergänzung zu Herrn Kollegen Becker darauf hinweisen, daß man sich mit dieser Thematik befaßt.

(Frau Beck-Oberndorf, GRÜNE: Aber sprachlich muß die tabuisiert werden!)

Sie versuchen, vor der deutschen Öffentlichkeit zu günstiger Fernsehzeit den Eindruck zu erwecken, als würde von dem Deutschen Bundestag...die Homosexualität sozusagen tabuisiert und als befaßte man sich politisch nicht damit.

(Oesterle-Schwerin: Wenn man Dinge nicht beim Namen nennen darf, werden sie tabuisiert!)

Das Gegenteil ist gegeben. Wenn Sie hier nicht bereit sind, auf die Anregung der Frau Präsidentin einzugehen, geben Sie solchen Verdächtigungen, nämlich daß es Ihnen im Grunde genommen nicht um die Sache, sondern um den politischen Schaueffekt geht, nur zusätzliche Nahrung. Das können wir natürlich nicht mitmachen....

**Beckmann** (FDP): ...Das Thema Homosexualität ist auch für meine Kolleginnen und Kollegen in der FDP-Bundestagsfraktion ein Thema, das angesichts der Bedeutung in der Bevölkerung nur mit größtem Ernst und seriös diskutiert werden kann. Nur unter diesem Aspekt ist der betroffenen Bevölkerungsgruppe, ist diesen Menschen, die zum Teil ein sehr schweres

Schicksal haben, zu helfen. Wir wehren uns dagegen, daß in diesem Zusammenhang im Deutschen Bundestag Kampfbegriffe eingeführt werden; damit ist den betroffenen Menschen nicht geholfen.... Wir werden uns für die Sache weiterhin einsetzen, aber seriös und ernsthaft.

...

**Kleinert** (GRÜNE): ...Ich will noch einmal in aller Deutlichkeit sachlich richtigstellen: Daß wir uns hier heute morgen damit befassen müssen, liegt daran, daß sich die Bundestagsverwaltung unter Bezugnahme auf das Präsidium geweigert hat, Anträge überhaupt auszudrucken, die die Begriffe "Schwule" und "Lesben" enthalten.
(Zuruf der CDU/CSU: Das ist richtig!)
Das nenne ich eine Sprachzensur der Fraktion DIE GRÜNEN.
(Bohl, CDU/CSU: Nein, das ist nicht richtig!)

...

**Renger:** Hier wurde seitens der...GRÜNEN der Antrag gestellt, das Haus möge entscheiden, ob der Antrag in dieser Form zulässig ist oder nicht. Ich lasse darüber abstimmen ob dieses Haus den Antrag mit diesen Bezeichnungen, die hier genannt worden sind, akzeptiert. [Wieder: Renger nimmt die Wörter "Lesben" und "Schwule" nicht in den Mund.] Es geht also um die Zulässigkeit des Antrags in der eingebrachten Form. Wer ist dafür?—Gegenprobe!—Dieses ist abgelehnt.

Noch am selben Tag informiert Oesterle-Schwerin die Öffentlichkeit in einer Pressemitteilung über das Ergebnis:

Mit...den Begriffen "Schwule und Lesben" hat die neuere deutsche Schwulen- und Lesbenbewegung ihren Anspruch auf Emanzipation und Akzeptanz statt bloßer Integration oder Toleranz—zu deutsch: Duldung—geltend gemacht. Dieser emanzipatorische Anspruch...stößt nun auf Widerspruch im Bundestag.
Der uns vorgeschlagene Begriff "Homosexuelle"...beinhaltet eine bestimmte Haltung gegenüber Schwulen und Lesben: Wer Homosexuelle sagt, spricht von einer "Gruppe, der wir zu helfen haben"...oder die ein "schweres Schicksal" haben....
Letztlich geht es um folgendes: Akzeptiert man oder frau selbstbewußte Schwule und Lesben, so wie sie sind und wie sie sich selbst bezeichnen...oder spricht man/frau *über* arme, vom Schicksal geschlagene Homosexuelle.
Wie sehr der CDU/CSU der Anspruch der Schwulen und Lesben nach Emanzipation zuwider ist, wurde deutlich, als auf ihre Intervention hin das Telefon des "Schwulenreferats" unserer Fraktion am 11. November 1988 wegen seines Namens von der Bundestagsverwaltung abgeschaltet wurde. Die Bekämpfung der Emanzipation ist einem also durchaus eine Rechtsverletzung gegenüber einer Parlamentsfraktion wert.

Am 29. November meldet die Deutsche Presseagentur:

> Bei der Abstimmung über die Zulässigkeit der Grünen-Anträge hielten sich viele SPD-Abgeordnete nicht an die Empfehlung ihrer parlamentarischen Geschäftsführung. Während die Prominenz in der ersten Reihe gegen die Anträge stimmte oder sich enthielt, wurde auf den hinteren Bänken fast durchgehend für die Behandlung der Anträge auch mit den Worten "schwul" und "lesbisch" gestimmt. Das sei "bemerkenswert" und "symptomatisch" für den inneren Zustand der SPD", sagte der CDU-Familienpolitiker...Hoffacker.

Am 8. Februar 1989 schreiben die Vorstandsfrauen des Deutschen Lesbenrings an die neue Bundestagsvorsitzende Rita Süssmuth:

> ...Bitte teilen Sie uns mit, wie Sie es mit der von Ihren Vorgänger/inne/n abgelehnten Bezeichnung für uns Lesben halten wollen.
> Die Zensur der Worte Lesbe/lesbisch...durch das Präsidium des Deutschen Bundestages können wir Lesben (nicht Lesbierinnen!!!) nicht hinnehmen. Diese Begriffe müssen von den Mitgliedern des Deutschen Bundestages akzeptiert werden, weil wir als Betroffene so bezeichnet werden wollen. Wir Lesben sind nicht gemeint, wenn von Homosexuellen und Lesbierinnen die Rede ist; wir können auch nicht akzeptieren, daß das Präsidium des Deutschen Bundestages darüber befindet, wie wir benannt werden wollen.
> Wir sind und bleiben Lesben!
> Mit freundlichen Grüßen, Lesbenring e.V.

Jutta Oesterle-Schwerin teilte mir am 20.10.1993 mit, daß Süssmuth sich ihres Wissens zu diesem Brief nicht geäußert hat. Sie hat sich überhaupt in dieser Frage nicht engagiert, sondern sich "neutral" verhalten.

## 3.3 Kehraus

Nachdem alle Bemühungen der Grünen um die Durchsetzung einer emanzipatorischen Sprachpolitik gescheitert waren, gingen sie sozusagen von der Offensive in die Subversive und bezeichneten Lesben und Schwule nunmehr als Urninden und Urninge. "Der Unbefangene glaubt, ein mittelhochdeutsches Wort zu hören", bemerkt dazu die FAZ vom 11.2.89 und fährt fort:

> Der Antrag der Grünen klärt aber auf, daß der Pionier "schwuler Emanzipation", der Jurist Karl-Heinrich Ulrichs, den Begriff "Urninge" in Umwandlung des Götternamens Uranus als erste Selbstbezeichnung für "Schwule" und "Urninden" für "Lesben" eingeführt habe (in der Schrift "Vindex", Leipzig 1864) (Herles).

> Der erneut eingereichte Antrag bezieht sich nunmehr also auf die "Beeinträchtigung der Menschen- und Bürgerrechte von Urningen und

Urninden durch die 'Sektion 28' der Local Government Bill in Großbritannien sowie vergleichbare Angriffe auf die Emanzipation der Uringe und Urninden in Bayern." Die Grünen begründen diese Wortwahl damit, daß sie eher auf eine antiquierte Selbstbezeichnung zurückgreifen wollten, als die pathologisierende Fremdbezeichnung "Homosexuelle/r" zu übernehmen.

Heute ist die ganze Sache nur noch ein Fall für die Lesben- und Schwulen-Geschichte und die Sprachgeschichte, nachdem der Bundestag 1991 klein beigeben mußte. Die Grünen stellten die weiterhin fremdelnden Abgeordneten vor die Wahl, den gängigen Sprachgebrauch der Lesben und Schwulen entweder endlich zu akzeptieren oder mit der ungeliebten Sache wieder durch alle Instanzen befaßt zu werden, einschließlich maximaler Beteiligung der Medien. Der Bundestag entschloß sich zum Einlenken, und die Grünen teilten am 4. Juni 1991 der Öffentlichkeit unter der Überschrift "Das Parlament erweitert seinen Sprachschatz" folgendes mit:

> Im Gegensatz zu den vergangenen Jahren, in denen die Begriffe "Lesbe" und "schwul" in den Überschriften von Bundestagsdrucksachen nicht zugelassen wurden, bekamen wir gestern vom Parlamentssekretariat die Nachricht, daß unsere Anträge auf die Einrichtung eines Lesbenreferats im Frauenministerium und eines Schwulenreferats im Familienministerium... zur Abstimmung zugelassen wurden.
>
> Der Zulassung, die diesmal ebenfalls zunächst verweigert werden sollte, gingen längere Beratungen auf verschiedenen Ebenen voraus. Das Verbot, durch das sich der Bundestag republikweit sowie im Ausland lächerlich gemacht hat, soll nicht mehr aufrecht erhalten werden.

4. Linguistisch-pragmatische Analyse und Beurteilung des "Streits um Worte"

4.1 Analyse

Die beiden Parteien stehen einander unversöhnlich gegenüber. Die Grünen haben einige Kompromißvorschläge gemacht, die das Bundestagspräsidium nicht akzeptiert hat. Das Präsidium hat einen Kompromißvorschlag gemacht, den die Grünen nicht akzeptiert haben.

Die Grünen haben zahlreiche Argumente vorgetragen, weshalb Lesben und Schwule auf ihre Selbstbezeichnung nicht verzichten wollen. Der Bundestag bleibt dagegen eigentümlich blaß in seiner Begründung: "Nicht alle Mitglieder des Hohen Hauses können diese Wörter akzeptieren". Warum—das wird eigentlich nicht gesagt. Das schwache Argument mit der "Hochsprache" zieht ja nicht mehr, seit Oesterle-Schwerin nachgewiesen hat, daß zumindest *Schwulenbewegung* vom Duden bereits als hochsprachlich abgesegnet ist.

Mein Eindruck ist, daß die Mitglieder des Bundestags, die schließlich gegen den "offiziellen" Gebrauch der umstrittenen Wörter gestimmt haben, gegen diese Wörter eine heftige und tiefsitzende Abneigung haben, die sie aber nicht weiter begründen können. Sie wollen sie übrigens auch nicht begründen, und anders als die antragstellenden Grünen "haben sie das auch nicht nötig". Mit der einfachen Ablehnung durch Handhochheben haben sie ihrer Pflicht genügt.

Ich möchte zunächst versuchen, die Gründe für diese Abneigung linguistisch-pragmatisch zu analysieren. Wenn die Gründe deutlicher werden, läßt sich besser dagegen argumentieren.

Etliche Mitglieder des Bundestags waren anscheinend peinlich berührt, wenn Oesterle-Schwerin die Ausdrücke benutzte, aber sie konnten nichts dagegen unternehmen. Was sie aber ganz entschieden ablehnen, ist die Übernahme der Ausdrücke in Texte, für die das gesamte Haus zeichnet. Sie wollen gegenüber der Öffentlichkeit nicht den Eindruck erwecken, als ob *sie selbst* solche schmutzigen, obszönen Ausdrücke "aus der Gosse" verwendeten. Mögen sich die Grünen damit bloßstellen, was für die "Würde des Hohen Hauses" schon schlimm genug ist—sie aber wollen sich damit nicht die Finger schmutzig machen.

Zugrunde liegt hier eine pragmatische Implikation etwa der Art: *Wer "schmutzige" Ausdrücke benutzt, ist selbst schmutzig.* Der Bundestag hat also ein Image-Problem. Er möchte auf die Öffentlichkeit nicht schmutzig wirken, sondern sachlich-klinisch-kompetent. Das Wort *Homosexuelle*—aus der medizinisch-pathologischen Fachsprache, wie Oesterle-Schwerin immer wieder geduldig ausführt—ist deshalb gerade das richtige. (Das Parlament gibt erst nach, als das eine Image-Problem von einem anderen überschattet wird: Man macht sich mit der deutschen Sturheit "republikweit und im Ausland" einfach lächerlich!)

Was aus linguistischer Sicht an diesem Streit besonders seltsam anmutet, ist, daß keine der Parteien auf die Idee gekommen ist, die beliebten Gänsefüßchen als Kompromiß vorzuschlagen. Die Springerpresse behandelte einen ähnlichen Konflikt zwischen Selbst- und Fremdbezeichnung jahrzehntelang stur mittels Gänsefüßchen. Sie setzten die für sie unakzeptable Selbstbezeichnung der Deutschen Demokratischen Republik, DDR, stets in Anführungszeichen.

Die eigentlich relevanten linguistischen Fragen sind aber:

a) Welche seltsame Kraft bewirkt, daß manche Ausdrücke "schmutzig" sind und manche nicht? Schließlich bezeichnen die Wörter *Homosexuelle* auf der einen und *Lesben* und *Schwule* auf der anderen Seite doch genau dieselben Leute, was auch von keiner Seite bestritten wird!

b) Trifft es zu, daß der Bundestag die Interessen der meisten Lesben und Schwulen besser vertritt als Oesterle-Schwerin und ihre MitstreiterInnen, wenn er sie mit dem "würdigen, seriösen" Wort *Homosexuelle* bezeichnet—und dann endlich zu den dringenden Sachfragen kommt? Es stimmt doch, daß sehr viele Lesben und Schwule diese Wörter als Selbstbezeichnung ablehnen, weil für sie der verletzende Schimpfwort-Charakter im Vordergrund steht.

4.2 Welche Ausdrücke sind schmutzig und welche nicht und warum?

Anscheinend sind Wörter wie Kleidungsstücke. Kleidung nimmt den Geruch ihrer Umgebung an, wie jede Nichtraucherin weiß, die längere Zeit in verräucherter Umgebung verbracht hat. Oder jede Frau, die Mottenpulver im Kleiderschrank hat. Die Kleidung riecht noch lange nach Mottenpulver.

Das Wort *schwul* ist—so sehen wir Lesben und Schwule es—behaftet mit der üblen Ausdünstung derjenigen, die es zur Demütigung der Schwulen erfunden haben. Trotzdem haben es die Schwulen angezogen, wobei sie sich sozusagen gegen den Gestank die Nase zuhalten mußten. Aber allmählich hat es den eigenen Geruch angenommen. Es ist jetzt ihr persönliches Kleidungsstück geworden. Das gilt aber nicht für alle Schwulen, sondern nur für die politische Avantgarde.

Für das "Hohe Haus" ist die Sache einfacher: Das Wort *Schwule* riecht übel nach Schwulen, und was die für Schweinereien machen, weiß man ja. Für Lesben gilt—*mutatis mutandis*—dasselbe.[18]

Wir sehen hier eine zweite pragmatische Implikation am Werk:

*Die Sprache des menschlichen Abschaums (Stichwort: Gosse) ist selber Abschaum, schmutzig,* insbesondere auch die Wörter, mit denen diese Personen bezeichnet werden und mit denen sie sich selbst bezeichnen.

Ähnlich gilt: Bestimmte Tätigkeiten sind schmutzig, ganz besonders alles, was mit Sexualität zusammenhängt und erst recht mit "abweichender Sexualität". Daraus folgt, die Sprache zur Bezeichnung dieser Tätigkeiten ist auch schmutzig, ausgenommen die klinische und die Verwaltungssprache, denn die ist legitimiert durch ihren Gebrauchskontext.

Wörter nehmen den Geruch ihres Kontextes an. Diese Aussage ergibt, umgedreht, folgendes: *Ein Wort, das als "schmutzig" eingeordnet wird, stammt aus einem—für die Einordner—"schmutzigen" Kontext.* Um genau dies geht es, und genau dies darf natürlich nicht gesagt, nicht zugegeben werden. Es muß unter dem Teppich bleiben—denn man ist ja soo tolerant, liberal und aufgeklärt! (Daß man es nicht ist, zeigen überdeutlich die Zwischenrufe "Was ist denn das?", "Das ist ja wohl nicht wahr!" und "Gott sei Dank!" zu den Vorschlägen, Lesben- und Schwulenreferate einzurichten bzw. zu dem Vorwurf gegen die Regierung, sie sei lesben- und schwulenpolitisch untätig.) Deswegen (u.a.) bleibt der Bundestag in seiner Ablehnung so unklar und verwaschen. Wenn der Gebrauchskontext (und das heißt: die bezeichneten Personen) nicht schmutzig wären, wären auch die von ihnen gewählten Selbstbezeichnungen nicht schmutzig, und dann könnte auch das "Hohe Haus" nicht durch sie beschmutzt werden.

Medizin, Verwaltung, Polizei und ähnliche ehrbare Institutionen haben sich von Berufs wegen auch mit "menschlichem Abschaum" zu befassen; sie tun es in ihrer eigenen Verwaltungs- und medizinischen Fachsprache. Sie reden in dieser Sprache *über* den betreffenden menschlichen Abschaum. Die Institutionen sind würdig und objektiv; sie enthalten sich aller Emotionen und folglich auch emotionaler abwertender Begriffe, wie *Schwule und Lesben*. Diese spezielle Sprache gehört zu ihrer Corporate Identity, um einen heute beliebten Begriff zu benutzen, genau wie ihre streng codierte Berufskleidung. Die Sprache stellt sicher, daß die Grenze zwischen den besprochenen frag- bzw. unwürdigen Subjekten und ihren Verwaltern klar markiert ist, damit Verwechslungen ausgeschlossen werden. Die wichtigste Funktion der fachsprachlichen Ausdrücke ist die der *Isolierung* und *Distanzierung*. Denn es gibt eine weitere pragmatische Implikation: *Wer die Sprache einer Gruppe benutzt, gibt sich als Mitglied der Gruppe zu erkennen.*[19]

Oesterle-Schwerin ist so gesehen wirklich ein Ärgernis, ein Pfahl im Fleische des Bundestags. Sie verwischt die Grenzen nicht nur durch ihre unerhörten Anträge, sondern schon insofern, als sie sowohl "diesem Hohen Hause" angehört als auch jenem Abschaum—und damit die Mitgliedschaft im Hohen Hause selbst gewissermaßen ein für allemal besudelt.

Es gibt im Deutschen die Redewendung "Den würde ich nichtmal mit der Kohlenzange anfassen". Das Wort *HomosexuelleR* ist wie so eine Kohlenzange, oder wie ein Gummihandschuh (vielleicht ein passenderer Vergleich im Zeitalter von Aids). Es verhindert den direkten Kontakt zwischen mir und dem ekligen Objekt. Es verhindert Kontamination, die mich zu einem der Ihren machen könnte. Der Bundestag fürchtet sozusagen, gemeinsam mit den Lesben und Schwulen in der Gosse zu sitzen, wenn er nachgibt, während Oesterle-Schwerin "nur" als genau so "normal" geachtet werden will wie die andern Abgeordneten.

Ich komme nun zur Beantwortung der zweiten Frage von oben: Trifft es zu, daß der Bundestag die Interessen der Lesben und Schwulen besser vertritt als Oesterle-Schwerin, wenn er sie mit dem würdigen, seriösen Begriff *Homosexuelle* bezeichnet? Zur Beantwortung dieser Frage möchte ich etwas ausholen. Der Vertriebenenpolitiker Wittmann beanstandete in seinem Beschwerdebrief über die "Gossenausdrücke" auch noch "sprachliche Erosionserscheinungen" auf einem ganz anderen Gebiet. Es gäbe immer mehr amtliche Schriftstücke, in denen die Bundesrepublik im Sinne der DDR "abwertend" bezeichnet werde, und zwar durch die Adjektive *bundesdeutsch* und *bundesrepublikanisch* (stattdessen möchte er lieber lesen: *deutsch*). Die Lesben und Schwulen sollen sich gefälligst so nennen, wie er sie nennen will. Aber er möchte nicht so genannt werden, wie die DDR ihn bezeichnet. Mit anderen Worten: Das Recht auf

Selbstbezeichnung verlangt er für sich selbst, und alle anderen sollen ihm folgen, aber er gesteht es den Lesben und Schwulen nicht zu.

Die Frage, wer die Interessen der Lesben und Schwulen besser vertritt, läßt sich leicht beantworten. Es handelt sich um Personen, die überwiegend im Versteck leben. Diejenigen, die sichtbar sind, und vor allem die, die sich politisch zu einer Gruppe formiert haben, nennen sich Lesben und Schwule. Es wäre also, wie Oesterle-Schwerin ganz richtig feststellt, ein Akt der Diskriminierung, sie mit einem Wort zu benennen, das sie explizit ablehnen. Die Unsichtbaren (die eventuell die Worte *Homosexuelle* und *Lesbierinnen* besser finden, was aber niemand herausfinden und somit exakt nachweisen kann, da sie eben unsichtbar sind) können die Grünen ohnehin nicht vertreten, weil sie von diesen Unsichtbaren kein Mandat haben, nicht haben *können*.

Es kommt außerdem hinzu, daß die Proponentin des Antrags, Oesterle-Schwerin, selber der besprochenen Gruppe angehört—im Gegensatz zu Jenninger, Renger und den Abgeordneten, soweit sie nicht Lesben und Schwule im Versteck sind. Renger, Jenninger und die Abgeordneten benehmen sich etwa so anmaßend wie mein Doktorvater, dem es beliebte, eine ehemalige Studentin und inzwischen arrivierte Professorin in den siebziger Jahren trotz ihres Protests weiterhin mit *Fräulein* anzureden, solange sie nicht verheiratet sei.

5. Ausblick

Eine der wichtigsten Entwicklungen im Bereich des Komplexes "Sprache und Homophobie" scheint mir der immer häufiger werdende Gebrauch des Wortes *heterosexuell*, bedingt wohl hauptsächlich durch den Aids-Diskurs. Das ist—trotz der Tragik des Anlasses—für Lesben und Schwule eine positive Entwicklung. Der Idealzustand, die einleitend angesprochene Emanzipierte Gesellschaft, ist diesbezüglich verwirklicht, wenn nicht nur Homosexuelle ihr Coming Out machen müssen, sondern auch Hetero-, Bi-, Trans- und Asexuelle und was es noch für "Bindestrich-Sexualitäten" geben mag. Kurz, wenn die Kategorie "sexuelle Orientierung" etwa den Status der Kategorie "Religionszugehörigkeit" in einer multikulturellen Gesellschaft erreicht hat: Es ist nicht gleichgültig, welcher Religion/Präferenzgruppe eine angehört, es ist aber keine bestimmte Religion, keine Religionszugehörigkeit und keine Gender-Präferenz vorgeschrieben, und daher ist Religionszugehörigkeit/Gender-Präferenz auch nicht festgelegt und vorhersagbar, zumal die Gender-Präferenz auch wie die Religion gewechselt werden kann.

Über das Thema Sprache, Lesben und Schwule bleibt noch viel zu sagen. Interessierte verweise ich auf mein Buchprojekt *Sprache andersrum*. Für Hinweise und Kritik bin ich immer dankbar.

## 6. Nachschlag

Eine vorläufige Fassung dieses Aufsatzes bot ich im Dezember 1993 der Zeitschrift *Das Plateau* zum Druck an, nachdem man sich sehr bemüht hatte, mich als Autorin des Hauptbeitrags—über ein Thema meiner Wahl—für eine der nächsten Ausgaben zu gewinnen. "*Das Plateau*", so hieß es in dem Einladungsschreiben, "will...eigenständige Standpunkte und Entwürfe präsentieren, will Auslöser sein für neue Wahrnehmungen". Und man garantierte "sorgfältigsten Druck, feinstes Papier, einen schön gestalteten Rahmen und einen anspruchsvollen Leserkreis". Meine Abhandlung über schmutzige Wörter und Schwulitäten auf feinstem Papier—das fand ich apart, deshalb sagte ich zu.

Lange Zeit hörte ich nichts von den Herausgebern und hatte die Sache schon fast vergessen, da bekam ich mein Paper zurück mit einer höflichen Absage. Der Entschluß sei ihnen nicht leicht gefallen, aber der zeitliche Abstand zwischen den Vorgängen, die ich analysierte und dem möglichen Erscheinungstermin wäre allzu groß—auch wenn das Thema selbst mit Sicherheit noch aktuell sei und wohl weiterhin bleiben werde. In jedem Fall aber danke man mir für das Vertrauen, das ich ihnen entgegengebracht hätte.

Wohl selten wurde der Inhalt eines Artikels durch ein Ablehnungsschreiben so schön bestätigt. Gossenausdrücke wie *Lesben* und *Schwule* gehören nicht ins Hohe Haus, und ein Aufsatz über Lesben und Schwule gehört nicht auf das "Plateau" erhoben. Aber das kann man nicht offen sagen, deshalb nennt man einen anderen Grund. Allzu viel Mühe muß man sich mit der Begründung aber auch wieder nicht geben. Plausibel muß sie nicht sein, nur den wahren Grund irgendwie verdecken helfen.

Hätte ich den Herren einen Beitrag über feministische Metapherntheorie, Bachmanns Libretti oder über sonstwas Ordentliches geschickt, hätten sie ihn vielleicht auch abgelehnt. Aber sie hätten mir nicht so einfühlsam für mein Vertrauen gedankt. Denn das Schreiben über Homosexualität kommt einem Coming Out gleich. Weshalb es denn auch meistens vermieden wurde und wird. Aber das Klima erwärmt sich langsam, sogar in Deutschland. Dennoch—dieser Aufsatz erscheint nicht zufällig zuerst in den USA.

## Anmerkungen

[1] Überarbeitete Fassung eines Aufsatzes, von dem ich am 30.10.93 bei der Jahrestagung der *Women in German* in Great Barrington, Massachusetts eine gekürzte Version vorgetragen habe. Den Frauen der Bostoner Gruppe der Women in German: Lisa Gates, Joey Horsley, Barbara Hyams, Monika Totten, Martha Wallach, Margaret Ward und Christiane Zehl-Romero danke ich herzlich

für die hilfreiche Diskussion einer vorläufigen Fassung und den Herausgeberinnen des Jahrbuchs für ihre sorgfältige Editionsarbeit und konstruktive Kritik.

[2] Die Idee, diesen berühmten Schluß-Satz des *Tractatus logico-philosophicus* im Sinne der Closet-Problematik zu interpretieren und hier als Motto zu verwenden, verdanke ich Joey Horsley.

[3] Nach meiner Habilitation 1978 bekam ich durch ein Heisenbergstipendium fünf Jahre Forschungsfreiheit, die ich für die Weiterentwicklung der feministischen Linguistik nutzte bzw. "zweckentfremdete". Damit war ich für eine Professur an einer der deutschen Männer-Universitäten disqualifiziert: Meine über 50 Bewerbungen blieben erfolglos.—Die Anzahl der Frauen auf deutschen Professuren beträgt noch immer rund 5 Prozent.

[4] In vielen Ländern gilt Homosexualtät noch heute als Verbrechen und steht unter Strafandrohung.

[5] Erving Goffman unterscheidet in seinem Buch *Stigma* (1963) zwischen "diskreditierten" Gruppen mit einem sichtbaren Stigma und "diskreditierbaren" mit einem unsichtbaren Stigma. Seine Überlegungen über die Besonderheiten unserer Situation fand ich schon in den 60er Jahren sehr hilfreich und erhellend.

[6] Die Psychologin Dr. Evelyn Hooker, die 1956 die berühmte Studie "The Adjustment of the Male Overt Homosexual" vorlegte, die schließlich dazu führte, daß Homosexualität nicht mehr als psychische Krankheit definiert wurde und 1973 aus dem *Diagnostic and Statistical Manual of Mental Disorders* gestrichen wurde, lehnte es ab, ihre Untersuchung auf Lesben auszudehnen (die damals *female homosexuals* "weibliche Homosexuelle" hießen). Eine solche Ausdehnung auf ihr eigenes Geschlecht, meinte sie, hätte sie selbst als "befangen" gebrandmarkt und die ganze Studie unglaubwürdig gemacht und in Mißkredit gebracht. Es reichte nicht aus, daß Hooker verheiratet war. Vgl. Marcus 16–25 und 172 f.

[7] Dies machte mir die feministische Linguistin und Aktivistin für Lesbenrechte Julia Penelope in einem Gespräch bewußt.

[8] Um die eine komplizierte Situation noch zusätzlich komplizierenden Assoziationen an sexuelle Akte zu umgehen, bevorzugte man zeitweise den Terminus *homophil*, der sich allerdings nicht hat durchsetzen können. Karen Peper spricht, sicher aus ähnlichen Gründen, von "affectional preference" statt von "sexual preference" (195).

[9] Lord Alfred Douglas (1870–1945), *Two Loves,* zit. nach Grahn (1).

[10] Einen sehr instruktiven und klaren Artikel über diese Debatte und ihre Implikationen für eine "gay history" schrieb James Boswell.

[11] Allerdings kenne ich etliche Feministinnen, die heterosexuell und mit ihren Partnern glücklich sind und andere heterosexuelle Feministinnen, die mit ihrer Gender-Präferenz unglücklich sind und lieber lesbisch wären, dies aber zu ihrem Bedauern nicht "hinkriegen".

[12] Die folgenden Zitate stammen, soweit nicht anders angegeben, aus einer vereinsinternen Dokumentation, die mir Brigitte Adler vom Deutschen Lesbenring zugestellt hat. Weitere Dokumente verdanke ich Jutta Oesterle-Schwerin.

[13] Die *Lesbierin* gleicht insofern der *Wöchnerin*, als es zu der "abgeleiteten" Form kein semantisch äquivalentes maskulines Simplex gibt—naturgemäß, sozusagen.

[14] Das gilt sicher erst recht von dem Wort *Urninden*, auf das sie schließlich listig ausweichen.

[15] Das gilt für *Lesbe*, eine Eigenschöpfung der Frauen- und der Lesbenbewegung, nicht. Es ist nur so gebaut wie andere Schimpfwörter für Frauen (*Putze, Tippse, Emanze*).

[16] Linguistisch ist das Unsinn. Wenn *Schwulenbewegung* hochsprachlich ist, dann auch *Schwulenszene* und *Schwulentreff*, weil *Treff* und *Szene* zweifellos "hochsprachliche" Ausdrücke sind.

[17] Der Ältestenrat (die GeschäftsführerInnen der Parteien) regelt parlamentarische Protokollfragen u.ä.

[18] In der Mottenkugel-Metapher steht "Ausdünstung" für die Gesamtheit des jeweiligen Gebrauchskontextes. Ich möchte das an einem weniger kontroversen Beispiel erläutern. Das Wort *lebenslänglich* bedeutet zunächst nichts anderes als "ein Leben lang". Verwendet wird es allerdings vor allem bei Verurteilungen von KapitalverbrecherInnen, die "lebenslänglich bekommen", d.h. zu einem Leben im Zuchthaus verurteilt werden. Wenn ich jetzt sage: "Sie ist lebenslänglich Beamtin" statt "Sie ist verbeamtet auf Lebenszeit," so suggeriere ich damit, daß das BeamtInnendasein dem Knast vergleichbar ist. Um diese unerwünschte Assoziation an den Knast zu vermeiden, werden in allen Äußerungen über Verhältnisse, die ein Leben lang andauern, die Worte sorgfältig gewählt. Vgl. auch das Wort *Maid*, das wegen seines extensiven Gebrauchs durch die Nazis unakzeptabel geworden ist, obwohl wir dringend eine feminine, nichtdiminutive Bezeichnung bräuchten.

[19] Das bekannteste Beispiel hierfür ist die Jugendsprache mit ihrem ständigen Zwang zur Erneuerung, weil die Jugend jeweils älter wird und die neue Jugend sich sprachlich gegen die Alten abgrenzen will.

## Zitierte Werke

Boswell, James. "Revolutions, Universals, and Sexual Categories." Duberman et al. 17–36.

Brantôme, Pierre de Bourdeille Seigneur de. *Das Leben der galanten Damen*. Trans. Georg Harsdoerffer. Frankfurt a.M.: Insel, 1981 (1665).

Duberman, Martin Bauml, Martha Vicinus, and George Chauncey, Jr. eds. *Hidden from History: Reclaiming the Gay and Lesbian Past*. New York: New American Library, 1989.

Faderman, Lillian. *Surpassing the Love of Men: Romantic Friendship and Love between Women from the Renaissance to the Present*. New York: Morrow, 1980.

Foucault, Michel. *The History of Sexuality, Vol. 1: An Introduction.* Trans. Robert Hurley. New York: Pantheon, 1978.

Goffman, Erving. *Stigma: Notes on the Management of Spoiled Identity.* Englewood Cliffs, NJ: Prentice, 1963.

Grahn, Judy. *Another Mother Tongue: Gay Words, Gay Worlds.* Boston: Beacon, 1984.

Gross, Larry. *Contested Closets: The Politics and Ethics of Outing.* Minneapolis: U of Minnesota P, 1993.

Grosse-Bley, Ralph. "Verwilderung der Sprachkultur gerügt: CSU-Abgeordneter prangert 'Gossen-Ausdrücke' an/Jenninger will helfen." *Nordpresse* 21 (24 May 1988).

Haeberle, Erwin J. "Swastika, Pink Triangle and the Yellow Star: The Destruction of Sexology and the Persecution of Homosexuals in Nazi Germany." Duberman et al. 365–82.

Halperin, David M. "Sex before Sexuality: Pederasty, Politics and Power in Classical Athens." Duberman et al. 37–53.

Herles, Helmut. "Urningen und Urninden." *Frankfurter Allgemeine Zeitung* 11 February 1989.

Marcus, Eric. *Making History: The Struggle for Gay and Lesbian Equal Rights 1945–1990: An Oral History.* New York: HarperPerennial, 1993 (1992).

Offenbach, Judith. "Feminismus—Heterosexualität—Homosexualität." *Feminismus: Inspektion der Herrenkultur—Ein Handbuch.* Ed. Luise F. Pusch. Frankfurt a.M.: Suhrkamp, 1983. 210–32.

Peper, Karen. "Female Athlete = Lesbian: A Myth Constructed from Gendex Role Expectations and Lesbiphobia." Ringer. 193–208.

Ringer, R. Jeffrey, ed. *Queer Words, Queer Images: Communication and the Construction of Homosexuality.* New York: New York UP, 1994.

Sedgwick, Eve Kosofsky. *Epistemology of the Closet.* Berkeley: U of California P, 1990.

———. *Tendencies.* Durham: Duke UP, 1993.

Smith-Rosenberg, Carroll. "The Female World of Love and Ritual: Relations between Women in Nineteenth-Century America." *Signs* 1 (1975): 1–29.

Wiedemann, H.G. *Homosexuelle Liebe: Für eine Neuorientierung in der christlichen Ethik.* Stuttgart: Kreuz, 1982.

Wittgenstein, Ludwig. *Tractatus logico-philosophicus/Logisch-philosophische Abhandlung.* Frankfurt a.M.: Suhrkamp, 1963 (1921).

Wood, Julia T. "Gender and Relationship Crises: Contrasting Reasons, Responses, and Relational Orientations." Ringer. 238–64.

# WIG 2000:
# Feminism and the Future of *Germanistik*

### Jeanette Clausen and Sara Friedrichsmeyer

The publication of this volume marks twenty years of Women in German and ten years of the WIG Yearbook. For a reminder of just how far we have come, we need only look at the first issue of the WIG newsletter, dated 10 December 1974, which invited GermanistInnen to exchange information on their research and teaching as well as their thoughts on how to combat sexism and increase the participation of women in the profession. As the editors wrote: "Everything remains to be done" (4). And they meant that quite literally, for not only did men outnumber women in academic departments at the time, but the works of women writers were often out of print, there were almost no useful publications or even bibliographies on German women writers of any period, feminist criticism was not widely considered to be a legitimate area of scholarly activity, and feminist theories were just beginning to be elaborated in various disciplines. The energy and creativity that feminist professors and graduate students applied to the filling of those gaps is a fascinating and encouraging story in itself. One WIG member has characterized the role of the organization as making possible "ein gewisses Vertrauen in die Möglichkeiten, den Beruf anders ausfüllen zu können, ein Bewußtsein, Teil eines kollektiven Projekts zu sein" and especially as supporting the belief "daß wissenschaftliche Arbeit und politische Diskussionen entscheidend zur Veränderung der Wissens- und Machtverhältnisse in einer Institution wie der Universität beitragen können" (Martin 169).

WIG's successes are apparent, first of all, in the very presence of a feminist critique in Germanistik and equally so in the fact that more German women writers are being studied and taught than ever before (Blackwell, Fries). Further, WIG members are highly visible and well respected within the profession, and the WIG Yearbook has become a valued publication, as attested to by the overwhelmingly positive reviews from scholars both within and outside of the organization. Numbers also help to tell the story: WIG membership has grown to over 600 and the yearbook has almost doubled in size since its early volumes; the editors receive many more manuscripts every year than can possibly be accepted and have entertained the idea of beginning twice-yearly publications. The range of theoretical perspectives, the sophistication of critical approaches, and the insistence on an interdisciplinary focus evident in the contributions of WIG members to conference programs and to recent issues of the yearbook all reflect the kinds of impressive changes our organization has brought to Germanistik.

Yet, our success in reaching an audience outside of WIG itself is still limited. Although WIG's membership list—as well as the names and affiliations of the yearbook's Editorial Board members, contributors, and referees—shows that we are becoming an increasingly international organization, *we* are our readers, for the most part. This situation is not unique to WIG or to Germanistik. In a recent *Signs* article titled "Issues for an International Feminist Literary Criticism," Amy Kaminsky laments that although feminist scholarship has become increasingly interdisciplinary, "it has paid little attention to feminist work on and in other literatures"; this she attributes in part to the capacity of "the already empowered center...to reproduce itself" (213), as well as to literary scholars' widespread lack of proficiency in other languages (222). In her description of an international feminist literary criticism, her distinction between a global and a universalizing perspective is especially germane: "The universalizing text starts from a fixed point that creates itself as a de facto center. Everything that enters its purview is seen with reference to that center and is incorporated, assimilated, or ignored according to the center's own point of reference and its demands. A global perspective, on the other hand, presupposes multiple reference points...[and] many sites for making meaning and interpreting reality" (215).

The importance of assuming multiple reference points has often been demonstrated in the context of avoiding falsely universalizing categories such as "woman," and this assumption can also be the spur for a feminist literary criticism that is truly international and multicultural. Among the questions that such a global perspective raises for us in WIG are: What is our relationship as feminist Germanists to the "already empowered center" of feminist scholarship and what do we think it should be? What is our relationship to feminist scholars of Latin American, Asian, African, and non-German European literatures, and what do we wish it to be? Have we in WIG created a eurocentric or "germanocentric" feminist scholarship? What is the relationship between a more international Germanistik and comparative literature? What and whom are we serving by the kinds of scholarly work we produce? How can we make our hard-won insights into German literary and cultural history accessible and useful to non-Germanists while also expanding our own horizons beyond the confines of the German-speaking countries? If we agree that a global perspective in feminist literary criticism is our aim, how can we contribute to its definition as well as to its realization? These queries lead us then to others with implications for the profession as a whole: What might/could/should our profession look like in the next twenty years? What is, or what should be, the relationship of feminist Germanistik to the future of our profession?

One way to begin answering some of these questions is to think in terms of what our academic workplaces will look like in the next decade. According to the widely cited government report *Workforce 2000,* women and people of color will make up two thirds of the work force in the United States by the year 2000.[1] The implications of these demographic changes for colleges and universities are obvious; indeed, at some campuses, the future is already here. Leaders of higher education institutions across the country are aware of the urgency to prepare for an increasingly diverse, multicultural student population, but, ironically, those same administrators are likely to think first of German and other foreign languages—outside of Spanish and possibly French—when reduced budgets force them to consider "downsizing." All of us have heard horror stories about program cuts, some of us have already experienced them, and probably few of feel completely sanguine about the future of our own departments and profession. Most alarmingly, we see the shrinking number of tenured positions and recognize that more of us will be teaching in temporary or part-time positions.

The need for American Germanistik to change if our profession is to survive into the twenty-first century has been much discussed (see, e.g., Nollendorfs, Van Cleve/Willson); however, to our knowledge, none of the studies dealing with this question address feminist involvement. We are not the first to recommend that Germanistik become more international, more heterogenous; but we are the first to suggest that WIG can and should play a leadership role in providing direction for that change—and not just because of the statistically documented "feminization" of the profession (Nollendorfs 6 ff.). Rather, our reasons concern the potential of feminism and feminist leaders for the future of the academy and our discipline. We refer to the history of feminism as a movement for positive change, for challenging existing structures. What we have learned and continue to learn from the ongoing struggle to neutralize male prerogatives of power we can also apply to issues of social equality beyond those constituted by gender or sexuality.

While it may be true that the work of feminist Germanists is still undervalued by non-feminists in our field (Fries, Joeres), it does not necessarily follow that engaging in feminist research and teaching has led to the marginalization of WIG members within academia. If feminist Germanists are somehow marginalized on individual campuses, this is, we would argue, the result of our connection to German departments with their dwindling enrollments and decreasing importance on those campuses as much as (if not more so than) because of our feminism. Although feminist research may have been judged questionable by some even a decade ago, it is now recognized as "legitimate" (even if not quite "mainstream") and a viable avenue to tenure and promotion. Moreover, feminism provides many of us with opportunities for leadership on our campuses and in the profession—many WIG members are or have been directors of Women's Studies programs and other interdisciplinary programs, serve as department chairs or deans or in other administrative capacities, and hold influential positions in professional associations. This is not to deny a continuing resistance to feminism in some quarters, nor do we want to minimize the plight of those who remain un- or underemployed. Rather, our point is the existence of a growing pool of leadership talent and experience within WIG and what that could mean for a Germanistik intent on becoming more multicultural and international.

Many WIG members are already engaged in diversity initiatives on their campuses and in professional associations, for example through the former AATG Committee on the Recruitment and Retention of Minorities, now the AATG Committee on Diversity. One outgrowth of the latter's work was the special "Focus on Diversity" issue of *Die Unterrichtspraxis* (Fall 1992), which contains articles on such topics as how to promote the study of German among students of color and on integrating information about Afro-Germans and other racial or ethnic minorities in Germany into the curriculum. WIG members who served on that committee organized a session titled "Addressing Cultural Diversity in the German Classroom" for the 1993 WIG conference. Other WIG members have organized sessions on related topics at the GSA, MLA, and other conferences. Recently, three WIG members announced plans for an anthology dealing with the ways that Germans through the centuries have represented foreignness. In a variety of forums, then, WIG members are asking questions about the cultural borders of the canon that parallel their earlier investigations into long-ignored women's writing: Who, for example, should be considered a German writer today? What about those who live in Germany and yet publish in other languages? Or those who live, say, in Turkey but write in German? Of course, feminist scholars are not the only ones pursuing projects that question constructions of nation, nationality, and national literatures. However, we must be the ones to ensure that gender continues to be included in such projects so that feminist issues are not overlooked and women's voices silenced once again.

Clearly, teaching and doing research on German literature, literary history, and culture from a multicultural perspective will continue to require new sensitivities. Redefining our relationship to the "already empowered center" of feminist scholarship will challenge us to reexamine our feminist convictions and priorities, and to build alliances with other programs having the transformation of knowledge as their goal. Dialogue with feminist literary scholars outside of American and European Germanistik will require a richer understanding of interdisciplinarity as well as of the triad—gender, race, and class—that we almost ritualistically invoke when speaking or writing on feminist topics. Recent issues of the German feminist newsletter *Frauen in der Literaturwissenschaft*[2] that focused on, e.g., Turkey, South Africa, India, Japan, and Eastern Europe offer a glimpse of work that feminist scholars in vastly different cultural contexts are doing, providing an abundant source of material and knowledge that most of us have not yet begun to explore. Such projects can and should draw inspiration from the feminist criticism that WIG members have long been doing, for feminist criticism has always been more than merely a way to work with literature and culture; it has also been about the ways in which power has been used through the centuries to include and exclude certain groups. And, more significantly, it has always been about transferring that knowledge, those insights, into life outside academia. The shared concerns of feminism and multiculturalism create an opportunity as well as a kind of moral imperative for change that can lead us beyond the borders of disciplines based in "national" literatures to a truly international and intercultural understanding of issues vital to us all. These are some of the elements of an agenda for "WIG 2000" that we hope will find their way into future issues of the yearbook, as well as our classrooms and our lives.

## Notes

[1] The phrase "women and people of color," which presumably means "white women and people of color," is itself an example of a universalizing perspective, one that assumes white people as the "norm"—unless we taken the statement to mean that all the "people of color" are men.

[2] For information, write to: Frauen in der Literaturwissenschaft, c/o Universität Hamburg, Literaturwissenschaftliches Seminar, Von-Melle-Park 6, 20146 Hamburg.

## Works Cited

Blackwell, Jeannine. "Deconstructing the Canon: A Ten-Year Comparison." MLA Convention. 30 December 1993.

Fries, Marilyn Sibley. "Zur Rezeption deutschsprachiger Autorinnen in den USA." *Weimarer Beiträge* 39.3 (1993): 410–46.

Joeres, Ruth-Ellen B. "'Language is also a Place of Struggle': The Language of Feminism and the Language of American Germanistik." *Women in German Yearbook 8: Feminist Studies in German Literature and Culture*. Ed. Jeanette Clausen and Sara Friedrichsmeyer. Lincoln: U of Nebraska P, 1993. 247–57.

Kaminsky, Amy. "Issues for an International Feminist Literary Criticism." *Signs: Journal of Women in Culture and Society* 19.1 (Autumn 1993): 213-26.

Martin, Biddy. "Zwischenbilanz der feministischen Debatten." *Germanistik in den USA: Neue Entwicklungen und Methoden*. Ed. Frank Trommler. Opladen: Westdeutscher Verlag, 1989. 165-95.

*NEWS from Women in Germanistik*. Madison: German Department, University of Wisconsin. 10 December 1974.

Nollendorfs, Valters. "Out of Germanistik: Thoughts on the Shape of Things to Come." *Die Unterrichtspraxis* 27.1 (Spring 1994): 1-10.

Van Cleve, John, and A. Leslie Willson. *Remarks on the Needed Reform of German Studies in the United States*. Columbia, SC: Camden House, 1993.

*Workforce 2000*. Washington, DC: U.S. Department of Labor, Workforce 2000 Project Office, 1987.

# ABOUT THE AUTHORS

**Susan C. Anderson** is Associate Professor in the Department of Germanic Languages and Literatures at the University of Oregon. She works mainly on twentieth-century German and Austrian literature, the interconnection of history and literature, and baroque literature. Her publications include *Grass and Grimmelshausen: "Das Treffen in Telgte" and "Rezeptionstheorie"* and articles on texts by such writers as P. Schneider, G. Grass, R. Huch, and A. Schnitzler. She is presently working on a book-length project on the literary approaches to German history by Huch, Döblin, Brecht, and Grass, all of whom deal with the Thirty Years' War.

**Jeanette Clausen** is Associate Professor of German and Chair of the Modern Foreign Languages Department at Indiana University Purdue University Fort Wayne. She is coeditor of an anthology, *German Feminism* (1984), and has published articles on Helga Königsdorf, Christa Wolf, and other women writers. She was coeditor of the WIG Yearbook from 1987 to 1994.

**Miriam Frank** is Master Teacher of Humanities in New York University's General Studies Program. She has written about German feminist publishing for *New German Critique* and *Connexions.* She is a coauthor of *The Life and Times of Rosie the Riveter,* and she has published and lectured widely on women's labor history in the USA. She has also coauthored *Pride at Work: Organizing for Lesbian and Gay Rights in Unions,* an organizing and bargaining guide. As the 1995 NYU Vladeck Fellow she is researching a book-length study on the history and contemporary organizing campaigns of Lesbian and Gay union activists.

**Sara Friedrichsmeyer** is Professor of German at the University of Cincinnati. Her publications include *The Androgyne in Early German Romanticism* (1983) and the coedited volume *The Enlightenment and Its Legacy* (1991). She has published articles on German Romanticism, feminist theory, and various nineteenth- and twentieth-century German women, among them Caroline Schlegel-Schelling, Annette von Droste-Hülshoff, Paula Modersohn-Becker, Käthe Kollwitz, and Christa Wolf. Her current project is a coedited volume (with Sara Lennox and Susanne

Zantop) tentatively titled *The Imperialist Imagination*. She has been coeditor of the *Women in German Yearbook* since 1990.

**Marjorie Gelus** is Professor of German at California State University, Sacramento. Her research interests include literature of the Goethe era, issues of literary theory, and feminist theory and criticism. She has published articles and reviews principally on Friedrich Hölderlin, Heinrich von Kleist, Franz Kafka, and Thomas Bernhard, and is currently working on a book of feminist revisions of the stories of Kleist.

**Brigid Haines** is a lecturer in German at University College of Swansea, Wales. She is the author of *Dialogue and Narrative Design in the Works of Adalbert Stifter* and of articles on Stifter, Lou Andreas-Salomé, Christa Wolf, and Helga Königsdorf. She is interested in nineteenth-century literature, women's writing, and critical theory, and is currently Treasurer and Membership Secretary of the British organization "Women in German Studies."

**Gail K. Hart** was born in Rochester, NY. She is Associate Professor of German and Associate Dean of Humanities for Undergraduates at the University of California, Irvine. She is the author of *Readers and Their Fictions in the Novels and Novellas of Gottfried Keller* (1989) and of a recently completed study of gender politics in *bürgerliches Trauerspiel*, as well as articles on Keller, C.F. Meyer, Lessing, Goethe, and Sacher-Masoch. She is currently working on a project involving the history of capital punishment, the social conventions of execution, and dramatic and fictional representations of scheduled death.

**Ruth-Ellen B. Joeres** is Professor of German at the University of Minnesota—Twin Cities and editor of *Signs: Journal of Women in Culture and Society*. She has published articles and books on German women writers in the eighteenth to twentieth centuries, the interpretation of women's lives through personal narratives, US feminist criticism, and the politics of the essay, among others. Her research is increasingly focused on the intersection of US feminist theorizing and German Studies. At the moment, she is completing a book on the representation and self-representation of German women writers in the nineteenth century as examined through the lenses of feminist and cultural theories.

**Ruth Klüger** is Professor of German at the University of California, Irvine. Previously she taught and was department chair at the University of Virginia and Princeton University. For seven years she was editor of *The German Quarterly*. Her research interests include Kleist, Austrian literature, and Jewish problematics. Her most recent publications are the autobiographical *weiter leben: Eine Jugend* (1992), for which she received several literary prizes, and *Katastrophen: Über deutsche Literatur* (1994).

**Sigrid Lange** studied at and received her *Habilitation* from the University of Jena. She has held positions as guest professor at the universities of Munich and Göttingen and has taught at the University of Massachusetts, Amherst. She has also lectured at a number of universities in both the USA and Germany. Her areas of concentration include German literature of the eighteenth century, contemporary literature, and feminist literary theory. The recipient of a fellowship from the Humboldt Foundation, she is presently at the University of Massachusetts, Amherst, where she is completing a book on women's writing in the eighteenth century.

**Richard W. McCormick** is Associate Professor at the University of Minnesota, where he has been teaching German cinema and twentieth-century German literature since 1987. He is the author of *Politics of the Self: Feminism and the Postmodern in West German Literature and Film* (1991) and a coeditor of the two-volume anthology *Gender and German Cinema: Feminist Interventions* (1993). Currently he is working on a book on the destabilization of gender in the culture of the Weimar Republic, focusing especially on film and literature.

**Elizabeth Mittman** is Assistant Professor of German at Michigan State University. She is coeditor, with Ruth-Ellen B. Joeres, of *The Politics of the Essay: Feminist Perspectives* (1993), and coeditor/translator of *Theory as Practice: A Critical Anthology of Early German Romantic Writings* (forthcoming). She has written articles on Christa Wolf and Novalis, and is currently at work on a book about constructions of gender and place in GDR literature. She studied in Leipzig in 1983-84, and taught at the Humboldt-Universität in East Berlin in 1987-88.

**Luise F. Pusch,** born in 1944, holds the title of Professor of Linguistics at the University of Konstanz. She is currently working as a freelance scholar and author and has published numerous articles and two books on traditional linguistics (1972 and 1980) and two books on feminist linguistics: *Das Deutsche als Männersprache* (1984) and *Alle Menschen werden Schwestern* (1990). Additional publications on feminist topics include *Berühmte Frauen: Kalender* (1987 ff.), *Ladies First* (1993), *Schwestern berühmter Männer* (1985), *Töchter berühmter Männer* (1988), and *Mütter berühmter Männer* (1994), as well as *WahnsinnsFrauen* (1992).

## About the Authors

**Karen Remmler** is Assistant Professor of German at Mount Holyoke College, where she teaches courses on contemporary German and Austrian culture, German language and literature, and Women's Studies. She has written articles on postmodern discourse and the representation of torture, Jewish female identity in the writing of contemporary Jewish women writers in Germany, body politics in the GDR, and recently coedited a volume with Sander L. Gilman, *Reemerging Jewish Culture in Germany*. Her current research includes a reassessment of Bachmann criticism and the significance of place memory for conveying Jewish identity in post-unified Berlin.

**Suzanne Shipley** (formerly Toliver) is Associate Professor of German and head of the Department of Germanic Languages and Literatures at the University of Cincinnati. This article is one of three she has published based on her sabbatical research into the lives of German and Austrian women in exile from Hitler's Germany. Her monograph on Erich Arendt, who spent his exile years in Colombia, includes the first translations of his work into English. Her current interest is in translating the works of living women poets from Austria and Germany into English.

**Silke von der Emde** is Assistant Professor at Vassar College in Poughkeepsie, NY. Her research interests include twentieth-century literature, feminist criticism, and German studies. The article included in this volume grew out of her dissertation "Entering History: Feminist Dialogues in Irmtraud Morgner's *Life and Adventures of Troubadoura Beatriz*." She is currently working on a book-length project on Irmtraud Morgner's aesthetics. She has published articles on women filmmakers, feminist aesthetics, and politics.

# NOTICE TO CONTRIBUTORS

The *Women in German Yearbook* is a refereed journal. Its publication is supported by the Coalition of Women in German.

Contributions to the *Women in German Yearbook* are welcome at any time. The editors are interested in feminist approaches to all aspects of German literary, cultural, and language studies, including teaching.

Prepare manuscripts for anonymous review. The editors prefer that manuscripts not exceed 25 pages (typed, double-spaced), including notes. Follow the third edition (1988) of the *MLA Handbook* (separate notes from works cited). Send one copy of the manuscript to each coeditor:

Sara Friedrichsmeyer        *and*        Patricia Herminghouse
Department of Foreign                    Department of Modern
  Languages                                Languages and Culture
University of Cincinnati, RWC            University of Rochester
Cincinnati, OH 45236                     Rochester, NY 14627


For membership/subscription information, contact Jeanette Clausen (Department of Modern Foreign Languages, Indiana University Purdue University, Fort Wayne, IN 46805).

# CONTENTS OF PREVIOUS VOLUMES

## Volume 9

**Ann Taylor Allen,** Women's Studies as Cultural Movement and Academic Discipline in the United States and West Germany: The Early Phase, 1966–1982; **Susan Signe Morrison,** Women Writers and Women Rulers: Rhetorical and Political Empowerment in the Fifteenth Century; **Christl Griesshaber-Weninger,** Harsdörffers *Frauenzimmer Gesprächspiele* als geschlechtsspecifische Verhaltensfibel: Ein Vergleich mit heutigen Kommunikationsstrukturen; **Gertrud Bauer Pickar,** The Battering and Meta-Battering of Droste's Margreth: Covert Misogyny in *Die Judenbuche*'s Critical Reception; **Kirsten Belgum,** Domesticating the Reader: Women and *Die Gartenlaube*; **Katrin Sieg,** Equality Decreed: Dramatizing Gender in East Germany; **Katharina von Ankum,** Political Bodies: Women and Re/Production in the GDR; **Friederike Eigler,** At the Margins of East Berlin's "Counter-Culture": Elke Erb's *Winkelzüge* and Gabriele Kachold's *zügel los*; **Karin Eysel**; Christa Wolf's *Kassandra*: Refashioning National Imagination Beyond the Nation; **Petra Waschescio,** Auseinandersetzung mit dem Abendlanddenken: Gisela von Wysockis *Abendlandleben*; **Dagmar C.G. Lorenz,** Memory and Criticism: Ruth Klüger's *weiter leben*; **Sara Lennox,** Antiracist Feminism in Germany: Introduction to Dagmar Schultz and Ika Hügel; **Ika Hügel,** Wir kämpfen seit es uns gibt; **Dagmar Schultz,** Racism in the New Germany and the Reaction of White Women; **Sara Friedrichsmeyer and Jeanette Clausen,** What's Missing in New Historicism or the "Poetics" of Feminist Literary Criticism.

## Volume 8

**Marjorie Gelus,** Birth as Metaphor in Kleist's *Das Erdbeben in Chili*: A Comparison of Critical Methodologies; **Vanessa Van Ornam,** No Time for Mothers: Courasche's Infertility as Grimmelshausen's Criticism of War; **M.R. Sperberg-McQueen,** Whose Body Is It? Chaste Strategies and the Reinforcement of Patriarchy in Three Plays by Hrotswitha von Gandersheim; **Sara Lennox,** The Feminist Reception of Ingeborg Bachmann; **Maria-Regina Kecht,** Auflehnung gegen die Ordnung von Sprache und Vernunft: Die weibliche Wirklichkeitsgestaltung bei Waltraud Anna Mitgutsch; **Maria-Regina Kecht,** Gespräch mit Waltraud Anna Mitgutsch; **Susanne Kord,** "Und drinnen waltet die züchtige Hausfrau"? Carolina Pichler's Fictional Auto/Biographies; **Susan L. Cocalis,** "Around 1800": Reassessing the Role of German Women Writers in

Literary Production of the Late Eighteenth and Early Nineteenth Centuries (Review Essay); **Konstanze Streese und Kerry Shea,** Who's Looking? Who's Laughing? Of Multicultural Mothers and Men in Percy Adlon's *Bagdad Cafe*; **Deborah Lefkowitz,** Editing from Life; **Walfriede Schmitt,** Mund-Artiges… (Gedicht); **Barbara Becker-Cantarino,** Feministische Germanistik in Deutschland: Rückblick und sechs Thesen; **Gisela Brinker-Gabler,** Alterity—Marginality—Difference: On Inventing Places for Women; **Ruth-Ellen B. Joeres,** "Language is Also a Place of Struggle": The Language of Feminism and the Language of American *Germanistik*.

## Volume 7

**Myra Love,** "A Little Susceptible to the Supernatural?": On Christa Wolf; **Monika Shafi,** Die überforderte Generation: Mutterfiguren in Romanen von Ingeborg Drewitz; **Ute Brandes,** Baroque Women Writers and the Public Sphere; **Katherine R. Goodman,** "The Butterfly and the Kiss": A Letter from Bettina von Arnim; **Ricarda Schmidt,** Theoretische Orientierungen in feministischer Literaturwissenschaft und Sozialphilosophie (Review Essay); **Sara Lennox,** Some Proposals for Feminist Literary Criticism; **Helga Königsdorf,** Ein Pferd ohne Beine (Essay); **Angela Krauß,** Wieder in Leipzig (Erzählung); **Waldtraut Lewin,** Lange Fluchten (Erzählung); **Eva Kaufmann,** DDR-Schriftstellerinnen, die Widersprüche und die Utopie; **Irene Dölling,** Alte und neue Dilemmata: Frauen in der ehemaligen DDR; **Dinah Dodds,** "Die Mauer stand bei mir im Garten": Interview mit Helga Schütz; **Gisela E. Bahr,** Dabeigewesen: Tagebuchnotizen vom Winter 1989/90; **Dorothy J. Rosenberg,** Learning to Say "I" instead of "We": Recent Works on Women in the Former GDR (Review Essay); **Sara Friedrichsmeyer and Jeanette Clausen,** What's Feminism Got to Do with It? A Postscript from the Editors.

## Volume 6

**Dagmar C.G. Lorenz,** "Hoffentlich werde ich taugen." Zu Situation und Kontext von Brigitte Schwaiger/Eva Deutsch *Die Galizianerin*; **Sabine Wilke,** "Rückhaltlose Subjektivität." Subjektwerdung, Gesellschafts- und Geschlechtsbewußtsein bei Christa Wolf; **Elaine Martin,** Patriarchy, Memory, and the Third Reich in the Autobiographical Novels of Eva Zeller; **Tineke Ritmeester,** Heterosexism, Misogyny, and Mother-Hatred in Rilke Scholarship: The Case of Sophie Rilke-Entz (1851–1931); **Richard W. McCormick,** Productive Tensions: Teaching Films by German Women and Feminist Film Theory; **Hildegard M. Nickel,** Women in the GDR: Will Renewal Pass Them By?; **Helen Cafferty and Jeanette Clausen,** Feministik *Germanistik* after Unification: A Postscript from the Editors.

## Volume 5

**Angelika Bammer,** Nackte Kaiser und bärtige Frauen: Überlegungen zu Macht, Autorität, und akademischem Diskurs; **Sabine Hake,** Focusing the Gaze: The

Critical Project of *Frauen und Film*; **Dorothy Rosenberg,** Rethinking Progress: Women Writers and the Environmental Dialogue in the GDR; **Susanne Kord,** Fading Out: Invisible Women in Marieluise Fleißer's Early Dramas; **Lorely French,** "Meine beiden Ichs": Confrontations with Language and Self in Letters by Early Nineteenth-Century Women; **Sarah Westphal-Wihl,** Pronoun Semantics and the Representation of Power in the Middle High German *Märe* "Die halbe Decke"; **Susanne Zantop and Jeannine Blackwell,** Select Bibliography on German Social History and Women Writers; **Helen Cafferty and Jeanette Clausen,** Who's Afraid of Feminist Theory? A Postscript from the Editors.

## Volume 4

**Luise F. Pusch,** Totale Feminisierung: Überlegungen zum unfassenden Femininum; **Luise F. Pusch,** Die Kätzin, die Rättin, und die Feminismaus; **Luise F. Pusch,** Carl Maria, die Männe; **Luise F. Pusch,** Sind Herren herrlich und Damen dämlich?; **Ricarda Schmidt,** E.T.A. Hoffman's "Der Sandmann": An Early Example of *Écriture Féminine*? A Critique of Trends in Feminist Literary Criticism; **Renate Fischetti,** *Écriture Féminine* in the New German Cinema: Ulrike Ottinger's *Portrait of a Woman Drinker*; **Jan Mouton,** The Absent Mother Makes an Appearance in the Films of West German Women Directors; **Charlotte Armster,** Katharina Blum: Violence and the Exploitation of Sexuality; **Renny Harrigan,** Novellistic Representation of *die Berufstätige* during the Weimar Republic; **Lynda J. King,** From the Crown to the Hammer and Sickle: The Life and Works of Austrian Interwar Writer Hermynia zur Mühlen; **Linda Kraus Worley,** The "Odd" Woman as Heroine in the Fiction of Louise von François; **Helga Madland,** Three Late Eighteenth-Century Women's Journals: Their Role in Shaping Women's Lives; **Sigrid Brauner,** Hexenjagd in Gelehrtenköpfen; **Susan Wendt-Hildebrandt,** Gespräch mit Herrad Schenk; **Dorothy Rosenberg,** GDR Women Writers: The Post-War Generation. An Updated Bibliography of Narrative Prose, June 1987.

## Volume 3

**Ritta Jo Horsley and Richard A. Horsley,** On the Trail of the "Witches": Wise Women, Midwives and the European Witch Hunts; **Barbara Mabee,** Die Kindesmörderin in den Fesseln der bürgerlichen Moral: Wagners Evchen und Goethes Gretchen; **Judith P. Aikin,** Who Learns a Lesson? The Function of Sex Role Reversal in Lessing's *Minna von Barnhelm*; **Sara Friedrichsmeyer,** The Subversive Androgyne; **Shawn C. Jarvis,** Spare the Rod and Spoil the Child? Bettine's *Das Leben der Hochgräfin Gritta von Rattenzuhausbeiuns*; **Edith Waldstein,** Romantic Revolution and Female Collectivity: Bettine and Gisela von Arnim's *Gritta*; **Ruth-Ellen Boetcher Joeres,** "Ein Nebel schließt uns ein." Social Comment in the Novels of German Women Writers, 1850–1870; **Thomas C. Fox,** Louise von François: A Feminist Reintroduction; **Gesine Worm,** Das erste Jahr: Women in German im Goethe Haus New York.

## Volume 2

**Barbara Frischmuth,** Am hellen Tag: Erzählung; **Barbara Frischmuth,** Eine Souveräne Posaune Gottes: Gedanken zu Hildegard von Bingen und ihrem Werk; **Dagmar C.G. Lorenz,** Ein Interview: Barbara Frischmuth; **Dagmar C.G. Lorenz,** Creativity and Imagination in the Work of Barbara Frischmuth; **Margaret E. Ward,** *Ehe* and *Entsagung*: Fanny Lewald's Early Novels and Goethe's Literary Paternity; **Regula Venske,** "Männlich im Sinne des Butt" or "Am Ende angekommen?": Images of Men in Contemporary German-Language Literature by Women; **Angelika Bammer,** Testing the Limits: Christa Reinig's Radical Vision; **H-B. Moeller,** The Films of Margarethe von Trotta: Domination, Violence, Solidarity, and Social Criticism.

## Volume 1

**Jeanette Clausen,** The Coalition of Women in German: An Interpretive History and Celebration; **Sigrid Weigel,** Das Schreiben des Mangels als Produktion von Utopie; **Jeannine Blackwell,** Anonym, verschollen, trivial: Methodological Hindrances in Researching German Women's Literature; **Martha Wallach,** Ideal and Idealized Victims: The Lost Honor of the Marquise von O., Effi Briest and Katharina Blum in Prose and Film; **Anna Kuhn,** Margarethe von Trotta's *Sisters*: Interiority or Engagement?; **Barbara D. Wright,** The Feminist Transformation of Foreign Language Teaching; **Jeanette Clausen,** Broken but not Silent: Language as Experience in Vera Kamenko's *Unter uns war Krieg*; **Richard L. Johnson,** The New West German Peace Movement: Male Dominance or Feminist Nonviolence.